ALSO EDITED BY
Philip José Farmer

Tales of Riverworld

Published by
WARNER BOOKS

QUEST TO RIVERWORLD

EDITED BY
PHILIP JOSÉ FARMER

WARNER BOOKS

A Time Warner Company

WARNER BOOKS EDITION

Cover design by Don Puckey
Cover illustration by Don Ivan Punchatz

Warner Books, Inc.
1271 Avenue of the Americas
New York, NY 10020

 A Time Warner Company

Printed in the United States of America

First Printing: August, 1993

10 9 8 7 6 5 4 3 2 1

CONTENTS

The editors would like to thank Steve Jackson and Steve Jackson Games for help in the production of this project, and in particular for providing copies of GURPS RIVERWORLD for use by the authors of these stories. GURPS RIVERWORLD summarizes the characters, story, and operational details presented in the five novels that comprise the primary portion of the Riverworld saga.

Up The Bright River

Philip José Farmer

1

Andrew Paxton Davis leaned into the fifteen-mile-an-hour wind. But not too far. He was standing at the end of a fifty-foot-long yew wood gangplank. It was three inches deep and four and a half inches wide. Thirty feet of it was supported by a single forty-five-degree angled beam, the other end of which was attached to the tower structure. Beyond that, the remaining twenty feet formed a sort of diving board. Davis, having ventured out to its end, felt it bend under him.

The ground was three hundred feet below him, but he could clearly hear the roar and screams of the crowd and sometimes fragments of words from an individual. The upturned faces were mostly eager or malicious. Some expressed fear or sympathy for him.

Beyond the end of the board was a twelve-foot gap. Then the projecting end of another gangplank, equally long and narrow, began. But his weight bent the end of the plank he stood on and made it five inches lower than the other.

If he could leap from one gangplank to the next he was free. The Emperor had promised that any "criminals" who could do so would be allowed to depart unharmed from the state. Attempting such a feat or refusing to do it was not, however, a choice. All major criminals were sentenced to the ordeal.

The people below were rooting for him or hoping he would fall. Their attitude depended upon which way they had bet.

Behind him, standing on the platform of the tower, the other prisoners shouted encouragement. Davis did not know two of them or what their crimes were. The others were his companions, if you could call them that, who had traveled far together and had been captured by the people of the Western Sun Kingdom. They were the Viking, Ivar the Boneless, the mad Frenchman, Faustroll, and Davis's bane, the beautiful but sluttish Ann Pullen.

Davis had been chosen by the Emperor Pachacuti to jump first. He would just as soon be the last in line. If he refused to leap, he would be thrown off the tower by the guards.

Ivar shouted in Old Norse. Though the wind hurled his words away from his lips, they came from the chest of a giant. Davis heard them as if they were far away.

"Show them you are not afraid! Run bravely and without fear! Run with the fleetness of Hugi, the giant whose name means Thought! Then fly as if you wear the birdskin of Loki! Pray to your god that you will not bring shame to him by hesitating! Nor to us!"

Faustroll's voice was shrill but pierced the wind. He spoke in English.

"It does not matter if you fail and fall, my Philistine friend! One moment of terror, quite cathartic for you and for us, and you will awake tomorrow as whole as ever! Which, if you will pardon my frankness, is not saying much!"

Ann Pullen either said nothing or her voice was snatched away by the wind.

What Faustroll said about him was, excluding the insults, true. He would die today; he would be resurrected at dawn. But he might be far down the River and have to start his journey all over again. That prospect made him quail almost as much as what he must do within the next twenty seconds. He had been given only two minutes to make the attempt.

"Ten feet, Andrew the Red!" Ivar had said when the Emperor pronounced sentence on him. "Ten feet! It is nothing! I will run on the board like a deer and will soar off its end like a hawk and land upon the other board like a lynx pouncing upon its prey!"

Brave words. Though Ivar was six feet six inches tall and was enormously powerful, he weighed over two hundred and thirty pounds. That was a lot of muscle and bone to lift. The heavier the runner, the more the wood would bend down. Not only would he have to leap across, he would have to leap up to attain the end of the other board.

Davis had an advantage in being only five feet six inches high and in weighing only one hundred and forty pounds. But the jumper's degree of courage made a difference. He had seen men and women who might have crossed the gap if fear had not slowed them down.

No hesitation, he told himself. Do it! Get it over with! Give it all you have! But his stomach hurt, and he was quivering.

He prayed to God as he trotted back to the tower and as he turned around to face the gangplank. Fifty feet was not long enough for a good runway. In that distance, he could not reach maximum speed. But that was how it was. No evading it; no excuses. Still praying, he bent down in the starting crouch and then sprang outward with all his strength. The sickness and the quivering were gone, or he was unaware of them. He felt as he had when, in 1845, he was ten years old and competing in a jump across a creek with other farm boys near Bowling Green, Clay County, Indiana. The glory of his healthy young body and intimations of immortality had blazed then.

Now, his spirit and body had become one as they had been one when he had made that winning jump on Earth. He was an arrow aimed at the end of the board beyond the void. The shouts of his companions, the roar of the crowd, and the captain of the guards counting off the seconds remaining became one voice. His bare feet slapped on the wood as they had slapped on the dirt when he had won the contest with his schoolmates. But, then, he had faced only getting wet if he fell short.

The end of the gangplank was coming far more swiftly than he thought possible. Beyond it was the space he had to travel, a short distance in reality, a long, long one in his mind. And the beam was dipping. Only a few inches, but the slight deviation from the horizontal might defeat him.

He came down hard with his right foot and rose up, up, up. The void was below him. He thought, Oh, God, to whom I have been always faithful, deliver me from this evil! But a rapture, completely unexpected, shot through him. It was as if the hand of God were not only lifting him but enveloping him in the ecstasy few besides the saints knew.

It was worth the price of horror and of death.

2

Yesterday, Andrew Paxton Davis had also been high above earth. But he was not under any sentence and was not afraid of dying immediately. He was clinging to the railing of a bamboo platform, the crow's nest as it were, while it swayed in the strong wind. He was seasick, though there were no seas on this world.

Bright in the early-morning sun, the city below him creaked as if it were a ship under full sail. He had ascended many staircases and climbed many ladders past many levels to reach the top floor of this sentinel tower, the highest structure of the gigantic skeletal building that was also a city. Though he had stood here for only two minutes, he felt as if he had endured an hour of watch on a vessel during a violent storm. Yet the view was certainly peaceful and undisturbed. The storm was within himself.

Northward, the River ran for thirty miles before turning left to go around the shoulder of the mountain range. That marked the upper border of this kingdom. Southward, twenty miles away, the River came from around another bend. That was the lower border of this small yet mighty monarchy. The Inca Pachacuti ruled both sides of the River within these borders, and he was disobeyed only at the risk of torture, slavery, or death.

Just past the edge of the City on the north was the Temple of the Sun, a flat-topped pyramid a hundred and fifty feet high and made of stone, earth, and wood. Below Davis was the Scaffolding City, the City of Many Bridges, the City Swaying in the Wind, the Airy Domain of Pachacuti Inca Yupanqui, who had ruled on Earth from A.D. 1438 to 1471. The Peruvians of that time knew him as the great conqueror and Emperor Pachacuti.

The City that Pachacuti had built was like none known on Earth and was, perhaps, unique on the Riverworld. The view from the top level of the highmost sentinel tower would have made most people ecstatic. It made Davis feel like throwing up.

The Incan sentinel was grinning. His teeth were brown from chewing the grail-provided cocoa leaf. He had seen Davis here many times and was enjoying his plight. Once, the guard had asked Davis why he came here if the place always made him ill. Davis had replied that at least here he could get away from the even more sickening citizens of the City.

But, suddenly inspired, he had added, "The higher I get from the ground, the closer I am to the Ultimate Reality, the Truth. Up here, I may be able to see the Light."

The watchman had looked puzzled and somewhat fearful. He had moved away from Davis as far as he could get. What Davis did not tell him was that it was not only the height and the swaying that made him nauseous. He was also sick with longing to see a child who might not be and many never have been. But he would not admit that that could be the reality. He was certain that, somewhere up the River, was a woman who had borne a baby in a world where no woman, so far, had conceived. Moreover, Davis was certain that the baby was of virgin birth and that it was the reincarnation of Jesus.

From below came, faintly, the voices of the people chattering away in Kishwa, Aymara, Samnite, Bronze Age Chinese, and a dozen other languages, the tinkling of windblown bundles of mica shards, the shrillnesses of whistles and flutes, and the deep booming of drums. All these floated upward, wrapped in the odor of frying fish.

Except for the temple and the city, the plains and foothills looked like most other areas along the River. The mushroom-shaped grailstones, the conical-roofed bamboo huts, the fishing boats, the large oar-and-sail war or merchant vessels, the people moving around on the plains bordering the River, were nothing unusual. But the city and the temple were extraordinary enough to bring men and women from far-off places up and down the River. Like Earth tourists, they were gawkers who had to pay a price for admission. Their dried fish; wooden, fishbone, flint, and chert tools and weapons; rings and statu-ettes; containers of booze, cigarettes, dreamgum, and ochre enriched the kingdom. Even the slaves enjoyed the bounty to some extent.

Presently, as Davis stood there, looking northward toward the invisible Light, the face of a man appeared just above the platform. He hoisted himself up from the ladder with powerful arms and stood erect. He towered over Davis and the sentinel. His shoulder-length hair was bronze-red; his eyes were large and light blue; his face was craggy yet handsome. He wore a kilt made of a blue towel, a necklace of colored fish bones, and a cap decorated with wooden pieces carved into the semblance of feathers. His tanned humanskin belt held a large stone ax.

Despite his savage appearance, he, too, had a quest. During the flight from his former kingdom, he seemed to have been seized with a revelation. At least, he had said so to Davis. What it was, he kept to himself. Davis had not been able to tell that the illumination or whatever it was had changed his character for the better. But Ivar was determined to travel to the end of the River. There, Davis supposed, the Viking thought that he would find the beings who had made this planet and resurrected the dead of Earth. And they would reveal the Ultimate Reality, the Truth.

Ivar the Boneless spoke to Davis in the Old Norse of the early-ninth-century Vikings. "Here you are, Andrew the Red, the Massager, enjoying the view and your sickness. Have you seen the Light?"

"Not with my eyes," Davis said. "But my heart sees it."

"What the heart sees, the eye sees," Ivar said.

He was now standing by Davis, his huge hands squeezing on the railing bar, his massive legs braced on the slowly rocking platform. Though he looked at the north of the Rivervalley, he was not trying to see Davis's Light. Nor was he looking for his own Light. As always when here, he was planning an escape route while seeing the entire kingdom spread out before him. Being the general of one of the Inca's regiments was not enough to detain a man who had been a king on Earth and in the Valley.

"We've tarried here far too long," he growled. "The source of the River beckons, and we have many a mile to go."

Davis looked anxiously at the sentinel. Though the Aymara did not understand Ivar's language, he still might report to the Inca that the two had been conversing in a suspicious manner. Pachacuti would then demand that Davis and Ivar tell him what they had said. If he was not satisfied with their answers, he would torture them to get the truth out of them. Suspicion floated through this land like a fever-breeding miasma. Hence, it was full of spies.

As Ivar had once said, a man could not fart without the Inca hearing about it.

"I go up-River tonight," Ivar said. "You may come along with me, though you are not a great warrior. Yet, you have some cunning, you have been useful in frays, and you do have a strong reason to leave this place. I tell you this because I can trust you not to betray me if you decide to stay behind. That is praise, since few may be trusted."

"Thank you," Davis said. His tone hinted at sarcasm, but he knew that the Viking was, according to his lights, being complimentary. "I will go with you, as you knew I would. What are your plans? And why tonight? What makes it different from all the others?"

"Nothing is different. My patience is gone. I'm weary of waiting for events to open the way. I'll make my own event."

"Besides," Davis said, "the Inca is too interested in Ann. If you wait much longer, he will make her one of his concubines. I assume that she's going with us."

"Correct."

"And Faustroll?"

"The crazed one may stay here or go with us as he wishes. You will ask him if he cares to accompany us. Warn him to stay sober. If he is drunk, he will be left behind, most probably as a corpse."

Davis and Ivar talked in low tones as Ivar revealed his plans. Then the Viking climbed down from the crow's nest. Davis stayed awhile so that the sentinel would not think that they had been conspiring and were eager to begin their wicked work against the Inca.

At noon, Davis was by a grailstone on the edge of the River. After the top of the stone erupted in lightning and thunder, he waited until an overseer handed him his big cylindrical grail. He went off to eat from its offerings, walking slowly and looking for Faustroll in the crowd. He did not have much time for this. His appointment with the Inca was within the hour, and that bloody-minded pagan accepted no excuses for lateness from his subjects.

After several minutes, Davis saw the Frenchman, who was sitting cross-legged on the ground. He was eating and at the same time talking to some friends. Faustroll's appearance was no longer so grotesque. He had washed out of his black hair the glue and mud forming a nest in the center of which was a wooden cuckoo egg. His hair now hung down past his shoulders. He no longer had a painted mustache, and he had also removed the painted mathematical formula from his forehead. He spoke only occasionally in the even-stressed words once distinguishing all of his speech. The change in him had encouraged Davis to believe that Faustroll was beginning to recover his sanity.

But his fishing pole was always at hand, and he still called himself "we." He insisted that using "I" made an artificial distinction between subject and object, that everybody was part of one body called humanity and that this body was only a small part of the even vaster universe.

"We" included the "Great Ubu," that is, God, and also anything that did not exist but could be named, and also the past, present, and future. This triad he considered to be indivisible.

Faustroll had irked, angered, and repulsed Davis. But, for some reason, Davis also felt a sort of fondness for him and was, despite himself, fascinated by Faustroll. Perhaps that was because the Frenchman was also looking for the Ultimate

Reality, the Truth. However, their concepts of these differed greatly.

Davis waited until Faustroll happened to look at him. He signaled with a hand raised level with his forehead, his fingers waggling. Faustroll nodded slightly to acknowledge the signal, but he continued his animated talk in Esperanto. After a few minutes, he rose, stretched, and said that he was going fishing. Fortunately, no one offered to go with him. The two met by the very edge of the River.

"What do we have in mind?" the Frenchman said, speaking in English.

"Ivar is going to leave tonight. I'm going with him, and so is Ann Pullen. You're invited. But you must not get drunk."

"What? Surely, we are jesting!"

"We are not amused," Davis said.

"We are sometimes intoxicated, but we are never drunk."

"Come off it," Davis said. "No clowning around tonight. Ivar said he'd kill you if you're drunk, and that's no empty threat. And you know what'll happen to us if we get caught. Are you coming with us or not?"

"We never leave a place. On the other hand, we are never in one place. That would be too mundane and scarcely to be tolerated. Yes, we will accompany us, though the answer to the Great Question, the uncompleted side of the formula, may be here in this minute metropolis of uncertainty and instability, not, as we hope, far up the River."

"Here's what Ivar proposes," Davis said.

Faustroll listened without interrupting, something he rarely did, then nodded. "We believe that that is as good a plan as any and perhaps better than most. Which is not to say that it has any merit at all."

"Very well. We'll meet at midnight at the Rock of Many Faces."

Davis paused, then said, "I do not know why Ivar insists on bringing Ann Pullen along. She's a troublemaker and a slut."

"Ah! We hate her so much, we must love her!"

"Nonsense!" Davis said. "She's contemptible, wicked, vicious, the lowest of the low. She makes the Great Whore of Babylon look like a saint.''

Faustroll laughed. ''We believe that she is a soul who had and has the strength of intellect and character to free herself of the bonds, limits, and restrictions imposed upon women by men since time began or, perhaps, shortly before that. She snaps her fingers under the puissant but pinched proboscis of the god you worship and the puny pinched penises of the men who worship him. She . . .''

''You will burn in hell as surely as a struck match burns,'' Davis said, his blue eyes slitted, his hands clenched.

''Many matches do not light because they are deficient in the wherewithal of combustion. But we agree with the dying words of the immortal Rabelais: 'Curtain! The farce is finished! I am setting out to seek a vast perhaps.' If we die the death of forever, so be it. There are not enough fires in Hell to burn all of us away.''

Davis opened his arms wide and held out his hands, indicating hopelessness. ''I pray that the good Lord will make you see the errors of your ways before it is too late for you.''

''We thank you for the kind thought, if it is kind.''

''You're impenetrable,'' Davis said.

''No. Expenetrating.''

Faustroll walked off, leaving Davis to figure out what he meant.

But Davis hurried away to be on time for his daily appointment. Just as he had been the royal masseur for Ivar the Boneless, when Ivar was king of an area far to the south of this state, so Davis was now premier masseur for Pachacuti. His job angered and frustrated him because he had been on Earth an M.D., a very good one, and then an osteopath. He had traveled to many places in the U.S.A., lecturing and founding many osteopathic colleges. When he was getting old, he had founded and headed a college in Los Angeles based on his eclectic discipline, neuropathy. That used the best theories and techniques of drugless therapy: osteopathy, chiropractic, Hahnemanism, and others. When he had died in 1919 at the age of eighty-four, his college was still flourishing. He was sure that it would grow and would found new branches throughout the world. But late-twentieth-centurians he had met had said that they had never heard of him or of the college.

Seven years ago, Ivar had been forced to flee from his kingdom because of treachery by an ally, Thorfinn the Skull-Splitter. Davis, Faustroll, and Ann Pullen had gone with Ivar. They did not know what to expect from Thorfinn, but they assumed that they would not like it.

After many fights, enslavements, and escapes while going up the River, they had been captured by the Incans. And here they were, enduring what they must and plotting to get freedom someday.

Ivar was as patient as a fox watching a toothsome hen, but his patience had been eroded away. Just why the Viking had not taken off by himself, Davis did not know. He would be burdened by them—from his viewpoint, anyway. But an unanalyzable magnetism kept the four together. At the same time that they were attracted to each other, they also were repulsed. They revolved about each other in intricate orbits that would have given an astronomer a headache to figure out.

About ten minutes by the sand clock before his scheduled appearance, Davis was in the building housing the Inca's court. This was a four-walled and roofed structure sitting on the intersection of many beams a hundred feet above the ground. The skeletal city creaked, groaned, and swayed around, above, and below them. It was noisy outside the building and only a trifle less so inside. Though the Inca sat on a bamboo throne on a dais while he listened to his petitioners, the people around him talked loudly to each other. Davis had threaded his way through them and now stood a few feet from the dais. Presently, the Inca would rise, a fishskin drum would boom three times, and he would retire to a small room with the woman he had chosen to honor with his royal lust. Afterward, Davis would massage the royal body.

Pachacuti was a short and dark man with a hawk nose, high cheekbones, and thick lips. Around the hips of his short squat body a long green towel served as a kilt, and a red towel, edged in blue, was draped over his shoulders as a cape. His headpiece was a turban-towel secured by a circlet of oak from which sprouted long varicolored fake feathers made of carved wood.

If Pachacuti had been naked, Davis often thought, he would not have looked like a monarch. Very few unclothed kings would be. In fact, even now, he was no more distinguished in appearance than any of his subjects. But his manner and bearing were certainly imperial.

Who was the woman who would share the royal couch today? Davis had thought that he did not care. And then he saw his bête noir, Ann Pullen, preceded by two spearmen and followed by two more. The crowd gave way for her. When she reached the dais, she stopped and turned around and smiled with lovely white teeth set in bright rouged lips.

Though Davis loathed her, he admitted to himself that she was beautiful. Those long wavy yellow tresses, the strikingly delicate and fine-boned face, the perfectly formed and outthrust breasts she was so proud of, the narrow waist and hips, and the long slim legs made her look like a goddess. Venus as she would be if Praxiteles had happened to dream of Ann Pullen. But she was such a bitch, he thought. However, Helen of Troy probably had been a bitch too.

The guards marched her toward the door of the room in which the Inca waited for her. A moment after she had entered the room, the guards admitted the little big-eyed priest who observed the virility of the Incan during his matings. When the king was done, and God only knew when that would be, the royal witness would step outside and announce the number of times the Inca had mounted his woman.

The crowd would rejoice and would congratulate their fellows. The kingdom would continue to flourish; all was well with its citizens' world.

Beware, though, if the Inca failed once.

Davis had never cursed. At least, not on Earth. But he did now.

"Go-o-o-od damn her!"

She had given herself to the Inca and now would become one of his wives, perhaps the favorite. But why? Had she quarreled with Ivar since he had been on the sentinel tower? Or had the Inca tempted her with such offers that she could no longer refuse him? Or had she, the Scarlet Woman, an abomination in the nostrils of the Lord, just decided that she would like to lie with the Inca before she left the kingdom tonight? The man was said to be extraordinarily virile.

Whatever the reason, Ivar would not ignore her infidelity. Though he had done so now and then in the past, that was because Ann had been discreet and he had been lying at the same time with another woman. For Ann to copulate with the Inca in public view, as it were, was to insult Ivar. Though he was usually self-controlled, he would react as surely as gunpowder touched with a flaming match.

"What's gotten into that woman?" Davis mumbled. "Aside from a horde of men?"

Ann Pullen was a late-seventeenth-century American who had lived—and she had lived to the fullest—in Maryland and Westmoreland County, Virginia. Born in a Quaker family, she had converted to the Episcopalian Church along with most of her tobacco planter family. She had married four times, a man by the name of Pullen being her final husband. Just when she took her first lover and when she took the last one even she did not know. But they had been coming and going for at least forty years during her turbulent life on Earth.

As she had declared—this had been in a public record—she saw no reason why a woman should not enjoy the same liberty and privileges as a man. Though that was a dangerous sentiment in her time, she had escaped arrests for harlotry and adultery. Twice, though, she had come close to being whipped by the court flogger because she was charged with attacking women who had insulted her.

Perhaps the isolation of the Maryland and Virginia counties in which she resided had enabled her to avoid the severe punishment she would have gotten in the more civilized Tidewater area. Or perhaps it was the fiery and pugnacious nature and the wild ways and free spirit of the Westmorelandians of her time. In any event, she had been a terrible sinner on Earth, Davis thought, and on the Riverworld she had gotten worse. His Church of Christ beliefs made him scorn and despise her. At the same time, he was grieved because she would surely burn in Hell. Sometimes, though he was ashamed of himself

afterward, he gloried in the visions of her writhing and screaming in the torments of Inferno.

So, now, the Jezebel had suddenly decided to couple with
Pachacuti. There was not much more she could do to make
trouble than this. Except for telling the Inca that Ivar, Davis,
and Faustroll were planning to leave the kingdom. Not even she
would be so low.

Or would she?

He wished to slip away from the court, but he did not dare to
anger the Inca. He was forced to listen to the cries and moans
of ecstasy from the emperor and Ann Pullen. The courtiers and
soldiers had quit talking to hear them, which made it worse for
Davis. Especially since they were not at all disgusted. Instead,
they were grinning and chuckling and nudging each other.
Several men and women were feeling each other, and one
couple was brazenly copulating on the floor. Savages! Beasts!
Where was the lightning stroke to burn them with a foretaste of
Hell? Where the vengeance of the Lord?

After several hours, the priest came out of the room. Smiling, he shouted that the Inca still had the virility demanded by
the gods and his people. The state would prosper; good times
would continue. Everybody except Davis and the man and the
woman on the floor cheered.

Presently, slave women carried in bowls and pitchers of
water and towels to bathe and to dry off the Inca and Ann.
When they came out, the chief priest went in to perform a
cleansing ritual. After he was done, a servant told Davis that
the Emperor was ready for him. Gritting his teeth, but trying to
smile at the same time, Davis entered the chamber of iniquity.
Despite the bathing, the two still reeked of sweaty and overly
fluidic sex.

Ann, naked, was lolling on a couch. She stretched out when
she saw Davis and then flipped a breast at him. One of her
chief pleasures was to flaunt her body before him. She knew
how disgusted that made him.

The Emperor, also naked, was lying on the massage table.
Davis went to work on him. When he was done, he was told to
massage Ann. The Emperor, after getting off the table, was
clothed by his dressers in some splendid ceremonial costume,

splendid by Riverworld standards, anyway. Then he left the chamber and was greeted with loud cheers by the crowd.

Ann got onto the table and turned over on her front.

She spoke in the Virginia dialect of her time. "Give me a very good rubdown, Andy. The Emperor bent me this way and that. I taught him many positions he did not know on Earth, and he used them all. If you were not such a holy man, I'd instruct you on them."

Two female attendants remained in the room. But they did not understand English. Davis, trying to keep his voice from trembling with anger, said, "What do you think Ivar is going to do about this?"

"What can he do?" she said flippantly. Nevertheless, her muscles stiffened slightly. Then, "What business is it of yours?"

"Sin is everybody's business."

"Just what I'd expect a smellsmock fleak preacher to say."

"Smellsmock? Fleak?" Davis said.

"A licentious idiot."

Davis was kneading her shoulder muscles. He would find it very easy to move his hands up, close them around her neck, and snap it. Though he was not a big man, he had very powerful hands. For a moment, he almost realized the fantasy flashing through his mind. But a true Christian did not murder, no matter how strong the provocation. On the other hand, he would not be really killing her. She would appear somewhere else tomorrow and bedevil others. Far from here, though.

"Licentious," she said. "You hate me so much because, deep down, you would like to tup me. The Old Adam in you wants to ravish me. But you shove that down into the shadows of your sinfulness, into the Old Horny crouching down there. I say that because I know men. Down there, they are all brothers. All, all, I say!"

"Whore! Slut! You lie! You would like to have carnal knowledge of every man in the world, and..."

She turned over abruptly. She was smiling, but her eyes were narrow. "Carnal knowledge? You mealy-mouth! Can't you use good old English? You wouldn't say tit if you had one in your mouth!''

Though he was not done massaging, he walked out of the room. The snickering and giggling of the servants followed him through the bamboo walls. They had not understood a word, but the tones of his and Ann's voices and her gestures were easily read.

Having recovered somewhat, he came back into the room. Ann was sitting up on the table and swinging her long shapely legs. She seemed pleased with herself. He stood in the door and said, ''You know what Ivar intends for us to do tonight?''

She nodded, then said, ''He's told me.''

''So you had to have one last fling?''

''I've done the double-backed beast with kings but never with an emperor. Now, if I could only find a god to take me as Zeus took Leda. Or the great god Odhinnr whom Ivar claims he's descended from. A god who has the stamina to keep going forever and no storms of conscience afterward and is always kind to me. Then my life would be complete.''

''I could vomit,'' he said, and he walked out again.

''That's one form of ejaculation!'' she said loudly.

He climbed down hundreds of steps, wondering meanwhile why these crazy pagans built such an inconvenient city. When he got to the ground, he searched for Faustroll along the Riverbank until he found him fishing from a pier. The Frenchman's bamboo basket held seven of the foot-long striped species known as zebras. He was describing to his fellow fishers the intricacies of the science he had invented. He called it pataphysics. Davis understood little of it. So, evidently, did the people around him. They nodded their heads at his remarks. But their puzzled expressions showed that they were as much at sea as most of his listeners. That Faustroll's Kishwa was not very good certainly did not help their comprehension.

3

''Pataphysics,'' Faustroll intoned, ''is difficult to define because we must use nonpataphysical terms to define it.''

He had to use French words interspersed with Kishwa, because "pataphysics" and many other terms were not in the Incan language. Thus, he bewildered his audience even more. Davis decided that Faustroll did not care deeply whether or not these listeners comprehended him. He was talking to himself to convince himself.

"Pataphysics is the science of the area beyond metaphysics," Faustroll continued. "It is the science of imaginary solutions, of the particular, the seeming exception. Pataphysics considers that all things are equal. All things are pataphysical. But few people practice pataphysics consciously.

"Pataphysics is not a joke or a hoax. We are serious, unlaughing, as sincere as a hurricane."

He added in English for some reason Davis could not figure out, "Pataphysics is synaptic, not synoptic."

Apparently, he had given up on the Incans. He switched to French.

"In conclusion, though nothing is ever concluded in the full sense of 'conclusion,' we know nothing of pataphysics yet know everything. We are born knowing it at the same time that we are born ignorant of it. Our purpose is to go forth and instruct the ignorant—that is, us, until we all are illuminated. Then, mankind as we unfortunately know it now will be transformed. We will become as God is supposed to be, in many respects, anyway, even though God does not exist, not as we know it, its backside is chaos, and, knowing the Truth, we in our fleshly forms will pupate ourselves into a semblance of the Truth. Which will be close enough."

Now here, Davis thought, is one who truly fulfills Ann's definition of a "fleak." And yet . . . and yet . . . Faustroll made some kind of sense. Remove all the folderol, and he was saying that people should look at things from a different angle. What was it that that late twentieth-century Arab he had met so many years ago had said? Abu ibn Omar had quoted . . . what was his name . . . ah! a man named Ouspensky. "Think in other categories." That was it. "Think in other categories." Abu had said, "Turn a thing over, look at its bottom side. A watch is said to be circular. But if its face is turned at right angles to you, the watch is an ellipse.

"If everybody were to think in other categories, especially in emotional, familial, social, economic, religious, and political areas, human beings would eliminate most of the problems that make their lives so miserable."

"It didn't happen on Earth," Davis had said.

"But here it may," Abu had said.

"Fat chance!" Davis had said. "Unless all turn to the Lord, to Jesus Christ, for salvation."

"And were truly Christian, not the narrow-minded, bigoted, selfish, power-hungry wretches which most of them are. I will offend you when I say that you are one of them, though you will deny it. So be it."

Davis had come close to punching the man, but he had turned away, trembling with anger, and walked off.

He still got indignant when he thought about Abu's accusation.

"Faustroll!" Davis said in English. "I must talk to you!"

The Frenchman turned around and said, "Commence."

Davis told him about Ann and the Emperor. Faustroll said, "You may inform the Boneless about this delightful situation if you care to. We do not wish to be in his neighborhood when he hears of it."

"Oh, he'll hear of it, though not from me. This area is a lava flow of rumor and gossip. Are you still willing to escape from this place tonight, as agreed?"

"With or without Ivar or Ann or you."

He pointed past Davis, then said, "Someone has already told him."

Davis turned around. The city proper, the towering skeleton city, began a half-mile from the Riverbank. The Viking was striding on the ground toward an entrance to a staircase. He gripped in one hand the shaft of a big stone ax. He was also carrying a very large backpack. Davis supposed that Ivar's grail was in it. It bulged so much, however, that it had to contain something else. Even from this distance, Davis could see that Ivar's face and body were bright red.

"He's going to kill the Inca!" Davis said.

"Or Ann, or both," Faustroll said.

It was too late to catch up with him. Even if they did, they could not stop him. Several times before, they had seen him in his insane rages. He would smash in their skulls with the ax.

"He'll not get through the Inca's bodyguards," the Frenchman said. "I believe that the only thing we can do is to follow our plan and leave tonight. Ann and Ivar won't be there. You and I must go without them."

Davis knew that Faustroll was deeply upset. He had said "I" instead of "we."

By then, the Viking had reached the third level and crossed over on it. For a moment, he disappeared behind a translucent wall formed by a lightweight sheet of dragonfish intestine.

"I feel as if I'm deserting him," Davis said. "But what can we do?"

"We have changed our mind, which is the prerogative, indeed, the duty, of a philosopher," Faustroll said. "The least we can do is to follow him and determine what happens to him. We might even be able to aid him in some way."

Davis did not think so. But he would not allow this cuckoo to show more courage than he.

"Very well. Let's go."

They put their grails in their shoulder bags and hurried to the city. After climbing up staircases and ladders, they reached the level on which were the Inca's quarters. They saw many people running around and very noisy about it. From a distance came a hullabaloo that only a large crowd could raise. At the same time, they smelled smoke. It had a different odor from the many cooking fires in the dwellings. Following the direction of the noise and sidestepping people running toward the staircases and ladders, they came out onto a small plaza.

The buildings around this, mostly two-story bamboo structures with half-walls, were government offices. The Inca's "palace" was the largest building, three stories high but narrow. Though it had a roof, its exterior had few walls. Its far side was attached to the main scaffolding of the city.

The odor of smoke had become stronger, and there were more men and women running around. The two men could make no sense out of the shouts and cries until Davis caught the Kishwa word for "fire." It was then they realized the commotion was not caused by Ivar. Or, perhaps, it was. Davis thought of the huge bulging bag on Ivar's back. Had that contained pine torches and an earthen jar of lichen alcohol?

The strong wind was carrying the clouds to the south, which explained why the smoke stink had not been so detectable in the lower levels. Getting to the palace would be dangerous. By now, the bamboo floor of the plaza was burning swiftly and they would have to go around the plaza. For all they knew, the floor on its other side was also ablaze. Near them, a crew was working frantically hauling up big buckets of water from the ground on six hoists. Through the many open spaces among the rooms and the levels, Davis saw lines of people passing buckets of water from the river.

It had all happened very swiftly.

Now Davis smelled the distinctive odor of burning flesh. And he could see several bodies lying in the flames. Several seconds later, a corpse fell through the weakened floor to the one below it.

It did not seem possible that one man could wreak all this.

"Will you go now?" Davis said. "Ivar is doomed, if he's not already dead. We'd better get down to the ground before we're caught in the fire."

"Reason does not always prevail," the Frenchman said. "But fire does."

They retreated, coughing, until the smoke thinned out enough for them to see. The exterior of the building was a few yards from them. Nearby were a staircase and several openings in the floor for descent by ladder. But they could not get to them because of the crowd surrounding them. The staircase and the ladders were jammed with a snarling, screaming, and struggling mob. Several fell off onto the heads of the refugees on the floor below.

"It is possible to climb down on the beams of the outer structure!" Faustroll yelled. "Let us essay to escape via those!"

By then, others had the same thought. But there was enough space for all. When Davis and the Frenchman got to the ground, they were shaking with the effort and their hands, bellies, and the inner parts of their legs were rubbed raw. They worked through the crowds until they were close to the River.

"Now is the time to appropriate a small sailing vessel and go up-River," Faustroll said. "No one is here to object."

Davis looked at the skeletal structure and the people swarming around it and still coming out of it. By then, the bucket brigades had done their work, though he would have bet a few minutes ago that the entire city was doomed. The smoke was gone except for some wisps.

He and Faustroll still had their grails. And a fishing vessel anchored a few yards out contained poles and nets and spears. That would have to be enough.

When they waded out to the boat, they saw a man, dark-skinned, black-haired, eyes closed, lying face up on the floor. His jaw moved slowly. He was not chewing a cud.

"Dreamgum," Faustroll said. "He is now somewhere in Incan Peru, his mind blazing with visions of the land he once knew but that never really existed. Or, perhaps, he is flying faster than light among the stars toward the limits of the limitless."

"No such splendid things," Davis said disgustedly. He pointed at the man's erect penis. "He dreams that he is lying with the most beautiful woman in the world. If he has the imagination to do so, which I doubt. These people are crude and brutal peasants. The apex of their dreams is a life of ease and no obligations, no masters to obey, plenty of food and beer, and every woman their love slave."

Faustroll hauled himself aboard. "You have just described Heaven, my friend—that is, the Riverworld. Except for the masters to obey and every woman being a love slave, as you so quaintly describe the velvet-thighed gender. Get rid of the masters and accept that many women will scorn you but that there are many others who will not, and you have the unimaginative man's ideal of the afterworld. Not so bad, though. Certainly, a step up from our native planet.

"As for this fellow, he was born among the poor, and he stayed among them. But the poor are the salt of the earth. By salt, we do not mean that excretion made by certain geological phenomena. We mean the salt left on the skin after much labor and heavy sweating, the salt accumulating from lack of bathing. That stinking mineral and the strata of rotting flaked-off skin cells is the salt of the earth."

Davis climbed onto the boat, stood up, and pointed at the man's jetting penis. "Ugh! Lower than the beasts! Let's throw the ape overboard and get going."

Faustroll laughed. "Doubtless he dreams of Ann, our local Helen of Troy. We, too, have done so and are not ashamed of it. However, how do you know that he is not dreaming of a man? Or of his beloved llama?"

"You're disgusting, too," Davis said. He bent over and clutched the man's ankles. "Help me."

Faustroll put his hands under the man's arms and hoisted him. "Uh! Why does gravity increase its strength when we lift a corpse or a drunk or a drug-sodden? Answer us that, our Philistine friend. We will answer for you. It is because gravity is not an unvarying force, always obeying what we call the laws of physics. Gravity does vary, depending upon the circumstances. Thus, contrary to Heraclitus, what goes up does not always come down."

"You chatter on like a monkey," Davis said. "Here we go! One, two, three, heave!"

The man splashed into the water on his side, sank under the surface, then came up sputtering. Waist-high in the River, he began walking to the bank.

"Thank us for your much-needed bath!" Faustroll said, and he laughed. Then he began hauling up the anchor-stone.

But Davis pointed inshore and said, "Here they come!"

Ten soldiers, wooden-helmeted and carrying spears, were running toward them.

"Someone's reported us!" Davis said, and he groaned. Two minutes later, they were being marched off to jail.

4

Ivar and Ann had not been killed. The Viking had fought through many soldiers, slaying and wounding many, yet had somehow reached his goal though he was bleeding from many wounds. His bloodstained ax had crashed down upon the head of the Inca, and Pachacuti had ceased to be the emperor. Ivar had made no attempt to kill Ann. That he was knocked out just after smashing the Inca's skull in may been the only reason he did not slay her.

Under the law of the Western Sun Kingdom, Ivar should have been kept alive to be tortured for days until his body could take it no longer. But the man who seized power had another idea. Tamcar was the general of a regiment but was not next in line for the throne. He immediately launched his soldiers against Pachacuti's, killed them, and declared himself the Inca. His assassins murdered the other generals, and, after some fighting, the survivors of the regiments surrendered to the new Inca. So much for the tradition of an orderly succession.

Though Tamcar publicly denounced Ivar, he must have been secretly grateful to him. He sentenced him to the Leap of Death, but that gave Ivar a thin chance to win his freedom and exile from the kingdom. Ann Pullen, Faustroll, and Davis had had no part in slaying Pachacuti, yet they were judged guilty by association with the Viking. Actually, the new Inca was just ridding himself of all those he considered dangerous to him. He rounded up a score of high-placed men and sent them out onto the gangplank. All but two fell. This pleased the people, though some were disappointed because not all failed. Tamcar sought out others whom he suspected might want to take the throne away from him. They, along with criminals, were forced to make the Leap. The mob loved the spectacles. After these warm-ups, the main event came. Ivar and his companions now had their opportunity to thrill the populace. Not to mention themselves.

Two weeks after Pachacuti's death, Davis and his fellow prisoners were taken to the tower at high noon. They had been held in a stockade, thus had had the space in which to exercise vigorously. Also, they had practiced long jumping on the runway and the sand pit provided for those who had to make the Leap of Death. The Emperor wanted his gamesters to come as near as they could to the receiving gangplank before falling. The people loved a good show, and the Emperor loved what the people loved. He sat on a chair on the platform from which projected the "freedom" plank.

The drums beat and the unicorn-fish horns were blown. The crowd below cheered at the announcement of the first jump.

Faustroll, standing behind Davis, said, "Remember, our friend. The degree of force of gravity depends upon the attitude of the one defying it. If there were such a thing as good luck, we would ask that it be given to you."

"Good luck to you, too," Davis said. He sounded very nervous, even to himself.

The captain of the royal guards shouted that he would begin the count. Before the two minutes were up, Davis had sped down the thirty-foot-long plank, brought his right foot down hard on its end, and soared up. It was then that the rapture seized him. Afterward, he believed that that was the only thing that bore him to safety. It had been given to him by God, of course. He had been saved by the same Being who had saved Daniel in the lion's den.

Nevertheless, he fell hard forward as his feet, just behind the toes, were caught by the end of the plank. His chest and face slammed into the hard yew wood near the edge of the plank. His hands gripped the sides of the plank, though he was not in danger of falling off. He lay for some time before getting up. Cheers, jeers, and boos rose from the mob on the ground. He paid no attention to them as he limped along the plank to the platform and was taken to one side by guards. His heart beat fast, and he did not quit trembling for a long time. By then, Faustroll was running down the gangplank, his face set with determination.

He, too, soared, though Davis doubted that the Frenchman was caught in the ecstasy he had felt. He landed with no inch to spare but managed to make himself fall forward. If he had gone backward and thus sat on the air, he would have fallen.

He was grinning when he got to Davis's side. "We are such splendid athletes!" he cried.

The drums beat, and the horn blew for the third time. Ann, as naked as her predecessors, her skin white with fear, ran along the gangplank. Bent forward, her arms and long slim legs pumping, she sprung over the void without hesitation.

"What courage! What audacity!" Faustroll cried. "What a woman!"

Davis, despite his dislike for her, admitted to himself that the Frenchman was right. But her bravery and strength were not enough to propel her to a good landing. The end of the plank struck her in her midriff and her elbows slammed onto the wood. Her breath whooshed out. For a moment, she hung, legs kicking over the emptiness. Her efforts to catch her breath were agonizing. Then she stretched out her arms, moving her hands along the edge of the plank. Her face was against the wood. She began to slip backward as her grip weakened.

Ivar bellowed, his voice riding over the clamor of the mob and the cries of the men on the platforms. "You are a Valkyrie, Ann! Fit to be my woman! Hang on! You can do it! Pull yourself up and forward! I will meet you at the platform! If I should fall, I will meet you again somewhere on the River!"

That surprised Davis. During the two weeks of their imprisonment, Ivar had not spoken a word to Ann. Nor she to him.

Ann grinned then, though whether it was with despair or pain or with joy at Ivar's words was a question. Sweating, her face even whiter, struggling hard, she pulled herself forward until her legs were no longer dangling. Then she rolled over and lay flat on her back while her breasts rose and fell quickly. Her midriff bore a wide red mark from the impact. Two minutes later, she got on all fours and crawled several feet. Then she rose and walked unsteadily but proudly to the platform.

Faustroll embraced her, perhaps more enthusiastically than modesty permitted, when she joined him. She wept for a moment. Faustroll wept too. But they separated to watch Ivar when again the drums rattled and the horns blared.

The huge man, his bronze-red hair shining in the sun, stepped onto the gangplank. As the other jumpers had done, he had been bending and flexing and leaping up and down in a warm-up. Now he crouched, his lips moving, counting the seconds along with the captain of the guards. Then he came up out of his crouch and ran, his massive legs pumping. The plank bent down under his weight, and it quivered from the pounding. His left foot came down just a few inches from the end. He was up, legs kicking.

Down he came, a foot short of the end of the victory plank. His hands shot out and gripped the sides of the wood near the end. The plank bent, sprang up a little, and sank down again. It cracked loudly.

Davis cried out, "Get on the plank! It's going to break!"

Ivar was already swinging himself backward to get momentum for a forward swing so he could get his leg up on the plank. Just as he did come forward, a sharp snapping noise announced that the wood had broken. Ann shrieked. Davis gasped. Faustroll yelled, *"Mon dieu!"*

Roaring, Ivar hurtled out of sight. Davis rushed forward and pressed his stomach against the railing. The plank was turning over and over. But the Viking was not in sight.

Davis leaned far out. There, thirty feet below him, Ivar was hanging by his hands from a slanting beam. His towerward swing had carried him far enough to grab one of the horizontal beams projecting beyond the main structure. Hanging from the beam with only his hands, he had managed to work closer to the building. But he must have slipped, and he had fallen. But, again, he had saved himself by clutching a cross beam slanting at a forty-five-degree angle in the exterior of the city structure. His body must have slammed hard against it, and his hands were slipping down along the slanting wood, leaving a trail of smeared blood.

When they were stopped where another angled beam met the one he was clinging to, he strove to pull himself up. And he succeeded. After that, he had to climb back up until he got to the platform on which Davis stood. If he did not do that, he would not be freed.

By then, Tamcar had left his throne to look over the platform and down at the Viking. He grimaced when he saw Ivar slowly but surely making his way up the outside of the structure. But even Tamcar had to obey the rules of the ordeal. No one was allowed to interfere with Ivar. It was up to him to get to the platform or to fall. Ten minutes or so passed. And the bronze-red hair of the Viking appeared and then his grinning face. After he hauled himself over the railing, he lay for a while to regain his strength.

When he arose, he spoke to Tamcar. "Surely, the gods favor us four. They have destined us for greater things than being your slaves."

"I do not think so," the Emperor said. "You will be freed, as the gods decree. But you will not go far. The savages just north of our state will seize you, and you will no longer be free. I will make sure of that."

For a moment, it looked as if Ivar were going to hurl himself at the Emperor. But the spears of the royal guard were ready for him. He relaxed, smiled, and said, "We'll see about that."

Davis felt drained. The ordeal had been terrible enough. Now, after having survived it, they would again fall into the hands of evil. Here, at least, they had plenty of food. But, just beyond the upper boundary of the Kingdom of the West Sun, the land on both sides of the River was occupied by people whom it was best to avoid. They gave their slaves just enough food to keep them working; they enjoyed crucifying slaves and tying them up in agonizing positions for a long time; they relished eating them. If you were their captive and you suddenly were given much food, you knew that you were being fattened to be the main course.

Davis thought that he wold have been better off if he had fallen to his death. At lest, that way, he would have had a fifty-fifty chance to rise again far north of here.

He was still downcast when the boat carrying them brought them within sight of what the Incans called the Land of the Beasts. The two crewmen were starting to haul down the lateen sail. He was sitting with the other captives in the middle of the vessel. Their hands were bound before them with thin cords of fish-gut. They were naked and possessed only their grails. On both sides of them stood guards with spears.

The captain of the guards said, "Within minutes, you will all be free." He laughed.

Apparently, the Emperor had sent word to the Beasts that they would soon have slaves as a gift. A group of dark-skinned

Caucasians stood at a docking pier on the right bank. They waved flint-tipped spears and big clubs while they danced wildly, the sun flashing on the mica chips inset in their flaring, light-gray, fish-scale helmets. Davis had heard that they were supposed to be a North African people who lived sometime in the Old Stone Age. Seeing them made him sweat and sick at his stomach. But, so far, they had not put out on boats to meet them.

Ivar, sitting close to him, spoke softly. "We are four. The guards are ten. The three sailors are not worth considering. The odds favor us. When I give the word, Faustroll and I will attack those on the sternside. You, Red-Hair, and you, Ann, will attack the others. Use your grails as hammers, swing them by the handles."

"The odds favor us!" Faustroll said, and he laughed softly. "That is a pataphysical view!"

Ivar bent over and strained to separate the cord securing his hands together. His face got red; his muscles became snakes under the skin. The guards jeered at his efforts. Then their mouths dropped open as the cord snapped, and he shot up, roaring, his grail swinging out. The hard lower edge caught a guard under his chin. Ivar grabbed the man's falling spear with his other hand and drove it into another guard's belly.

The Incans had expected no resistance. If they did get it, they were certain that the handicapped slaves would be easily subdued. But the Viking had removed two guards from the fight seconds after it had started.

Davis and Ann swung their grails with good effect. His came up and slammed into the crotch of the nearest guard. After that, he had no time to see what his companions were doing. A spearhead gashed the front of his thigh, and then the man who had wounded him dropped when Davis's grail smashed into the side of his head.

It was all over within five seconds. The sailors leaped into the water. Ivar ran toward the steersman, who jumped overboard. Following the Viking's bellowed commands, the woman and the two men hoisted the sail. A great shout went up from the savages on land, and they immediately manned boats.

Drums sounded, apparently signaling those farther up the River to intercept the slaves' boat.

They came close to doing it. But Ivar, a consummate sailor, evaded them and then left them behind. They sailed northward, free for the time being.

5

Eighteen years had passed since the flight from the Land of the Beasts. They had fought much, been imprisoned a few times, and had suffered several hundred mishaps and scores of wounds. But they had lived in this state, Jardin, for seven years with relative tranquility and content.

Andrew Davis's hutmate was Rachel Abingdon, a daughter of an American missionary couple. He had converted her to his belief that the Redeemer had been born again on the River and that they must find him someday. Meanwhile, they had preached to the locals, not very successfully, but they did have a dozen or so disciples. Materially, Davis thrived. Many men and women came to him daily to be massaged or manipulated osteopathically. They paid for their treatments with artifacts which he could trade for other goods, if he so desired, and with the gourmet foods their grails delivered. Life was easy. The citizens were not power-hungry, at least not politically. The days passed for Davis as if he were in the land of the lotus-eaters. Golden afternoons fishing and happy evenings sitting around the fires and eating and talking merged one into the other.

Ivar the Boneless was general of the army, which was organized solely for defense. But the neighboring states for a thousand miles up and down the River were nonbelligerent. Militarily, he had little to do except keep the soldiers drilled, inspect the boundary walls, and hold maneuvers now and then.

Ann had long ago quit living with Ivar. To Davis's amazement, she had gotten religion. If, that is, the Church of the Second Chance could be called a religion in any true sense.

The missionaries he had talked to and heard preach claimed to believe in a Creator. But they said that all Earth religions were invalid in stating they were divinely inspired. The Creator—they avoided the word "God"— had made a being superior to man shortly before the great resurrection of the Earth dead. These were a sort of flesh-and-blood angels, called Makers, whose mission was to save all of humanity from itself and to raise it to a spiritual level equal to that of the Makers. The man or woman who was not so raised was, after an indeterminate length of time, doomed. He or she would wander the void forever as conscious matterless entities without will.

"The Chancers' ethics are very high," Davis had sneered one day while talking to Ann. "They pay no attention to sexual morality as long as no force or intimidation is involved."

"Sexual mores were necessary on Earth," she had answered, "to protect the children. Also, venereal disease and unwanted pregnancies caused great suffering. But here there are no such diseases, nor do women get pregnant. Actually, the largest, the most powerful element of sexual morality on Earth was the concept of property. Women and children were property. But here there is no such thing as property, no personal property, anyway, except for a person's grail and a few towels and tools. Most of you men haven't absorbed that idea yet. To be fair, a lot of women haven't either. But all of you will learn someday."

"You're still a slut!" Davis had said angrily.

"A slut who doesn't desire you at all, though you desire me. The day you realize that, you'll be one more step closer to true love and to salvation."

As always, Davis, teeth and hands clenched, body quivering, had strode away. But he was unable to stay away from her. If he did not talk to her, he could never bring her to the true salvation.

Faustroll, two years ago, had declared that he was God. "You need look no more, our friend," he said to Davis. "Here before you is the Savior. The fleshly semblance of a man that we have adopted should not deceive you. It is needed to prevent you and the rest of us from being blinded by our glory.

Accept us as your God, and we will share our divinity with you.

"Actually, you are already divine. What I will do is reveal to you how you may realize this and how to act upon the glorious realization."

Faustroll was hopeless. His philosophy was blather. Yet, for some reason, Davis could not help listening to him. He did not do so for amusement, as he had once thought, or because he might make Faustroll see the Light. Perhaps it was just that he liked him despite his infuriating remarks. The Frenchman had something, a je ne sais quoi.

Davis had not seen Ivar for months, when, one day, Ivar hove into his view. "Hove" was the appropriate word; the Viking was a huge ship, a man-of-war. Behind him was a much smaller man, a tender, as it were. He was short and thin, black-haired and brown-eyed. His face was narrow; his nose, huge and beaked.

Ivar bellowed in Esperanto, "Andrew the Red! Still dreaming of finding the woman who gave birth to a second Christ? Or have you given up that quest?"

"Not at all!"

"Then why do you sit on your ass day after day, week after week, month after month, year after year?"

"I haven't!" Davis said indignantly. "I have made many converts to people who had rejected Christ! Or who had never heard of Him, who had not been in a state of grace!"

Ivar waved his hand as if dismissing their importance. "You could put them all under the roof of a small hut. Are you going to be satisfied with hanging around here forever when, for all you know, your Jesus is up-River and waiting for you to appear so that he may send you forth to preach?"

Davis sensed a trap of some sort. The Viking was grinning as if he were ready to pounce on him.

"It makes better sense to wait here for Him," Davis said. "He will come someday, and I will be ready to greet Him."

"Lazy, lazy, lazy! The truth is that you like to live here where no one is trying to kill or enslave you. You make feeble efforts to preach, and you spend most of your time fishing or tupping your wife.''

"Now, see here!" Davis said.

"I am here, and I see. What I see is a man who was once on fire, has cooled, and is now afraid to dare hardship and suffering.''

"That's not true!''

"I reproach you, but I also reproach myself. I, too, had the dream of going up the River until I came to its mouth. There I expected to find the beings who made this world and who brought about our resurrection. If they would not answer my questions willingly, they would do so under duress. I say that though it would seem that they are immeasurably more powerful than I am.

"But I forgot my dream. To use your own phrase, I was at ease in Zion. But this place is not Zion.''

Davis nodded to indicate the man with Ivar. "Who's that?''

Ivar's large hand pushed the little man forward. "His name is Bahab. He's a newcomer. Bahab the Arab. He was born in Sicily when his people held that island. I do not know when he lived according to your reckoning, but it does not matter. He has an interesting tale, one that reminded me of what I had forgotten. Speak, Bahab!''

The little man bowed. He spoke in a high voice and in a heavily accented Esperanto. Though some of his words were not in local usage, Davis figured out their meaning from the context.

"You will pardon me, I trust, for such an abrupt approach and possible intrusion. I would prefer sitting with you and having coffee and getting to know you before beginning my story. But some people are barbaric or, I should say, have different customs.''

"Never mind all that!" Ivar said loudly. "Get on with your story!''

"Ah, yes. Some years ago, I was up-River a long way from here. I talked to a man who had the most amazing news. I do not know if it was true or not, though he had nothing to gain from lying to me. On the other hand, some men lie just for the pleasure of it, sons of Shaitan that they are. But sometimes, if the lie is merely for amusement's sake . . .''

"Are you going to make me regret bringing you here?" Ivar shouted.

"Your pardon, Excellency. The man of whom I spoke said that he had a curious tale. He had wandered far, up and down this Valley, but had never encountered anything so wondrous. It seems that he was once in an area where a certain woman, who claimed to be a virgin, conceived.''

"Oh, my God!" Davis said. "Can it be true?"

Bahab said, "I do not know. I did not witness the event, and I am skeptical. But others who had been there at the time swore that what the man said was indeed true."

"The baby! The baby!" Davis said. "Was it a boy?"

"Alas, no! It was female.''

"But that couldn't be!" Davis said.

Bahab paused as if he were wondering if Davis had called him a liar. Then he smiled. "I merely tell you what the man and his fellows, actually, five in number, told me. It does not seem likely that all would be conspiring to lie to me. But if I offend you, I will say no more.''

"Oh, no!" Davis said. "I'm not insulted. On the contrary. Please continue.''

Bahab bowed, then said, "All this had happened years before I came to that area. By now, the baby would be fully grown, if there was such a baby. The woman may not have been a virgin, as she claimed, and some man might be the father. But that would be miracle enough since all men and women seem to be sterile.''

"But a baby girl?" Davis said. "That's can't be!"

"I have talked to wise men and women of the late twentieth century, by Christian reckoning, scientists they call themselves," Bahab said. "They told me that, if a woman could be induced to conceive by chemical methods, the child would be female. I did not understand their talk of 'chromosomes,' but they assured me that a virgin female can conceive only a female. They also said that, in their time, this had never happened. Or in any time before theirs.''

"They leave God out of their science," Davis said. "It happened once . . . when Jesus was born."

Bahab looked incredulous, but he said nothing.

"What you think should happen," Ivar said, "and what does happen are often not the same. You still do not know the truth. The only way you can find that is to venture forth again and determine for yourself. Surely, you can't be uninterested because this child was female? There were women goddesses, you know."

"God does what He wishes to do," Bahab said.

"You are right, Ivar," Davis said. "I must search out this woman and her daughter and talk to them. You are also right, I confess, in that I have let sloth and peace lull me to sleep."

"We go! I, too, have been asleep! But I am tired of this purposeless life. We will build a boat, and we will take it up the River!"

"Rachel will be pleased," Davis said. "I think."

Rachel was eager to go, though she also was disappointed that the Savior was a woman.

"But then, we don't know that this story is true," she said. "Or it may be a half-truth. Perhaps the child was male. But evil people have distorted the story, changed it to make the baby a female. It's a lie which the Devil begat. He used many devices to lure the faithful into error."

"I don't like to think that," Davis said. "But you could be right. Whatever the truth, we must try to find it."

Faustroll said that he would go with them. "This virgin birth could be a pataphysical exception. Pataphysics, as we have remarked more than once, is the science of exceptions. We doubt that it happened since we do not remember having done it. We will be pleased to expose the charlatans who claimed that it did happen."

Ann Pullen said that she was staying in Jardin. No one, however, had asked her to accompany them. Davis thought that he should have rejoiced when he heard the news. But he felt a pang. He did not know why he was disappointed or why he felt a hurt in his chest. He detested the woman.

A month later, the boat was complete, a fine ship with a

single mast and twenty oars. Ivar had picked the crew, brawny men and their battle-tested women, all eager to put the soft life behind them. Only two of Davis's disciples had been allowed to go on Ivar's boat, and that was because they did not object to fighting in self-defense. The others, pacifists all, would follow in a smaller vessel.

At dawn of the day set for their departure, they gathered at a grailstone. After the stone had shot its thundering and white flash upward, they removed their grails, now filled with food of various kinds, beer, cigarettes, and dreamgum. Davis would pass out the tobacco, beer, and gum to the crew, though he would have preferred to throw them into the River. Since they would eat breakfast on the vessel later in the morning, they began boarding from the pier. The air was cool, but Davis was shivering with excitement. For a long time, he had been aware that something was missing from his life. Now he knew that it was the desire to explore and to find adventure. On Earth, he had been a traveler over much of the United States, lecturing and founding colleges of osteopathy. He had been faced with the hostility of local doctors and of the crowds provoked by the M.D.s. He had charged head-on into the jeers, boos, death threats, and rotten eggs thrown at him. But he had persisted in a campaign he and his colleagues had finally won.

On the Riverworld, he had seldom stayed long in one place except when detained in slavery. He was a walker-to-and-fro of the earth and a far-venturing sailor, too. Real happiness was not his unless he had a quest beckoning him to far lands.

Ivar stood on the rear deck by the steersman and bellowed orders. He, too, was happy, though he complained of the crew's slowness and clumsiness.

Two burly Norsemen began to loosen ropes securing the vessel to the pier. They halted when Ivar bellowed at them to wait a moment. Davis heard a man shouting, and he looked shoreward. The top of the sun had just cleared the mountains; its rays swept away the grayness and shone on the stranger. He was running across the plain, waving his arms and yelling in Esperanto.

"Don't go yet! Wait for me! I want to go with you!"

"He'd better have a good reason for delaying us," Ivar said loudly. "Otherwise, into the water he goes!"

Davis was curious about the mysterious stranger, but he also felt something unaccountable. Was it a premonition of dread? Did this man bring unsettling news? Though Davis had no reason to suspect this, he felt that he would be happier if the man had never showed up.

The fellow reached the pier and halted, breathing hard, his grail dangling from one hand. He was of middle height and rangy. His face was strong and handsome, long, narrow, though partly obscured by his black, wide-brimmed, high-crowned hat. Under the shadow of the hat were dark eyes. The long hair falling from under the hat was glossy black. A black cloak covered his shoulders. A black towel was around his waist. His jackboots were shiny black fish-hide. His black belt supported a wooden scabbard from which stuck the fish-hide-bound hilt of a rapier. If the weapon was made of iron, it was unique in this area.

"What brings you croaking like a raven of ill omen to us?" Ivar yelled.

"I just heard that you were leaving for up-River," the man said in a deep voice. His Esperanto was heavily tainted by his native language, which must have had many harsh sounds. "I've run all the way down from the mountains to catch you. I would like to sign up. You will find me handy. I can row with the best, and I am an excellent archer, though recent events have robbed me of my bow. And I can fight."

He paused, then said, "Though I was once a peaceful man, I now live by the sword."

He drew out his rapier. It was indeed of steel. "This has pierced many a man."

"Your name?" Ivar shouted.

"I answer to Newman."

"I expect and get immediate obedience," Ivar said.

"You have it."

"What is your mission?"

"The end of the River, though I am in no hurry to get to it."

Ivar laughed, then said, "We have something in common,

though I suppose that many are also trying to get there. We have room for you as long as you pull your weight. Come aboard. You will take your turn at the oar later.''

''Thank you.''

The boat was pushed from the pier, and the two Norsemen jumped onto the vessel. Presently, it was making its way up the River. When the morning breeze came, the rowers shipped their oars, and the fore-and-aft sail and the boom sail were hoisted. The crew sat down to eat from their grails.

Ivar came down from the deck to talk to people amidships. He stood above the newcomer. ''What tale of interest do you bring?''

The man looked up.

''I have many.''

''We all do,'' Ivar said. ''But what have you found most amazing?''

Newman half-lidded his eyes as if to shut out the light while he searched his inner darkness. He seemed to be feeling around for some treasure.

Finally, he said, ''Perhaps the most amazing is a man who claimed to be Jesus Christ. Do you know of him or did you live in a time and a place on Earth where he was unknown?''

''My gods were Odin and Thor and others,'' Ivar growled. ''I have sacrificed many Christians to him on Earth. But, near the end of my life, I became a Christian. More from a desire to hedge my bets, you might say, than from true faith. When I came to this world and found that it was neither Valhalla nor Heaven, though much more like Valhalla than Heaven, I renounced both beliefs. But it is hard not to call out for my native gods when I need them.''

''Those who had never heard of Jesus on Earth have heard of him here,'' Newman said. ''But you know enough about him so that I do not have to explain who he is.''

''I could not escape knowing more of him than I care to hear,'' Ivar said. He pointed at Davis. ''That man, Andrew the Red, is constantly prating about him.''

Davis had been inching closer to Newman. He said, ''I'm eager to hear your story, stranger. But this man who claimed to be Jesus cannot be He. He is in Heaven, though He may have been reincarnated as a woman on this world. Or so some say. My wife and I are going up-River to find her."

"Good luck, what with all the many billions here and the chance that she might now be down-River," the man said. "But you will not be offended, I hope, if I say that you will be disappointed even if you find the woman."

"Enough!" Ivar said. "The tale!"

"I came to a certain area shortly after the man calling himself Jesus was crucified by a fanatical medieval German monk. He was called Kramer the Hammer. The crucified man was still living, so you will see how soon after the event I arrived. The short of it is that I talked to him just before he died. And then I talked to a man who had lived in the dead man's time and place on Earth and knew him well. This man confirmed that the dead man had indeed been Yeshua, as the witness called him.

"I was very near him when he spoke his last words. He cried out, 'Father! They know what they're doing! Do not forgive them!' He sounded as if his experiences on this world had stripped him of the faith he had on Earth. As if he knew that mankind was not worth saving or that he had failed in his mission."

"Impossible!" Davis said.

Newman stared coldly at Davis. "I'm lying?"

"No, no! I don't doubt your story of what happened. What I don't believe is that the man on the cross was really Jesus. He's not the first nor the last of those who said that they were the Savior. Some may have genuinely believed that they were."

"How do you account for the testimony of the witness?"

"He was lying."

Newman shrugged. "It makes no difference to me."

Rachel touched Davis's shoulder. "You look troubled."

"No. Angry."

But he was also downcast, though he knew he should not be.

That evening, the boat was moored near a grailstone. After the stone thundered, the crew ate the offerings of the grails. They also devoured the freshly caught and cooked fish offered to them by the locals. Davis sat in a circle around a bamboo wood fire. Faustroll was at his side.

The Frenchman said, "Your wife was correct when she said you seemed troubled by Newman's tale. You still seem so."

"My faith is not broken, not even shaken," Davis said.

"You say so. Your body, your voice declare that you are plunged into black thoughts."

"The Light will clear away the darkness."

"Perhaps, friend," Faustroll said. "Here, have some fish. It's delicious. It's something you can have faith in."

Davis did not reply. The sight of Faustroll's greasy lips and the thought of Faustroll's shallowness sickened him. Or did the sickness come from another cause? He was far more disturbed than he had admitted to Rachel or the Frenchman.

"The stranger, he talked as if with authority," Faustroll said. "Of course, all crazies do."

"Crazies?"

"There is something deeply disturbing in that man, though he has much self-control. Did you not perceive it? He is dressed in black as if he is in mourning."

"He just seemed like one more mercenary adventurer," Davis said.

Faustroll put his hand on Davis's shoulder.

"There is something we must tell you. Perhaps our timing is wrong, seeing that you are so melancholy. But, sooner or later, you who seek the Light must face it, though the Light may not be the color you expect."

"Yes?" Davis said. He was not very interested.

"We speak of the time when you leaped across the void between Pachacuti's gangplanks. You said that you were seized by a spiritual rapture as soon as your foot left the gangplank. The rapture lifted you as if it were a gas-filled balloon. You soared higher than you should have, higher than you were capable of leaping. It was, you said, given by God. But . . ."

Davis sat up straighter. Some interest flickered in him.

"Yes?"

"You crossed the gap and landed upon the plank. But your feet struck its end. As a result, you landed hard and painfully."

You might have fallen off the plank then if you had not grabbed its sides."

Faustroll paused. Davis said, "What about it?"

"Rapture is fine. It carried you across safely. But then you struck the plank. Reality entered; the rapture was gone."

"What about that?"

"We are making an analogy, perhaps a parable. Think about that leap, friend, while you journey in a quest for what may be imaginary. Rapture is nontangible and temporary. Reality is hard and long lasting and often painfully crippling. What will you do if you find that the woman did not conceive and that there is no child?

"Reality may be a club which shatters your ability to ever feel that rapture again. We hope, and it is for your own good, that you never find that child.

"Think about that."

If the King Like Not
the Comedy

Jody Lynn Nye

"Nay, *listen* to the lines you say," William Shakespeare pleaded with his cast. "If you merely recite you'll not gain the sympathy of your audience. And you, sir," he turned to confront one of his players, "they're not supposed to feel for you. You're a vile, wicked caitiff, a tale-teller, a liar, and a slanderer. Your punishment at the last is richly deserved."

"Guilty as sin, my lord." Washington Irving grinned, leaning back against the rail of the boat, the *City of London*. "I can't help hoping for sympathy. It's human nature. Sorry, Will. I'll try again to be an unrepentant Lucio. I'll repeat it again, measure for measure."

Will turned away to smile slightly at the young man's pun.

"Do you, then. And you, Duke, pray attempt more majesty. You are the central figure, he who compels all things to happen."

Aristophanes nodded sharply at him. With his winged black eyebrows and ram-curly hair, he looked stern all the time, but Will learned the expression concealed a mighty sense of humor. He was also an unrepentant landlubber, and suffered each time the Shakespeare Company journeyed along the River to one of its engagements. He tottered uneasily across the deck and clung to the rail beside Irving. His olive face was pale.

"Do we land soon, amiki Will?"

"When we see the banner, my friend," Will promised, "but not unless the nation of Alcapolando falls within the pale of

41

those which are prepared to receive and release us as we are. The line, please, Master Hang.''

"Upon mine honor, thou shalt marry her." Hang Yi, seated on a barrel against the cabin doors, spoke up at once. Their prompter never needed to refer to the text: it had been written down from his own capacious memory.

A burst of sound interrupted their conversation. "Hey, Will," called out Haroun Baxter, waving his wooden horn. "Are we doing the finale or not? Webber's got just enough juice for one more run through before we have to stop and recharge."

"Right you are, Haroun. Very well! Cast!" Will clapped his hands and shouted over the hubbub of voices on all three of the lead boats. "Final number, please. And a one, a two . . .''

When he awoke, naked and hairless on this world, Shakespeare had been fortunate enough to land among a goodly number of folk who came from his own time, seventeenth-century England, including the miraculous presence of two actors from his own company of Stratford. As there was no need to strive for mere survival, it seemed utterly natural to take up again where they had left off. Within a short time, Little Stratford, as the narrow band of trees and clearings had come to be known, boasted the only organized theater group up- or down-River.

The lead dame of the company was Sister Margaret, a former nun who adored Shakespeare's dramas, and burst into hysterical laughter whenever she heard the line, "Get thee to a nunnery," though she would never tell him why. Once she got over the loss of her religion, clothes, and the security of the cloister, she and Will had taken up together. Not a beautiful woman, as other men saw her, she had lustrous, dark eyes, and thick black hair, two features that Will had always found compelling. Her figure was not the stick-straight set of bones favored by the twentieth-centurians, but a warm, curvy armful. In this comedy she played Mistress Overdone, but she had been Juliet's Nurse, Elizabeth Woodville, the Abbess Aemilia, all with equal aplomb. She acted as godmother to the chorus and minor parts, and still had energy left for those times when the two of them were alone together. God did indeed call to His service formidable women. She made a wonderful subject for sonnets.

The other three dramatists had come to Little Stratford one at a time. In the second year after Resurrection, Irving had come poling up the River with Hang Yi on a boat like a bamboo coracle. The American was friendly and goodhearted, always ready to defuse an argument with humor. Hang Yi was a gem, a treasure. He carried within his mind the texts for anything that he had ever read, no matter how trivial, but among them all of Will's plays. Another twentieth-centurian called the talent an "eidetic memory." Whatever it was, Will blessed it, for every time a stranger from the sixteenth century forward heard who he was, he demanded a snatch from one of the plays. As the father of his works, he retained a certain amount of what he wrote within him forever, but as a playwright, he was always conceiving new projects, and was disturbed when all his audience wanted was the same old thing.

Aristophanes had traveled to Little Stratford with a cluster of Second Chancers, and when they moved on, he stayed, saying that he had found *his* church. His English was strained but comprehensible. It improved rapidly over the years while he learned to translate his works until he was able to compose in English and Esperanto. Will was familiar with the classicist, having shamelessly lifted some of his story lines from the Athenian's plays. Aristophanes was philosophical about having been used as a reference. He confessed that he, too, had drawn ideas from previous dramatists and historians, and wondered what *they* thought of *him*. What made him unhappy was that when all else was equal in language, availability, and quality of performance, modern audiences still preferred Shakespeare's works to his own.

The twentieth-century Englishman, Webber, had awakened by Little Stratford's central grailstone in the fifth year after Resurrection. In him the troupe gained a marvelously talented musician. Upon the electronic "piano" that the colony had managed to trade for an entire season of plays performed by the Shakespeare Company, Webber had composed a range of stirring melodies, both instrumental and song. In nearly every case his tempos were far faster than the songs and ballads of Will's own day. Webber assured him these would be popular with the modern folk who comprised a good quarter of the population anyhow. Other musicians, like Baxter, some with homemade instruments of wood, bone, and gut string, found their way to the theater community, until they had a goodly orchestra under Webber's baton.

Over the years, Little Stratford had its share of twentieth-centurian folk from the entertainment industry. Nearly all those engendered in the beginning by the grailstones moved on within a few years, calling the company's venue "primitive." Some stayed, including two tall actresses, one with pure, ice-fair skin who said she'd once played Hamlet's mother, and the other with gold-red hair and a quirky smile who could turn her hand willingly to any part she was given, be it sword carrier, star, or properties mistress. He was also grateful for the presence of a dark-skinned American woman, Sharee Bangs, who had been a "technical director" on "Broadway." Will thought hard, trying to picture the great city the lass talked about superimposed on the tiny Cotswold village Broadway had been in his day. Webber, his chief adviser about the last human era, scorned most of the folk who moved on, dismissing them as spoiled brats from "Broad Hollywood."

Properties were among the only practical effects available to the company. Costumes, in the absence of wool, linen, silk, or cotton, could only be suggested by a collection of towels, of which they had collected a mort. Likewise the scenery, made largely of wooden standards draped with painted towels, and printed placards to explain what they represented. *Macbeth* was the easiest to stage, requiring only "a blasted heath," and the staircase, reversed, which had been constructed for a down-River run of *Romeo and Juliet*. The very paucity of set pieces made it easy to transport play and players to a venue aboard their sailing vessels, chiefest among them the *Anne Hathaway* (Will cherished a hope that one day the original would see her namesake, and call out to him), the *City of London*, and the *Elizabeth R*. Will's cabin, which he shared with Margaret, and the more delicate and valuable of the props, was abaft the main deck on the *City of London*. Forty people could sleep on each of the larger boats, and the flotilla of smaller vessels held the rest of the traveling company as well as the majority of the sets.

Aristophanes had no difficulties with sketchy scenery or the lack of costumes. He taught Will a thing or two about carving masks. Together they staged *The Clouds*, put on plastic paper by the incomparable and irreplaceable Hang Yi, and set to music by Webber. Shakespeare was delighted by the production, and couldn't wait for its premiere.

The printer box was another item for which the company had served a season or more elsewhere. It took the hard-won Riverworld technology, chaining a box called by the twentieth-centurians a "storage battery" to the gigantic exploding mushrooms that fed them thrice daily, and transformed it into music, light, and speech. Inserted where a grail would go, the leads fed the lightnings to a great ceramic object in the shape of an urn that was packed in powdered clay insulation. From the urn, smaller leads branched out through an adjustable carbon-clay stack, feeding the charge in smaller doses to that half of the printer device which lacked the movable spots that under Webber's tutelage Will had come to call "keys." He learned also to spell in modern English and to use "software." Using the same voltage, the urn lightnings also fed Webber's piano, and the two klieg lights, precious beyond worlds, which had come to them from Parolando, many thousands of grailstones up-River. All of these devices traveled with them every time the company set sail.

And sail they did. Though blessed by the Ethicals with food and clothing and the means to build shelter, the theater folk yearned for the applause of audiences. Entertainers had a desperate need to entertain. Adulation made them fly higher than any ten pieces of dreamgum. Not only that, but after a few years, Little Stratford needed more wood, more cloth, more paint to make the plays to make their audiences want to come back again and again.

Will had a recurring fantasy that one day he would run into his patroness, Queen Elizabeth. He had no doubt that one of the tiny kingdoms along the River was hers, but none of his advance men had yet reported having found it. He knew not what benefit having a patroness would accrue him on this world where every man had what he had already—that was to say, nothing plus a grail, plus what his mother wit could gain him. There was no gold, no lands to bestow, little protection against the grail slavers and pirates, the torrential rains. Yet he craved the approval he had enjoyed during her lifetime.

Lacking the exchange medium of money, the company collected goods as the price of admission to their performances. A portion of wine, or a length of wood, or a few precious sheets of paper served to admit one to the traveling theater. Wood and pigments were the most necessary items. For the price of sixty packages of blue eye shadow, his troupe had staged an entire performance of *The Legend of Sleepy Hollow*, book by Irving, music by Webber.

With difficulty, once a season the little sailing ships tacked upstream to return goods to Little Stratford. Pirates were an eternal threat. More than once the company had fallen victim to concerted raids that got uglier when the attackers realized that they had nothing more to offer than a few lengths of wood and discarded lipsticks. Sooner or later one of the pirates would come from a previous audience and know that concealed somewhere on the fleet of bamboo boats was electronic equipment, and all would be lost. The company needed to look harmless, poor, unconcerned, but unapproachable—a difficult combination of circumstances.

And yet, all had gone well for the last few years. Every step backward was matched and overmatched by four steps forward. Those in the theater, including Will himself, were superstitious to an extreme, clutching tight to various lucky pieces, and invoking gods and saints that no longer existed to allow them safe passage through tricky waters. Their fame spread within a few thousand grailstone's distance until they were looked for and welcomed, and yet the company sought to enlarge its territory to encompass even more fans. Entertainment was little and far between on the Riverworld, so Will's troupe was nearly always received well. He felt he could happily go on forever.

The very uneven spread of technology made it imperative that the troupe choose their landings well. They had to avoid landfall where no other boats were anchored. If a nation lacked metal, the sight of Will's carefully made wooden scenery and trim boats would drive the inhabitants to turn over every trunk and bag until they found the blades to cut with. And will-he-won't-he, Will found he needed to train an armed militia to guard the Fuller urn, piano, lights, and computer while those artifacts were on shore.

He leaned over the side of the boat and watched slim silverfish picking up the crumbs he dropped as the waves swirled against the side. Each of the sailing vessels was built in the fashion of a Spanish galleon, deep in the waist but high to prow and stern. Will's cabin, which he shared with Margaret, was abaft the main deck.

"Master Shakespeare! Ho!"

He glanced up to the girl in the lookout, and let his eye follow in the direction toward which she pointed. On shore to their right was a banner made of white towels stretched across a tall, broad picket gate. It said "Welcome Showboat!"

"At last!" cried Aristophanes. "We're there!"

Margaret stood proudly at his side as Will made a leg to the Triumvirate who ruled in Alcapolando. The first consul, after whose name the nation had been called, bowed over her hand.

"Nice to meetcha, Lady Margaret, Mister Will," said Consul Capone, straightening up. He was a big, broad man with a nose that looked as if it had been knocked askew. He had scars on his arms and face, some of which looked deliberately inflicted. Tattoos in blue and green decorated his chest and upper arms.

"We were delighted by your banner, Lord Consul," Margaret said, smiling prettily. "Not often do we have such a . . . pronounced welcome. No one has ever made a banner for us before."

"Ah, well, we do things big around here," Capone said airily. "I been an admirer of yours for a long time, Mister Will." The other two consuls pushed forward, and Capone presented them. Like Capone, they were large men with long black hair reined in by narrow fillets. "Philip of Macedon, and Cochise of the Great Plains. They're big fans of yours, too. We also have honored guests coming from a couple of places down-River." Capone squinted out beyond the boats of the Shakespeare Company. "They ain't here yet."

Shakespeare laid a friendly hand on the big man's forearm and drew him along into the fenced compound. His people and the other two consuls followed. Inside was a large town of small bamboo huts, loomed over by a grand three-lobed building on the bluff overlooking the River plain. The place was as clean as a beggar's bowl, and all the inhabitants he could see who were not milling around the arriving theater company moved purposefully on other tasks.

"Then allow us, good consul, to negotiate the ... *unattractive* part of our relationship, before company comes. In the meanwhile," Will glanced over his shoulder at the others, "my troupe will set up so we may begin as soon as your visitors arrive." Irving threw a humorous glance at Will, and followed the Greek dramatist back to the boats to begin supervising the unloading.

"What a fascinating country this is," Margaret said, gazing around them with wide eyes. She sought to appear innocent, but took in every detail as completely as possible. In her former life, Margaret had taught in a church school, and Will knew she missed nothing. A prearranged series of pressures from her fingers on his arm told him that she spotted iron tools and electrical equipment. It was safe to reveal their own technology. That was good news. he had come to depend on the devices.

"My lord consul, we are glad of the opportunity to entertain and amuse you," Will said, leading the conversation back to the matter at hand. "We propose to perform two plays this day. One can be made ready shortly after luncheon, and the other to be performed after dinner. As an entr'acte, we have musicians, jugglers, and a conjurer who tells jokes in modern English while he performs his wonders. In the morning, we would be on our way again, leaving you our thanks, and, we hope, happy memories."

"That sounds good," Capone said. The other two understood more English than they spoke, leaving the first consul to do most of the talking. They nodded among themselves. "About the plays ... ?"

"The daylight play will be a comedy in the style of ancient Greece. A musical version of *The Clouds*, by Aristophanes and

Webber.'' Shakespeare, taking a turn around the dirt ''square,''
pointed back toward the gate. A thirty-foot phallus made of
cloth and wood was being brought onshore by a handful of the
spear-carriers, more than usually living up to their designation.
''Here is the centerpiece of the scenery. Bold, but traditional.''

''Take it away,'' said Cochise, waving an angry hand toward
the enormous member. ''It offends us. Such a thing is indecent
in public.''

''Tell you the truth, Will,'' Capone said, throwing a massive
arm over the playwright's shoulders and pulling him to one
side, ''I'd rather have one of your own plays than something by
an ancient Greek, if you know what I mean.''

''Our postprandial delight would be *The Comedy of Errors*,''
Will protested, ''which I wrote.''

''We'd rather see *Richard the Third*,'' the consul said. His
voice dropped still further. ''I got my reasons, so I want you to
do that one. Any objections?'' There was threat in his words,
which Will affected not to notice.

''None, sir. Then,'' Will said gallantly, expanding his speech
to include the other consuls, ''we will spare you the *Comedy*,
which is errant foolishness, my lords, and give you instead a
fine performance of that drama. I think you will find merit in
my compatriot's offering.''

''Nah. We want two by you, traditional sure, but nothing
new or too dirty. I don't know this Aristocratites, or whatever
you said.''

''Sire, his name is Aristophanes, as worthy of recognition as
you or I.''

''Forget it. We'll have both or neither. The customer is
always right, right?''

''Right.'' Will sighed, thinking of having to explain to the
Greek that once again the modern audience had failed to
recognize his merits. The only thing which kept the news from
being entirely bad was that Aristophanes himself enjoyed the
lead in *Richard the Third*, nearly a one-man drama, with plenty
of opportunities to ''chew scenery,'' as his modern cohorts put
it. ''How large an audience shall we plan for?''

''Everybody,'' Capone said expansively. ''Alcapolando is

what you might call a democracy in the, uh, *Roman* pattern, so when one of us gets a treat, everybody gets it."

"Did you bring enough for *everyone*?" Margaret muttered under her breath.

Will negotiated a fair price for the company's services, and escorted Margaret back to the boats with both the news of their employment and their observations. The giant phallus was carried back on board and stowed away, replaced by thrones, barrels, and the ever-interchangeable standards. The Fuller urn was dragged out of the hold, grounded, and its lead inserted into the grailstone to await the noon burst.

It was easy for the repertory company to change over from one script to another. All the costuming they had was on hand, and the props could be made to fit any play. The cast certainly knew their parts. Some of the women from the chorus in *The Clouds* would have to tuck away their hair to play the young princes condemned to the Tower and a few of the odd lords to be murdered by Richard.

As Will predicted, the Greek dramatist was perturbed.

"All these modern people, they don't know good theater," Aristophanes complained. He swept his white capelet around his chest with a dramatic arm and struck a histrionic pose. "I shall go rehearse my lines with Hang Yi. At least he sees the merit in classic theater."

Will didn't argue with him, being deep in his own thoughts. What reason could Consul Capone possibly have for insisting on such a specifically historical drama as *Richard the Third*? None of the consuls came from Shakespeare's era. It had to be one of the coming guests to whom it was important. Will felt a tingle of excitement. *Richard the Third* was the hearty condemnation of the Plantagenet monarch. Perhaps it was for Elizabeth that Capone wanted them to perform it. He felt a thrill at the idea of seeing her again, of laying his works at her feet, after so long. He resolved that the performance would be the best that had ever been done of that libretto, to please her.

Will ate his lunch in high good humor. The cast gathered around him about a hundred yards from the grailstone that had filled their cornucopias, running through lines from the play between bites of chicken in spiced saffron cream sauce. Everyone seemed "up" for the performance. Even Aristophanes had come over his snit and exploded with laughter at sophomoric jokes told to him by the irrepressible Irving between recitations of his own lines.

"What a brute this Capone is," Hang Yi said. "Your own line suits him well: 'they imitated humanity so abominably.'"

"There's a large population here, Will," Margaret said, wiping her hands daintily on the grass. "Not great enough to overwhelm the grailstones, but it seems unusually crowded. From the few boats in the harbor, I thought there would be less."

"It may be that Capone and his minions are leaders of such power that none wish to leave," Aristophanes suggested. "Everything runs well; look, they have many more devices than we do, and so many of the citizens are fat."

"It seems too good to be true," Sharee said, overhearing the last. "Except for the usual hassle we're getting from the muckamucks, everything runs like a Swiss watch."

"I, too, believe in your 'no pain, no gain' maxim," Will said, thoughtfully, coming back to ground from daydreams of kneeling before Elizabeth and receiving accolades and honors. "Do you take a few of your folk into the heart of the village. Trade for pigments and wine, or whatever seems in plentiful supply, but keep your ears sharpened for gossip."

Sharee and her spies returned feeling uneasy. "There's more here than I can see, brother. Except for one thing: there's grail slaves. I saw these skinny dudes splitting irontree leaves into fibers. They don't look strong enough to do any other work. Big Man Capone's talk about this being a Roman-patterned democracy's a crock of shit."

"Caution is the wisest path," Margaret insisted, tapping an insistent finger on the top of her grail." Anyone not involved in the performances, stay with the boats. If you look superfluous, they will think you are superfluous, and . . ."

"Now, now, sweet chuck," Will chided her. "We have no evidence that these people mean us any harm."

"Better safe than sorry," Webber said, pushing out his full

lower lip. "I want full guards around the orchestra at all times. That Indian consul was eyeing my piano with what I can only call extreme covetousness. I'm not having *The Comedy of Errors* turn into The Surprise Symphony."

In no time, the company had put up the three-sided curtained enclosures which served as the wings, orchestra, and lighting booth. The Alcapolandoans watched with interest as the scenery went up, and as each player appeared from makeup in his or her guise for the first play.

The performance of *Richard the Third* went wonderfully well. The Greek dramatist loved the crowd's response to his dragging limp and lightning-fast changes of mood, and played to them. The humorist in him reveled in the glory of overplaying Richard's villainy. The crowd gasped at the murders of Clarence and the children, cringed as the deformed Duke of Gloucester set about his slimy wooing of the delicate Anne.

Richard's queen was played by Song Hai, the slender fourth-century Chinese lass who was the company's ingenue. She would also be taking the part of Adriana in the *Comedy* later on. Sympathetic sounds came from the audience as she shrank from Aristophane's embrace. Webber contributed a tremolo that increased the mood of terror.

A large, fair man himself, Shakespeare portrayed the doomed George, Duke of Clarence. He enjoyed his drunken lurch about the stage, ending head up in a huge malmsey cask that was only a half-front. As he plunged into it, a stagehand threw a beaker of watered wine into the air and Will let out a drunken wail that swiftly died away into a murmur. Not subtle, but effective. While the audience cried out their alarm, Will patted the stagehand's shoulder, dropped to elbows and knees, and crept off the stage.

After that, he was free to watch from the wings. Aristophanes did a fine job. His initial disappointment at having his play superseded by one of Will's "old things" had obviously dissipated, and he held the audience captive in one clenched fist. In the center of the front section, the Consular court sat clustered around the Triumvirate, rapt with wonder.

Will scanned each face, looking for Elizabeth. He'd been too busy before the play began to come out and meet the arriving guests. She must be here; all his senses told him he was in the presence of undoubted royalty.

Nowhere among the strangers did he see a head of red hair. Seated beside a stocky man with dark hair and an eagle's beak for a nose was a light-skinned lady with brown hair wound about her ears, but she was the only female in the first ranks. Will was disappointed. Wait—behind them there was a tall woman with a turban would around her head, an austere profile— No, it was not she; another disappointment. The lady had not come. Shaking his head at his own unbridled fantasies, Will went to the rear of the "house" to check on the lighting director.

As he approached Sharee's tent, a burly man with a crossbow stepped in front of him.

"Where're you going?" he growled.

"I wish to see to the rest of my staff," Shakespeare said with dignity. "I am the master of this theater company." As the man hesitated, he added boldly, "I may go where I like. Your first consul told me I have the freedom of the city."

"Oh, yeah." The man grinned, lowering the crossbow. "You go on ahead."

Thee were too many guards stationed thereabout for Will's comfort. At the lighting table under the three-sided tent, Sharee gave him a nervous look, and shrugged meaningfully toward her left shoulder. Will glanced that way. An archer stood with his back propped against one of the standards. He dropped a calming hand on her forearm and went out. More guards dogged the scene-shifters as they carried props up and back from the boats. Still another detached himself from the company and followed Will all the way to the boats. Two crossbowmen stood on the pier, glaring at passersby.

"It's more than an honor guard, Will," Margaret whispered to him when he returned backstage for the last scenes and the curtain call. Aristophanes was soliloquizing. The audience matched his fierce grin with their own. "Capone doesn't fear for our safety. It's our departure he doesn't want."

"Nonsense, lady," Will said. "I don't care for the man's countenance, but he doesn't worry me. I'm sure he'll try to cheat us out of our fee, as all the other lords and ladies up and down the River always do. No one puts a value on our time, as what we make is insubstantial."

"Will," Baxter interrupted him. "Will, they paid in advance."

Shakespeare stopped short, and glanced at the horn player for confirmation. Baxter nodded vigorously, pointing to a pile of bundles in the wings. It was an event almost unprecedented in their career. The others turned concerned faces toward him.

"*Now* I am worried," Will said.

Danny Bacardi, the first seat in woodwinds, put in his own comment. "I heard rumors while we were off trading that the Triumvirate wants to keep us here for good. They need our boats, Will. They'll enslave us, take the ships, and whatever it is the cables are feeding on board the *London*."

"They'll not have my equipment," Webber said. "Or me, either."

"One of them pinched my . . ." Song Hai said, pointing behind her and blushing.

The others whispered stories of similar transgressions. Hang Yi kept the play moving onstage by signaling and hissing to each actor before his or his cue came. It was incredible that any could concentrate on their roles, considering what was going on behind the curtains.

"I saw, too," Aristophanes confirmed, when he came offstage for a brief rest. "A woman who sought to defend her honor with a slap was punched to the ground by a guard. There is no respect here for them at all."

"What can we do?" Irving asked. "They're between us and the boats."

The play came to its conclusion. Richard fell in his battle with Richmond, who spoke with Derby about the future of England. During the long curtain call, Will thought furiously. He made his mop and mow, smiled, bowed, and retired behind the curtain to allow the stars to take longer drafts of the heady applause.

The only plan that came to his mind was daring, and required at its worst the sacrifice of only a single player. There was no reason the others should suffer for his stupidity in landing them here without more information about the true nature of the nation of Alcapolando—it would be he who took the lumps as the others went free. In exchange for their allegiance, he owned the responsibility for their safety. He whispered his plan to Margaret and Hang Yi as the final curtain closed. Margaret went white with shock, but the unflappable Hang promised to spread the word throughout the rest of the crew without fail.

The consuls come to congratulate the company at the end of the play, heaping especial praise upon the chief actor.

"This Aristocracites is a hot property, okay," Capone said, slapping the Greek dramatist on the back. "Tomorrow you can do something else that's equally wonderful, or maybe we'll let you have a day off. I dunno yet."

"I beg your pardon, sir," Will interrupted. "We leave on the morrow, after breakfast, as we agreed."

"The hell you are," the consul said. "We like you, you stay. Right? We're . . . extending your contract indefinitely. You want an audience, we'll give you the best audience every night." Capone's small, light, piggy eyes grew dreamy. "I'll be the envy of every don up- or down-River. They'll have to come to me to see you." He became more businesslike. "Besides, I could use your boats, so I'm confiscating 'em. Not too fast, but flashy. And big! I like them. Them high sides'll take a lot of arrows before they sink. Great for an advance guard. So you're staying. That's final. So what did you have in mind for tomorrow?"

His fears confirmed, Shakespeare took the first consul aside. "We'll talk about future programs later, won't we? It's bad luck to plan more than a day in advance."

"Okay," Capone agreed uneasily. Will realized the American might harbor as many superstitions as his own folk. It was something he could play upon in days to come.

"My lord, we wish to offer something more thrilling than the *Comedy* this evening. I hope you will forgive the substitution."

The consul looked annoyed. "Something by you? I don't

want any foreign crap. I mean, the guy's a good actor, but still . . . the big wanker really put some of my people off.''

''Nay, sir, I have forsworn any of my brothers' works for today, though by my head, you will come to like them one day,'' Will said, radiating confidence he did not feel. He fixed his large, intense eyes on Capone, willing him to believe what he said. Capone shook off the spell with difficulty, then shrugged.

''Yeah, sure. So what is it?''

''I would have us play for you *The Tempest*, my favorite among my own works. I myself,'' he said with a feigned modesty, ''shall pay Prospero. There is no better role. In days to come, I will no doubt hear your praise about this finest night.''

''Terrific!'' the man exclaimed.

Dinner was a subdued event. Crossbowmen hung about at a distance as the company huddled together upon its adopted hillside, talking in an undertone.

''You can't be serious, Will,'' Song Hai said, still weeping. She had refused to eat though Irving, her longtime mate, tried to tempt her with the choicest morsels from both their dinner buckets. ''You can't mean to sacrifice yourself.''

''I am prepared,'' Will admitted, ''but if all goes well, I shall not have to. The ruse will work; it must.''

''The plan is simple,'' Hang Yi explained, methodically tearing up the chunk of bread from his grail. ''The stage gradually empties of players at the end of *The Tempest*. As each of you completes his or her part, make your way in whatever fashion you can to the boats, carrying whatever you may so as not to attract attention. Not all the boats are watched. The three largest seem to have commanded the most interest, and the guard is only on the pier to which they are moored. The others are not observed except cursorily. You can slip into the water at any point on the shore and swim or wade under the pilings.''

''We are too many,'' Aristophanes complained. ''We'll never get away.''

His words were pitched just a little too loudly. The guard must have heard the last phrase, for they moved in closer. Will nudged Song Hai with his elbow.

"Scene two," he whispered.

The girl sat up straight and declaimed at the top of her voice. "If by your art, my dearest father, you have put the wild waters in this roar, allay them!"

The guards halted, and looked puzzled.

"Rehearsal, gentlemen," Will called. "Hast thou any fancies to tread the boards?"

Pointedly, the guards turned their backs on the company. Hang Yi's austere face creased in a lipless grin.

"We will get away," Shakespeare promised. "Play your parts, and go your ways, and one day we will look back on this night and laugh."

Torchlit, the scenery for *The Tempest* looked wild and eldritch. Will felt it to be a perfect setting for his most daring performance of all. In various small ways throughout the play, the members of the company tried to make their farewells to him, and he made an attempt to foresee any difficulties that might befall them in starting anew without him. Mourning he must put off until later.

"If we should not meet again, sweet Margaret," Will said, standing next to her in the wings while the first scene of the drama unfolded, "I want you to take over the leadership of the troupe. All trust you. You see the more practical needs of the community, and can settle squabbles better than any of my three fellow playwrights. There will be some grumbling, but in the end they will be grateful to you for sparing them the petty day-to-day trials."

"Why do you keep those duties yourself, then?" Margaret asked, trying to keep her tone light as she nestled securely into the curve of his arm. He squeezed her.

"I revel in all those small tasks," Will said cheerfully. "I cry you mercy, my dear: you knew that already. Go. It is your cue. Farewell. Until we meet again. I love you."

With his kiss upon her lips, she crept out to conceal herself behind a low draped form that represented a mossy rock. He tasted the salt of her tears and tried to push aside all regrets as he adjusted his false beard in place, and made the mental transition from playwright to magician.

The performance went forward with great success. Song Hai as Miranda was suitably dainty. She was much admired from the front row where wine was freely circulating in large earthenware mugs between the consuls, their trusted henchmen, and the guests. One of the men exclaimed in his cups that he'd have that one for his own. The girl's porcelain cheeks reddened, and she shuddered, but, a genuine trouper, went on with her lines without interruption. Margaret, as Sycorax, mother of Caliban, seen only in shadow during the first mention by her loathly son, had whirled up from behind her rock and vanished into the wings. She'd have gone down to make the ship ready and muster all the junior members of the troupe, if not prevented from doing so by Capone's men.

As planned, each cast member left in turn. First Caliban, then the courtiers, then Miranda and Ferdinand, and lastly the dancing sprite Ariel, leaving Prospero majestically alone in the gloom, lit by a single torch that he held between his hands. If his stagehands could work fast enough, the hot stage lights could be carried on their standards to the gangplank. If not, the equipment would be left behind with Will.

By now, the other boats had doubtless slid quietly from their slips, turning the slats of the sails to catch the wind. They'd be sailing the wrong way, following the night wind instead of the day's, but once away, the folk of this nation would not stop them. Will knew that it was mere opportunism that had dropped him and his troupe into the hands of the Triumvirate, that only he would pay the penalty for his error in landing them here. If the Triumvirate's treatment was too harsh, he would need only to provoke a fatal attack, and by morning he would be free, somewhere else. Still without his beloved company, but free to begin again.

Time for the final declamation came at last. The stage was empty and dark, with only Will, firelit, as a focus. He had to hold his audience's attention long enough to make certain all made it to safety.

He stepped forward onto the apron of the stage, knowing by the smallest fraction how close he was to the edge, as if he'd been born upon it. Prospero's speech was like a plea to the

Triumvirate. It spoke to his circumstances as though it had been written for the occasion. He cleared his throat silently, and began:

> "Now my charms are all o'erthrown,
> And what strength I have's mine own,
> Which is most faint: now, 'tis true,
> I must be here confined by you,
> Or sent to Naples. Let me not,
> Since I have my dukedom got
> And pardon'd the deceiver, dwell
> In this bare island by your spell;
> But release me from my bands
> With the help of your good hands:
> Gentle breath of yours my sails
> Must fill, or else my project fails,
> Which was to please. Now I want
> Spirits to enforce, art to enchant,
> And my ending is despair,
> Unless I be relieved by a prayer,
> Which pierces so that it assaults
> Mercy itself and frees all faults.
> As you from crimes would pardon'd be,
> Let your indulgence set me free."

With a regal gesture, Shakespeare turned the torch upside down and plunged the flame against the stage before his feet, blanketing all in total darkness, the signal to his ships to get under way. He experienced a keen knife-thrust of regret, feeling that last guttering spark from the torch as the end of his dramatic career. Tomorrow, grail slavery, starvation, and frustration would be his lot. No more Shakespeare, writer, director, manager of Shakespeare's Company of Little Stratford. He stood, waiting for the guard to come up and take him.

The audience was silent for a long, long moment. And then the applause began, growing from a few pattering echoes like the sound of rain on the roof, increasing to a veritable thunderstorm of approbation. Standing with head bowed, he accepted it all as his swan song.

It did not stop. As the applause went on and on in the darkness, Will felt a moment of hope. Perhaps he need not remain behind. Perhaps his spell could hold them long enough. He raised his eyes. If the deafening sound continued even a few more heartbeats, he would have plenty of time to run the distance to the boat. It was worth the essay. He knew every inch of the stage, even in the dark. Raising the skirts of his robe up around his hips, he backed away from the fallen torch and fled silently off stage left.

Behind him, the applause continued, with cries of "Author! Author!" and rhythmic stomping ringing through the clearing.

Ah, Will, he thought, the finest moment of your career, and you're hotfooting away from it. And yet, if you stayed, it would be the longest curtain call you'd ever know.

Away from the stage, his eyes began to be accustomed to the dark. He saw stars twinkle through the haze of smoke from the village huts. Pattering barefoot through the center of town, he found the little path to the quay. There were no guards. Evidently Capone had told the truth when he said all—or nearly all—would be allowed to enjoy tonight's performance. There would surely be guards on the quay near the boats. He could only hope that the militia had dealt with them.

Prospero's heavy robe impeded his progress. As he ran, he shucked it over his head, flinging it to one side. Margaret would be cross, clucking over the lost time it took for her to do the exquisite embroidery, but Will might have to swim for it to catch up with the boats. No amount of work was worth his life; she's acknowledge that, gladly.

The sharpened pickets loomed up before him, limned by the starlight and the light of torches on the other side of the fence. He was almost to the unlocked gate when a shadow moved between him and freedom. It shifted, and the torchlight outside the gate illuminated the face of a man he'd seen in the audience, a middle-sized man with black hair and a moody, thoughtful face. Will stopped, rocked back on his heels with shock. Caught, so near to freedom! He looked around, expecting Capone to come out of the shadows next.

The man laid his right hand on the iron-headed Thor-hammer stuck through a loop on his leather belt. The weapon was dark with fresh blood that dripped on the ground at his feet. Shakespeare gulped. He feared for the members of his company. He could hear no sounds but wind and water beyond the gate.

"Master Shakespeare!" It was a hiss, not a shout, from the dark-haired man. "William Shakespeare, formerly of Stratford?"

"I am he, sir," Will said, forcing his voice from a tight throat.

"Richard, formerly Duke of Gloucester, at your service."

Will felt all his blood drain to his feet. He swayed. He should have known immediately: the handsome Plantagenet features were printed as cleanly on this face as the words on the damning script. *King* Richard, whose brief reign had immediately preceded that of his patrons the Tudors—of all the joints in this town he walks into mine, he thought, paraphrasing a line one of his actors kept saying to underline an unlucky coincidence. For grievously insulting him, the king would stove in his head with the mighty war hammer. Will would wake up at a grailstone far from here, away from all he had worked for for almost three decades. He nearly wept for all his destroyed dreams, thinking of having to start again, possibly millions of miles away. Or worse, Richard would hold him here until the triumvirate and their guards figured out that their birds had flown, leaving him to answer their questions. But his inbred respect for the Crown of England still held true; all he could do was answer and await the consequences. He bowed deeply.

"My lord!" he said.

"Hsh!" Richard cut him off with a gesture. His eyes burned with an inner fire that Shakespeare had seen many times in the eyes of his great-grand-niece Elizabeth, and feared. "Am I a deformed, misshapen, vile thing, sir? Am I a bottle spider, a foul, bunch-backed toad? Do you find the least suggestion of a hump here?" He turned a well-muscled back toward Will. Except for enlarged muscles in the right arm and shoulder that no doubt corresponded to the hammer he carried, the body was as true as any man's on Earth or Riverworld.

"Nay, sir," Will admitted meekly, "I do not."

Richard turned back and bowed, a mere inclination of the head. "I wished only to have the facts set straight. I thank thee. Nought of the other condemnations you made are true, either. A fine and stirring performance this afternoon, Master Shakespeare. I quite hated the bastard myself. The villein Capone meant to insult me, but I've more perspective than he dreams. Come down-River to Boarsmarch some time. You'll be welcomed.'' He looked over Will's shoulder. ''And now you'd best go, man. I've thrown cloths over the surveillance cameras, but they'll shortly reckon the facts as I did, and be out here in pursuit of you and your company. The pier guards,'' he grimaced, ''are dead. I'll hold these others back some little time. Go!''

''My lord, I thank you,'' Will said. He knew he babbled, but shock upon shock had loosened his wits.

''Go!'' Richard said impatiently. He pulled the hammer out of its loop and turned to face the gate, shoving Will behind him.

Will needed no further impulse. He ran.

The gangplank of the *City of London* was already up, but Irving and Aristophanes threw Will a rope that landed on the pier, trailing slowly as the ship moved away. Will dashed past the shattered bodies of Capone's guards and snatched it up before it fell off the end. He leaped off the pier into the water, and let them haul him aboard after they turned the sails into the wind.

''All's well that ends well, eh?'' Irving said as Will reached the rail and fell, sodden, onto the deck.

Gasping, Shakespeare nodded. The others knelt over him, checking for bruises and broken bones. ''What a narrow escape! Never, never again!''

''Oh, you'll do it again,'' Margaret said, gathering him to her in a crushing grip and dabbing at his face with a towel. ''And again, and again, you silly man, because you can't live without the applause.''

The four dramatists looked at each other. Irving grinned.

''Methinks the lady's protest is all too correct.''

''That's a terrific quote!'' Webber said when Will told the group the story of his escape and unexpected meeting with the late king. "Quick, write it down before you forget it. We can put it on the playbill next place we do *Richard the Third*. 'I quite hated the bastard myself.' Marvelous."

"We won't be doing it again like that," Will said thoughtfully, staring up at the stars as they sailed away. "I'm going to rewrite it."

Because It's There

Jerry Oltion

With an ear-splitting blast from its steam whistle and a great rattling of anchor chain, the riverboat *Not For Hire* engaged its motors and churned the water into a froth, slowly building up speed against the current.

"There they go," Roald Amundsen said with a wistful note in his voice. He was standing on the bank, a little away from the thickest knot of the crowd that cheered and waved the riverboat on. He was a tall man, dark-haired, with piercing blue eyes and an aquiline nose, but the way he hunched his shoulders and scuffed his feet on the ground made him look like a schoolboy who'd just flunked a spelling test.

"Ah, good riddance to the sons of bitches," said his companion. Robert Peary was a bit shorter than Amundsen, auburn-haired, and his eyes were more gray than blue, but at the moment they sparkled with fire.

"Sour grapes?" Amundsen asked.

"Shee-it." Peary turned away to climb up the bank toward the village of bamboo huts. "It's getting so you can't swing a cat without hittin' another goddamned polar expedition."

This was the second riverboat in as many years heading up-River with that goal in its crew's minds, and most bank-dwellers had lost count of how many sailboats, rowboats, pedalboats, and even submarines had come by in the last decade with the same objective. Everyone wanted to reach the North Pole, and the mysterious tower rumor placed there.

"There aren't any cats here," Amundsen pointed out.

Peary spat on the grassy Riverbank. "That's another thing I hate about this place. No cats, and no goddamned *dogs*. What kind of polar expedition's got no dogs in it?"

"Oh, come on. You can make it to the pole without dogs. Scott did it." Robert Scott had been a month behind Amundsen in reaching the earth's South Pole, and he'd walked nearly the whole way.

"Sure he did. And then he starved to death on the way back." When he reached the level plain above the Riverbank Peary turned around and looked over the heads of the crowd. Out on the water, dozens of wind-surfers skipped gaily across the riverboat's bow-wave, their brightly painted triangular sails stretched tight in the perpetual downstream breeze. The riverboat blew its steam whistle again. "Most of those poor bastards will starve, too, if they don't get killed by the natives on the way. They're not real explorer material."

Amundsen tugged a knee-high stalk of grass from the ground and chewed on the soft end. "At least they're going somewhere," he said. "They're trying."

Peary took a deep breath, building up for one of his blasts of invective for which he was famous, but after a moment he just let it all back out in a sigh and said wearily, "Screw you, Amundsen, and the horse you rode in on."

Peary turned away and began to walk up the bank again, but Amundsen couldn't resist getting in the last shot. Grinning, he said, "There aren't any horses here, either."

The village tavern served three or four different styles of home-brewed beer and a home-distilled liquor that could pass for vodka on a cold night. None of it matched the quality of the stuff provided by the mass–energy converters the locals called "grails," but what they lacked in refinement they made up for in quantity. The grails never provided more than a drink or two per meal; people who wanted more had to make their own or buy it from someone who did.

Neither Amundsen nor Peary were regular drinkers, but after charging their grails at the community stone that evening they found themselves drifting with the dinner crowd toward the tavern, where the discussion naturally centered around the riverboat.

Predictably, somebody asked them why they hadn't joined the expedition, and just as predictably Peary had said, "Because it's a fucking waste of time, that's why. They're going to struggle up how many *million* miles of river, crisscrossing the planet hundreds of times in the process, then climb the mountains at the end of it and sail the sea beyond that—for what? To plant their flag on the tower somebody else already built there? What's the point?"

"What's the point to staying here?" The speaker was a tall, solidly built woman with platinum-blond hair down to her waist and a fine coat of downy soft white fur over the rest of her body. Her name was Gressa, and she claimed to be a yeti. Her fur was a pretty good endorsement of her claim, but her otherwise human features made some people skeptical.

Peary was one of the skeptics. "Madam," he said, "I don't see you heading for the polar regions either, and you would seem to have more reason to go than most, if your claims of ancestry are to be believed."

"Polar, shmolar," she said with a snarl. "For the first time in my life I'm *warm*. Besides, we're talking about you. Hardly anybody on the River was resurrected within a thousand miles of anybody they knew from before, yet you and Amundsen were resurrected side-by-side. Don't you figure there's a reason behind that?"

A loud chorus of agreement swept the room, but Peary put a stop to it by banging his empty beer mug on the polished oak bartop. "Maybe there *was* a reason," he said "Maybe the beings who put us here *do* want us to reach the North Pole. Well, as far as I'm concerned, that's reason enough to stay away. I do what I want, not what some piss-ant alien god tells me to do."

There was a moment of silence in the bar. Nobody was happy to be at the mercy of the Riverworld's creators. Most people's entire system of belief had been destroyed at a stroke on resurrection day, and the Church of the Second Chance's Hindu-like doctrine of redemption through self-purification was a poor substitute for the lost ambition that had driven humanity for so long. The Riverworlders needed a new direction to give meaning to their new lives, and they didn't like being reminded of it.

Amundsen's voice broke the uncomfortable quiet. "That's why I think we should go south. With all the attention on the North Pole, nobody's thought to go the other way."

Peary snorted. "North, south, what difference does it make? We're living on an artificial construct. Any exploration we do has no more meaning than ants exploring your kitchen."

"Does sitting on your ass have any more meaning?"

Peary had no answer to that, save to wave his empty beer mug at the bartender.

"You know what I think?" Amundsen went on. "I think you've lost your nerve. You used to be the most restless man I knew, but ever since we woke up here you've been afraid to walk around the bend. You bluster around like a crochety old sea dog, but you act like an old woman. You—"

"That's enough." Peary set his mug down.

Amundsen shook his head. "No, it's not enough. You were the first man to stand on the top of the earth, but you've let this world beat you without a fight. You've become a whimpering, cowardly—" Whatever else he might have said couldn't make it out around Peary's fist.

With both of them sitting down it wasn't a hard punch, but it was enough to knock Amundsen off his stool. He crashed to the wooden floor, taking Gressa down with him. The other people in the tavern whooped with delight as he struggled to his feet again and took a swing at Peary, knocking him back against the bar.

It might have ended with that, but the shouts of "Fight! fight!" made words of reconciliation impossible, and Peary didn't look as though he was in a mood to reconcile anyway. He rocked forward on the rebound from Amundsen's punch, growling like a wolf, and drove another straight jab into Amundsen's chest. That gave him the room he needed to stand up.

The tavern patrons backed away with a great scooting of chairs and tables to form a shouting, jeering ring around the two fighters. Neither paid the crowd any attention. They squared off an arm's length apart, trading punches like boxing puppets, totally absorbed in beating one another silly. At first Amundsen's greater reach gave him the advantage, helping him bloody Peary's nose and knock out a tooth, but that only seemed to fuel Peary's anger. He finally let loose a roundhouse that sent Amundsen over backward, striking his head on the edge of a table on the way down. He didn't get back up.

Panting for breath and bleeding from both nose and mouth, Peary bent down to check that Amundsen was still breathing. Satisfied, and also satisfied that he'd defended his honor, he draped Amundsen's left arm over his shoulder and lifted him up. "Somebody help me get him home," he said.

Gressa lent another shoulder, and together they dragged the unconscious explorer out of the tavern.

They'd have missed breakfast if Gressa hadn't spent the night, but when the first hint of morning light came in through the hut's single window she rose from Peary's cot, gathered their grails, and took them down to the community grailstone for recharging.

A few minutes later the thunder of mass–energy conversion echoed through the valley. Amundsen sat up, groaning with pain from his bruises. On his cot across the hut, Peary propped himself up on his elbow. "Are you all right?" he asked.

"I think so. You?"

"Fine."

"Good." Amundsen rubbed his neck, tilting his head from side to side as if checking for loose parts.

Peary cleared his throat a time or two, then asked hesitantly, "Have . . . have I really lost my nerve?"

Amundsen eyed him warily. "Let's just say you're not the same Robert Peary I knew on Earth."

"Shit."

That brought a grin. "You still talk like him."

"But I don't back it up with actions, do I?" Peary sat up and began pulling on his pants. "You're right; I've been afraid to explore around the bend."

Amundsen shook his head. "I just said that to make you mad."

"Well, it worked. Probably because it's true."

The silence stretched for half a minute while Peary finished dressing. Finally Amundsen asked, "So what are you going to do about it?"

Peary shrugged. "Go to the South Pole with you, I guess."

Amundsen's face lit up like a little boy's. "You mean it?"

"Yeah, I mean it. As you so delicately pointed out to me last night, I've got nothing better to do."

Gressa appeared in the open doorway, carrying the grails. "What was that, some kind of male bonding ritual?" she asked.

"Huh?" they both said.

She set their grails on the wickerwork table against the wall opposite the door. "The male yetis used to do it, too. They'd get all pissy at each other from living all winter in a cave, so one day they'd fight like hell and the next day they'd go off hunting together like nothing had happened. I never did understand it."

Amundsen laughed. "I suppose it is some sort of primitive ritual. Dogs do it, too."

Peary ignored him and opened his grail. "Hah, sausage and eggs. Save the sausage; we can make pemmican with it."

"Pemmican?" asked Gressa.

"Dried meat and fat," Peary explained. "High-energy food for traveling, and it stores well. We can stock up on it while we're making the airship and the rest of our gear."

Amundsen and Gressa both said, "Airship?"

Peary looked at them as if they were both idiots. "Of course we go by air. None of this fighting our way back and forth along the River for the next hundred years; we can make a blimp and get there in a couple of months."

Amundsen got out of bed and began dressing. "How long have you been thinking about this?" he asked.

"Since about three o'clock this morning," Peary replied. "Come on, let's go; time's awasting and we've got lots to do today."

Looking from Peary to Gressa, Amundsen raised his eyebrows in a What-have-I-done? sort of gesture, but he was smiling.

* * *

Once he got started, there was no keeping up with Peary. Over the next few months he became a whirlwind of activity, learning to make pemmican from fish and from the food provided by the grails, designing and building polar clothing with heavy cloth made from a local variant of the cotton plant, and constructing the airship from the intestinal linings and flotations bladders of the man-eating dragonfish caught in the River. He and Amundsen were perfectly matched in their meticulous attention to detail, each having learned the value of advance preparation in their explorations on Earth.

The other people in the village pitched in enthusiastically, either from a sense of pride at having the expedition start from their section of the Valley or simply because it was a fun diversion from the pervasive boredom of river life. People saved food from their grails for pemmican, fishermen held contests for the biggest dragonfish for the gasbag, and engineers from all ages collaborated on designing an engine for maneuvering. Metal was rare on Riverworld, so they built a closed-cycle steam engine out of ironwood and bamboo, using an easily vaporized and recondensable fish oil instead of water for a working fluid.

"You're nuts," Peary told them when they showed him the working model. "Who ever heard of a fish-oil engine?"

The engineering team included a computer hardware designer, an early-twentieth-century sailor, a Roman aqueduct builder, and a short guy with a sloped forehead and heavy brow ridges who claimed to have invented the wheel. "It's just like the naphtha engines we used on motor launches back on Earth," the sailor told him. "Those were closed-cycle engines, too. The beauty of using fish oil is that the oil will seal and preserve the wooden parts, and also provide lubrication. You should be able to go around the world before the engine wears out."

"If we could carry enough fuel, maybe," Peary admitted. "But we can't, and besides that I don't want an open flame anywhere near all that hydrogen."

"Who said anything about flame?" the engineers said. "The whole thing will be solar powered."

They proceeded to show an incredulous Peary how the gasbag could be made nearly transparent by saturating it with fat, and how a reflective lining could be spread inside it to focus sunlight onto a tube-shaped boiler suspended along the bag's long axis. The lining could be manipulated magnetically from outside, using the ultrastrong magnetic fasteners salvaged from clothing provided by the grails, allowing it to track the sun as it arced overhead throughout the day and also correcting for changes in angle due to latitude. The system would only generate a few horsepower, not enough to buck much of a headwind, but enough to let the blimp seek out favorable air currents and save hundreds of hours of drifting in the wrong direction.

Staying aloft for the weeks it would take to drift to the pole would require careful conservation of their hydrogen supply. The gas would come from electrolysis, using the electrical discharge from the grailstones to split water into hydrogen and oxygen. Once they were under way, they would regulate their buoyancy by venting hydrogen or dropping ballast as required.

When they ran out of ballast there would be only one direction: down. And the odds of finding another stretch of Riverbank where they could land to recharge without being killed or enslaved weren't good, so they planned for a heavy ship at first, growing slowly lighter as it neared the pole. That was the same basic strategy they had used in their dogsled expeditions on Earth as well; they had started out with dozens of men and hundreds of dogs pulling heavily laden sledges, and as they used up their supplies and cached them for the return journey, they had sent men and dogs back a few at a time until only a lightweight, fast group with a single sledge made the last sprint for the pole.

There would be no caching of supplies for the return journey this time, but even so, after calculating their worst-case rate of consumption and accounting for all the equipment they could imagine they might need, they realized they would be able to carry a third person. Gressa quickly seized the opportunity, pointing out that she'd spent her whole life on Earth in cold climes without any special equipment at all. Peary was glad to have her along, and if Amundsen wasn't as enthusiastic he at least didn't seem to mind.

At last the day came when everything was ready for launch. Their supplies were loaded, the gasbag was straining against the ropes, and people from miles around had gathered to see the explorers lift off. They gave a little farewell speech from the open door and windows of the enclosed gondola, then amid cheers and applause they cast off the mooring lines and drifted slowly into the sky.

They had taken dozens of practice flights already; the only difference today was the crowd below, which slowly dwindled to insignificance. The mountains separating the convolutions of the River slid downward as well, until the blimp leveled off a few thousand feet higher than the peaks. The air was cold at that height, and silent save for the gentle creak of rope against wood as the gondola swayed beneath the oblong balloon.

As soon as they leveled out, they hauled on the control ropes strung through the roof and around the outside of the bag, ropes bearing magnets that pulled the reflective inner lining into position to focus the morning sunlight on the boiler in the balloon's axis. A few minutes later the engine at the rear of the gondola began turning with a soft *chuff . . . chuff . . . chuff*. The propeller, a long, steep-pitched wooden blade, slowly picked up speed as the system heated up, steadying out within a few more minutes to a low-speed blur. The blimp began to swim through the air, responding sluggishly to the elevator and rudder controls. Now the soft hum of the propeller and the whisper of wind slipping past the windows filled the gondola.

Recirculated oil vapor flowed from the engine through an inside radiator, heating the living space before returning to the boiler. The passengers would stay plenty warm, at least during the day, and they had heavy clothing and sleeping bags for nighttime. The piles of equipment and ballast stacked all around would help provide insulation as well. With a full load of supplies, the quarters were close; there was room for little more than a small table to sit at and a few feet of open floor to stand on or lie down on beside it. It was like living in a closet, with food, skis, tents, backpacks, and more filling every corner.

Fortunately, the world outside the windows was as spacious as the gondola was cramped. Below them the planet looked like a gigantic plowed and irrigated field, with long parallel rows of Rivervalley stretching off to the east and west as far as they could see. Clouds and mist in the air above the open water made that distance considerably less than the natural horizon, but none of them doubted that the channels extended for thousands of miles.

The blimp began drifting southwest with the prevailing wind, crossing the valleys at an angle. Its three passengers watched the tiny wakes of boats on the water below, and the even tinier specks of people on the banks, people who lived only a few miles away but due to the mountains would forever be strangers to the people just one valley removed.

All morning they drifted, eating their noon meal when the echo of thunder from the grailstones below announced the hour. Shortly afterward, Amundsen slid into his sleeping bag and pulled a mask over his eyes so he could sleep. The blimp would need constant piloting to ensure that it didn't blow up against a mountain or pass into a northerly air current, and he had volunteered for the first night shift.

Peary and Gressa amused themselves throughout the afternoon by watching the landscape below. After a hundred miles or so the east–west trend of the valleys gave way to a more north–south orientation, then they veered off to run southwest–northeast for a while. It became apparent that not only did the River itself meander all over the planet, but long parallel sets of valleys also meandered in larger patterns of their own. Peary speculated that the super-bends might spell out some sort of message from space, but they couldn't decipher any hint of one from the narrow strip of the planet they could see as they drifted.

By evening Gressa had tired of the spectacle. Stifling a yawn, she said, "It's pretty up here, but I somehow thought there would be more adventure to it."

Peary laughed softly. "I've always said, 'The more dramatic your expeditions are, the more incompetent you are.'" Then his smile slipped a little and he said, "Besides, we have plenty of time for adventure. Don't go asking for trouble; it'll show up soon enough on its own.''

Despite Peary's warning, the next few days were just as event-free. With no major land masses or oceans to complicate things, and with no axial tilt either, Riverworld's weather patterns were much more cooperative than those on Earth. The explorers drifted slowly southward, rising and falling and occasionally steering east- or westward to find favorable currents or to detour around storm clouds, but they covered thousands of miles without a hitch. They'd started a little north of the equator; on the morning of the eighth day Peary took a sighting with the sextant and calculated that they were now at forty-five degrees south latitude, over halfway to their goal.

A couple days after that they saw another airship far off to the west of them. It was much larger than theirs, a true dirigible, and under power—northward. ''Another shot for the wrong pole,'' Peary said with a grin.

''Unless they've already been to the south and are going home,'' Amundsen said.

The thought made Peary scowl. He stared silently after the dirigible until it had disappeared from sight, and he was in a foul mood the rest of the day.

''He remembers the trouble he had with Cook,'' Amundsen told Gressa when Peary had gone to bed. ''Frederick Cook claimed to have reached the North Pole a year before Peary did, but he made his claim only a week before Peary returned from his expedition. Cook stole all Peary's thunder, and even when people began doubting Cook's word it was too late to stop the tongues from wagging. Some people even doubted that *Peary* had made it. It was all a terrible mess. Destroyed their friendship, of course, and nearly destroyed ours when I refused to vilify Cook along with the others.''

''Was he telling the truth?'' asked Gressa. ''Did he make it to the pole first?''

Amundsen shrugged. ''Who knows? He says he did, but even I have to admit that he wasn't above fudging his facts when it was convenient.'' He smiled, remembering. ''Another explorer named Peter Freuchen used to say, 'Cook was a liar and a gentleman; Peary was neither.' He was certainly right on the latter count, and maybe on both.''

Gressa laughed, glancing over at Peary in his sleeping bag. ''He's been a perfect gentleman to me,'' she said.

Amundsen laughed too. ''Chivalry, my dear. He died before it did.''

As they neared the pole the air grew colder and the surface winds less predictable. The frequent changes in altitude to find southerly currents meant venting hydrogen and dropping ballast much faster than before, using up both at an increasing rate. The mountains in the polar regions tended to be lower and more gently sloping on their southern faces, presumably to allow more sunlight into the valleys, but that didn't help the explorers any since the lower elevations were nearly always swept by south winds. They had to stay high to catch the air mass being drawn inward to feed the constant outward flow.

''That's actually good news, in a sense,'' Amundsen said when Gressa asked him why that was. ''It means there's probably a polar plateau where the air can lose its heat to space without being warmed again from below. When it cools off it falls, and when it hits the ground it has no place to go but outward, provided the ground's cold. If it's warm then it just rises again, but if it's cold then the air keeps cooling and picking up speed as it flows downhill and as more air pushes it from behind.''

''Why's that good?'' Gressa asked. ''It means headwinds all the way, doesn't it?''

''Only if we go in low, which we won't. We'll go in high, with the air drawn into the low-pressure cell. On the way back we'll fly low and get a tailwind that way, too. But what I meant was it's good news there's a plateau; that means the pole is on land—or at least on ice—and it's much more likely that we'll be able to ski to it from wherever we have to set down. It would be too much to ask that the winds take us exactly to the pole.'' He paused, then said softly, ''And besides, if there's an ice cap then it's less likely that anybody is living there.''

''Oh,'' Gressa said, glancing over at Peary, who stood at the bow window looking southward as if he wanted to be the first person to even *see* the pole. "Yes, I guess that is good news, isn't it?"

That night, instead of descending as the gasbags cooled and lost buoyancy, they dropped ballast to maintain their altitude in the southerly current. Peary went to sleep when Amundsen awoke for his shift, and a few hours later Gressa followed him. Amundsen spent the cold early-morning hours sitting by the forward observation window with his sleeping bag wrapped around him while he listened to his companions' soft snoring. Now that the solar engine had shut down for the night, that was the only sound in the gondola.

Moisture from their breath kept frosting over the windows, so he had opened the forward one a few inches and peered out through the crack. Starlight provided just enough light to see a rough outline of the terrain below. The land was covered in light and dark strips, snowcapped mountain ranges separating the rivervalleys. Earlier in the night the river had been dotted with the tiny orange specks of hundreds of campfires, but now they had burned out while everyone slept.

The stars shone steadily where the gasbag didn't block them out. From this high altitude and with the air as cold as it was, this was by far the clearest night the explorers had seen yet. It seemed to Amundsen as if they were floating on the edge of space itself. As he watched the unfamiliar constellations wheel slowly around the pole, he thought about how different his life would have gone if he had been born fifty years later than he had. So many things had happened on Earth after his death. Men had walked on the moon. They would have gone on to the planets, maybe even to other stars if the Riverworld project hadn't stopped their expansion. And he would have been among them.

He might yet have a chance at it. Who could say? Life on the Riverworld was a complete enigma. Death had been robbed of its sting, and with it the barrier of time. He and the rest of humanity might be captives on this alien planet now, but who knew what the future might hold for them? The stars were still out there, still beckoning, and Amundsen, at least, still yearned for them with an explorer's heart. The aliens couldn't take that away from him.

His ears popped, and when he looked back inside at the instruments he realized he had been woolgathering for too long. The airship had lost altitude. Quietly, so as not to wake Peary or Gressa, he opened a bag of sand and poured it out through a hole in the deck made just for the purpose. He checked the statoscope, a more sensitive altimeter that registered slight changes in altitude, and saw that they were still dropping, so he poured out another bag.

They were still dropping. Puzzled, he looked out the window and saw the ground still quite a ways below, but appearing less distinct than it had earlier. A thin layer of cloud covered it now.

He poured out another bag of ballast. The statoscope leveled out, even showed a slight ascent, but within a few minutes they were falling again.

Had the gasbag sprung a leak? Amundsen poured out more sand until the balloon reached neutral buoyancy again, then checked the pressure gauge. It was holding steady. But within a minute, they began descending again.

It couldn't be a simple downdraft, not this high in the air. Down on the ground, convection cells would be churning as warm air rose over the River and cold air sank down from the icy mountaintops, but that would all balance out only a few thousand feet above the mountains, and the airship was much higher than that.

It wouldn't be for long, though. The rate of descent kept increasing as Amundsen watched. He poured out more ballast, then looked out the window again. The cloud cover was getting thicker. He didn't want to drop into it; they would have no idea where the mountains were then, and could easily be blown into one.

Then it dawned on him what was happening. If they weren't losing hydrogen and they weren't in a downdraft, then they had to be gaining weight somehow. And the only way that could happen was ice. The clear night had allowed the planet to radiate its heat to space, and down on the ground the air had finally reached the dewpoint. The cold gasbag gave it a perfect surface to condense on as well. "Uh-oh," he said aloud. Then, stomping his feet on the floor, he shouted, "Ice! Wake-up!"

Peary sat upright like a pop-up figure in a book. "What's wrong?" he asked.

"We're icing up," Amundsen told him. "Start tossing out ballast; I'm going up top to knock it loose." He snatched a ski pole from one of the piles of expedition equipment, wrapped a shirt around the end and tied it in place to make a soft club, then opened the overhead hatch and climbed up into the rigging between the gondola and gasbag.

Peary climbed out of his sleeping bag and pulled on his heavy parka and leggings. When he'd given her room enough to maneuver, Gressa did the same, and the two of them began emptying ballast sacks.

"We're going to run out of ballast at this rate," Peary said after a few minutes. "And it's not doing a fucking bit of good anyway; we're still falling."

They could hear Amundsen overhead, thumping the blunted ski pole against the underside of the gasbag and cursing, "Come on, damn you, break free!" Ice chips rattled against the gondola when he managed to knock some loose, but he wasn't doing much more good than the two pouring out ballast.

"Yank on the reflector ropes," he called down through the hatch. "That might knock some of this stuff loose."

"Good idea," Peary said. He tugged on the adjustment ropes leading up to the magnet-lined bands encircling the balloon. They resisted his pull at first, then gave way. More ice rained down past the windows, but the blimp continued its descent.

"The filthy whore's still falling!" he shouted. To Gressa he said, "Keep pouring out ballast," then he grabbed another ski pole, wrapped its end, and climbed up to join Amundsen.

The space between the gondola and the gasbag was a maze of frost-covered ropes spreading out upward to form a net over the top. "We're going to have to climb all the way up," Amundsen told Peary. Using the net like a ladder, he pulled himself upward, hooking his hands and feet in under the ropes to hold himself in place under the overhang and pausing every few rungs to flail away at everything within reach with his blunted ski pole. Peary did the same on the other side, zigzagging his way back and forth as he climbed in order to cover most of the balloon's surface.

They thought the first part was the worst, hanging like spiders beneath the curved sides with thousands of feet of empty space below them, but when they reached the halfway point the ice grew much thicker and the flakes their poles knocked loose slid straight into their hands and faces. Plus cold air rushed upward past them now as the airship fell, fluttering the ice all around them. The fog bank below rose steadily to meet them.

"I'm running out of sand!" Gressa shouted from the gondola. Her voice rang clear in the freezing night air.

"Toss out the furniture," Peary shouted back. "Toss out anything we can do without."

"What about the people below us?"

"Fuck the people below us! You think they'd rather get hit by a blimp?"

The ropes creaked and the airship surged against their feet as Gressa opened the door and threw the chairs out into the night, but even that didn't stop their descent. Peary and Amundsen pounded frantically on the balloon, but the ice on top clung to the surface like glue and the rope netting caught much of what they were able to knock free.

Gressa yanked the table free from the wall and sent it out after the chairs. "What next? Food or equipment?" she shouted.

"Throw out the tents," Amundsen told her. "We can make more out of the balloon when we get there."

Gressa gasped. "Make tents out of the balloon? How are we going to get home?"

"It looks like the Suicide Express, unless we're lucky enough to get help from the locals to repair the blimp."

"The Suicide Express! Is it worth it just to get to the pole? I think I'd rather just go home the regular way and try it again."

Peary snorted. "Hah. You don't turn back at the first lead in the ice. Throw out the goddamned tents, and the sleeping bags, too. We'll sleep in igloos and in our clothes. Throw out some of the *food* if you have to; we won't be needing it all anyway on a one-way trip."

Growling with frustration, Gressa began following his orders, checking the statoscope after each armload went out the door. The blimp plummeted into the clouds, terrifying them all with the possibility of smashing blindly into a mountaintop, but at last it slowed to a halt without hitting anything.

"We're rising again!" Gressa shouted.

Peary and Amundsen quit beating on the gasbag. "How fast?" Amundsen asked.

"A few hundred feet per minute. Wait, it's getting faster."

"Uh-oh. We overdid it. We'll probably have to vent some hydrogen or we'll go too high now."

Sure enough, within a few minutes they had punched back up through the clouds like a rocket, the ropes creaking and more ice falling free as the gasbag expanded in the ever-thinning air. Amundsen scrambled back down through the rigging into the gondola and helped Gressa stabilize their altitude, tugging on the rope connected to the hydrogen valve on the top of the gasbag and trying to vent as little as possible, but knowing that if they overshot in the other direction the gasbag would burst from the internal pressure and they would fall like bricks to their deaths.

They finally stabilized at about 15,000 feet, but it was like riding a yo-yo. The thinner air at high altitude made for much less resistance to motion, so even a few pounds of imbalance would send them climbing or falling for hundreds of feet before they could get it turned around. When accumulating ice weighed them down again, Peary, who had remained outside, would have to knock loose chunks of it, but if he broke away too much Amundsen would have to vent more hydrogen to prevent rising too high. They spent the rest of the night doing that, the three of them trading places from time to time so none of them would freeze to death outside on the icy balloon.

"This reminds me of driving a stubborn mule," Amundsen said during one of his shifts. "Beating the poor creature to keep him moving."

"Hah, you're not so different from Scott after all!" Peary said with a laugh. Robert Scott had started his polar expedition using Siberian ponies to haul his sledges.

Amundsen didn't laugh. "I hope not," he said. "Scott's horses died before he even made a real start."

"We've made more than a start," Peary said. "Don't worry; we'll get this oversized mule-member there yet."

Dawn was slow in coming at their high latitude, but when the sun finally peeked above the horizon the ice began to melt and they had to release more and more hydrogen to keep from rising too high.

"Well, this looks like it," Peary said, pacing back and forth in the now-spacious gondola. "We're out of ballast, unless we want to toss out the last of the equipment and food. We can stay aloft the rest of today, but when we cool off again tonight we're going down for the last time."

"If only I hadn't panicked and thrown out so much!" Gressa wailed. "It's all my fault."

Amundsen said, "Nonsense. If you hadn't thrown out what you did we'd have hit the ground and been killed, or drowned in the river. As it is we've got one more full day of flight, a south wind at our backs, and only a few hundred miles to go. We'll set down as far south as we can and see if we can get help from the locals. And if not, then we'll go the rest of the way on foot."

"I wish we could tell which River channel goes farthest south," Peary said, looking out at the side-by-side valleys miles below. Now that they were only a few degrees of latitude from the pole, more and more sections of the River made one final bend and retreated to the north again, leaving the ones on either side of it to close up the gap and continue on. One of them had to go farther than the rest, and if the explorers had to set down on the River, that would be the valley to choose. But there was no way to tell until they actually reached the end which one it would be.

All day long the fish-oil engine pushed them along with its steady *chuff-chuff*ing, adding a few miles to their southerly drift, but with the sun so low on the horizon it ran at only a few percent of its equatorial efficiency. Peary cursed it for the useless deadweight it had nearly become, and if his words could have heated the boiler the blimp could have flown around the world in a day, but he succeeded only in warming his own lungs and his companions' ears.

Then, just as evening was setting on and it was looking as if they might have to pick a valley at random, they saw the polar ice cap in the distance. "There's the southernmost branch of the River over there," Gressa said, pointing far off to the west where a dozen or so parallel north–south canyons swept around the others in a smooth curve and hugged the base of the ice cap like a moat around a castle.

"Should we make for that, or should we try for the ice cap itself?" Amundsen asked Peary.

"We're at eighty-five degrees latitude," Peary said. "Only a few hundred miles to the pole. If we can make it to the ice cap, we could ski that distance in a few days."

"And if we don't make it, we could spend the rest of our lives climbing mountains just to cross these last few dozen valleys," said Amundsen.

"If we make for the southernmost channel, we're going to *have* to climb at least one mountain," Gressa pointed out. "And that last cliff before you reach the ice looks almost twice as high as the rest."

She was right. The mountains separating the bends in the River were low enough to scale, but the polar plateau stood thousands of feet higher than its surroundings. It was hard to tell from a distance, but the boundary looked to be a smooth cliff.

"I say we go for the ice cap," Peary said.

Amundsen, watching the landscape below, said nothing for a long moment. Their solar engine provided very little thrust at this latitude; they were largely at the mercy of the wind, and Coriolis force was sending them eastward as the air mass was drawn in over the pole. If they tried to steer westward, they almost certainly wouldn't make much headway; all it would accomplish would be to slow their southerly progress. "All right," he said at last. "We go for the ice cap."

It became a race with the night. At their altitude they had a longer day than the land below, but they still weren't high enough to be in the tiny region of twenty-four-hour light above the pole. At any rate, sunlight penetrating the atmosphere at such a shallow angle had little heat in it, and as the gasbag began to cool, the blimp began its last descent. When the engine at last wheezed to a stop they threw it overboard, but that gained them only a brief thousand feet or so of elevation before they began to drop again. They went through their backpacks, tossing extra clothing, cooking equipment, more food—everything they could spare. Peary even began sawing off pieces of the gondola toward the end.

At last they drifted over the final stretch of the River. The cliff bounding the polar plateau was indeed a sheer drop of at least a mile, and as they floated past it they cheered and hugged one another and bounced up and down until the entire blimp swayed like a drunken moth. But even then they weren't home free. They were still thousands of feet above the ground, in air moving southward, but below them blew the headwinds they had been fighting to avoid for two days now. They would have to drift far onto the polar plateau and then make a fast descent to the ice before the headwinds blew them back over the River again.

They stretched it as far as possible, heaving out their irreplaceable skis and backpacks full of gear and even their grails to gain another half mile, knowing that anything they dropped to the ice they could pick up again after they had landed, but at last the gondola was stripped clean and still they were descending into northward-moving air.

"Let 'er rip," Peary said when he saw they were moving backward, and Amundsen yanked on the release rope. Hydrogen whistled out the top of the gasbag, and they started down in earnest. They weren't falling as fast as they had when they'd iced over, but they would land hard.

"Get ready to ditch as soon as we hit," Peary said, but instead of going to the door he climbed up through the hatch on top of the gondola and pulled his sheath knife from its holster.

"What are you doing?" Amundsen asked him.

"I'm going to scuttle the gasbag when we set down," Peary said. "Otherwise it'll blow right back over the cliff."

Amundsen looked like he wanted to argue, but he knew as well as Peary that the wood in the gondola and the fabric of the gasbag and even the rope holding it all together could mean the difference between life and death on the ice cap. He nodded and said merely, "Be careful."

They descended at an ever-increasing angle as the surface winds took hold of them. The closer they drew to the ground, the more texture it took on, becoming a rolling plain of snowy hills, like a stormy ocean frozen in midwave. Dark ridges of rock stuck up through the ice, and smaller boulders lay scattered at random. The low sun angle created pools of shadow that could have hidden anything.

The cliff edge only a few miles distant seemed to sweep upward toward the horizon, a sharp line of snowy white obscuring the topography beyond even as it drew closer. When it was only a mile or so distant and the balloon was still hundreds of feet in the air, Peary shouted, "Blow gas! Give 'er God's own flatulence or we'll never make it!"

"We'll hit too hard!" Amundsen shouted back, but a moment later he evidently decided that was better than being dashed to death on the mountains bounding the River beyond. He tugged on the release rope as if he could pull the blimp to ground with it.

The ice rushed up to meet them, but so did the cliff edge. Gressa crouched in the doorway, ready to leap if it looked like they would blow over before they hit, but the gondola touched down a hundred feet shy of the edge. It struck with a sideways twist that spun her free and threw her a dozen feet closer to the chasm, but the foot or so of soft snow on top of the ice cushioned her fall and she bounced to a stop amid a cloud of swirling white powder.

Amundsen had been pitched to the gondola's floor, but a moment later he crawled to the door and tumbled out into the snow. Peary hung from the rigging, slashing madly at the gasbag with his knife.

"Let it go!" Amundsen shouted. "Jump free!"

The blimp, lighter by the weight of two people, lurched into the air again. The gashes Peary had made in the underside hardly affected its lift. Cursing, he leaped from the gondola and fell fifteen feet to the snow, where he stabbed his knife downward like an ice ax and skidded to a stop with only a dozen feet to spare.

The blimp cleared the edge of the cliff, swirled around once, and disappeared in the downdraft beyond. In the sudden silence, Peary said, "Well, here we are. Now for the fun part."

They hiked westward in the deepening twilight, searching for the equipment they had thrown overboard, but their equipment found them instead. They were working their way up the flank of a long north–south drift when they heard a low growl from above, and half a dozen white, furry creatures appeared like wraiths over the top. Their arms were filled with skis and backpacks and food, like rioters coming home from a good day's looting at a sporting goods store.

When they saw Peary and Amundsen and Gressa they dropped their booty with a surprised chorus of hooting and grunting. Then Gressa shouted, "Holy shit, I know these guys!" and took off running toward them.

They scattered, shrieking, but Gressa warbled something in their own tongue and one of them paused, did a double take, and took a few hesitant steps back, obviously recognizing her but just as obviously not sure what to make of her clothing or her companions. Gressa walked up to him, speaking softly, and after a moment his tension eased and the two of them hugged like long-lost lovers.

When he finally let her go, she turned to Peary and Amundsen and said, "Hey, come meet my brother!"

The yetis belonged to a tribe of about thirty who lived in caves surrounding a single grailstone a few miles to the west. They took the explorers in and fed them their first warm meal since they'd left home, then everyone sat around a fire at the mouth of the largest cave and swapped stories. The yetis had little to tell; the grailstone provided food and wood for fires, but there was no game to hunt on the plateau and no one had yet found a way down to the lands below.

Peary had just one question for them: Had they or anyone else ever made it to the pole?

Gressa translated his question, and when her brother answered she said, "Kijika says he's never heard of anyone doing it. Nobody from here has ever gone more than a couple of days' hike southward, because there aren't any more grailstones in that direction. He says there are other tribes of yetis far around the perimeter of the ice cap, but he's never heard of any of them going to the pole, either.''

"Ask him if he'll help *us* do it," Peary said.

Gressa did so, and when he responded she laughed and told him, "He says, 'Why not? There's nothing else to do around here.' ''

Peary smiled. "Good. Then here's what we do." He began describing how to shuttle food forward from cache to cache, making a chain of support from the base camp all the way to the point where the last team could make a final push for the pole.

They spent the next few days storing up food and repairing the skis and backpacks that had broken in their fall to the ice. Both Peary and Amundsen were impatient to finish what they'd started, but they'd both learned from previous failures on Earth not to push their luck. So they waited until everything was ready before setting out once again, this time with a dozen yetis for support.

They skied for ten or twelve hours a day, and built igloos to sleep in at night. The yetis didn't ski, but their wide, furry feet acted like snowshoes and what they lacked in speed they made up for in stamina. They turned back in pairs, two more returning down the chain each day while the rest pushed onward.

At last, only fifty miles or so from the south pole, the final pair of yetis turned back, leaving Gressa, Peary, and Amundsen to finish the journey they'd started half a planet away. They made half that distance in one day, then had to spend two days more in the igloo while a storm blew snow all around them and reduced visibility to nearly nothing.

They emerged on the morning of the third day to a landscape covered with jewels: the facets of fresh snowflakes reflecting the reddish, low-angled sunlight in every direction. This close to the pole the wind was little more than a breeze, and they set off again to the south, skiing in long, impatient strides and covering three or four miles per hour. As they drew closer to their goal they scanned the horizon ahead of them for any signs that others might have passed their way, but nothing broke the monotony of the ice.

Then, when they figured they were only five miles or so away, Amundsen pointed a few degrees off to their right and said, "What's that?"

"What's what?" Peary asked, turning to look.

"I see something sticking up on the horizon."

Peary squinted, then said, "It's a rock."

"It's a pretty tall rock."

"Then it's a tall fucking rock."

"Maybe it's a cairn,' Gressa said. "Maybe somebody beat us here after all."

"No," said Amundsen. "That thing's got to be twenty feet tall."

"Then it's the damned aliens," Peary said with a sigh. "They put a tower at both ends." He looked back the way they'd come, as if actually thinking about turning around without even finishing the last few miles, but then he shook his head and started forward again. Amundsen and Gressa followed him silently.

It seemed to grow taller the closer they approached, and they began to realize it was both much bigger and much farther away than they had guessed. Relying on dead reckoning, they had misjudged the distance to the pole. They covered another ten miles before they reached it: a cylindrical steel shaft twenty feet wide and a hundred feet tall. A deep rumbling noise, almost subsonic, filled the air and shook the ground around it, and after a few minutes it became apparent that the shaft was turning slowly counterclockwise.

"An axle," Amundsen said, laughing. "What a grand joke!"

"I piss on their joke," Peary said, and opening his pants, he did so. His urine frozen where it splashed on the metal.

Gressa skied around to the other side, then gasped. "Come here!"

Amundsen and Peary rushed around the pillar and found her kneeling beside two bodies. Both were frozen solid, but perfectly preserved. One was short, with long, dark hair and a heavy nose, and the other was more slender and fine-boned.

"Cook," Peary said, staring at the swarthy one.

"Scott," Amundsen said, staring at the other.

Peary shook his head sadly. "Maybe I shouldn't have sworn I'd see him in Hell."

Gressa bent down and pried a piece of paper from Cook's clenched fist. "They left us a note," she said.

Peary took it from her as if it were a poisonous snake, holding it at arm's length and reading, " 'On the seventy-third day of the twelfth year post-resurrection, Frederick A. Cook and Robert F. Scott reached this spot, the South Pole of this most unusual planet we perforce call home.' Holy mother of dogs, they've been here for years. 'To any others who come this way, we extend hearty congratulations for completing a most difficult undertaking, and we entreat you all to remember that the only winners in endeavors such as these are the ones who find what they are looking for in their own hearts.' What a load of crap."

"No, it's not," Amundsen said. "It's the truth, plain, and simple. And it's a damn sight more charitable than the note I left Scott when I beat him to the South Pole on Earth."

"Hah. Listen to this: 'If Robert Peary or Roald Amundsen ever reach this point, we consider the score now even, and leave our bodies here as proof positive of our accomplishment. We invite you to join us in our next quest, to scale the highest peak on the planet, wherever it may be. We are in no great rush to be at it, and since Scott has already frozen to death once and he tells me it is less than pleasant, I imagine you can find us in more tropical climes for some years to come. Yours truly, Frederick A. Cook.' " Peary crumbled the note and tossed it on his dead rival's chest. "Arrogant bastard," he growled.

Amundsen nodded. "Of course he is. Don't you see, that's his whole point."

Peary didn't answer. He just stared off into the distance.

"What's his whole point?" asked Gressa.

Amundsen said, "He's telling us not to give in. If somebody beats you, don't give up, because you'll always have a chance to win at something else. The people who put us on this planet are trying to stifle our ambition, to tame us. Domesticate us. But we can't let them do it. It's up to people like us to keep the wild spark alive, to keep exploring even in the face of superior knowledge. To keep our ambition and freedom even in captivity.''

He waved an arm at the pillar beside them. ''Peary had the right attitude a minute ago: Piss on it. Piss on the whole situation, on anyone who tries to control your life. Do whatever you please, here or anywhere.

''You're reading some mighty fine print between the lines,'' Peary said.

''It's there to be read.''

Peary scowled. ''Piss on it, huh? Just go on as if it meant something?''

''It *does* mean something. It means you're alive. What are you going to do, go back to moping on the Riverbank and watching everybody else have all the fun? Let's do what Cook suggests: find the tallest mountain in the world and go climb it.''

''Even if he's already waving a flag from the top of it?''

''Even then. We'll plant our flag beside his and thumb our noses at the gods together. And then we'll find an even bigger challenge. Maybe we'll build a rocketship and go to the stars.''

Peary looked down at the two bodies at his feet. It was somehow comical to see his and Amundsen's rivals lying stretched out on the ice and know at the same time they were roaming free somewhere else, wreaking havoc with the carefully planned order of things.

His frown slowly melted away. Grinning, he said, ''The stars, eh? What the hell. Sure. It'll be something to do.''

A Place of Miracles

Owl Goingback

Screams of agony and suffering filled the night. Long, piercing screams that chilled the flesh like the blade of a finely honed knife scraping against bone. Sitting Bull paddled slowly, struggling to keep his canoe in the center of the River, well away from the madness transpiring along the shore.

With grim face, he watched as fire licked crackling tongues to thatched huts, destroying what had once been a small village. As the flames—deliberately set by conquerors from the opposite side of the River—shot into the night, shadowy shapes fought and died in an orgy of violence.

It was not the first time he'd witnessed such scenes of violence or heard such heartbreaking cries. As a boy, he'd heard his mother wail the song of mourning shortly after a Crow warrior cut short the life of his father, Returns Again. In her sorrow, she'd cut her hair and sliced her arms with a flint knife. As a young warrior, he'd heard the screams of women and children as their bodies were torn to pieces by the white man's bullets. Later when he was a broken old man, he'd shed bitter tears over the cries of undernourished children suffering and dying from epidemics of measles, influenza, and whooping cough. White man's diseases. Their cries had haunted his dreams till the day he died.

Sitting Bull did not question that he was dead. He remembered his death quite clearly. It happened on a bitter cold night of a Canadian winter. He'd been rudely awakened from a sound sleep by the shattering of wood as the door of his tiny cabin burst open and a dozen or so tribal policemen barged in.

Though the tribal policemen were also Indians—some from his own tribe—they'd been bought by the white man's dollars and whiskey to do his dirty work for him. They'd come all the way to Canada to arrest Sitting Bull and take him back to the Standing Rock Reservation.

It seemed the whites were afraid there was going to be another Indian war. They thought that the ghost dance—started by Wovoka, the Paiute prophet—was the beginning of a bloody uprising. They did not understand that the ghost dance was just a religious ceremony, a prayer to the Great Spirit to change things back to the way they were before the white man came.

Sitting Bull had tried the ghost dance, but found that it was not for him. He no longer believed there was any hope to be had for his people. Nor did he think the dance could turn back the tide of white settlers that ate up the land like locusts. But because his name was well known, the whites blamed him for the sudden popularity of the ghost dance and accused him of instigating trouble. They didn't see him as he really was: an old, tired Indian who's set aside his weapons, leaving the warpath, to spend his final few years in peace.

As his followers gathered outside, looking in through the open doorway, the tribal policemen dragged Sitting Bull from his bed, forcing him to stand naked and shivering in the center of the room. Indignant at how he, a holy man, was being treated, he resisted arrest. During the struggle, someone fired a shot. Sitting Bull wasn't sure if it was a policeman or one of his people who fired the shot. It didn't matter. Whoever did it, he was blamed. Though Sitting Bull was unarmed, one of the tribal policemen pulled a pistol and shot him in the side.

Crying out in pain, Sitting Bull grabbed his side and fell to the floor. Lying there, his blood slowly seeping through the cracks, he watched as Henry Heavy Head, a "hangs-around-the-fort Indian," stepped forward, cocked his pistol, and shot him in the head. There was a blinding flash of pain as the bullet entered his skull. And then darkness.

Sitting Bull ran a hand over his head, searching for the spot where he'd been shot. His fingers detected nothing. No bump, no cut, or patch of dried blood. Nothing. Not even a scar. He was healed. Gone, too, were the scars he'd inherited in a lifetime of battles and hardships. Even his limp, the result of being shot in the foot by a Crow chief, was no more. In fact, his body was no longer the tired, wrinkled vessel of a man well past his prime. It was youthful and strong, as it had been when his life had seen only twenty or so winters.

He rubbed his hand over his head again and shuddered. Gone, too, were the long, silky braids of hair he'd been so proud of in life. His head, as bald as a baby's backside on the day of his resurrection, was covered with a very short cropping of hair.

It is only hair. It will grow back.

Sitting Bull frowned. If he was really in the spirit world, it was like nothing he'd been led to expect. It was not the vast plain of golden grasses and quiet streams as foretold by the medicine men and tribal elders. There was a plain, but it was rather narrow, extending only for a mile or so on each side of a wide river. Beyond that, wooded hills led into towering mountains.

No buffalo herds wandered lazily across the grasslands. No eagles soared overhead. In fact, since his awakening, he'd seen no animal or bird of any kind. True, there were fish in the River, and worms crawled from the ground at night, but he never considered fish or worms to be his brothers.

But while the spirit land may have been lacking in animal life, it was not so with people. There were plenty of people. Lots and lots of people. All of them white.

Oh, Grandfather, you have made a terrible mistake. You have sent me to the wrong place. This is not the spirit land of my people. It is the white man's heaven.

It angered him that he would have to spend all eternity with those who stole the sacred Black Hills, burned the villages of his people, and slaughtered all the buffalo so the children would starve. He would paint his face and go on the warpath again, but there were no guns anywhere to be had and he was too outnumbered to fight with just a bow and arrows. So instead of fighting, he'd decided to carve a canoe from the trunk of a fallen tree and travel down-River in search of his people. So far he'd been unsuccessful in his journey.

The flames engulfing the village grew higher, illuminating even more of the battle taking place on the shore. The heaviest fighting was around one of the mushroom-shaped rocks on which the food pails were filled.

Three times a day the voice of the Great Spirit boomed across the land, and his spears of real fire shot into the sky from the mushroom-shaped rocks. During those times, any pails sitting on one of the rocks would be miraculously filled with food. Unfortunately, many of those in the spirit land were unhappy with what their pail contained and sought to steal the contents from others. Greed, it seemed, was not something the white man left behind when he crossed over.

He glanced at his metal pail with contempt. It reminded him of the tin cups the guards had served beans and rancid pork in when he was a prisoner of war at Fort Randall. Two tin cups per day per Indian. Even in the white man's heaven things were rationed.

He looked away from the fighting to the little girl lying in the bow of his canoe. She was young. Nine or ten summers at the most. Someone had beaten her. There were bruises on her face, and her upper lip was cut and swollen. Quite possibly she had been molested too, for there were cuts and bruises on her thighs and pelvis.

He thought she was dead when he pulled her naked body from the river, but he'd detected a faint heartbeat. Very faint. And when he blew his breath into her body, her tiny lungs had started working again. He watched now, as her chest slowly rose and fell, her lungs laboring to draw breath into a damaged body.

Her spirit is strong. It refuses to cross over.

Cross over? Cross over to where? How could one die if they were already dead? But Sitting Bull knew it was possible. He'd seen several people die since starting his journey a week ago.

But where does the spirit go from here? Is there another land beyond this?

Perhaps after dying a second time the spirit was allowed to pass on to a better place, a country of open prairie and roaming herds of buffalo, like the land he longed for. Then again, maybe it just entered another world as equally bizarre as the one he traveled through.

As he sat there, looking down upon the girl, she coughed and opened her eyes.

A look of fear quickly stole across the girl's face. She whimpered and tried to scoot backward.

Sitting Bull slowly held up his right hand, palm facing forward in a gesture of friendship, and spoke to her in his native tongue. The blank look he received told him that she didn't understand. He smiled and tried again in English.

"Do not be afraid. I will not hurt you."

She stared at him, perhaps pondering whether or not to trust him.

"Where . . . where am I?" she finally asked.

"You are safe," he answered. "I pulled you from the water."

She sat up and looked around, staring at the burning village for a moment. "I'm cold," she said, crossing her arms across her chest.

Sitting Bull had no blanket, but he did have a large piece of brightly colored fabric, like that his breechcloth was made from. Draping it over her shoulders, he tucked the edges of the fabric beneath her legs.

Reaching behind him, Sitting Bull grabbed his pail and set it between his legs. The girl had no pail; someone must have taken it from her. The pail would do the thief no good, however, for it was impossible to open another person's pail. But without the container, the girl would surely starve to death.

He opened his pail and removed a small glass of whiskey from it. Sitting Bull never drank the white man's poison, but kept it in case he wished to trade with others along the river. In this case it might be just the thing to warm a small body.

Leaning forward, he held the glass to her lips so she could drink. She took a sip and coughed violently. He tried to get her to take another sip, but she refused.

"What is your name?" he asked, returning the glass of whiskey to his pail.

"Krissy," she whispered.

"It is a good name," he said, nodding. "It reminds me of the sound crickets make. Kriss . . . s . . . sy, Kriss . . . s . . . sy."

Krissy smiled. "What's your name?"

"I am Tantaka Iyotake."

She wrinkled her nose. "That's a silly name."

"To you it is silly, but to my people it is a very strong name."

"What does it mean?"

"Sitting Bull."

Her eyes opened wider in recognition.

"You have heard of me?"

She nodded. "My third-grade teacher read a story about you."

Sitting Bull was pleased to be recognized, especially by someone so young.

"What did your teacher say about me?"

"She said you were a chief . . ."

"Not chief," he corrected. "Medicine man."

". . . and that you killed General Custer."

"They say I killed him. I don't know. There was much confusion that day . . . soldiers riding everwhere. Women screaming. People shooting." He shrugged. "Maybe I did kill him."

Krissy thought it over for a moment. "I don't think you killed him, cause if you did you wouldn't be in heaven."

Sitting Bull frowned. "Maybe we're not in heaven."

"We are too in heaven," she said, anger leaping into her voice. "My momma said that all good people go to heaven when they die. And I've been good!"

Sitting Bull pointed to the burning village. "They have let some bad ones in too."

Krissy was undaunted by the remark. "That's because Jesus hasn't been here yet. When he comes, he'll kick the bad ones out—send them to the *other* place—and everything will be all right. Heaven is beautiful. You'll see."

They debated the issue. Krissy, believing they were in Heaven, told of all the things she'd learned in Sunday school. Sitting Bull refused to be swayed. He refused to believe they were in a place as wonderful as the Heaven Krissy described— the place of miracles. He'd yet to see anyone who flew around on wings—angels, Krissy called them—or fields of flowers where children laughed and played all day long. So far, all he'd seen was the same unhappiness and misery he'd known in life.

But despite their differences of opinion, Sitting Bull enjoyed Krissy's company. She was a breath of fresh air in a somewhat foul world. He'd always been fond of children, no matter what color their skin was.

Frustrated at being unable to sway Sitting Bull to her way of thinking, Krissy tapped her foot impatiently.

"Well, you just wait till Jesus gets here," she said, wrinkling her nose. "He'll prove we're in Heaven. He'll—"

THUNK!

Blood sprayed across Sitting Bull's face as the arrow burst from the center of Krissy's chest. A narrow shaft of wood, smaller around than his little finger, with a jagged stone point.

"Oh . . ." Krissy said, her mouth dropping open. She looked down at the arrow sticking out her chest, blood dripping from its shaft. "Oh, oh, oh . . ."

Krissy slowly raised her head, looking at Sitting Bull questioningly. She started to say something, but her eyes glazed over and she toppled forward. A feathered shaft protruded from her back.

"NOOOO . . . !" Sitting Bull yelled, grabbing his spear and standing up in the canoe.

He'd been so engaged in conversation that he'd allowed his canoe to drift dangerously close to the shoreline. They'd been spotted. A canoe, filled with six men, rushed to intercept them.

The canoe was less than fifty feet away and closing rapidly. The man in the very front was standing up, refitting an arrow to his bow Before he could get off another shot, Sitting Bull drew back his arm and threw his spear.

The spear flew straight, hitting its target, burying itself deep in the man's stomach. The man screamed in agony as the spear—its tip the horn from a horn fish—ripped through flesh and internal organs, severing muscle and spinal cord. There was a loud splash as he fell into the river.

Sitting Bull did not have another spear. Nor was there time to snatch up his bow and arrows. The other canoe was already upon him. Grabbing his stone-head war club, he leaped from his canoe, landing in the middle of the other.

In life, Sitting Bull had been a fierce warrior. At age twenty-five, he was a leader of an elite military society called the Strong Hearts, a sash wearer. In death he was no less brave, nor was he any less skilled as a fighter. Though outnumbered five to one, he was like a crazed grizzly bear as he landed among those who dared attack him.

No sooner had he landed in the other canoe than he crushed a man's skull with a powerful blow of his war club. Stepping quickly over the quivering body, he attacked the next man in line who was rising, a stone knife in hand.

Sitting Bull parried a knife thrust meant for his abdomen and countered with a vicious blow to the man's jaw, scattering teeth out across the water. The man fell overboard. The sudden displacement of his weight capsized the canoe, throwing Sitting Bull and the three other men into the water.

Diving beneath the overturned canoe, Sitting Bull pulled a stone-bladed knife from his belt and came up behind his next victim. Grabbing the man around the neck, he dragged him underwater. The man kicked and fought, struggling to get free, but Sitting Bull held on, stabbing him repeatedly in the back. Feeling his opponent's body finally go limp, Sitting Bull released his hold and swam for the surface.

Treading water, he looked around for the other two men, but they were nowhere in sight. Apparently, they had either drowned or made it to shore. Exhausted, Sitting Bull swam back to his own canoe, pulling himself carefully up and into the tiny craft.

Krissy lay facedown in the bow of the canoe, in a pool of her own blood. Leaning forward, Sitting Bull lightly placed his fingertips against her neck. She was still alive. A faint pulse could be felt. Careful of the arrow sticking from her body, he reached under Krissy and gently rolled her over on her side. As he did, her eyes opened.

"Hello, my little cricket," he said, forcing a smile.

"I don't feel so good," Krissy said, her voice straining. "It hurts real bad."

"Shhh . . . lie still."

She coughed and looked up at him, studying his face. "Am I dying?"

Sitting Bull did not lie. "Yes."

Tears ran down her cheeks. "Not fair. I'm already dead. Why do I have to die again?"

He had no answer for her.

"Will I get to see Jesus?"

Sitting Bull thought of all the things he'd learned in life . . . all the things he'd been told by the tribal medicine men, whom he believed, and by the white priests, whom he didn't.

"Yes," he said nodding.

A tiny smile touched the corners of Krissy's mouth—a frail, little smile, like the wings of a butterfly—and then disappeared. "Will you hold my hand?"

Sitting Bull reached out and grasped Krissy's hand, interlacing his fingers with hers.

"Thank you," she said, slowly closing her eyes.

Sitting Bull watched as her chest rose and fell, rose and fell. And then stopped.

Sitting Bull buried Krissy's body a mile or so down the River, about a hundred feet back from the shore, in an area void of people. He covered the grave with large stones he'd gathered from the River's edge, marking it with a crude wooden cross. She would have liked the cross.

Once the stones were in place, he'd sat down with his pipe and offered prayers for the spirit of a little girl who'd touched his heart. He'd just finished with his prayer, tapping the ashes from his pipe, when he noticed a man approaching.

Though he'd seen hundreds of white men since his resurrection in the spirit land, there was something different about this one, something vaguely familiar. He was certain he'd seen him someplace before, but he couldn't place where.

Laying his pipe aside, Sitting Bull stood up. He turned to face the white man who approached, studying his every feature. The man was lean and muscular, and walked with his head erect, his shoulders squared. He had the bearing of a leader, of one who was used to giving commands.

It wasn't until the man was only ten feet away that Sitting

Bull finally recognized him. The man recognized Sitting Bull at the same time.

"You!" the man snarled, drawing a stone knife from the waistband of his breechcloth.

He looked quite different in death than he had in life. The bright blue uniform and polished brass buttons had been replaced by a brightly colored breechcloth and sandals made from fishskin. Gone, too, was his long hair and droopy mustache. But his eyes were the same—cold, piercing eyes that burned with the light of ambition, greed, and—yes—maybe even a little madness.

Sitting Bull drew his war club.

Even though he was much younger than the last time he saw him, and he lacked his army of long knives, Sitting Bull would have known him anywhere. He was the man who'd stolen the Black Hills. The man who caused so much suffering and grief to the Indian people.

"Custer!" Sitting Bull whispered between clenched teeth. He lunged forward, swinging his war club.

The war club struck General Armstrong Custer on the side of his head, knocking him to the ground. He tried to rise, but Sitting Bull hit him again, killing him.

Breathing hard, Sitting Bull stared down at the lifeless body of Custer. He'd seen hundreds, if not thousands, of white men since his resurrection. There were probably millions of them living along the River. To come across the one man he hated most in life, here, now, it was amazing. Why, it was . . .

A miracle.

A chill danced along Sitting Bull's spine. He looked up, almost expecting the sky to be filled with flying people.

Angels.

He smiled as he remembered what Krissy had said, for those words now gave him hope—hope that he would one day find his people and the land of open prairie he longed for. After all, in a land of miracles anything was possible.

Yes, Krissy. Heaven is truly a wonderful place.

Diaghilev Plays Riverworld

Robert Sheckley

I will skip the beginning, senors, of how it all began for me, since it begins the same for everyone who finds himself reborn in this place they call Riverworld. All of us begin naked and hairless, lying on short grass near the bank of an interminable river. Close at hand, attached to the wrist by a short strap, is the implement they have named the grail: a cylindrical object with recesses inside. It is a magical food provider. When put into one of the depressions in the great gray stones they call grailstones, at certain times, accompanied by a devilish discharge of blue electricity and a booming noise like a sudden storm in high mountains, it becomes filled up with food and drink, and with the narcotic they call dreamgum, and with spirits, too, and sometimes wine, and nearly always tobacco.

When I came back to life, the first thing I thought of was my death on that gray morning in 1587, sitting in my chamber in Salamanca, with the weariness coming over me, and the sudden weakness in the veins that told me the end was at hand. I had little chance to recommend my soul to God. I didn't think much about it, to tell the truth, because for one who has lived his life as a conquistador and companion of the Pizarro brothers in the new world of the Indies, it doesn't do to think too much about whether one has lived a good life or not. We Spaniards of the Conquest set ourselves to do a certain thing and we didn't much care how we went about it. Life was cheap in those days and in that place, our own as well as everyone else's. We lived by the sword and died by it, and I for one had been surprised to find myself a survivor of those hectic days, to discover that I had lived long enough to grow gray hairs and to die in bed in the university city of Salamanca, the place where I had taken my arts degree so many years before. I remember thinking, as the priest bent over me and the pain and lassitude seized me, "Well, let's make an end of it." But I could never have guessed that this land of Riverworld lay beyond.

In those first days, on the banks of that great river, I learned, along with others newly reborn, the use of the grails, and a little about the conditions of life in this place. Later I found that I had been singularly fortunate in the gradual manner of my introduction to this world, reborn in a quiet fold of the Riverbank claimed by no one, an equal among others recently reborn like themselves, and equally ignorant.

My companions in those first days after rebirth were mercenary soldiers from the Free Companies, which had done such notable deeds in Italy in their time. They were a collection of English and German men-at-arms, not a Spaniard among them. We conversed in a mixture of Spanish, French, Italian, and a little Catalan. It was not too difficult to exchange our thoughts, which were rudimentary. As usual in such places, there were some who had been born a day or a week before the others, and they showed us how the grails worked. And so we talked and speculated about our lot in Riverworld, and tried to decide what to do with ourselves.

The decision was soon made for us. Not long after my rebirth, a group of about fifty men came marching along the banks of the river toward us. We saw at once that they were armed, and we were all too aware that we were not. We had found nothing to fight with in this uncanny place, not even sticks and stones. So we huddled together and tried to look formidable despite our nakedness, and waited to see what the newcomers intended.

They marched in good order, forty or fifty hard-looking men armed with wooden staves and odd-looking swords that we later learned were fashioned from fish bones. They had armor made from the tough dried hide of some species of great fish that lurked in the River's depths. The foremost among them was more splendidly attired than his fellows and wore an insignia in his fishscale helmet. He asked to speak to our commander.

We hadn't concerned ourselves with such matters up to now. Our novel surroundings had taken up all our attention. Since I was the most familiar with the newcomers' language, which was Latin, and which I had studied during my year at the University of Salamanca, it fell to me to be the spokesman.

"Who are you people?" I asked, deciding to take a bold line.

"We are Roman soldiers of the Flaminia Legion," the officer replied. "I am Rufus Severus, and I have been elected tribune to represent these men. Now, who are you?"

"We are new in this place," I told him. "We are fighting men and we have no leader, though I, Rodrigo Isasaga, am spokesman by default, as I have more of your language than the others. We are awaiting information as to what our possibilities are."

"You should be glad you ran into me," Rufus said. "You look like a good enough group of men. But you are under several severe handicaps. First, you do not speak the language of this place, which is called Norse, though I understand it is a corrupted and simplified version. I advise you to learn it as quickly as possible. Second, you are masterless men in a place where the strong quickly enslave the weak. There are many here in the settlements along the River who will be happy to bind you and make you serve them. They will take most of the food and all of the drink from your grails, and leave you only enough to live on half-starved. I suggest that you join my legion until such time as you can provide for yourselves."

"You are about fifty men," I said. "That is not a very strong army."

"No, it is not," Rufus agreed. "But we are disciplined, and we have the advantage of having known each other in our former life. That is a rare circumstance in this place."

I thanked him for his information and asked permission to discuss what he had said with my men. Then I told my companions of the Free Companies what I had learned. They decided to a man to join up with Rufus. I decided to also. Not that I was much taken with the Roman. But it seemed best to belong to something until I had some idea of conditions in this place.

So we fell in with Rufus and his soldiers. There were a dozen of us. The Romans had a few spare cudgels, which they let us use. And we marched on, traveling up-River.

I spent several days with this Roman army and learned that they had little more idea of what they were doing than we had. A lucky turn of fortune had caused them to be all reborn together. Rufus was the ranking officer. Seeing the conditions, he had quickly organized them and found what weapons he could for them. They soon saw soon that it was dog-eat-dog in this place. They decided to march, one direction being as good as another. They hoped to find other legionnaires, perhaps a whole Roman City, or, failing that, a Gaullish town, for some of them were Romans from that country.

And so our first days passed, during that march along the flat Riverbank, and we passed people from many different civilizations.

That was a pleasant stroll, senors, even though the Roman soldiers set a good pace. Our route lay along the left bank of the great river that dominated this world. It reminded me of the Amazon, where I had the honor of serving under don Francisco de Orellana, whose presence I sorely missed now. But there was no real resemblance between the two rivers. The Amazon was a world of riotous jungle vegetation. Once in it, it had seemed more like a sea than a river. It had been difficult to get to either bank, since it was so overgrown. Our river, by contrast, was an orderly sort of place, running between flatland on either side. A mile or so back of this flatland were hills, and they soon gave way to towering cliffs, the highest I have ever seen, and I have seen the Alps in France.

As I say, it was at first almost a stroll rather than a route march, because we were not encumbered with belongings. Provisions could be had every evening, and water was always close at hand. Our grail cups were light. We also carried some towels along with us, which had appeared beside us at our birth. They served as clothing and bedding. The Romans had even joined some of them together by their magnetic strips, to provide themselves with something like togas. Other towels served as knapsacks, and by tearing strips from them (with difficulty, for they were of extremely tough material), they were able to fasten these objects to their bodies, a practice that we copied.

Spaced along the Riverbank were the great gray grailstones, where we were able to stop and reprovision. Of people we saw but a few at first. This was a deserted stretch of the River. We were on the march almost a week before we ran into groups of any size. And then we were taken by surprise, because they were not European, but Chinese.

We first saw the Orientals at dawn of the eighteenth day of our march. They were a group of twenty or so. They had tied back their dark hair with cloth headbands. They were armed with weapons such as those the Romans possessed. Their faces were flat, and of a yellowish hue, much as Messer Marco Polo had described them in his account of his travels.

We stopped and tried to talk with them. Several of them had some measure of Italian, and we learned that they were servants of Kublai Khan, who had built a fortified town nearby. We were told that the great khan welcomed strangers, because he liked to hear about the habits and customs of men from far places. The Romans had not heard of him, since he came long after their time. But I was able to tell them that the Great Khan was the head of an empire larger than that of Rome.

I also questioned the Chinese as to the whereabouts of Marco Polo, but they had no knowledge of him. We talked it over among ourselves and decided to go with the Chinese to their camp.

Xanadu was a large bamboo village set on the plain and surrounded by a wall made of branches from the limbs of the great trees that grow in the hills nearby. The place was very orderly, with carefully stamped-out dirt passageways, and houses built of bamboo. The Orientals had wrought cleverly. Their city looked like a prosperous place.

We were brought to see the Great Khan almost immediately. Kublai Khan was not Chinese himself, as I learned, but Mongol. He was an individual of middle size, rather plump, with a flat round face and a dignified expression. Speaking for my fellows of the Free Companies, I told him where we came from and what had befallen us. Kublai said he had been born into Riverworld like the rest of us, but some years earlier, and, seeing the social disorder into which everyone was born, sought to impose some structure on political institutions. Chinese and Mongolians had rallied to his banners, and so far things had gone well for his state.

He was disappointed that we had no goods to sell or trade, but told us we were free to continue on our journey, or to stay as long as we pleased. In either case, we were free to use the grailstones that were scattered across his territory, as long as we did so in an orderly manner.

"But think carefully about whether you want to continue," he said. "I have sent out messengers to see who my neighbors are, and some of them are quite barbaric. You will not find matters so well arranged as you travel farther up-River. I suggest that you settle down here. We will find women for you, since we enjoy at present a modest surplus in them, and you will be safe."

This suggestion, reasonable though it was, did not sit well with me. I hadn't gone through all the strangeness and dislocation of being reborn in a new world in order to sit down now in a bamboo village and get my rations every day like a good little fellow. I was one of that generation that sailed to the Indies with Francisco Pizarro. Even though I had died once, I wasn't ready yet to retire.

Most of the Free Company mercenaries agreed with me, but Rufus and most of the Romans thought better of the idea, and they decided to stay. The rest of us set off again, totaling now about forty men.

After several more weeks of travel across sparsely populated territory, we came to a large Riverside village of tenth-century Saxon fishermen from the lowlands along the Elbe. There were also some eighth-century Hungarians living among them, and a few nineteenth-century Scots who kept to themselves. These Saxons had never migrated to England as so many of their countrymen had done. Here in Riverworld they had set up their village in a wide bend of the River. They had constructed boats of bamboo and other woods, and made quite a good thing of fishing.

Their boats were small but handy, and quite seaworthy. Neither the Chinese nor the Romans had taken to the water yet, but we saw the advantages of that mode of travel almost at once. Travel by water seemed safer than any other way, faster, and less tiring.

We stayed with the Saxons for a while, and it was here that I met Hertha. It happened one evening when a group of us were sitting around a campfire telling stores and singing songs of our homeland. The talk turned to dances, and each man showed the steps of a dance native to his region.

When my turn came, I danced a jota for them. I had been well versed in dancing as a boy, and if I do say so myself, our native dances of Spain are more beautiful than those of most races. The jota required a partner, however, and so, looking into the faces around the campfire, I chose a pretty flaxen-haired young girl and asked her if she would dance with me.

Hertha picked up the steps at once, and we performed to considerable applause. Back in Salamanca, in my student days, I had danced once or twice for pay, and had been told I would be able to make a good thing of it if I chose to continue.

Hertha was grace itself. Her small well-shaped body, revealed and concealed by the clinging towels, moved in and out of the stately figures of the Spanish dance. We won a resounding round of applause, and those around us plied us with food and drink.

When we talked later, we found we had little in common in the way of a language. But Hertha was already picking up the Norse that was the lingua franca of the River, and soon we were conversing nicely, and finding that we had as much in common as a man and maid can hope to have. We became hutmates that very night, and we are together still.

Since there were few ways of passing the time, there on that slow bank of the River where food came by itself to our grails and one day was much like the last, Hertha and I practiced other dances. I showed her the steps to the fiery flamenco dances of Andalusia, the Sevillanas and the Seguiryas and others, and she showed a fine poise and grace in the performing of them. With her smooth blond hair tied back beneath a black towel and her back arched imperiously, Hertha could have been a gypsy from Granada or from the Triana in Seville. The only thing missing was the sound of stamping feet, which so characterize the dances of Andalusia. But these depend on well-shod shoes and plank floor, neither of which we had.

Nevertheless, we persevered. One day I constructed a comb for her in the Spanish fashion, and showed her how to put up her hair in a typical gypsy fashion. A towel had to serve as a mantilla.

These careless days seemed as though they would continue forever. But then, quite unexpectedly, our Saxon camp was attacked by a strong force of raiders, who came up unseen in the night and attacked just before dawn. They came from the city of Oxenstierna, a large encampment of Northmen that had moved into the vicinity recently. They were mostly Swedes and Danes from the seventh and eighth centuries, former soldiers of the army that ravaged Europe and England for so many centuries before the Norman Conquest. They were turbulent men and strong fighters, much given to strong drink and to the random practice of violence. They burst into the Saxon camp late one night when the sentries were dozing. There was a general battle throughout the camp and up and down the Riverbank. When it was over, most of our Saxon friends had been killed, and Hertha and I were hauled in front of their king, Eric Longhand, to see how he wished to dispose of us.

"What can you do?" Longhand asked.

"We can join your forces and serve you well," I told him.

He shook his head. "We have enough soldiers at present. Nor do we lack for grail slaves." He turned to his men. "Might as well put these to death."

"Wait!" I cried. "Hertha and I have something that might be of use to you."

"And what is that?"

"Time hangs heavy in this world," I pointed out. "There is sufficient food and drink, but little in the way of entertainment. My wife and I are dancers, skilled in the exciting steps of my native Spain. We will entertain you."

Longhand was amused by this suggestion. "Very well," he

said. "Let us see you dance. We will postpone execution for a
few minutes until we see how well or poorly you shamble."

Hertha and I gave the performance of our lives. I must say, it
was very good indeed. What we lacked in finesse we more than
made up for in desperate fury. Hertha remembered her steps,
and we danced a series of jotas, then several sets of Sevillanas,
and then the mysterious Seguiryas, which never fail to move
onlookers. At the end, the Vikings applauded, and our lives
were spared.

Once that first evening of bloodshed was over, the Vikings
proved to be amiable people. Hertha and I moved freely among
them, and life soon returned to an even temper. The days
passed, and nothing of any note happened until about two
weeks later, when a group of prisoners was brought in from one
of the guardposts.

"We caught them using the grailstones," the guard said.

I was present at the interrogation of the prisoners. Hearing
them speak Spanish, I was immediately alert. There was one
face among them that I recognized. "Gonzalo!" I cried. For it
was indeed my old captain, Gonzalo Pizarro, brother of Francisco
Pizarro, at one time captain-general of Peru.

"Hello, Rodrigo," Gonzalo said to me. He was cool in this
desperate strait, a tall, well-made man, with a big hawk nose
and keen dark eyes "What are you doing here?"

"I am making my living as well as I can," I told him. "I am
a dancer, Gonzalo, and I suggest that you become one, too. As
I remember it, you had a lively turn with jota and the zapateado,
and you could perform some of the South American figures as
well, though not as well as Francisco."

Gonzalo Pizarro immediately asked me if I had seen his
brother, for whom he had been searching. He was disappointed
when I told him I had not. As for becoming a dancer, at first he
scoffed at the idea. For him, one of the original conquistadors,
the conqueror of Quito and other famous places, once for a
brief time the controller of Peru after the assassination of his
brother Francisco, this seemed a step downward. He swore he
would prefer to die with his honor intact. But that was mere
bluster. When the time came to make a choice, he announced

himself to Eric Longhand as a dancer just like the rest of us, only better than most. And on the strength of his boast he was allowed to join Helga and me.

It was clear that he would need a partner, and he lost no time in finding one. He picked a Russian woman who had been recently accepted into the Viking settlement. Her name was Katrina, and she was part gypsy, a dark-eyed, wild-haired beauty who might have been from Córdoba or Jerez de la Frontera as far as her looks were concerned. She was graceful and light on her feet, and she picked up the steps quickly. She and Gonzalo quarreled with each other from the moment they met, for Gonzalo was randy as a billy goat and had his eye on the slow-moving Scandinavian beauties from the start. But he and Katrina seemed to like each other well enough despite their arguments, or perhaps because of them. Whatever it was, the relationship seemed to suit them both.

Our dances went better now with two couples, and soon after that we added another when Pedro Almargo joined us. This old comrade of Gonzalo's had been his archenemy in the stirring days in the Andes, when central South America had been a prize fought over and wrenched back and forth between the various conquistadors. In fact, Gonzalo had had Almargo executed when he captured Quito, a fact for which he apologized now. Almargo said he didn't hold a grudge over so slight a matter. What was important now was what lay ahead. And he studied hard at the dance with his new partner, a small, vibrant Provençal woman from Aix.

More Spaniards from the days of the Conquest found their way to us, for rumor travels faster in Riverworld than a bird can fly. Alberto Tapia came, and the Valdavia brothers of the Chilean conquest, and Sebastian Romero, who soldiered with Balboa. Even gallant Hernando de Soto found his way to us in Oxenstierna. And we were joined by others not of Spain, most notably the Russian woman Bronislava, who brought her brother, whom she claimed was a famous dancer in his own time named Vaslav Nijinsky.

This Nijinsky was an odd sulky creature who claimed he didn't dance any longer, but who did offer to choreograph for us, and to provide numbers for the whole company to perform en ensemble. I was suspicious of him at first; he was an odd-looking creature with his long skull and his strange, graceful, effeminate movements. He was very strong but very strange, too, and he shied away from people.

He was always watching when new people come in to Oxenstierna.

"Who are you looking for?" I asked him one day.

"Never mind, it is better not even to say his name."

"Come, Vaslav, saying his name won't hurt."

"It will make him appear."

"Is he such a devil, then?"

"The worst that ever was. He captured my soul long ago, and he will be back to get it again."

I learned from Bronislava that he was referring to a man named Diaghilev, who had been a ballet impresario back when they were all alive in the closing years of the nineteenth century and the beginning of the twentieth. Under the direction of this Diaghilev, Nijinsky had scored his greatest triumphs: *The Spectre of the Rose*, *The Nutcracker*, *Les Sylphides*, and many others. He had been the leading dancer in the company, and the company itself had been world-renowned.

"So what was wrong with that?" I asked her. "What did Vaslav have to complain of?"

She shook her head, and her eyes took on a faraway look. "There was something about Sergei Diaghilev, something terrible and abnormal. He drove everyone hard. But that was not it. Ballet dancers are accustomed to working hard. But it was something else. I can only call it something diabolic. He terrified Vaslav, and finally drove him insane."

Somehow, even with all the millions, the billions of people being reborn in Riverworld, I knew that Diaghilev would find Nijinsky. And so it did not surprise me when one day a new group of people came to Oxenstierna. They were travelers, traders, and they had come from far away. They carried some trade goods—dried packets of fishskin and other fish products, and they had some boards, too, rough-hewn out of the great ironwood trees. This last had been done at some place down-River where they had made iron tools.

Along with this troop came a man of medium height, with sad dark eyes and a flat, rumpled face. He was in no way handsome, but there was a commanding air about him. He came up to our tent, where we were having our rehearsal.

"You are the dancers?" he asked.

"That is what we are, senor," I replied "And who are you?"

"I am a man who has a way with dancers," he replied.

Vaslav, who had been in one of the other tents, rehearsing the dancers, now came in, saw the newcomer, and his jaw fell open.

"Sergei!" he cried. "Is it really you?"

"None other, my friend," the newcomer said. "Suppose you tell your friend here who I am."

Vaslav turned to me. His dark eyes glowed as he said, "This is Sergei Diaghilev. He is a great impresario, a great producer of dance troupes."

"Interesting," I replied. "I don't need you, Diaghilev. Our troupe is already organized."

"No doubt," Diaghilev said. "I merely want to watch your performance."

Diaghilev attended our evening show, and came to see us after the performance. It had gone well enough. Our audience seats were better than half full, which was doing well for us. I poured Diaghilev a glass of wine. We Latins had traded our spirits for it with the northern men. It seemed to be a French vintage, but I missed our rougher Spanish stuff.

I was full of suspicion of this Diaghilev. Especially since he was in the same business I had set myself to. I was well aware of my own deficiencies in this line of work. Luck had thrown me into the impresario line, mainly because I had a gift of languages that, though meager, was greater than that of my fellows. I had no high regard for my talents. If this man was indeed world-renowned, as Nijinsky had assured me, he could no doubt do a better job at leading a dance troupe than I could. But I saw no reason to assist him in putting me out of work. I swore to myself that I'd kill him before letting that happen. There was little enough to do in Riverworld except fight or be a slave. A man didn't give up a good job lightly if he had the luck to find one.

Diaghilev tried to put me at my ease at once. "You have done a fine job, Senor Isasaga. It is obvious that you are not schooled in the dance. But what of that? You have done as well as a man could. I do suggest, however, that there is an improvement or two that could well be wrought without loss to you or your people, and with considerable gain."

"What is that?" I asked.

"First accompany me to my camp," Diaghilev said. "I have something I want to show you. Bring all of your people, too. They will be interested."

We accompanied Diaghilev down to the River, and then about a mile downstream along its right bank. All of our troop went along. Gonzalo had taken the precaution of arming himself. He carried a copper dagger that he had won at dice from one of the Northmen. A half-dozen of the other Spaniards carried cudgels. Even the women dancers had little flint knives or sharp-edged stones, which they carried in their sashes. Diaghilev must have noticed, but he affected an air of unconcern.

There were only eight people in Diaghilev's group, and they appeared to be unarmed. This was a relief for us: this bunch would give us no trouble. And half of them were women, anyhow.

Diaghilev served us a beer his people had brewed from roots and leaves and wild yeasts. It was not bad. Then he proposed that his people entertain us. And so we lay back on the grass while his people danced. Among them were names whose fame I only learned about later: Alicia Markova, Michel Fokine, and the divine Anna Pavlova.

None of us had ever seen anything like his performance before. Perhaps the Russians had not the fire of our Spaniards. But that was the only fault you could find, if fault it was. In every other capacity, including that of sheer breathtaking artistry, they surpassed us in every way. Markova floated like a butterfly, and alighted like a piece of down. Pavlova was poetry personified. They were all incredible. We applauded strenuously. Nijinsky watched with tears in his eyes. And at the end, the

Russian dancers held out their hands imploringly to our Nijinsky, who had watched all this in a despairing silence. He turned away from them, shaking his head, muttering, "I no longer dance." But they persevered, and Diaghilev included his pleas, and at length Nijinsky relented and repeated, as I was told later, one of his solos from *The Spectre of the Rose*.

At the end we all sat together and drank wine, and Diaghilev said to Nijinsky, "I knew I would find you, Vaslav. We are together again."

"I did the dance for you, Sergei!" Nijinsky cried. "But I will never dance again!"

"We will see," said Diaghilev.

Once this Russian turned up, our situation changed. It was only logical to combine our companies. There was no talk of who was in charge. But without ever exerting himself, Diaghilev bit by bit took over. He did it with a suggestion here, an idea there, and his ideas were first-rate. He was the one who directed the construction of a wooden platform so that our dancers' heels could be heard stamping out the rhythms. And of course he was also the one who devised shoes so that they could be heard. He had curtains made for greater dramatic effect. He introduced stage lighting and scenery. Nor were his suggestions disconsonant with the spirit of Spanish dance. He was far better at it than I was, foreigner though he was. There was no doubt about it, this man was a conquistador of dance. I struggled with my stubborn soul, and finally decided it was better to be assistant to a genius than mediocre sole impresario of a second-rate dance troupe.

Most of us got used to it. Not Gonzalo. He hated the idea of Sergei lording it over him. He bristled, resisted, but even he was convinced in the end. Diaghilev's improvements made the performance so much better.

Soon, our fame began to spread. People came from far and wide to Oxenstierna to watch our performances. And Sergei Diaghilev began to turn to the production of musical instruments.

He was aided in this by another newcomer to our ranks, Manuel de Falla, a Spaniard born well after my time, famous in his day, so I was told, as a composer. This de Falla was a dark little fellow, and he had lived many years in Paris and was in some ways quite Frenchified. Even in our rudimentary clothing of towels and leaves, he stood out as something of a dandy. He began by devising simple percussion instruments for us, making them of bamboo and wood. Next he improvised a guitar. The sound box was made of bamboo pieces closely joined with fish glue, and carefully polished and then varnished. He made a keyboard with a fish's backbone, cut it down to half round, and carefully fitted it with frets of shell. His strings were of fish-gut shaved down to proper diameter. It was difficult getting strings that matched, but de Falla worked with massive patience, and after a while he had constructed the first stringed instrument ever seen in Riverworld. There was no problem tuning it: the man had perfect pitch.

Once he struck it up, the effect was electrifying. With the sound of the guitar, even such a rudimentary guitar as this one, our dance really came to life. Now our troupe ceased being little more than a novelty. We were able to turn out true performances.

We lacked only a singer. And soon we had two, a man and a woman. She was Spanish-Algerian, he a Moor from Algeria. They had been husband and wife on Earth, and had succeeded in finding each other again in Riverworld. On Earth they had performed in Cádiz and in the Casbah of Tangier. They sang the true Flamenco, the cante jondo of ancient days, and now the focus of our performance shifted, for they were true artists. De Falla composed for them, and Nijinsky choreographed new dances for our troupe.

Our dance company entered a period of expansion, and many new dancers tried to join us. Diaghilev's Company of Spanish Dance, as it was now called, was one of the few employers in that region of Riverworld. Perhaps in all of Riverworld, for all we knew. You could find work as a soldier anywhere, or a slave, or a concubine. After that, the jobs were few and far between.

The kingdom of Oxenstierna was too small to set up as a powerful state. But the Northmen didn't want to attach themselves to any of the other powers in the region. The Slavic kingdom of Stanislas II was on one side, and on the other, a Japanese group. Both outnumbered the north Europeans by a factor of ten to one. Eric Longhand showed some talent for diplomacy then, when he declared his area a free-trade zone and put himself under the protection of the three largest powers in the vicinity. His territory included a small island that had formed up half a mile offshore, and he had almost four miles of shoreline. To this territory anyone was welcome who came in peace. Weapons were bound with peace-strings when you entered Oxenstierna, and they were not meant to be broken until you left. Those who broke the law were turned over to their own tribal or city authorities for judgment and punishment.

And so our enterprise prospered, senors, and so did the city of Oxenstierna. People came from far and wide to trade in our borders. And not just to trade. Oxenstierna offered something no other place in our vicinity could give: a sense of security, a chance to relax from the cares of state, and the constant scheming of who ruled whom, and what to do about it. In this new Earth of Riverworld, since the cares of getting food and erecting shelter had been more or less provided, what remained were the matters of who should rule whom, and what god they should worship. Men now had the chance to devote all of their time to matters of religion and state. But this interest was taken up by the more aggressive men. The others, who constituted the majority, were singularly uninterested in such matters, and cared even less for questions of color, race, and language. Language was a hodgepodge anyhow, and finally all of us had to learn the artificial language of Norse in order to converse. We could well be called the planet of Babel.

Most of those reborn on Riverworld concerned themselves with thoughts of dominance. For them the highest good was the ability to lord it over their fellows, often in the name of some obsolete doctrine such as racial purity. The preponderance of men, however, now as in the past, cared little for such matters and wanted only to live in peace.

Foremost among those who preached a racial purity were our Spanish conquistadors. I say it with regret. You will notice that

I separate myself from them, senors. The world has always been a polyglot place, and no place is more so than this Riverworld, where our languages are clumped along a river-bank some millions of miles long.

But our conquistadors were perhaps not so much racist as naively self-important: the old Spanish doctrine of *Viva yo!* Whatever the reason, they came flocking to our banners, Spaniards from all times and places, as well as criollos from Mexico and South America.

Gonzalo Pizarro, in the meantime, had not been idle. The name Pizarro had a certain glamour among Spanish speakers. There was a thrill to remembering the old days of conquest, when Spanish arms had been preeminent around most of the known world, and this was aided by the fact that most of the other Spanish heroes didn't show up in Riverworld. No one knew the whereabouts of the Cid, or Cortez, or Francisco Pizarro, or Balboa, or the other great figures from the con-quest. This was not surprising, of course, in a land of thirty to thirty-five billion souls. It was amazing enough that Gonzalo himself was here.

Other Spaniards began finding their way to our camp. Not just conquistadors, of course, and not just Spaniards from Spain. Spain's population was never that large. They came from Castille, Aragon, and Extremadura, the heart of Spain, which was small indeed. Other Spaniards came: Andalucians and Catalans, and criollos in large numbers, too, Spaniards born in the overseas provinces of Mexico, Colombia, Venezuela, Argentina.

And so, slowly, as the weeks and months passed, the Spanish world began to reconstitute itself around Diaghilev and Gonzalo Pizarro. Not all as dancers, of course. And the territory of Oxenstierna prospered, even without direct taxes on the new-comers who came to trade there. There were taxes, of course, on those of us who lived there as full-time residents. But these taxes were low, because the Northmen, now in the minority, saw they were onto a good thing and the only way they could keep it was by treating us very well indeed.

Meanwhile, Diaghilev, in despair of ever getting together a pure ballet troupe, and lacking a good accompanying music and orchestra, was looking into sources of dramatic entertainment from all over Europe. He introduced elements from the commedia dell'arte and other little plays and skits. But the Russian ballet and the Spanish dance continued to dominate, and this was the situation when a messenger came to Eric Longhand and announced that less than three hundred leagues up the River they had found a great Indian kingdom.

These were Incas, he said, and they were under a ruler who called himself Atahualpa.

The news of Atahualpa's Incas being so near up-River electrified the Spaniards. The conquistadors, who formed the core of the dance troupe, had never gotten used to their status as entertainers. Gonzalo least of all. His mind was still inflamed by the memory of the great status he had attained in South America. Although he had been completely loyal to his brother Francisco, it hadn't disturbed him that Francisco had never shown up. Nor any of his other two brothers. He was the only Pizarro around, and there was little doubt he liked it that way. Now his job was clear to him: he had to rouse the Spaniards to the greatness that lay ahead of them.

When the Spaniards heard he was contemplating taking over the kingdom of the Incas for the second time, they thought at first he was crazy. But it was the sort of craziness they liked.

"We did it once," he pointed out. "The odds were heavily against us. There must have been a million of them. And we were one hundred and eighty men. We are more than that now!"

"Not many more," Tapia pointed out.

Gonzalo harangued them at night over the campfire. He was a good speaker, and his tones carried utter conviction. He reminded them of past victories of Spanish arms. He told them that their lives now were nothing, less than nothing. They were men at arms, conquistadors. And what were they doing? Earning their keep as entertainers! It could not be tolerated. Especially not now, when there was a chance at something better, of doing a deed that would set Riverworld on its ear and make their fame everlasting.

Talk of the conquest was heard all over the camp. Impossible to keep it a secret. These men talked. And the more they talked, the better the idea seemed. The Viking rulers of Oxenstierna heard, but decided to take no official notice. They didn't want a civil war on their hands among several hundred crazed Spaniards. Eric Longhand had been waiting for something like this. He needed to extend his trade connections. The more people he could form alliances with, the better off his situation would be. And so he determined now to send his troupe of dancers and flamencos up the River in what craft they could get together and see if some arrangement could be made with these Incas.

He was also pleased to give letters of introduction to Gonzalo and the others, graciously permitting them to keep all that they could conquer up-River. It was Gonzalo's idea to get this worthless paper, because Gonzalo wanted to follow a strict form, and pretended that he believed that Eric was his chieftain to whom he owed loyalty, as he had once owed it to the King of Spain. (He had forsworn that loyalty, but it had been a long time ago.)

The Russians thought the plan was crazy, but went along for the dancing. When it came right down to it, they didn't believe the Spaniards would really attempt anything. It seemed ridiculous to them to fight for the rulership of barbaric kingdoms when the dance troupe was coming along so well. Diaghilev agreed to go along and introduce the troupe to the Indians. He saw it as a further chance to spread culture up-River. Nijinsky, as usual, said very little. He was a strange fellow. Not even being reborn in Riverworld had rid him of his solitary ways. Nor had it cured him of his habit of staring into space vacant-eyed. He was as crazy in Riverworld as he had been back on Earth.

We Spaniards put together a fleet of canoes and rafts, and began our trip up the River. The neighboring principalities that lined the banks let us pass. A strange, ominous mood accompanied us. The River itself was in a calm mood, but strange dark clouds haunted our passage. The heavens themselves seemed to presage the coming of some great event.

After several weeks, we came into the Incan territory. At an outpost staffed with several officers we were to wait while they sent ahead for permission to enter the Kingdom of the Sun, as their empire was called.

At length permission was received. We continued up-River, with several Indian officials aboard to act as guides. After another two days, they told us to pull into shore. From here we would have to walk.

Gonzalo was feeling in a nervous, hectic, exalted mood. His Spaniards were armed as well as men could be in this land. They had several steel swords, and a lot of wooden ones with flint knives embedded in their ends. They had lances and knives, and even one or two crossbows, constructed at great effort and expense. The Indians they saw on their way into the hills didn't appear to be armed.

At length we reached the Inca city, which had been named Machu Picchu in honor of their lost capital on Earth. This place had been constructed on the upper ranges of the tallest hills, those that lay just before the main unscalable mountains. It looked like unfriendly territory. Why had they built here rather than in the more comfortable lowlands? No one could tell us. The city of Machu Picchu was constructed mostly of bamboo, but it was taller and more grand than anything we had seen before, much more impressive than Oxenstierna. Many of the buildings were three and four stories high, and instead of being individual huts like elsewhere, the buildings had been run into each other to construct a dozen great buildings that covered several acres.

We dancers assembled in a square on the flattened top of a hill. At the head of the square, with three-story bamboo buildings behind, the Inca sat in the midst of his retinue. They were gorgeously attired in costumes made from the omnipresent towels, armed with a variety of fantastic bamboo swords, shields, bows and arrows. The retinue watched impassively as the Spaniards approached.

"Your excellency," Diaghilev said, speaking in his excellent Spanish, which the Incas spoke to the outside world, though they conversed among themselves in a language called Quechua, "we come to you from a far country down-River." Diaghilev was dressed as formally as he could manage. He had found no substitute for the monocle he used to wear. Haughty and supremely confident, he bowed to the Inca. The Inca nodded. "Let the spectacle begin."

With a flourish, the dancers come on. They were accompanied by drums of various sizes, and by flutes, and there were several primitive bagpipes in this orchestra. It was a bright sight: the flamencos, male and females, stomping and whirling in front of the Inca, who, with his nobles behind him, watched without expression.

The Spanish dancers were in full career. I heard Diaghilev say to Nijinsky, "What is this dance they are doing now? I don't remember anything like this."

"They must have choreographed and rehearsed it on their own," Nijinsky said. "I have never seen this one before."

The dance reached a climax. The final note sounded and the dancers froze in position. And then Gonzalo Pizarro cried, "Santiago! By God, let it begin!"

The dancers whipped off their costumes. Beneath them they were encased in fishscale armor and were carrying edged weapons. I stood with Gurdjieff, dumbstruck, aghast at their foolishness, yet wishing I were with them, as they advanced threatingly toward the Inca. But Atahualpa stood his ground, and, as the Spaniards approached, made a slight gesture with his right hand.

The foremost rank of Indians behind the Inca knelt down. There were more Indians behind them, and they were armed with guns. The weapons were crude, more like harquebuses than rifles, but they were indeed guns, and they appeared to be primed and ready to fire.

Gonzalo and his men stopped dead in their tracks.

Atahualpa said, "So you are Gonzalo Pizarro."

"Yes," Gonzalo said. "I am."

"I have met the Pizarro family before," the Inca said.

"The results of that meeting are well-known," Gonzalo said.

"This time," the Inca said, "we have firearms. It makes all the difference, doesn't it?"

Gonzalo had no answer to that. The Inca raised his arm. The door of one of the huts opened, and a man was led out between two Indian guards. He was tall, broad-shouldered. His arms were bound behind him, and he had a rope around his neck by which the Indians led him. I knew at once who he was. So did Gonzalo.

Gonzalo finally managed to gasp, "Francisco! It is you!"

"Yes, it is me," Francisco Pizarro said bitterly, speaking with difficulty due to the rope.

The dance troupe gathered together in a circle, back-to-back, weapons at the ready, ready to sell their lives dearly. But the Inca said, "Hold! We have no quarrel with you dancers. No, and not with Spaniards, either. It is the Pizarros we want. We have Francisco. Now Gonzalo Pizarro is here, and he must stay here."

The dancers muttered among themselves, but they were only a few hundred men, and they were surrounded by thousands of Indians, some of whom had guns.

Diaghilev was the first among us to recover. "What do you want with the Pizarros?" he asked.

"I have made it my lifework to collect them," Atahualpa replied. "I have two of them now, and there are two still to go."

"And what will you do with these Pizarros?" Diaghilev asked.

"That is none of your concern," Atahualpa said.

"This is a new world," Diaghilev said.

The Inca nodded grimly. "But there are old scores still to pay from the old one. You might consider what the Pizarros did to me and to my people. Here the worst we can do is kill them, and they will return to life elsewhere. But if any of you think this is unfair, I will permit you to substitute for either of the Pizarros, and we will let one of them go."

There was a long silence. No one was going to take the offer. Certainly not Diaghilev, whose concern this was not, and certainly not me, who was no longer a conquistador but a dance director and assistant to a genius.

The Inca laughed. "Now, all of you, senors y senoras, get out of here before I change my mind."

And that was the end of it. And that is the story, senors, of how the Diaghilev dance troupe became preeminent for a second time, and entertained humanity throughout the Riverworld. It is also the story of the Pizarro brothers, and how once for a second time they found their destiny in a world of Indians.

Secret Crimes

Robert Sampson

The wind blew stronger now. It pushed against the gray length of the skiff and tore at the meter-thick mist that lay along the River's surface like frosting on some dark cake.

Pinkerton hunched deeper into the skiff. He glanced resentfully into Riverworld's night sky. It blazed overhead, rich with sheeted stars, studded by suns of bright apple-green, scarlet, topaz, and frigid blue.

He thought grimly that even the night of this cursed world was wrong. It was light, too light, the sky too vivid. He was opposite New Rome territory now, a place of probing eyes. Guarded. Dangerous territory for a lone man arriving after sunset.

He squinted over his shoulder toward the western bank. At this distance from shore that part of his body visible above the mist would seem only a drifting snag. For a few minutes more, he could remain unseen. But he must declare himself soon. Presently the stone dock would slip into view, the last point at which he would be permitted to land.

Beyond that dock, extending down-River no one knew how far, lay the gardens of Tiberius. Gardens sealed and secret, the Danes had warned him, exquisite in their formal beauty. And utterly lethal to the uninvited visitor.

During that final meeting with Canute IV, nearly a hundred kilometers upstream in Danish territory, the king had warned him to express no interest in the gardens. For his own safety, he must arrive openly at the dock, oars splashing, boat visible, hailing the concealed guards.

It was the only practical way to approach New Rome. Arrive openly. Not that they would take him at face value, no matter how guileless he appeared. They challenged and suspected everyone. Good military doctrine, if uncomfortable civil policy.

He would find no one unsuspicious in the New Rome of Tiberius Julius Caesar Augustus.

Cold air flowed against his face, chilling his forehead, where the hair already receded in shallow bays. Briefly releasing the oars, he shivered and drew the shawl closer around blocky shoulders.

Perhaps half a kilometer ahead, he caught a fugitive pale glimmer against the black Riverbank. After a few more minutes of drifting, he could make out the stone dock, just as the Danes had described. At some distance behind the dock squatted bamboo huts, indistinct in the vague light. He could see no guards. But they would be there.

He spit foul taste from his mouth and gripped the oars. The boat angled across the current toward the dark bank. The dim bulk of a grailstone slipped past. Excitement tingled in his throat, the same edgy joy he had felt when traveling disguised through the confederacy so long ago, sniffing out rebel secrets for General McClellan.

Finally the dock rose ahead of him, pallid against the black water. He shipped dripping oars. The skiff rasped against stone. As it did so, three figures materialized from the night, where he had seen no figures stand. They trotted toward him. Skyshine outlined the shapes of their helmets. Roman legionnaires, no less. Round shields rode their left arms. Stubby javelins, the famed Roman pilum, angled ready in their hands.

It was, he thought, like being set upon by illustrations in a book.

In loudly confident Esperanto, the universal language of the River, Pinkerton called, "Good evening. Can I dock here for the night?"

The guards halted abruptly on the land side of the dock. One of them shouted urgently, "Out of there. Quick! Quick, man!"

Pinkerton stubbed his ropes around mooring posts. "Coming." Moving deliberately, he heaved his personal bag onto the dock.

"By the balls of Jupiter," a guard snarled, "get away from that boat!"

He ran heavily toward Pinkerton, right shoulder up as if fending off a blow. Hard fingers gripped Pinkerton's arm. He was heaved onto the dock, dragged toward the shore. Another guard swept up Pinkerton's bag and bolted off the dock. His strained face peered toward the misty water.

They plunged frantically some yards up the grassy slope. Dropping Pinkerton's arm, the guard whirled to examine the River. Breath gusted from his mouth. He rubbed one big hand across his face.

"Dragonfish," he explained. "River's swarming with them. Worth your life to get near the bank this time of night. They heave up over the edge to snag you."

Dragonfish! Pinkerton thought. He knew them well. The knowing slipped cold along his bones. Dragonfish grew to enormous size and ferocity. Usually—not always—they scavenged. They also attacked. Not two weeks ago he had seen one burst foaming into the sunlight, its immense mouth hollow as a tunnel and spiked with dirty white teeth. That one had snapped away the whole stern of a small boat—and both people sitting there.

He sighed faintly. "Dragonfish," he said. And spat. "What makes dragons so thick around here?"

"Who knows. Let's have a look at you."

Their hands ran efficiently over him, checking for weapons.

"Only his knife," the leader said. "I'll borrow this awhile. Let's go, then."

They closed around him, boxing him in with smooth professionalism. One on each side, one behind, big men, heavily built, formidable in armor.

"You escort all your visitors?" Pinkerton asked.

The guard on his right grinned. "You got to see the Goddess. She decides whether you're a visitor or not."

"Or dragonfish food or not," the guard on the left rumbled. He sounded distantly amused.

"What goddess?" Pinkerton asked. "I thought Tiberius governs here."

"When he's here, he does," the guard said. "Just you thank your household gods he's not here tonight. You might get more justice than you'd like."

On that dour note, they marched toward the village across grass that felt as springy underfoot as fine wire. As they approached the cluster of huts, Pinkerton smelled the sourness of drying fish skins. Somewhere inside the dark, a woman's voice wailed a thread of incoherent misery.

A large settlement, Pinkerton thought, as they threaded among the buildings. Likely four or five hundred people in this area alone. Perhaps as many more clustered on the far side of the grailstone.

No, he thought. No. Too early for an estimate. The bitterness of old shame moved inside him. As McClellan's intelligence officer on the Peninsula, he had estimated Lee's army at two hundred thousand troops. Wrong. Grossly wrong. Grossly misjudged. The worst failure of his career. One of the two worst failures.

It was that second failure he regretted the most.

Memory hardened his face. Yes, Dingus, he thought, we failed with you, you insolent, murdering thief. Others called you Jesse James or Robin Hood, or Lord knows what foolery. To the Pinkertons, you were Dingus, our shameful failure. We would have had you at last, were closing in. Only Bob Ford shot first. Sending Dingus to where Pinkertons could never follow.

A failure.

With an effort he cleared his mind. Wait and watch, believe the evidence of your eyes. Be patient. Skeptical. On the Peninsula, he had relied on the reports of deserters, spies, slaves. And twenty years after the War for the Union, ex-Confederates still derided him, mocked at his reputation.

Surely his estimates had not been so wildly incorrect. Surely not.

Dull light fanned up behind the huts, casting a pale yellow shine on the split-bamboo walls. The guards herded him forward into a broad area, brightly lit. Some twenty meters away sprawled a large bamboo structure, faced with wooden beams elaborately carved and tinted rose, blue, and green. Fish-oil lamps flared before a massive door upon which had been painted in red and black an Egyptian-like figure gripping a staff.

By the door four helmeted guards stood rigidly erect. They gripped pilum tipped with chipped flint blades. Along the side of the building loomed the shadowy figures of other guards.

An officer materialized from the shadows to confer with the guards. One of these edged the great door open, releasing an unexpected odor of sandalwood. He vanished inside.

They waited in silence for nearly fifteen minutes. During that time, the guards by the door did not move or drift their eyes toward Pinkerton. But he doubted that he could run five steps before collecting his death of flint points.

As he stood examining the painted door, a fragile thread of lamentation lifted distant among the huts behind him. Pinkerton glanced sharply around. "What's that?" he asked the nearest guard.

For a moment he thought the guard would ignore his question. Then the man's eyes crawled sideways. Stiff-lipped, he muttered, "One of Tiberius's widows."

"Widows?"

"Quiet down there," the officer snapped.

Disciplined silence followed. Behind them the distant wailing rose and waned like a string flowing in the wind.

Finally the door rasped open. A guard beckoned them inside. They passed through a small, dimly lighted room and down a wide corridor hung with colored cloth and woven rush mats. Perfume thickened the air. At the end of the corridor, the officer paused to jabber a language Pinkerton could not identify. Unexpectedly, a bare feminine arm reached from the wall draperies and swept aside a curtain. Warm yellow light flooded into the hall.

Pinkerton was ushered into a bright room, heavily perfumed, draped in colored hangings, and populated, as far as he could tell, only by women.

Before him, erect in a chair, sat a young woman swathed in filmy cloth. Her eyelids were painted blue and her eyes seemed

immense within their rings of kohl. Beneath elaborately dressed
dark hair, her face was slender and long, with a straight nose,
somewhat sharp, and pale skin powdered to pallor.

She lifted a small-fingered hand. "Come forward, sailor by
night." Her voice was softly impersonal.

White light burst behind Pinkerton's eyes. The blow drove
him forward. He fell, aware only that he had been struck on the
back of the neck and that he must not lose consciousness.

After time he could not measure, the blackness around his
vision crept away. He found himself crouching on hands and
knees, sickness in his mouth.

Behind him the officer's voice rumbled, "Kneel before the
Goddess."

He blinked his eyes to focus. He said gutturally, "In my
country we do not kneel."

"A strange country," she said. "You may look on me and
say your name."

Swaying back on his haunches, he lifted his head against
pain and looked into her face. Her lips blazed harlot red against
the pallor of her skin. She seemed a painted child. But
authority's cold iron rang in her voice, and her eyes, intelligent
and unsentimental, were darkly mature.

He said, in precise, cold tones, "My name is Allan Pinkerton.
Founder of the Pinkerton National Detective Agency in Chicago,
Illinois, the United States of America."

Allan Pinkerton, born in Glasgow, Scotland, 1819, son of a
police sergeant. Emigrating to the States in 1847 with his wife,
he found law enforcement more pleasing than his profession of
coopering. He became a deputy sheriff, then was appointed as
the first detective on Chicago's new police force. But ambition
gnawed him. In 1850 he resigned to organize his own private
detective agency with his two sons.

"A detective agency," the young woman said. "I do not
know the meaning."

"It is an organization to protect against crime. To seek out
criminals. A detective exposes secret crime and brings it to
punishment."

Faint emotion drifted behind the paint-masked face. "Secret
crime," she murmured. "A pleasing phrase, Mr. Pinkerton

detective. And have you always brought secret crime to punishment? Have your efforts never failed?"

"We have been successful," he said curtly. "Even extremely successfully. But perfection is found only in Heaven, not among the affairs of men."

"Or the affairs of goddesses." She laughed, a shining white sound. "Even goddesses may fail, for a time. As I fail, I confess, to discover why a lone man comes by night across the terrors of the water seeking our hospitality."

When you lie, tell as much of the truth as possible. So he said promptly, "I followed the advice of the Danes upstream. They warned of grail slavers on the far bank. They said that it would be safer to travel at night until I passed that danger. They suggested I ask for shelter at New Rome."

Every word was true. If not the whole truth.

"We have encountered the grail slavers before," the girl told him. "They understand the sword. But what do the Danes understand? Their king, Canute IV, is said to be a saint. I have observed that saints make uncomfortable neighbors. The splendor of their moral kingdom leads to pettiness in administering their more temporal realm."

Pinkerton shook his head. "I know nothing of that. They were civil enough to me."

She was not beautiful but powerfully feminine. The rich softness of her femininity glowed around him, as if warm wind rushed against his body. At the same time, he saw how closely she measured him, and that her intelligence was calm and cold and dangerous.

The Goddess smiled. "I find much about you I do not understand. Enlighten me. Have you found no woman's comfort that you travel alone?"

"I am hunting my people," he said. "When I woke—or resurrected—whatever you call what has happened to us, I found myself not in the Heaven I hoped for, or the Hell I feared. Nothing so comprehensible."

He paused, knowing that most men explained too much, and so trapped themselves with their own tongues. But reticence in this place was more dangerous. He said slowly, "I woke among strangers. They were a friendly, aimless people. They lacked ambition and energy. They worshiped sticks. And my wife was gone, you understand. My sons gone. My profession lost. My country unknown. I am not prepared to give up family, profession, and country. So I hunt for them."

And Dingus, too, some quiet part of his mind whispered. One day I will find Dingus, and on that day I will scratch that failure from my record.

He discovered that the Goddess was regarding him with an amused tolerance he found deeply irritating.

She said, "Wise men say that more people live along the River than all the grains of sand in Egypt's deserts." She slowly shook her head, ruefully amused. "Of these large matters, I suspect none of us may claim knowledge. I only know that to each of us the Ka has again returned. Once more the holy sun warms our blood. Again we embrace life. Is this not enough, Pinkerton detective, that life extends once more before you?"

"Not enough," he said brusquely. "I left too much uncompleted."

"Death has canceled all previous obligations," she said. He felt that he was being admonished by some unreal doll. "Into your hands has been yielded a second life, fresh and new. Do with it as you will."

"Obligations," he said, eyes fixed on the scarlet curve of her mouth, "are never canceled. We are obligated to complete what was left unfinished."

Her tiny hand executed a floating gesture that seemed to him expressive of amused contempt.

"I fear our philosophies will never agree," she said, offering him a ghostly smile.

Under the fragile stuff of her dress rose the soft protrusions of her breasts. He wrenched his eyes away. Dislike for her softness, her perfumes and garish makeup, her indecent clothing, her attitude of remote, superior laughter, drifted through him like poisoned smoke.

She crooked one finger. The big officer moved from behind Pinkerton and to stand at attention by her chair.

"Marius," she said, "allow our weary searcher a hut for the night."

She did not look directly at Pinkerton. He felt that her eyes shone with delicate mockery, as if she had sensed his gaze on her breasts.

"Allow him the privilege of the grailstone," she added, and bent forward to murmur inaudible words. More loudly, she remarked, "Perhaps he and I shall speak again, do I feel so inclined."

Pinkerton struggled to his feet and was led from the room. As they passed through the draperies, he glanced back, saw her small body, exquisite in white, slip from sight among the attending women.

To his astonishment, he felt a sudden transient warmth toward her, as if she were some pretty child requiring his care. Then the dislike returned. Shameful, he thought fiercely, that his body should respond to this wanton child. Satan constantly mocks men. Battle Hell's lust with discipline and denial.

Once outside the building, he inhaled deeply, purging his lungs of her perfumed air. The guards eyed him curiously. Marius dropped a big hand on Pinkerton's shoulder.

"We've got an honored guest here, boys," he remarked pleasantly. "I'll march him around to the Dignitary's Hut. Flavius, you quick-step the section back to the River. The Goddess expects you to finish tonight's patrol for the glory of New Rome. Meaning for the sake of your valuable skins."

Turning away, he clapped Pinkerton heavily on the back. "Well, my honored friend, you just come on along with me."

They moved from the lighted compound into a succession of passages winding among unlighted huts. Once again he heard the long wail of grief. For a time, they walked without speaking, Marius striding energetically along a course that, as Pinkerton suddenly realized, held to no direction for long and ended circling back upon itself.

Apprehension stirred in him. The Goddess had spoken inaudibly to the guard. His mind darted among possibilities. Delay argued that time was needed for preparations that surely involved himself. But if they wished his death, he thought pragmatically, he would have been killed by now. Effectively he was their prisoner.

Unless they played cat and mouse, intending to pounce without warning and so terrify a confession from him.

That was possible. He eyed the great shoulders of the man striding in front of him, and felt blood flush his cheeks and forehead. He felt a dizzying need for action.

As if overhearing his thoughts, Marius said, "You're a lucky man. You came out of that interview unskinned." He chuckled to himself. "That's more than some. The Goddess must like your looks."

Pinkerton sucked in a great breath. "I thought Tiberius ruled New Rome. Who is she?"

He felt, rather than saw, Marius' astonishment. Then the big man guffawed. "Cleopatra."

"Good Lord," Pinkerton said, "That child?"

"That's her. *The* Cleopatra. Cleopatra VII, Philadelphus Philopator Philopatris. The same one who played those fancy tricks with Caesar and Mark Anthony. By the belly of Mars, you wonder why. She's not got that much chest. But she can think the clouds out of the sky. Maybe that's what Julius liked."

"So what is she to Tiberius? Queen? Wife?"

"Not wife, not her. Joint rule with Tiberius, you can call it. She makes Tiberius sweat. He doesn't stay around much."

"That's very strange."

"She rules. He rests." He uttered a harsh sound, too cold to be a laugh. "At his resting place. There's nothing you want to know about Tiberius and how he rests."

Apparently they had walked long enough. Marius halted before a small bamboo hut with a roof of heavy grass fringe hanging down like uncut hair.

He told Pinkerton, "Here's your hut, courtesy of the Goddess, who could have tossed you to the dragonfish as easy as sending you to sleep in all this comfort. I'll have somebody walk you to a grailstone in the morning."

"I'd like my knife back."

"Patience. Can't have you cutting yourself while you're our guest."

Marius tramped away. Pinkerton stood for a moment in the doorway of the hut, inhaling the moist night air. The odor of her sandalwood still clung to his clothing. Those imbecile Danes had not mentioned Cleopatra. It was slovenly, careless work. Leaving him with the queasy feeling that they had neglected to explain other important facts. For one savage moment he felt that he fumbled blindly through high grass swarming with poisonous snakes.

Had he recognized their incompetence, he would have refused Canute's commission, simple as it was.

He made a controlled gesture of irritation. If he could ransack the Confederacy for its secrets, he could certainly assess New Rome's strength. Nothing easier.

Impatiently, he wheeled and stepped into the hut.

Inside, a small fish-oil lamp glowed dimly on a bamboo table, illuminating a platter of fruit and cold meat. Against the far wall stood a bed on which his personal bag had been tossed. Near the bed stood a bamboo chair.

In the shadows by the chair, half visible in the wavering light, stood a figure wrapped in dark-gray stuff.

His heart leaped. He set his feet.

"I have been waiting for you," the figure whispered. "The Goddess wishes you to undertake a commission."

He stood silently for a moment. His expression was not as a man surprised but as one adjusting his thoughts. Abruptly he gestured toward the chair.

"Welcome, Goddess," he said. "Please sit down. These accommodations aren't grand enough for your rank. But, as you understand, I am merely borrowing them."

She moved forward into the light, shaking loose the gray robe. "I have been detected," Cleopatra said in a pleased voice.

In a movement as graceful as the flowing of smoke, she seated herself. She wore much perfume. Her huge eyes shone.

"How clever that was," she cried. "You knew me instantly. Do sit down." She smiled up at him with deprecating humor. "We may forgo such tiresome formalities as kneeling. That is a matter of formal protocol we insist upon, in its place, to encourage our subjects in the habit of reverence."

He seated himself gingerly. In this unsteady light, her face, masked by vivid colors, seemed the face of a teasing child.

She said, "Tonight when you described your unusual profession, I was filled with interest. Now that you have demonstrated your skill, I confess myself filled with admiration. You grasp the truth from shadows."

"You are very gracious."

"In New Rome, she told him, "a lone woman, although highborn and powerful, needs many friends. In the same way, a stranger in New Rome may well benefit from the gratitude of high office. Given these mutually dependent circumstances, I hope you will agree to become my friend."

At once he understood that she had elected to use him as part of a private intrigue. His arrival at the hut had been delayed so that she could enter first. The heavy perfume clinging around her assured that he would identify her easily. Allowing her to complement him, disarm him, bring him to her service.

Leaning forward, she exposed her face to the delicacies of the lamplight. "You cannot know how urgently your friend requires your skills. You have long sought out secret crimes. Is that not so?"

"It's a detective's job."

"Then Isis has certainly led you to us. In this place, as you shall see, we are creating a new city, a city dedicated to the purities of the sun. The sun, for most of us here are Egyptian, braced by the sturdy metal of a few Romans. Regrettably few, since they are determined builders.

"Together we shall raise a city more extraordinary than Memphis of Alexandria, more honored than Rome herself. To this end we have consecrated our new lives. Yet at the very beginning of our selfless work, secret crime confronts us. Abominable crime, my heart tells me. You have heard the women wailing in the night?"

"Yes."

"If men lamented as do women, you would hear their voices, too. The women lament because their husbands are gone. The men, perhaps, lament their wives. Who can tell? Man and woman, they vanish in the night. They do not return."

He said carefully, "They might have migrated elsewhere."

"Leaving behind family and possessions. I think not."

He considered. "Your borders are well-guarded?"

"Every state must assure its borders against the malice of neighbors. The guards report no one passing."

"Then it's a simple matter, you see. It must be one thing or another. Either the guards have been bribed or the missing people are still in New Rome."

"Not so simple a matter, Pinkerton detective." She lowered her eyes, drew her knees together, clenched her hands whitely into her lap, the image of a confused and frightened woman. He watched with wry admiration. It was a remarkable performance.

She whispered, "They were all my supporters, you understand. My friends. Each received a personal invitation to visit Caesar's Gardens."

His face remained blank. "Gardens?"

"The Gardens of Tiberius. They lie not far south of where you docked. There the Emperor built a villa and a private lake. There he lives in self-imposed exile. A few Praetorian Guards protect his privacy."

"He can hardly govern from there."

"He governs by memorandum," she said. "I receive a sufficiency of those, you may well believe."

Her wide eyes caught at him. "You must understand. Tiberius is a masterful administrator. He has the Julian family genius for planning within political realities."

She waited for him to speak. Finally he asked, "And what else?"

"He, also," she said, shading her words with exquisite diffidence, "is cursed by darker moments. His ability is, perhaps, shadowed, as we may say, by moments of ferocity. They come as they will and they pass. As storm frets the sky."

"You feel he may have killed them?"

"Who can know. Who can know. You see the difficulty, friend detective. As joint ruler, I must know. I feel he cannot have slaughtered those people in his madness. But I must be sure. For New Rome, I must learn this."

He leaned away from her, closing his eyes. He felt buffeted by her femininity, her cleverness, the silky beseeching of her voice.

She said, "You seem somehow offended. Have I erred in consulting you?"

The swiftness of her perception was unnerving. He shook his head. "I am trying to understand what you wish."

"Tonight he has invited certain of those I admire and trust to dine with him in the Gardens. If they recognize danger, what can they do? Who may refuse an invitation from the Emperor of us all? I wish you to go to the Gardens, watching unseen. To observe, if you must, the Emperor's secret crimes. Or not, if there are not. Can you do this as a friend for a friend?"

"You said there will be guards."

"Marius is an officer of the Praetorians, although assigned to command my faithful Egyptian guard. He will lead you into the Gardens. You will not be seen."

"And when I return?"

"Tomorrow night, I will receive your report in this room."

When he did not answer immediately, she added gently, "There are those who whisper that you are the Danes' spy, come from Canute himself, to pick out our secrets. On your return, how delighted I will be to refute these slanders."

No need for that silken threat, he thought. In the end he must agree to help her. What other choice had he?

He fashioned an empty smile and reached to touch the warmth of her hand. It would be something to tell later that he had touched Cleopatra.

"Fools see spies everywhere," he said. "I can do this for you. When will Marius come?"

"In an hour. Eat something and rest. I regret that your night will be long."

"A detective is used to that," he said, and saw her to the door.

After she had melted into the night, he returned to the table and began to eat. Much as he disliked her, he felt only admiration for her skill. What an operative she would have been.

And now he had an hour to work out what it all meant. Thirty years in the detective business had given him an infallible sense of when a client lied. And she had lied. Lord, yes, toward the end, one lie on another.

Whatever her reason for involving him, it almost certainly had nothing to do with Tiberius' secret crimes.

When he had finished eating, he dumped his bag out on the bed. From what seemed a thickened seam along the bottom edge, he removed a narrow slung-shot some twenty centimeters long. Made of dragonfish skin and bound with scraps of cloth, it contained a knob of ironwood tightly packed in sand.

He examined it critically, frowning at its wear and fraying. A poor substitute for lead and woven leather. But you made do.

He slapped its reassuring weight into his palm. Something to hold in reserve while wandering through the night.

Slipping the weapon into his belt, under the loose shirt, he stretched out on the bed and closed his eyes.

In less than an hour, a quiet tap came at the door. He rose, yawning and rubbing his face, and cursing the foul taste that never seemed to leave his mouth. He tramped heavily from the hut. Marius stood waiting, wrapped in a heavy cloak. Without speaking, he gestured for Pinkerton to follow and moved away. The air smelled cold and moist.

In a few minutes, they emerged from the labyrinth of trails among the huts onto a rough grass plain that sloped gradually toward the River. Marius walked ahead, moving with the even stride of the legions, steady as a drumbeat. His head and shoulders bulked indistinctly against the fantastic glitter of the stars.

After twenty minutes of silent plodding, the big officer halted. To the left glinted the River. Ahead and extending to the right into darkness stretched a tall black mass, a wall or hedge of some kind. Distant beyond the hedge came the remote pulsing of a drum and a rumor of laughter sounding less substantial than Pinkerton's heartbeat.

He felt edgy. His skin seemed tight and dry, his hands stiff. The conclusions of his reasoning disturbed him. Not that he had enough information to reason. But then, you never got enough information. You used what you could get and then you listened to the ambiguous whispers of intuition.

Marius said into Pinkerton's ear, "Bamboo thicket ahead. We take caretakers' path through. Garden's other side."

Pinkerton gripped the back of the big man's belt and was led into confused darkness. They jogged left and right around clumps of bamboo—planted, Pinkerton suspected, to conceal the entrance. For an extended period they groped along a lightless track, treacherous underfoot, the faintly bitter scent of bamboo surrounding them.

They came suddenly to open grass. Before them stretched the dark gloss of an artificial lake nearly three hundred meters wide. Some form of stone construction joined it to the River. Curving deeply inland, the lake ended near a merrily lighted villa.

On a stone patio between villa and water, a cluster of men and women lounged on couches. Before them a group of dancers pranced to drums and bleating shell horns.

Marius chuckled. "How these patricians do live."

"We need to get closer," Pinkerton said.

His edginess had passed. Now his mind felt calm and quick. He followed Marius along the edge of the bamboo thicket to a point where the lake bank bent toward the villa. The activity on the stone patio was less than one hundred meters away. They crouched to watch.

"Which one's Tiberius?" Pinkerton asked.

"Doubt he's come out yet." Marius nodded toward a lighted window in the nearest wing of the villa. "That'll be him. Tallying up expenses. He loves to chase those coppers."

"I'd like to see what he looks like."

"Old Man Glum with a face full of pimples. He'd not welcome you."

"I suppose not," Pinkerton said.

Excitement shuddered through the group on the patio. A few men scrambled to their feet, staring toward the entrance of the lighted courtyard that bisected the villa front to back. Guards standing inconspicuously in the shadows came striding forward. Armed men began emerging from the courtyard.

Marius jerked to his feet. Squinting back in the direction of the River, he said, "Patrol coming!" in an astonished voice.

Pinkerton swiveled to look. His eyes, dazzled by the patio lights, saw nothing.

Marius snarled softly, "No patrol scheduled this hour. They'll sweep this area clean. Move!"

"Where?"

"It's the villa for us. You might see our jolly emperor, after all. Come on."

The hard shackle of his hand locked around Pinkerton's arm. They scrambled off, keeping close to the bamboo hedge.

Pinkerton glanced toward the patio. The party had fallen to disorder. A double file of soldiers tramped across the patio. Within the marching line, like an embedded jewel, strolled Cleopatra, her head arrogantly tilted. She wore white, set off with bright scarfs, and an elaborate golden headdress.

Pinkerton stared blankly at her, his mind momentarily disengaged. "Cleopatra!"

Marius jarred to a stop, looked, muttered to himself in bouncing Latin that needed no translation. He seemed completely bewildered. He jerked at Pinkerton's arm.

"Come on."

Opposite the villa now, they loped across open grass to the wing, then glided beneath the lighted window, barred and covered with translucent material. Marius slowed, listened, eased around the corner of the plastered wall. They plunged into darkness thick as paste.

"Door here," Marius said. "Always locked. But you can lever it open, if you know how."

Warmth began behind Pinkerton's ribs and spread joyously through his body. He was too disciplined to smile. So, for all his doubts, his reasoning was correct. This excursion was a charade, top to bottom. A design of lies. Not that the profound skepticism of a professional detective would ever have accepted the absence of a guard, the isolated door, the easy access.

But Cleopatra's arrival. That jarred. That did not fit the design he saw.

Metal whispered on metal. Marius grunted. With a sharp click, a slice of dull light opened in the darkness.

Pinkerton slipped the slung-shot free and followed Marius into a long, dim hallway smelling strongly of damp plaster. Twenty meters ahead lay the intersection of a wide corridor paved in red tile. Lamplight trembled against the cream-colored walls.

Marius gestured him forward. The hallway offered no concealment. Bare walls, closed doors, a fine trap. As they moved up the hall, an unseen door grated open in the lighted corridor, releasing a confusion of voices. Footsteps clattered toward them.

Marius wheeled across the hall. He thrust open a door in the left wall and drew Pinkerton through. Swinging the door not quite shut, he clamped an eye against the crack.

In the corridor, a peevish voice grumbled, "Yes, yes. I'll come at my leisure. I will not be rushed."

Pinkerton secured his back against the wall. Fingering the slung-shot, he glanced swiftly around. They stood in a long, wide room oversupplied with tables, backless benches, cupboards of various sizes, and an uncomfortable amount of darkness. This world, he thought, would benefit from kerosene light. Across the room fish-oil lamps flickered on a big table strewn with scrolls and writing implements.

Pinkerton inspected the shadows beyond the table, his eyes vacant under heavy eyebrows.

From the corridor, the peevish voice cried, "Keep that woman under close watch. Offer her guard refreshment. Keep them away from the patio. And tell those gatemen to watch for my sig l. Or by Juno's tits, they'll swim too."

Footsteps stamped toward them. Marius eased the study door shut and recoiled to the center of the room. Unpleasant thoughts tugged his face.

Pinkerton stepped to Marius' side. He said soft-voiced, "Room's full of soldiers. Don't touch your sword."

Surprise shocked Marius' eyes. His body swayed slightly, as if he had been clubbed across his chest.

"Forget the assassination," Pinkerton said pleasantly. He slipped the slung-shot from sight.

Marius did not touch his sword or look at anything but Pinkerton's face. While he stared, the door thumped open. Caesar Tiberius strode into the room.

The Emperor was a tall man, with imposing shoulders and a spare, hard body. He moved as if his joints hurt him, not swinging his arms much, carrying his head canted forward. Across his forehead and chin festered a spray of dark-red pimples. The scars of former eruptions cratered his cheeks.

He scowled at the two men as if he had a bellyful of scorpions.

Marius angled up his arm in salute. "Hail, Caesar!"

Tiberius glowered, said curtly, "You're late. This is intolerable." Then more sharply, "Is this Canute's man?"

Marius' eyes crawled sideways to stare at Pinkerton. With difficulty, he said, "This is the man you ordered brought here."

Tiberius growled, "That rare one, Cleopatra, the preening queen herself, the one you grin attendance on day and night, Marius—she has deigned to inform me, tonight, not an hour ago, that this man arrived with messages, or so she claims, from Canute."

He regarded Pinkerton with glum suspicion. "All honeyed words, no doubt. All windy promises, not worth a belch in the wind. Here to talk and talk and spy and spy."

Pinkerton said stolidly, "To talk only."

Caught without warning. Blind, confused, understanding nothing. Clutching at Tiberius' words. Wringing each syllable for meaning.

Tiberius was regarding him glumly. "Your friend Canute is a fool, and you another for serving him."

Anger stiffened Pinkerton's face and darkened his eyes. He said mildly, "Canute is neither my friend nor my master."

Mockery twisted Tiberius' mouth. "I know every time you talked to him. In secret. I know when you left the Danes. In secret. I know when you landed in New Rome. All in secret, no secret at all."

Roman spy at the Danish court. Or spies. Cleopatra also knew.

"Plots," Tiberius said. "Liars and pretty words." He inspected Pinkerton with bitter eyes. "We will not talk tonight. Come without warning and you need expect no audience. You may attend tonight's entertainments. Perhaps tomorrow or the day following. . . . I have little time to waste. Guards!"

From the shadows deep in the room stepped four armed

guards, silent as the coming of death. Nothing moved on Marius' disciplined face.

Tiberius said, "Escort these men to the Lake. They may watch the entertainment with the rest of the guests. With That Woman."

The guards escorted Pinkerton from the room, down corridors to the courtyard, and left them at the edge of the stone patio.

After the guards marched away, Marius casually looked around him. No one stood within hearing. He muttered to Pinkerton, "So the Queen of the Nile didn't entirely fool you?"

Pinkerton said, "Assassination was the only thing that made sense. She needed a dead man to blame it on. No other reason for me to be here. Not to report on the Emperor's crimes. Who'd take a stranger's word about those."

Marius grinned faintly. "Well, I owe you a favor or two. I never sniffed those guards."

"Would you really have killed Tiberius?"

The grin faded. Marius' eyes wandered. He said indistinctly, "I don't know."

Silently they walked toward the semicircle of couches. Self-reproof tore Pinkerton's mind like an angry animal. He'd been so sure of himself. So confident. So unaware that his reasoning penetrated too shallowly.

Among these people and their practiced treacheries, slovenly reasoning would be fatal. They would tear him to pieces.

He spat to clean his mouth. He had died once, such a death as few men had. He did not wish to die again, not so soon.

They approached the lake. A few meters from the water, Cleopatra stretched gracefully on a dining couch. Two women and half a dozen men chattered around her. She looked profoundly bored. The golden headdress rested beside her couch.

Pinkerton asked, "Why did Cleopatra tell Tiberius I was an envoy of the Danes?"

"Who knows the Queen's mind." He shrugged and came to a halt. "We part here. You ambassadors can sit with queens. Common soldiers stand patiently in the rear." He drifted away.

As Pinkerton approached the couches, Cleopatra glanced

toward him, smiling as a knife blade might smile. "Ah, the detective."

"The glorious envoy," he said.

A touch of real amusement crossed her face. "I had not suspected you of wit."

And to those surrounding her, she said, "It is so wearying, but state business constantly presses. I must speak to this man. Would you greatly mind? There seem interesting activities at the water's edge."

That velvet request sent the crowd chattering toward the edge of the lake. There young women lighted clusters of candles mounted on eight small rafts. The young women did not appear to be wearing much.

Cleopatra touched the couch beside her. "You may sit here. Clearly Tiberius received my message. I only just learned that he demanded you be brought instantly to him. His agents infest Canute's court. Had I not hailed you as a secret envoy, he would have butchered you for a spy."

"Your note irritated him," Pinkerton said.

"He lives perpetually irritated. Now, sir envoy, what service shall you offer me for preserving you from Tiberius?"

Anger came on him without warning, leaving him unsure of his voice. He glowered toward the water's edge, where the young women adjusted structures of bamboo and opaque material over flaring candles. Lanterns, he realized. Ovals of rose, light blue, gold, and green that shone pleasantly against the black water.

"You sent me to die," he growled. "You expect my service?"

"I sent you. I saved you. You live by my grace."

He said, "A man has friends or enemies. One or the other. Someone lies to me, tricks me, he's enemy. Enemy. Only that. Nothing but that. Eternally that."

Young women laughed as they waded into the lake. Uncoiling lines from the rafts, they swam softly off, towing the lanterns behind them. On shore the men shouted encouragement.

"Control your voice," Cleopatra said mildly. "Words carry far in this lake air." She examined him curiously, eyes shrewd under the painted arches of her eyebrows. "No resentment, my poor detective, so astute and so inflexible. Surely you know that all alliances are temporary. Accept them when offered, when it is to your advantage to do so. That is the wisdom of governing villages or empires. So the Divine Julius taught me."

Stiffly upright, keeping space between them, he growled, "I live by other standards."

Men laughed and yelled after the swimming women. Two or three plunged into the lake and splashed toward the lanterns.

"I do not mock your standards. But we are far from your America and its ways."

"Far! We've been dead. That's far as you can get."

"Then accept that we live. Why or where is of small importance."

He did not answer her at once, but sat scowling at his square hands, an unyielding block of a man, reviewing hateful memories. The air reeked of her perfume.

He said finally, "It was disgusting how I died. It was gangrene—gangrene of the tongue. Was completely paralyzed then. Had been for years, God help me. You die like that, you smell it, taste it. Even drugged, even asleep. You smell yourself rotting. The stink's still in my mouth."

More men plunged into the lake to pursue the lights. A few men and women scampered along the shore, shouting encouragement to the swimmers.

Cleopatra said, "Death was once death. But no longer, not in this strange place. I know this for a certainty—that when you die here, you come to yourself again at another place along the river. Your body is returned to you without stain or flaw, however you died."

"Your mind remains unchanged," he said. "It remembers everything. It is not permitted to forget. I remember too much. Memories of failures, memory of death, foul memories. Unendurable!"

"In Old Egypt we accepted the progression of the soul from life to life, purifying itself through endless cycles."

"We are not in Old Egypt or America," he said. "We are in Hell itself."

She did not answer him. From the lake drifted a shriek of feminine delight. A lime-green lantern rocked wildly.

Finally he said, heavy voiced, "That room was guarded tonight."

"Tiberius is ever careful." She gestured toward the lake. "Even here."

He already noticed guards posted at intervals along the shores.

Watching her face, Pinkerton said, "The guards weren't to protect Tiberius from me. They were to protect him from Marius. I believe he thinks Marius is no longer reliable."

"My conclusions also," she said gravely. Which told him that her note to Tiberius was calculated to divert suspicion from Marius to himself. She added, "And now I see Tiberius approaching. Have you more to tell me?"

He turned fiercely to her. "Call your soldiers. Save yourself, if you can. I think he will kill us all tonight."

"My soldiers are trained and faithful. I have taken certain steps. Ah, Caesar, you come at last. How charming the lanterns look on the water."

Tiberius loomed over them, his inflamed face petulant. A heavy dark cloak wrapped him from neck to ankle. "These young fools will douse every light, splashing around like maniacs."

He lifted one powerful arm to wave. At the water's edge, a guard touched flame to a long torch and began swinging it in blazing orange arcs.

"Enough. Enough," Tiberius shouted. "Do you want to burn out our eyes?" He sprawled onto a nearby couch. "How can they swim? The air's ice. This cloak is too light."

The torchman sizzled out the flame in the lake. He retreated swiftly from the water, looking back with sharp attention. Watching those tense movements, Pinkerton felt memory, like a spectral light, flicker in his mind.

To Tiberius, Cleopatra said, "Since you delight me with lanterns, I have bought a few fire toys to amuse you."

She extended a languid arm toward three rough sacks sitting upright by the lake edge.

"Those stinking Greek devices. They choke you with their filthy smoke."

"These are quite special," Cleopatra told him. "They were especially prepared in your honor."

The guards at the River, Pinkerton remembered. Their frantic race for the bank, as they stared back at the water.

Cold plunged into his body. Jerking upright on the couch, he squinted across the lake.

Under the incandescent sky, a skin of grayish light spread over the water. Ripples from the splashing swimmers marred the surface. Nothing else.

". . . stables so filthy," Tiberius was saying, "that Hercules flushed them with an entire river. You know the story. It contains a profound moral. The Deified Augustus howled with rage when my mother, that hag Livia, kept pounding at him to read these stories, think about them. I howled, too. But she didn't permit me to ignore them."

From the direction of the river, thin lines elongated across the surface of the lake. Pinkerton could not see them clearly. He felt the frigid rocking of his heart.

Cleopatra said cheerfully, "And what moral, my emperor, did your mother impel you to draw?"

Many lines creasing the lake surface. Lines swiftly extending themselves, a network of lines, weaving toward the floating lights, the shouting swimmers.

Tiberius had signaled his men to open watergates between lake and river. Dragonfish, the swarming night hunters, were pouring in.

"The moral is obvious. Whatever you must clean, clean completely. Use what is necessary to do the task and do it grandly, without weakness or regrets."

"Whether a stable or, to stretch the analogy, an empire."

"Correct," cried Tiberius, rolling over to face her. He seemed affable and amused. "Sweep the filth away, enemies, problems, ambiguities, in one conclusive stroke. A single great violence is less distasteful than many small ones."

Near a golden lantern, a swimmer, leisurely backstroking, abruptly vanished in a suck of water.

Pinkerton flung himself from the couch. "Dragonfish!" he roared.

"Ah, yes," Tiberius said in a gratified voice. "They seem rather sluggish tonight."

The surface of the lake churned, bobbing the lighted rafts. Someone shouted frantically. Water sprayed as a sleek blackness heaved through the surface and plunged crashing back. Falling water beat against the swimmers. Their white arms flailed. A rose lantern was flung into the air and vanished. There was much screaming now, imposed upon a heavy splashing, as if massive weights wallowed through the water. Between the reeling lights slipped long bodies, shining darkly in the starlight. They slashed and twisted. They tore at the swimmers.

Two men, swimming hard, raced for shore. One vanished in an explosion of water, as a mouth like a fanged cave closed on him. The second man reached the bank. As he heaved himself out, a guard darted forward, clubbing with the butt of his javelin. The swimmer toppled backward into the lake, was dragged under, pale legs beating.

Cleopatra said, "My emperor, I cannot understand the Roman appetite for public murder."

"Excitement," Tiberius remarked. He seemed almost cheerful. "Cleansing. Admiration of bravery. Look there."

On the far bank, soldiers behind a thicket of javelins herded the rest of Tiberius' guests toward the lake. Two men resisted, were stabbed and driven back. Another threw himself against a flint point. His corpse splashed among the tangle of people driven into the lake. They screamed and fretted the water with their legs. Among them twisted dragonfish, viciously striking. The screaming did not last long.

"Such a quantity of death is tedious," Cleopatra remarked. "I can hardly approve your taste, Tiberius."

"Shall we walk along the shore?" he asked, waving his big hand. "The fish are noble killers, well worth seeing."

"It seems a dubious pleasure. Sit with me instead and talk, in your charming way, of Rome after Caesar."

"I must insist," he said, and a thing got into his face that rippled and shook it and hung quivering, quite horrible, at the edges of his mouth.

Tossing her head indulgently, Cleopatra slipped from the couch. "Ah, if I must. But allow me the pleasure of strolling in your company by the sparkle of my pretty fire displays. With my own hands, I will light them for you. Do I not honor you royally, Tiberius?"

Taking up a candle, she glided toward the sacks lined at the lakeside.

Tiberius turned to Pinkerton. "Join us. I won't have an emissary from the admirable Canute claim neglect."

He clapped one powerful arm around Pinkerton's shoulders, and as he did so, the sword scabbard concealed under his cloak bumped the detective's leg. "Have you enjoyed our little entertainment?"

"My God," Pinkerton cried. "Your murders!"

"Flushing the stables clean," Tiberius said, showing his great square teeth.

Vivid light came then. It flared against them, sudden as a blow, a glare agonizing their eyes with its violence. Surprise dragged open Tiberius' mouth. With unexpected agility, he hopped away from Pinkerton, and one hand drove under his cloak.

Cleopatra ran toward them, protecting her head with a fluttering cloth. A fury of sparks cascaded around her. Behind her slender figure trembled thick pillars of white and scarlet flame.

"Isn't it lovely?" she cried breathlessly.

From the direction of the villa began a confused shouting and the heavy pounding of running men.

Without checking her pace, Cleopatra flicked out a long knife and slashed it across Tiberius' throat. Cut shallowly, the Emperor lurched back. He bellowed and ripped free his short sword. Blood spattered his toga. Again she cut at him. He caught the blow on his bare wrist, stumbling away from her. His sword swung level.

Pinkerton took one step forward and lashed the slung-shot at the Emperor's head. The blow missed, but drove into his heavy shoulder at the neck.

Tiberius staggered, nearly dropping the sword.

Cleopatra darted at him, her face serene, eyes enormous within their black rings. With a dainty movement, she thrust the knife into the side of Tiberius' neck.

Crazy howling spilled from Tiberius' mouth. The blade had driven under the skin along the left side of his neck, a bloody wound but not fatal. He hacked at Cleopatra, missed, lifted one hand to shield his eyes from the ferocious light. She darted away from him to the edge of the lake.

Pinkerton beat the slung-shot twice against the side of Tiberius' head. The Emperor plunged forward, staying upright by an immense effort. Dropping to one knee, he supported his weight on one arm.

From the villa came a confused roar, the shouting and hard clang of fighting. Pinkerton saw a tangled mass of soldiers battering at each other. The flares, he thought, his mind still neatly compiling solutions—the flares had signaled Cleopatra's men, who now engaged the Praetorian Guards.

His eyes refocused. To his horror, he saw the Emperor struggle to his feet. Cleopatra stood erect at the lake edge. She gripped her left arm. Blood flooded through her fingers.

Behind her in the tattered water rushed a thick black length.

Pinkerton saw it and, yelling incoherently, drove the slung-shot against Tiberius' head. Nothing whatever happened. He felt no contact, no solid blow tingling his hand. He saw that the weapon had split down its length. Spilled out the sand. Fallen to pieces. His fingers gripped only a few limp rags.

Tiberius drove the sword into Cleopatra's body. She fell sideways, hands picking at the blade. Tiberius yanked the weapon free and tumbled to his knees beside her. He began to hack at her with furious strokes, throwing the power of his shoulders into each blow. He grunted, as if cutting wood.

Pinkerton ran forward. He locked his fingers under the Emperor's chin and wrenched back his head. For an instant, he looked down into the twisting horror of that bloody face.

Then he broke Tiberius' neck.

Some time later, he released the convulsing body. It lay twitching and stinking across the inert white mass that had been Cleopatra.

Pinkerton sobbed air into his dry mouth and forced himself erect. And it was as if that movement conjured up the Devil.

The edge of the lake exploded. A colossal thing reared from the water, a tower of glistening black. Spray slashed across his face. He had the blurred image of an egg-white mouth, stiff with fangs, that plunged down on him. He found himself rolling, shouting kicking across the flooded stone. Near him, a thick body slammed hard against the patio.

In the blindness of terror, he scrabbled away from it. Arms caught at him. He fell over, kicking furiously, sure that the dragonfish flopped toward him. A man's weight sprawled across his body. They struggled.

"Wait," a voice shouted. "It's all right."

Found himself staring up into Marius' contorted face.

Pinkerton gasped, "Cleopatra," and rolled to his feet. His legs collapsed under his weight. Clutching Marius for support, he tottered a few steps toward the lake edge. Then stopped.

On the stone pavement before them lay only a short sword. No bodies remained.

Past the patio edge, thick shapes searched the water.

"Couldn't come in time," Marius explained, his voice slow and unnatural. "Fought the Praetorians. My own people. Couldn't cut through."

Men ran toward them. They turned to face the flint points of half a dozen javelins. Behind the shafts stared faced stiff with excitement.

Pinkerton's legs had no bone in them. He felt incapable of thought. Spitting away the reek in his mouth, he shouted into the faces, "The Emperor is dead. Nothing you can do now."

Blankness grew in their eyes. The disciplined line of flint blades grew ragged.

Pinkerton asked, "Whose men are you?"

"Cleopatra's guard, sir. We came at the signal of the lights, as ordered. We came at once."

Pinkerton said, "Cleopatra's dead. Both of them dead. The dragonfish got them. The Emperor's pets came out of the water and ate their master."

Marius stepped up beside Pinkerton. Locking one arm around Pinkerton, he boomed, "You men know me—Centurion Marius Domitius, Chief of Cleopatra's Guard. All these months, we protected her. You did. I did. Tonight we couldn't protect her. Not against Tiberius and his fish. Well, it's no shame to you. Nobody could have stopped this. And remember, you whipped

Tiberius' boys here tonight. You and I did, shield to shield. You can be proud of that. Now we got to go tell the others. We've lost an emperor. So we'll do what soldiers do in this kind of mess—we select our own emperor, and let the civilians like it. We'll do that tomorrow. Understand?''

He scowled fondly at them, and Pinkerton felt the terrible, steady shaking of muscles inside the man's body.

"Now we'll have discipline here. Align those weapons. They're wobbling like temple harlots. Ground pilum!''

Javelin butts whacked crisply against the paving.

"Artelius, march them to the villa and dismiss them.''

They watched the soldiers tramp away. When the men were out of hearing, Marius' shoulders went limp. Corroding anguish got into his eyes. He said thinly to Pinkerton, "I loved her, maybe you know, maybe you don't. I am a Roman, faithful to my emperor, and still I loved her. Can you reconcile that?''

Pinkerton shook his head.

"I never could,'' Marius said. He moved slowly off, picking his steps across the stone patio.

So now, Pinkerton thought, I have three failures, not two. His mind ached with shame and self-contempt. Three to think of every day, all day and night. Three. And no way to die. No way to get clean of them.

"I am in the belly of Hell,'' he whispered.

He walked unsteadily to the edge of the patio. Indifferent to the dark water, he bent and lifted the sword from where it lay in puddled blood. From its cutting edge he picked a tuft of dark hair, smelling strongly of sandalwood.

"Love,'' he said. "My God, was it love with me, too?''

He flung away the sword. The scented wisp of hair he held awhile, rubbing it between his fingers. Then he threw the hair into the lake, violently, as if it were a thing that might destroy him. He turned and walked toward the villa.

Hero's Coin

Brad Strickland

The habit of writing was strong in me while I lived, old in me when I died, and insistent in me after that strange awakening beside the River, with so many of my brothers and even the abbot himself around me. I recall how, upon awakening, we eyed each other in astonishment, each monk wanting but not daring to ask the question: Is this Heaven? Or Purgatory? Or—

And those strange ones amongst us, men colored brown and jabbering in an outlandish tongue, other men with yellow hair speaking words we could almost understand, and the strange grailstones and all the rest. Father Lupian (he whom I had seen die, ten years before I myself coughed out my life) took charge of us, brought us to ourselves, set about re-creating the order, reestablishing the Chronicle. Almost before we had shelter he had devised a way to peel the bamboo and work its fibers into paper, and he had discovered the fish bones that gave us pens and the berries that gave us ink. If this be Purgatory, he said, then let us repent our sins in the only way we know how: by living our praise, by writing for the glory of God.

So the months passed, and I, Brother Aelfstan, resumed the work I had done on Earth, that of recording the passage of time, of capturing the fleeting years with ink and pen. Wars flared around us; but the Brotherhood, being poor and inoffensive, weathered the storms. From time to time we took in newcomers, men and women of our own age and native land and others. Gradually we learned other ways of speech, other means of keeping the Chronicle.

And thus it happened that I met the man who was destined to be my greatest annoyance and my greatest friend. Before daybreak one morning I had gone to the River to fish, and there he lay, naked, his grail at his wrist, a translated soul. I revived him, and he spoke in the strange inflection that a thousand years after my time on Earth was English: "What place is this?"

I told him where he was and spoke of the Brotherhood. He nodded his understanding, rose, and we returned to the monastery. Father Lupian welcomed the stranger, offered him shelter and kiltcloth, and bade him stay as long as he pleased. The stranger thanked him—thanked him in our own tongue, not in Esperanto, though his accent was outlandish and strange. I saw him to a cell and then hurried to prayers.

Afterward, Father Lupian took me aside to ask, "What manner of man is this?"

"I do not know, Father. He is a man of the latter times, I think. His stature is great."

"True, but that proves nothing. As scripture tells us, and as God has seen fit to reveal to our eyes here, there were giants in the earth in ancient times." The old man—curious how even now, when we looked the same age, all the monks regarded Father Lupian as the old man—sighed. "Watch him closely, Brother Aelfstan. Something about him mislikes me."

Watch him I did, to the extent of becoming his friend. Nemo—for he never told his name, and this is what Father Lupian began to call him—Nemo, I say, was a goodly-shaped man, with strong features and quizzical blue eyes. He gladly worked alongside us monks at our humble tasks of building, cleaning, and clearing, but never did he join us at worship. At mealtimes he took from his grail whatever food was given, and to others he offered the alcohol, tobacco, and dreamgum. He drank abstemiously, preferring water to wine. And at first he talked but seldom.

At first, I say, for with the passing of time he began to tell me bits of his story, which in my understanding gradually assembled themselves into a mosaic. Of his life on Earth he spoke not at all, but he recalled that terrible and strange day of awakening here. He and a few others of his speech found themselves among fierce men, Maoris he called them, who bore ill will against those of whiter skin. He talked of slaughter that began not soon after the resurrection, of how he and his companions fled madly, and of how he and a few others had at last escaped.

This was the surface of the tale, but beneath that I caught glimpses, as it were, of other things moving. Nemo did not stress his part in the escape, but I divined that he it was who devised his group's resistance to the warriors, he it was who led them away at last, him to whom they looked for leadership thereafter.

"And did you then lead them?" I asked as we labored side by side at erecting one wall of a new dormitory.

Nemo looked away and softened his deep voice. "I did not," he said. "On a night when all were asleep, I slipped away from them and left them to other leaders. You see, I was not the man they believed me to be." I expected him to speak of his death and translation here, for most people who thus found their way to the monastery would do so in wonder and half in fear. However, he chose never to mention it, and to this day I do not know what fate sent him to our place on the River, only that it must have been a most painful and unpleasant one. Always afterward he took the utmost care not to die, even in times when dying would have released him from troubled times and from oppression.

For more than a year he remained at the monastery, quiet and undemanding, glad in heart to assist us, quick to advise us when the storms of war rose between those on the other side of the River, an Eastern race who coveted the holdings of our neighbors up-River, who were a hairy, heavyset folk who scarcely seemed to house a human soul. Thanks to his intercession and his advice, we were spared the battles, and both sides looked to us as a place where their wounded could be cared for until their bodies healed themselves. In the end, he it was who reasoned with both sides and who resolved the war in a peace that looked fair to last.

By this time Father Lupian had changed his opinion of Nemo. "Tell us who you are," the abbot requested more than once. "For I sense in my heart that you are truly a hero."

"No," Nemo said firmly. "I am no one. Let the name you gave me be my whole story."

More than once I heard this exchange, or variations upon it. When the heretical Second Chancers came to proselytize, some of the brethren heeded their speech and followed them, but Nemo did not, and so I did not. For by this time I had decided that the old faith held no truth, at least regarding the afterlife. This place was no Heaven, no Hell, no Purgatory. It simply was, and we were along with it. Yet old habits are hard to kill, and so with the others I remained faithful to the form of worship.

At least, I did until the day when Father Lupian called together all the brothers and told us that he had been given a vision in a dream. "We are blessed beyond imagining," he told us. "For in my revelation, God told me who our peace-maker is and revealed to me the name of our Nemo. He worships not with us because he has no need of worshiping as sinners do. Nemo is the blessed Saint Peter himself, the rock upon whom the holy Church was built."

Some of the others believed him, but when Nemo noticed their changed behavior toward him, he grew suspicious. When at last he heard the tale, he grew angry, although too many held the opinion too firmly for him to deny it with any lasting success. Within a day, Nemo left the Brotherhood. Feeling more at home with him than with my former brothers, I went with him.

"I am not Saint Peter," he complained to me after many days of travel. "In fact, I'm no hero at all. Why can't people see that?"

"People want heroes," I told him. I added, after a few moments, "I myself saw King Alfred, later called the Great, during my days of life on Earth."

"And was he heroic?" asked my companion with a bitter smile.

I remembered that day very well. I was fifteen, and new in the monastery, my parents having decided that the youngest son of too many was clearly destined for the priesthood. The king came in with Father Lupian, and the rest of us stood in ranks, soldiers in the army of God. I shook as the King approached me. He smiled and touched my shoulder. "Kings do not bite, boy," he said, and moved on.

"No," I answered slowly. "He was a man."

"That's what everyone forgets in this place," growled Nemo. The next day we wandered on.

I could spin a long tale of our wanderings, of the times when both of us grew quarrelsome, of the women who nearly won me away from following this man, this hero who denied his gifts. Our steps spanned many years and led us to many changes. We saw sections of the River where fire-breathing machines labored for humankind, and sections where hairy giants lived as they lived in the days long before civilization. We saw wars and we saw peaceable kingdoms. We tarried in some places and sped through others. And we met heroes by the score, by the hundred.

In a place torn by a four-way war, we met a man called Sherman who had gathered together others of his age, who had molded them into an army, and who seemed bent upon destruction for the sake of itself. He imprisoned us, until Nemo devised for him a strategy that set two of the enemies against each other and left Sherman free to deal successfully with the third. By the time he released us, the other two parties to the war had so reduced themselves that Sherman held sway over all. "You must be General Lee," insisted Sherman. "You don't look like him, but by God, you must be General Lee."

"I am no one," said Nemo, and having purchased our freedom with the pain and the deaths of hundreds, we moved on.

We came to a poor country on one of the River's islands, a place that often suffered raids by River pirates, that often lost men and women to slavery. There we spent two Earthly years, and there Nemo devised an ingenious and simple invention that changed the islanders' way of life. He had noticed how the current split, stronger on one side of the island than the other. He had the islanders weave strong nets of Riverdragon intestine, and he had them troll not for fish, but for treasure. For by this time traffic upon the River was constant, and each day brought news or rumor of new wrecks, new loss. The nets seldom failed to bring up something worthwhile: metal, weapons, or free grails. By barter and by plan, the islanders grew strong enough to defend themselves, and came a day at last when they offered Nemo the kingship of their realm. "For surely," one said, "you must be Archimedes himself."

And so we moved on.

We rode for a while on a great steam-driven riverboat, trading our labor for our passage, and met a man named Clemens who seemed consumed with bitterness and sour humor. We met a woman who claimed to be Cleopatra, and one who claimed to be Guinevere. Both were women, nothing more. Once we met a dark-haired passionate woman who laughed when she heard my companion's name. "I'm Nobody," she said playfully, "who are you?" Her name was Emily, and for some months she and Nemo were lovers; and then in a pirate encounter she died, and he was saved, and so was I. Nemo searched for her, knowing that somewhere on the River she had been reborn, but the River is long, and we never found her again.

As we traveled, changes came, faster and faster it seemed. The air began to fill with commerce, as had the River: balloons and dirigibles and flying machines passed over us, fought in midair, and fell like plummeting angels. We met a man named Lindbergh who pursued a dream of flying all the way around the world in one of these crafts, a man driven by a species of madness, I thought.

After each encounter, after each new hero, Nemo would ask me if I had learned my lesson. I always told him that I had not. He wanted me to say that there are no heroes, that there are only men and women, some who accomplish more than others, but at heart all the same. I could not say that, for after all, we had met only a few hundred so-called heroes, and although they had all turned out to be mere mortals, that might not be true of the others. We spent some time among the Second Chancers in one of their gathering places, and they endeavored to persuade Nemo that all men and women were heroic in potential, that our hope for salvation lay in perfecting ourselves in this existence. He listened politely, helped when he could, and moved on.

And I? Truth to tell, as long ago as my days upon Earth I had lost the substance of my belief, though even here I continued to follow its form. Perhaps I prayed to an empty heaven, but then who knows? And though my belief was gone, in a curious fashion my faith remained, even if it had become merely faith in faith and not faith in God.

So came the time when the translations halted, when resurrections ceased. Unease and fear ran up and down the River, and wars—which one would suppose would end, now that Death was permanent—broke out afresh, with new venom and new violence. And then, just three weeks ago, we fell into the hands of one who called himself Judeus the Terrible, who had heard of our coming and who imprisoned us together in a cell of stone. Nemo he took for hard questioning, and when he returned my friend to our cell, Nemo was broken in body.

"He thinks I am a miracle man," Nemo murmured. "He believes I can give him weapons with which to conquer all of Riverworld."

As so often on Earth, I tended the sick and listened to confession. Nemo had gained a reputation in our wanderings, a reputation as a deviser and inventor, as an adviser and counselor. Like many powerful and small-minded men, Judeus assumed that one golden key unlocked the secret of domination, and in my friend he saw that key. Three times he tortured Nemo, and each time my friend grew weaker. This morning was the last. In the courtyard, before the scowling, swarthy Judeus, I saw them smite Nemo's head from his body. On the way back to my cell, the two guards spoke to me, asking when Nemo would raise himself.

"He will not," I said sorrowfully.

"Yes, he will," one of the guards insisted. "Go quickly, Aelfstan the Hero-Friend, and when you speak to him in prayers, say a word for the guards who released you."

And so here I am in a night of sorrow, drifting down the River on a trading vessel, scratching out these lines in memory of a friend. Already people treat me with awe, and some have whispered that Nemo was the Messiah himself.

He was not.

In his last, pain-racked hours, Nemo told me his Earthly story: He had lived in the twentieth century of Our Lord, in a city of the New World, and he had been—a night watchman. He had lived for sixty-four years and had died of a heart attack, alone, late one night in the library where he worked. For two years, he said, he had been a soldier in a great war; and then for forty years he had guarded a library by night and had read. And his reading, he said, had convinced him that in the end there were no heroes, only men and women doing whatever they could to meet their troubles and to survive them. His reading had given him the knowledge of many tongues and many devices, and that knowledge had followed him to Riverworld, where it was his fame and in the end his doom.

Perhaps he was right about himself, and perhaps he was but an ordinary mortal after all. But here, on Riverworld, his name is already great, and I fear that people look to me to write his gospel. What is its creed, I wonder? That we are all ordinary, even those we misname "great"? Or the reverse, that we are all uncommon, even those we think mean and low?

For like heroism, faith is a coin with two sides. May the God I no longer believe in help me, may he help all of us. We all drift toward that end that now awaits us, and whatever it reveals, obliteration or transfiguration, it cannot come too soon for me. I will welcome whatever I find there.

As for Nemo, whose true name I now write for the first time, may his doubt and his faith, which were two sides of the same coin, be also mine. Farewell, John Adams Smith, and *requiescat in pace.*

Human Spirit, Beetle Spirit

John Gregory Betancourt

When I awoke by the water's edge, I was naked as an animal. A polished stick as big around as my leg and made of wood—though from what tree it came I could not say—hung from my wrist by a thin cord. I threw the stick off, leaped to my feet, and gave a cry of alarm: "Ai-ai-ai!"

The sound echoed up and down the river's bank. Silence followed, then a hundred other throats picked it up and echoed it back in a thundering roar.

"Ai-ai-ai-ai-ai—"

The sound swelled like a chant to fill the air, and as I stood there, I could smell my own sweat pouring forth like an animal's musk.

"Ai-ai-ai-ai-ai—"

I had to be in the spirit-world, since I remembered my own death clearly. I could still hear our tribe's spirit-man chanting over me, trying to drive the sickness from my body. I remembered pain in my gut like a knife, and I remembered a fever that made the world seem to shake like a tree in a storm.

"Ngosoc," I had whispered with my dying breath, naming the man who had bewitched me.

Why was I here? What spirit or god was punishing me? Had I named the wrong man—had Ngosoc been innocent? I pressed my eyes shut and bit my lip until I tasted the warm sweetness of blood. *Spirits go away, go away, go away!*

The cries of fear slowly died. I opened my eyes, but nothing had changed. Everyone on the bank of the River was looking around with fearful, panicked expressions. A few took tentative steps this way or that; far off, I heard a woman screaming on and on and on.

Of all those around me, I stood nearest the River's edge. I ran down to the water, squatted, and stared at my reflection. It was a nightmare. You can tell man from animal by his decorations, I knew: tattoos for cheeks and eyelids, paint for chests and arms. All those who had awakened with me had looked human enough in form—dark-brown skin like mine, broad cheeks, flat noses—but they were completely hairless from head to crotch. Now, staring at my reflection, I touched my own bald scalp, felt the emptiness under my arms, gazed down at my naked male sex. I was hairless as a newborn, and my foreskin had been cut away, leaving my penis pink and exposed. Worse still, the hundreds of tattoos with which I had so carefully covered my body over the fifty-eight years of my life had vanished.

I found I barely knew myself. What game was being played on me? What spirit would do such a thing?

It must be Glasha the Snake, I thought, standing: he was the trickster. Who else would wake me in the spirit-world in such a manner? Or perhaps it was a test. Cocoti the beetle had always tested us, trying to prove man no better than the monkeys in the trees.

Scowling, I strode up the River and tried to understand where I was, my bare feet splashing through shallows, small silvery fishes darting away from me. A clear area perhaps twenty paces wide extended between the River and a vast field of waist-high grass. We had all awakened on the River's bank. Far across the grass I could see hills dotted with trees. Ahead I spotted a grove of thick old bamboo that came down almost to the water's edge.

If this were some spirit's test, I would master it, I decided. I had led the two hundred men, women, and children of my village through thirty-three rainy seasons, and I knew the ways of the spirits almost as well as our tribe's elders. I had walked with the spirits of plants and animals more than a hundred times. They were sly, the spirits: some playful, some serious; some helpful, some not . . . but they never did anything without cause. It would be my task to discover that cause if I could. Whether I helped that cause along or resisted it would depend on how it suited my own desires. Here, in the spirit-world, only one thing was certain: I could rely on little but my own wits.

Several branches as big around as a man's thumb had washed onto the River's bank. I picked them up one by one and tried their strength. The first two snapped like twigs. The third felt strong as fire-hardened oak, and its edge came to a point suitable for digging. I quickly stripped it of leaves.

If man is not animal, he must prove it with his decorations. That must be my first goal, I thought: decorating myself. Paint would do, since I had neither ink nor bone needles for tattoos.

Twenty paces from the bamboo I reached a place where the River had cut more deeply into its bank. I waded out cautiously until the water came to my knees. My toes curled deep in the warm, soft muck of the River's bottom, feeling for sinkholes and stones, finding neither. It seemed a likely spot, so I dug into it with the pointy end of my stick until, a few handspans down, I reached clay. When I dug out a handful and held it up to the light, it was a pale gray, almost white. I fingered it skeptically. It was coarse and crumbled easily, but it would have to do.

I spat into it, working my mucus into the clay until it had the right consistency, and dabbed circles and lines across my cheeks and nose. Then I painted four straight lines—warrior's lines—across my chest and arms.

Clothed in my decorations, no longer looking like an animal, I started to wade to shore—and came to an abrupt stop. A whole village worth of brown, hairless men and women were standing at the edge of the water, watching me.

"Where are we?" one of them asked. His accent was strange, twisting the words so they were barely understandable, but I could figure them out. He was tall and broad of shoulder, with a warrior's look in his eye, and I took an instant liking to him: this is a good man, something inside me said.

"It is the spirit-world, of course," I told him. "We are being tested."

Several of the women shrieked. I glared and they fell silent.

"I am Hiwyan, son of Yagna," I called to all of them, "headman of the Moboasi."

"You lie!" one woman called, coming to the front. She put her hands on her hips. "I knew Hiwyan. He was an old man!"

I looked her up and down, and though she was thin as an eel and twenty years younger than when I'd last seen her, suddenly I knew who she was. "Maraga," I told her, "your brother Kianano was my best friend when we were boys. Your husband Kotabi and I raided the Onomi a dozen times together. I *am* Hiwyan. Do you not recognize me?"

She squinted, then said, "You are too young, too handsome. Hiwyan was old and scarred when he died."

"My body has been made new," I said. "The spirits have done this to us all—even to you."

The warrior who had spoken to me had been nodding his hairless head all the while. "I have heard of the Moboasi," he said slowly. "They are said to be fierce as enemies and generous as friends."

"This is true," I told him.

"I am Eona of the Avai, forty years a hunter."

"Forty?" I scoffed. "You are a stripling, barely a man."

"It seems the spirits have changed us all," he said. He spread his arms to the heavens. "I thank you, spirits, for making me young again!"

Someone called, "It is true. I had seen forty-five years when I died!"

Someone else called, "And I had seen fifty-two!"

"If we are all here," I said, "it must be for a reason." There were murmurs of agreement from everyone present. "We must make a village," I continued, "and learn what that reason is. Only then will the spirits be content."

Maraga continued to study me. "You speak as Hiwyan spoke," she admitted. "His soul burns within you; I see it in your eyes."

"Come help me, Maraga," I told her. Bending, I scooped out a handful of clay and offered it to her. "We are men, not animals. We must paint ourselves, and then we must build a village.''

Maraga waded out beside me, took the clay from my hand, and like a headwife, began calling orders to the women and girls watching from the Riverbank. To my surprise nobody argued: they were all looking for someone to lead them, I realized. Several girls ran to fetch leaves from the trees, and still others fanned out into the waist-high grass, looking for maggots and berries to mix with the clay to make colored paints.

Eona waded out beside me and began digging for clay with his bare hands. When a dozen more men waded out to help, I handed my stick to Eona so he could dig for them all.

"You will be my right hand," I whispered in his ear. "Gather enough clay to paint every man, woman, and child, then join me by the trees. We must select a place for our village."

He nodded and bent to the work, the muscles in his back rippling like wind in the grass. As I watched, sweat began to bead on his forehead and upper lip. He was very strong.

I waded ashore, motioning to the men who had hung back. There were twenty or thirty of them, some as young as eight or ten, a few as old as I now looked. Reluctantly, it seemed, they approached. I saw fear and confusion in their eyes and knew these were people who needed a strong leader to guide them.

"You will be our hunters and warriors," I told them. I still had a little clay left on my hands, and I used it to dab circles under their eyes and draw lines down the bridge of their noses. Eona sent a boy to bring me more clay when I needed it, and I managed to paint every man there before it ran out. The marks weren't much, but they would show these men as human for now.

"You must make spears from the bamboo," I told them. "The life of the village depends on you and what game you can catch. We will set up our village while you hunt. Be back before dark. Now go!"

They slapped their chests and took off for the bamboo at a run. My gaze lingered on the last to leave, a lanky young man of perhaps twenty-two or twenty-three, hairless as the rest, but with an angry cast to his dark-brown eyes. There was something familiar about the way he moved, I thought, something that made me distinctly uneasy. Had I known him back in the real world? I frowned. If so, we must have been enemies—truly, I thought, I would have to watch my back around that one.

As headman of my village for thirty-three years I had learned well the dangers of treachery. Many had spoken against me over the years, but I talked with a monkey's limber tongue. I could outspeak any man in the village, so crafty and convincing were my arguments.

Strong of arm and sharp of eye, I had assumed the feathered mantle of the headman in my twenty-fifth year and brought my people their greatest power. Fearless were the Moboasi under me, and well feared by their enemies. It was my leadership that helped us seize new hunting grounds from the Gonaci and the Acoloas. It was my leadership that stole canoes and women from the despised Mowando and drove them from their shit-stinking village forever. The spirits had smiled over my leadership, and by the time I died the name Hiwyan already lived on in many songs and stories.

As I paused at the top of the River's bank, I noticed another cluster of hairless men and women gathered far to my left. They weren't brown-skinned, but white as a coconut's meat.

Are they ghosts? I wondered. Could they be the spirits who brought us here?

They all stood around a strange tree like none I had ever seen before. The tree's surface was the silver color of a fish's scales, but not so shiny. It was low but broad—its top covered the space a whole village would take up—and it had holes cut deep into its silver surface. Its trunk was small and scarcely seemed strong enough to hold it up.

Several of the white-skinned men were climbing across its lightly sloped surface, sticking their hands in the holes. Like my own people, they seemed to have strange wooden sticks attached to their arms by ropes. As I watched, first one then another of them fitted their sticks into the tree. The sticks seemed to slide into place naturally.

Ah, I said to myself, that must be what the sticks are for. But why bother to fit them into holes? It made no sense to me.

Perhaps the spirits who had brought us here would make the tree's purpose clear later. For an instant I regretted casting my own stick away, but then I realized it would still be where I had thrown it . . . after all, who would take it?

Swallowing, I got up my courage to speak to the white-skinned ghosts or spirits or whatever they were. As I walked toward them, several noticed me and pointed, jabbering in a harsh, flat language I did not understand. They seemed excited to see me, and not unfriendly.

Halting twenty paces away, I studied them. Although their skins were white, they did not look like ghosts: their faces had a strange sharpness to them, and their noses stuck out too far. They also seemed just as confused as my own people had been. Perhaps they were from a distant tribe?

I moved closer very slowly, opening my hands with the palms up to show I meant no harm. The white-skins had no spears or knives that I could see, but they could throw rocks and use their hands against me . . . or even those sticks attached to their wrists. Perhaps a few of them spoke my language, I thought. Perhaps they could explain what the spirits meant by bringing us all here.

Their headman and what must have been two of his spear-carriers, though they had no spears, came forward to talk with me. The headman had a huge nose—I tried not to stare, but it stuck out at me like a pointing finger—and his eyes were the blue of a shallow pool of water. Pale reddish-brown speckles covered his shoulders. Truly I had never seen his like before.

"Haitheyr," he said to me in a low, soothing voice. He stuck out his hand cautiously, and when I looked at it, he slowly reached out, took my right hand in his, and moved them both up and down a moment before letting go.

"I am Hiwyan of the Moboasi," I told him.

He shook his head and touched his chest. "William Byrd," he said. "Byrd. *Sahvie?* Byrd."

"Burd," I said, nodding solemnly; I could follow that much. I pointed to myself. "Hiwyan."

"Hi-wee-an," he said.

I smiled and he smiled back. I pointed to the strange tree.

"Did the spirits send it here?" I asked.

He shook his head and said something incomprehensible. I shook my head back. We were going to have to teach him our language if we were going to get anywhere. Still, he was clearly headman of these strange white-skinned people, since he had come to talk with me, so I decided to show him all the courtesies his position called for. He might prove to be a valuable ally if another tribe or wild animals attacked, I thought. If his people proved dangerous, we could always drive them away.

He pointed to the man to my left, who was equally pale-skinned and with an equally big nose, though his eyes were the brown of overripe bananas. "Carver." Then he pointed to the man to my right, who was smaller and thinner, with eyes as brown as my own. "Shay," Burd said.

"Carvar. Shay," I repeated, nodding, and the two white-skins nodded back.

"Come," I told Burd. I pointed to part of the River where Eona was still digging out clay for the women to mix. I took a step toward it. "Come, Burd."

He seemed to understand what I wanted; he turned and spoke quickly to his Carvar, and Carvar turned and trotted back to stand by the strange silver tree.

Burd took three steps toward Eona and looked at me inquiringly. I caught up and from there we walked side by side like equals, with his spear-carrier named Shay trailing. As we went, I pointed first to the sky and spoke its name, then to the River, then to the grass and trees. Each time Burd dutifully repeated what I had said. His willingness to learn was a good sign, I decided, and boded well for the future of both our villages. He'd speak my language like a civilized man in a few moons.

As we neared, Eona and the other men stopped their work and stared at us warily. There was recognition in Eona's eyes, I thought; he had seen Burd's kind before.

Burd and I stopped at the River's edge.

"This is my friend Burd," I said in a loud voice. "He is

headman of the white-skinned people up the River." I pointed toward their strange tree. "The other man is called Shay, and he is Burd's spear-carrier."

Eona approached, wading out of the River. "We don't want anything to do with the white-skinned men," he said in a low but serious voice. "They are dangerous."

"Why?" I asked, my voice low also.

"I have seen white-skins like Burd before. They came to live in the forest not far from my village. All the time they talk-talk-talk of their white goddess, *Virgin Mary*, and make us worship her as chief of all the spirits." He spat. "They gave presents to make us worship *Virgin Mary*—knives with blades that shine like the sun, bright beads, cloths like they wear, and bowls and cups that do not break."

"Do you speak their language?" I asked.

"A few words, no more. Others here may speak it, though. A great many people went to worship *Virgin Mary* and live among the white-skins as their slaves."

I frowned. This was bad news indeed; instead of friends and allies perhaps I had brought spiders into our midst. From the corner of my eye I studied Burd, who was staring at the men digging clay with an unreadable expression on his face. What did he see in us . . . slaves? Allies? Something else entirely?

"We must keep away from them," I decided.

Eona nodded. "That is wise."

"Unless," I continued, "they choose to join us and live among us as people."

"They will not," he said.

"We shall see."

The other clay-diggers had gone back to piling clay on the riverbank while we spoke, and Maraga and most of the other women were coming back from their scout work with colored berries and leaves. The women sat and began working with the clay. Some chewed berries and leaves, spitting them out when they were pulped; others ground up maggots and other insects with little bamboo sticks. Maraga herself mixed berries, leaves, insects, and clay together with well-practiced fingers, producing first red and blue, then also green and yellow paints, which she spread out on more broad green leaves.

I brought Burd and his spear-carrier over to the women, squatted, and gestured for Burd to do the same. After a moment's hesitation, he did so, and his spear-carrier followed suit.

Using the first two fingers of each hand, I took dabs of red and blue and began painting circles and lines on Burd's cheeks, arms, and chest. He made no movement until I was done, and then just nodded once.

When I moved toward his spear-carrier, though, Shay leaped to his feet, making fists of his hands. A burst of angry words came from him. I stared, puzzled. Did he not want to be human again?

I looked at Burd, and Burd spoke sharply to his spear-carrier. The spear-carrier shook his head, took a step back, and set his feet defiantly.

One of the women—little more than a girl, really, with small budding breasts and narrow hips, perhaps a year into the bleeding that marked entry into the female mysteries—leaned forward and caught my eye.

"Pardon for interrupting, headman," she said, eyes down as was proper. "The white man says, 'Keep your filthy hands off me, you savage.'"

"You understand their talk?" I said.

"Yes, headman."

"What is your name?"

"Nonu, headman."

"Come sit beside me." I patted the ground to my right. She moved up and crouched there, still staring at the ground. "How did you learn the white-skin's language?"

"I was born in their *hospital*."

The word meant nothing to me. That must be what they call their village, I thought.

"You tell him this," I said. "If he is not an animal, he must paint himself to prove it. If he is an animal, he must leave."

She spoke the words, and I watched Shay's face turn red as the sun at sunset. He snarled something to Burd, turned, and stalked off toward the strange silver tree. I grunted at his back, then spat after him: "Animal." What kind of spear-carriers did

Burd choose? They would be useless in a fight, with so little discipline.

Burd said something to me, which Nonu translated as: "Do you know what has happened to us?"

"We are in the spirit-world," I said, and from then on, with Nonu translating, we managed to have a conversation of sorts.

Burd and most of the other white-skins, it turned out, were from a village far to the east of ours, a place called *New Zealand*. The name meant nothing to me. He, too, thought the gods had brought us here—one named *Jeezuz* in particular—but for what purpose he did not know.

Our thoughts were much in agreement, it seemed. When I told him my plans for building a walled village, he agreed it was a good idea: neither of us knew what animals prowled the nearby forests. He offered help from the white-skins, and I accepted. Any of the white-skins could share our village, I promised, as long as they learned our language, decorated themselves as people, and accepted me as headman. He agreed quickly.

"I will tell my people," he told me. Rising, he backed away, then turned and walked toward the strange silver tree.

"Follow after him," I whispered to Nonu. "Listen to all they say, then come back and tell me."

"Yes, Headman," she said, and she crawled into the waist-high grass on her hands and knees. I saw a few stalks move, and then she was gone.

Maraga knelt beside me. She had used berries to stain several stalks of grass red and blue, and as I watched, she braided the strands together around my upper arm. I had been the first to paint myself; now I was the first to wear a badge of bravery.

"You have made it well," I said, studying her work.

"My husband is not here," she said. "I need a man to look after who can protect me. I work hard, Hiwyan, as you know."

"I do know that," I said, puzzled.

"Make me your wife," she said. "We are both old enough not to play games with ceremony. We need each other."

"What about your husband Kotabi, who is my best friend?"
I asked. "How can I steal my best friend's wife?"

"Kotabi died a year after you died. He has not been reborn
in the spirit-world; I have looked. Therefore, why should you
not make me your wife?"

What she said made sense. "It shall be so," I said.
"Henceforth, you are my woman."

"And you are my man."

I nodded, and that was our marriage. We spent the next hour
decorating ourselves. Maraga painted my head and back; I
painted hers. Around us, the one hundred and twenty-two
members of my new village did the same.

Nonu returned as quietly as she had left and came at once to
report to me. She had done exactly as instructed, she said,
creeping through the grass until she was within spitting distance
of Burd and the other white men. None of them had so much as
looked in her direction. As she sat before me to tell me what
she'd overheard, Maraga began to paint blue and red circles on
the girl's face, neck, and head.

"Byrd told them of your offer," Nonu said, "and they
argued much about it. The women and men do not want to
paint themselves—truly, headman, it is not their way!—but
Byrd argued that they needed our protection from animals.
'What animals?' some wanted to know. They have seen nothing
but a few rats scurrying in the grass, and one of the men caught
a fish. Most of them have decided not to come. Byrd and a few
of the men want to join you. They say our people know how to
survive in the wilderness and they need to learn what we
know."

Eona had also been listening. "They are a danger," he said.
"We should accept none of their kind!" Several others echoed
his words: many here had heard of the white-skins and their
spirit *Virgin Mary*, it seemed, but only Nonu spoke their
language.

"*I* am headman here," I said. "It is my decision. We can
use more strong arms to help build our village. If they do not
become people like us, we will drive them out."

On that, they agreed. Even so, I felt an undercurrent of

resentment toward the white-skins, and anger toward my decision. Still, I *was* headman, and my decision would stand.

Burd and five other white-skins—three men and two women—showed up not long after that. Two of the men held poorly made bamboo spears and shifted nervously from foot to foot as everyone gathered around to look them over. They all wore mats of woven grass to cover their genitals, which made Maraga and the other women giggle in amusement. I was not so amused.

"Tell them to remove their mats," I told Nonu. "If they are to join us, they must dress as we do. They cannot be better than us and hide behind grass."

When Nonu repeated my message, Burd immediately removed his mat. The other three men did so more slowly, almost reluctantly. The women did not.

"Maraga," I said softly, "take the women and decorate them."

She called to the other women of our new village, and as one they moved forward, taking the two white-skinned women by the arm and leading them away from us men. Maraga would get rid of their mats, I knew: she was already making a good headwife. Nonu hesitated, looking at me, but I shooed her after the rest. She should stay with the women; if I needed her to translate for Burd and the others, I would call her.

The white men looked very uneasy. One of them was half aroused and trying to hide it behind his hands without much success. I snorted; they were like children, I thought, ignorant of the world around them and how it worked. We would make people of them.

"Do not frighten them," I called to the men around me. "Move slowly. They are animals now, but we can make them into people with time and patience. First we must paint them. Who will help me?"

"It is a mistake, but I will help," Eona said. He picked up a leaf covered with blue paint and came to stand at my side, and together we began to paint the rest of Burd's body. More slowly, the rest of my village took up leaves of paint and began to decorate the three remaining white-skins.

When we finished and stood back to admire our handiwork, I

had to admit it helped: Burd looked almost civilized, with a pattern of black dots running down his arms and cheeks, set off by bold red and blue lines. His scalp was painted blue, like mine. Later, after the village walls were up, I knew we would have time to make penis sheaths and braid more grass and animal-hair into decorative ropes for arms, legs, and necks; then we would be truly civilized again. For now, though, we had to concentrate on the basics of survival.

Next I led all the men into the bamboo. There I could see signs of my hunters' passage: using stones, they had cut down bamboo stalks, then sharpened them to make spears. Eona picked up stones from where the hunters had left them, passed them out, and we began breaking down the tallest and heaviest old-growth bamboo for our village's walls. Every so often I glanced out toward the grassy field, where most of the women—including the two decorated and now matless white-skins—were busily gathering grass and knotting it into rope. Others were searching the field for edible plants and insects to supplement whatever the hunters brought back. Still others were gathering up the wooden sticks that had been attached to our wrists when we woke, which I decided was a good idea, since we might yet find a use for them.

It would take half a day to put up a bamboo wall around our village site, I knew, and several months to get everything else comfortably arranged. We had a lot of work before us. Still, it had to be done, and the sooner we started the sooner we would finish.

I began hauling bamboo poles as big around as my arm and twice my height from the grove, piling them not far from where the women worked. Our village would circle the place the women now sat, I decided.

Pausing, I squinted up at the sky. The sun was beginning to settle to the west; soon it would paint the skies with bright reds and yellows and oranges. With a start I realized there were *two* suns in the sky, the bright one lighting the land and a smaller, paler one beside it. The smaller sun was too tiny and too bright to be the moon. We truly were in the land of spirits, I thought, awed.

Eona carried more bamboo poles out and threw them down

with mine, and suddenly there was a small army hauling
bamboo out. As Eona headed back for more, I joined him. It
was good to work, to stretch strong young muscles in arms
grown used to being old and weak. The white-skins worked
alongside us, and though they said nothing to anyone, their
work was as good as any other's. When I pointed that out to
Eona, he merely frowned.

We had just begun to set up the stockade walls when a huge
noise like thunder came. I looked back toward the white-skins'
camp and saw blue lightning flicker around the huge silver tree
where the white-skins gathered, but then it vanished just as
quickly as it had appeared.

Everyone else had paused, too, and in the distance I could
hear the white-skins shouting—though whether they were joy-
ful or angry, I couldn't tell. I glanced around, spotted Nonu,
and told her to take Burd and Eona to see what had happened.
She translated quickly, and the three of them ran toward the
tree.

"Back to work!" I ordered, and everyone resumed their
duties, the men raising huge bamboo poles while the women
tied them in place with bamboo ropes. The women still worked
in the field, gathering armfuls of grass for beds and roofs,
weaving more rope, making hammocks and sleeping mats.

We had just finished the outer wall and were tying the
village's gate in place when Burd and Eona returned. Nonu was
carrying one of the strange wooden sticks that had been
attached to everyone's wrist when we woke, only this one's end
had been removed, revealing a hollow interior. It was full of
colorful objects.

Nonu set the container upright in the center of the village,
and everyone gathered around to see. "This one was Byrd's,"
Nonu told me. "He set it into the giant stone tree before
coming to stay with us, and after the lightning came, it filled
itself with food and treasures!"

"They aren't sticks, but spirit-boxes," Eona said. "All of
the white-skins' spirit-boxes were filled!"

Everyone murmured with excitement.

Burd was talking to the other white-skins, and they all turned
and ran toward the silver tree. I didn't blame them; if my

spirit-box had filled up with food, too, I would also want it . . . but was it wise to eat food given by spirits?

I thought of our own spirit-boxes then, but Maraga had already thought to check them. "They are empty," she reported, showing me one she had managed to open. "The spirits did not fill ours."

At that there were grumbles around me, but when I glared they stopped.

Byrd sat cross-legged before his spirit box and began pulling out object after object. He seemed to recognize many of them, though I did not. One was a small stick with a silver tip on one end. When he flipped his thumb across it, a little flame appeared.

I took a step back. "What magic is this?" I demanded.

"It is not magic," Nonu said. "The white-skins call them *lighters* and use them to make fire. A little stone rubs sparks, which catch fire on a bit of oil-soaked cloth."

"It has been sent by the spirits," I said with a confidence I did not feel. A little stick that made fire! A miracle! "We will dine well when our hunters return!"

That seemed to cheer everyone up. Then Burd pulled a strange-looking brown food from the spirit-box, smelled it, smiled, and offered it to everyone near him. Nobody would take it. Shrugging, Burd bit into it himself. The spirits had also filled a cup inside his spirit-box with a steaming dark brown liquid. He sipped cautiously. When I leaned forward to smell it, he offered it to me, but the bitterness of its scent made my eyes water. I waved it away.

The other white-skins were returning with unhappy expressions and empty spirit-boxes. They muttered something to Burd, who shrugged, then passed them some of the food from his own spirit-box. They divided it and devoured it within the space of a few heartbeats.

They say the other white-skins stole their food and treasures," Nonu told me.

Maraga bent to whisper in my ear, "Must we tolerate thieves, who steal food and treasures from our villagers?"

"The food was not in our village," I said. "How were the white-skins to know these white-skins would return? We would have taken their food and treasures ourselves, too, if we had the chance.''

She had to admit I was right.

Burd had finished his meal and begun pulling objects from his spirit-box again. At the bottom he found large squares of red and green cloth. Maraga moved forward, fingered the cloth wonderingly, and looked at Burd.

''Mine?'' she asked. Nonu translated.

Byrd smiled and handed it to her, and then everyone in the village rushed forward, grabbing and saying, ''Mine! Mine!'' in loud voices.

When the youngest boys emerged from the scramble with Burd's fire-stick, I pulled it from his hand. ''Only the headman can make fires,'' I told him. He looked like he was going to cry, but instead dove back in and soon emerged with another treasure, Burd's cup, which was now empty. He ran off with it, shouting happily.

Maraga was already cutting Burd's red cloth into strips with a reed she had sharpened on a stick. The first strip she wrapped around my left arm. It make a striking contrast to the deep brown of my skin, and I strutted proudly this way and that, letting her admire it.

Burd touched my arm. I looked at him warily.

With Nonu translating, Burd said: ''You must have your people put their spirit-boxes in the stone tree.''

''We cannot take gifts from the spirits until we know why we have been brought here. If we accept their food, we must serve them and their purposes.''

''How will you find out what their purposes are?'' Burd asked.

''I must walk with them and talk with them,'' I told him. ''They will tell me which spirit brought us here, and why. Only then can we decide what to do next.''

''How will you find these spirits?''

''They are everywhere,'' I said impatiently, waving at the grass, at the bamboo, and the River itself. ''They fill the world. Every object, living or not, has its own spirit.''

He nodded, understanding at last.

Maraga touched my elbow. ''The hunters,'' she said.

"We will talk again later," I told Burd. "If you have any questions, ask Nonu. She will be your teacher among us."

"Thank you," he said, but I was already following Maraga to where the hunters stood, in the center of our little walled village.

The oldest came forward and threw the day's game before me: two small, ratlike creatures and a snake hung on a bamboo pole. "The hunting is bad here," he said. "There is no game to be found larger than these."

I frowned; they had found hardly enough to feed an entire village.

"A few of the boys had gone down to the River to spear-fish," the oldest hunter went on, "and they had better luck." He motioned, and two boys ran forward. They carried about twenty fish strung through the gills on a bamboo pole. Some of the fish were small and thin, but a couple were fully as large as small dogs. Most were in between in size. That made me smile. It would not be a feast, but we certainly would not go hungry tonight.

The women had gathered enough wood for a fire, and after he had instructed me in its use, I lit the fire with Burd's spirit-given *lighter*. Since the spirits had given it to Burd, and Burd had given himself to us, I figured it was safe to use.

As flames rose, snapping and crackling through the wood, the women began to prepare the evening meal. I looked up at the sky and saw stars beginning to appear: they were strange, not in the familiar patterns I had seen all my life, and I wondered what that foretold. The spirit-world is now our own, I reminded myself.

With darkness, we began hearing strange noises from the direction of the white-skins' camp. I picked up a spear, motioned for Burd to do the same, and we went out together to see what was causing the commotion.

It was a strange scene at the spirit-tree: most of the white-skins had shed their grass mats and spirit-box-given cloths and were rolling around on the ground screwing like dogs in heat. It is natural to turn one's gaze away and pretend not to notice when men and women join together, but there was something *wrong* about it here, something both terrible and frightening. It was as though the white-skins' souls were possessed by evil spirits. These were not the acts of men and women, but of beasts.

Then I found a dead white-skinned women—strangled, it looked like. A few feet beyond her, a man had been stabbed to death dozens or hundreds of times with a bamboo knife. The knife was still buried in his chest.

"Stay ready," I told Burd, hefting my spear to show him what I meant. He lifted his own spear and took a stronger grip on it.

We circled around the spirit-tree, finding a couple more dead bodies. Then, among the joined couples, I spotted Clay and pointed him out to Burd. Burd ran to his friend, spoke to him, but Clay only snarled murderously and swung a fist.

When Burd backed away, Clay rose and charged at him, screaming, flailing his arms. I rushed to Burd's side to defend him. When Clay turned on me, his eyes wild and senseless, I drove my spear into his belly.

Gasping, he stopped and just looked at me, then slowly sank to his knees. I jerked my spear free and hit him in the face with its butt. He collapsed and did not move, either dead or dying.

Face pale, Burd stared at me. He jabbered something, then turned away, fell to his knees, and abruptly vomited. Had he never seen blood or death before? I wondered. He was acting like a boy on his first village raid.

The woman Clay had been screwing leaped to her feet and padded silently off into the darkness. I picked up a couple of pieces of red cloth she had left lying in the dirt. The spirits would not mind my taking them, I thought.

Now I had seen enough to confirm my suspicions. Whatever happened to the other white-skins hadn't affected Burd: the decorations on his face and chest had marked him as human, and the evil spirits had left him alone.

"Let's go back," I told him, and when I started for our village he picked himself up and followed.

As we neared the village gate, a small brown figure suddenly hurtled out of the grass at me, screaming like a monkey. I dropped my spear, caught small arms, and heaved a small body up into the air.

It was Joqua, one of our village's youngest boys. He was only eight or nine years old, thin as a reed, but still strong and wiry. He kicked until Burd grabbed his feet, and together we wrestled him to the ground and sat on him to keep him from biting and kicking us.

He was chewing something in his mouth. Burd reached out, pried Joqua's jaws open, and pulled it out, barely avoiding losing his fingers to Joqua's teeth in the process.

It looked like a white slug in the dimness. Burd smelled it suspiciously, then passed it to me.

It was soft, sticky, and warm to the touch. It had a sweet, spicy scent.

"Gum," Burd said. He mimed pulling something out of a container—and I realized he meant this strange *gum* had come from his spirit-box. I had been right; the spirits had tried to trick us with their presents. If we'd put our spirit-boxes into the spirit-stone, we would have fared no better than the white-skins.

I looked back at the spirit-tree, listening to the cries and sobs and moans of white-skinned men and women in the power of evil spirits. Perhaps, I thought, this *gum* was like the *javara* we made and snorted to bring us closer to the spirit-world. That seemed likely.

Little Joqua had quieted. He let me pick him up, and I carried him the rest of the way into the village. I kept the *gum* in my hand the whole way.

We pulled the village's gates shut. While the women saw to Joqua, I called all the men together. They gathered around me, and I told them all I had seen at the white-skins' spirit-tree.

"The spirits tricked them," I said, holding out the *gum*. "This *gum* is like *javara*. It opened their souls to the spirits."

"Then they are possessed now," Eona said.

"That is true," I said. "They did not protect themselves as

we did. None of them had painted their bodies to mark themselves as human.''

''We must drive them away from here,'' Eona said firmly. ''There will only be more trouble if they remain.'' A number of others echoed his words.

I shook my head, though. ''We must not do anything until I have walked with the spirits,'' I said. ''I have the *gum* now. I will chew it, and I will see who has brought us to this place, and for what purpose. Only then may we act.''

Eona thought about it a minute, then nodded. ''That is wise,'' he admitted.

I sat by the fire, stared into the flames for a heartbeat, then put the *gum* into my mouth and chewed slowly. The taste was odd, sweet and bitter at once, like nothing I had ever eaten before.

Little happened at first. Slowly the flames began to turn green, then blue, rising before me like a mountain of color. I felt the heat through my whole body, closed my eyes, and felt myself soar over the land like a bird.

I came to land in a clearing in a place very much like the forest in the real world where I had lived. There were bright birds in the surrounding trees, and monkeys chattered down at me as gold and red butterflies flitted about my head. I could smell the rich moistness of the earth and feel the warm breeze on my skin. I looked at my arms and found my tattoos had returned; I looked as human as I ever had.

A wide trail led through the clearing. I followed it. Tree branches wove together over my head, and it grew darker. I came to an old stone ruin, and seated on top of the ruin was an enormous black beetle.

''Are you Cocoti?'' I said to the beetle. I felt myself tremble with fear. Never before had I come face-to-face with this great spirit.

''I am Cocoti,'' said the beetle. Its voice was sharp and strong. ''Why have you come to the spirit-world, manling?''

''I have come seeking answers.''

''What answers do you seek?''

''Why have we been born into the spirit-world?''

"You are no better than monkeys," the beetle said, "no matter how you decorate yourselves."

"Answer my question, Cocoti," I said, bolder.

"Do you raise your hand against me?"

"No," I said. "You are greatest of all the spirits, Cocoti, and all men fear you. But answer my question, Cocoti, and perhaps I can help you in return."

"It is a high price to pay."

"I will pay it."

The beetle paused, its six huge black arms waving in the air. "You are in the spirit-world," it said at last. "You are not dead, manling, but neither are you alive yet. You who are the dung of a wild dog must know that."

"Then what are we?"

"You are the future," it said. "You are all the future." And then it leaned forward and bit off my head with its shiny black jaws.

I woke cold and stiff, gasping in pain. A thin light was bleeding into the village through the bamboo walls to the east; the sky looked gray. I felt a drop of rain strike my forehead, then another.

The fire had gone out. I rose and looked around me.

Eona and Maraga were both watching me. Their eyes were puffy; they hadn't slept all night, it seemed. Eona's spear lay at his feet. He had been guarding me.

"Are you well?" Maraga asked.

"Yes," I said.

"The spirits—?"

"I saw Cocoti," I said. "He says this is not the spirit world. It is another test."

"We already knew that," Eona said.

"Yes," I said.

Men, women, and children were sprawled here and there throughout the village, one head pillowed on another's stomach or thigh, arms intertwined. Men and women were already pairing off. Only the white-skins all slept singly, off in one corner.

There was also one man lying behind Eona and Maraga. He wasn't breathing, I saw.

"What happened to that one?" I asked.

"Burd killed him," Eona said simply.

"What?" I cried.

Maraga said, "He tried to murder you when you were in the spirit-world."

I shuddered at the thought. A man who died while his soul was in the spirit-world would have his soul trapped there forever. It was a horrible fate.

"Why would he do such a thing?" I asked. "It makes no sense."

"Look at his face," Maraga said.

I went to the man, knelt, turned him over. Blood had pooled in his right cheek, turning it black where it had touched the ground, and the paint on his face had all smudged. It was the hunter I'd worried about the day before. I'd thought I'd known him then. Today, in the morning light, I knew I did.

"Ngosoc," I whispered.

"You named him as your murderer before you died," Maraga said. "Then men of our village killed him that night."

It was true: he had bewitched me in the real world, sending evil spirits into my stomach to kill me. He was forty years younger now, and I did not know how I had failed to recognize him. It must have been more of his witchery.

"Burd killed him?" I asked.

Eona nodded. "The white-skins set the grass on fire by the spirit-tree. We were all at the gate, watching the flames, when we heard a warrior's cry behind us. It was this one"—he nudged Ngosoc with his toe—"running at you with a spear. He would have driven it through your back. Burd grabbed a spear, threw it, and killed Ngosoc."

"Was it a clean blow?" I asked.

"Straight through the heart," Maraga said. "The spirits must have helped him."

I thought back to how I'd saved Burd from Clay the night before. Now Burd had saved me in turn. If throwing away the spirit-boxes had been our first test, letting Burd and the other white-skins join us must have been the second.

I told Eona and Maraga as much.

"It is true," Eona admitted. "The spirits have been guiding you. Though I still do not like or trust white-skins, Burd is different."

"He will become a human being," I said.

I walked slowly to the gate, untied it, pushed it open. Eona and I stood shoulder to shoulder looking out toward the spirit-tree. The grass-fire still smoldered a bit, sending smudgy gray pillars of smoke toward the sky, but a heavier rain began to patter down around us. I knew it would put out the last of the flames.

You are the future. How many more tests would Cocoti pose for me before he was satisfied? What would the next test be?

"They must become human beings," I said, realizing the truth at last. It had been before me all the time. It was the greatest test ever posed by Cocoti. "You said the white-skins came to your people in the old world, making them worship *Virgin Mary*. The white-skins were wrong. There is no *Virgin Mary*. There is only Cocoti here, and he is still testing us."

"What must we do?" Eona asked.

"First we must decorate the white-skins," I said, "to protect them from evil spirits. Then we must take their spirit-boxes and destroy them, for they are the source of the evil. The white-skins must join our village and live as people among us."

"All of us together?" Eona asked, brows creasing.

"Yes," I said, and I could see it in my mind: White and brown, all working together, building the greatest village the spirits had ever seen. It could happen. It *would* happen.

You are all the future.

All of us. That included the white-skins, I knew.

I leaned on Eona's shoulder and told him of my vision, told him all Cocoti had revealed to me. He agreed on my interpretation.

"But what if the white-skins will not join us?" he asked. "They have never lived among us as people."

"You have your spear," I said, "and I have mine. If they

will not become people, we must treat them as dangerous animals and kill them. When their souls are reborn, they will know the truth."

"The truth," he echoed. Then he smiled. "It is a good plan. Cocoti is right. When will we start?"

"Now," I said. "Wake the other men—and Nonu. She must speak to the white-skins for us. It is early; the white-skins will be sleepy and disorganized. Perhaps some will still be possessed by evil spirits."

"Yes, headman."

That was the first time he'd ever called me that, I realized. He had accepted me fully. *That was another test,* I thought. *Will you never stop, Cocoti?*

As Eona woke the others, I looked out across the grassy field and dreamed. We would all come together, I thought, every man and every woman in the world, all of us serving Cocoti and the spirits. White or brown, green or purple, the color of our skin would not matter. Our rebirth in the spirit-world was only the beginning.

You are the future. You are all the future.

I would make sure of that.

Nevermore

David Bischoff
and
Dean Wesley Smith

1

Ah, broken is the golden bowl! The spirit flown forever!
Let the bell toll!—A saintly soul floats on the Stygian river.

"Lenore"
Edgar Allan Poe

The sun hurt his eyes.

The man lowered his cowl and readjusted the rough cloth for better shade. He squinted across the mile expanse of the whiskey-dark River to the other side. Yes, there was the usual grass plain, and the usual vast majestic sweep of the eternal mountains that bordered this insane Valley of the Not-Dead. Between them, the rocks and the low trees and the iron trees. Shreds of smoke wisping above them like escaping souls from tombs attested to settlements. Nothing vastly unusual about that. However, just at the edge of this monotonous forest before these monotonous mountains rearing above this monotonous river was a building, and upon this large, singular, two-storied building were chimneys and gables.

There looked to be seven gables, but he couldn't count them from here. Still, in the fifteen years he had roamed the Afterlife, he'd never seen such architecture.

Seven gables. Hawthorne would be proud.

Then again, perhaps Hawthorne was there.

Edgar Allan Poe lifted the satchel containing all that he owned in this life—his grail, some extra clothing, a writing utensil, a sheaf of his scribbling, his bottles, his gum, and the peculiar item that had led him here—and tossed it over his shoulder. His eyes were still bleary and Demon Drink still rattled its chains in his head. He was tempted to take a sip from his bottle to gentle it a bit, but decided not to. If his Earthly tenure had taught him nothing else, it had taught him that one did not seek employment reeking of alcohol. He'd had his share last night, his grail's supply of ale and wine tossed down with dinner, followed by too much lichen-derived stuff that the group of fifteenth-century Germans on this side of the river had provided him with. As he moved his twenty-five-year-old body down to the shore toward the pier, he felt almost as old and sick as he'd felt when he'd died at the age of forty in Baltimore. "Lord Help my poor soul," he'd gasped in the hospital of Washington Medical College, and then died.

This was not at all what he'd had in mind.

The familiar River smells were in full flow, and as always they made him sick. They reminded him of the smells of the Fells Point area where whiskey and a diseased brain had made an end of him, amongst the din and stench of harbor taverns. Nonetheless, he quieted his ill spirit, promising it again that there would be peace at the end of this journey, peace in the arms of his dear lost Sissy.

Poe made his way to the pier, which served as a docking area for a number of boats. A man was sitting on one of the dock pilings. Poe made his way over. The dock swayed as he stepped on it, and his stomach lurched. But he kept his balance and his gorge, making his way to the man at the end.

In rough German, Poe inquired of the man as to if he owned any of the boats. "*Ja,*" the man replied, and gestured toward a sturdy-looking rowboat, made of wood, far superior in Poe's opinion to the dragonfish-skin boats he'd had to use too often in his roaming. Poe then asked if the man spoke English and was relieved when he said "Yes." By now, he could get by in many languages, including the silly Esperanto that seemed to be becoming so popular. However, he still felt by far more comfortable with English, even though he was quite fond of the

French who, led by critics and writers like Baudelaire, had, from what he'd heard, kept his tales alive on Earth.

"My good man—that house over yonder. Would that happen to be the House of the Seven Gables?"

"Yes."

A remarkable vocabulary so far! "Excellent! Then a man of your literary erudition would doubtless know of me when I say that I am Mister Edgar Allan Poe!" He said it with a flourish of his hand, wishing he had a fine beaver hat to take off instead of the blasted cowl. How he missed the clothing of his day! His topcoat, his boots, his bow tie . . . A literary man had to look a certain way. . . . But with these bland but serviceable garments, there was no telling each other apart. Not really. It would be nice to be able to grow back his mustache and his side whiskers and well as the long wispy, curly black hair around his bulb of a head. All that was left of his signature countenance was the brooding dark eyes, the pouty, sneering lips, and the aristocratic nose, all inherited from his actress mother.

The man—a thick suet of a lug—just looked at him blankly, then shrugged with incomprehension.

"Hmm. Well, then . . . surely my tales have reached you, even o'er a campfire one gloomy night. I have been led to understand that the stories themselves have survived, if not the actual order of words or my name. . . . 'The Fall of the House of Usher' . . . 'The Black Cat' perhaps. . . . Surely 'The Masque of the Red Death' . . ."

With each ticking off of a title, the man shook his head.

Poe straightened to his full five foot eight inches, pulled on his clothing with a huff of wounded dignity. "Well . . . I suppose you will be privileged to hear them someday. I can't imagine they could have traveled to this area, come to think of it. Still, a man of brilliance would like to think that his works travel at the speed of light!" He cleared his throat. "In any event, I need a ride across the River."

"Certainly. I can provide you with that, sir. However, I do not give rides for free."

"But good sir. I am a writer . . . Over there is my destination, a household that will surely appreciate the arrival of such as me. They will no doubt repay you for your time and effort."

The man had begun to lose interest. He turned back to what he'd been doing before: repairing a net.

This was not going well. Poe's temperament would have him storm off and sulk for a while, and then find some other means of transportation. However, his desperation and his headache stopped him from going more than a few steps.

He spun around and walked back to the man.

"Look here, my friend. I'm not a wealthy man. My royalties have not reached me in this existence. I have very little to offer in the way of barter."

"What have you got?"

Poe lowered his sack and pretended to go through it.

"A small amount of delicious alcoholic beverage . . . some dreamgum . . ." He shuddered at the thought of having to give up either of these items.

"*Ja*. Maybe."

"Some new poems of mine, scribbled in my hand and signed . . . I can promise you a copy of my new effort 'Bells of the River' will doubtless be worth a great deal one day!"

The man turned up his nose. "Poetry! What use does a fisherman have for poetry! It comes free from singing bards if we should want it!"

Poe swallowed his fury. "And of course, this paltry item of merchandise." From his sack he drew the curious piece that had brought him to this place.

It was a book. Or perhaps a magazine of some sort. Poe could not really tell, since it was such a slipshod publication. But then, any publication at all was something of interest to a writer and editor like Edgar Allan Poe. Such an item spelled the existence of a publishing house, which meant work for a soul who seemed doomed to a poverty-stricken existence even though his books seemed to have sold millions of copies in many languages. A book indeed, with a cover of fishskin, binding a collection of quite rough paper, messily stamped with printed words. Upon the cover was engraved the title and the author:

TARZAN RESURRECTED
by
Edgar Rice Burroughs

Poe handed the man the book.

The man's eyes widened and lightened. He smiled. "Yes! Yes! Tarzan!" He slid the book within his own clothing before Poe had the opportunity to change his mind. "An excellent trade. Get in, get in! I'll take you."

A little nonplussed, but happy for the acceptance, Edgar Allan Poe followed the man to his boat, preparing himself for river-sickness.

2

Oh! that my young life were a lasting dream!
My spirit now awakening till the beam
Of an eternity should bring the morrow.
Yes! thought that long dream were of hopeless sorrow

"DREAMS"
Edgar Allan Poe

Trash, of course. Poe had read the book, naturally. Several times. There wasn't much else to do on this world to pass the time, and even though the novel was badly written nonsense, the very fact that it was words of fiction made it a pleasure to a man who had devoured books in his day. Had he paper to spare, he would have written one of the caustic reviews for which he had been so famous, even though there was no periodical in sight to publish it.

Of course it was all balderdash! A man brought up by apes in Africa discovers he is an English lord. He has a lifetime of the most unlikely adventures, laboriously alluded to with the most tasteless of titles. And then . . . he is resurrected on the World of the River and proceeds to seek someone named Jane.

Despite the awkward sentence structure and the garish sensibilities displayed, Poe had to grant the effort had a certain narrative drive. And his own search—for his dear lost Virginia, who had died in 1847 at the age of twenty-five—made Lord Greystoke's search quite involving and appealing. Still, this Burroughs fellow was clearly far beneath his own literary level.

However, the book and the implied existence of a publishing house . . . that was an entirely different matter!

The German deposited him on the other side of the River without much ceremony and then rowed back with his new prized possession tucked in his clothing. No matter, thought Poe, brushing off his cloak as though divesting himself of the dirt of the entire transaction. If this was the place it was supposed to be, then surely he shall be able to have another if he pleased. . . . And frankly, if any more, hopefully better literature.

Poe reached for the bottle of spirits and took a nip. Damn the fumes! He'd die if he didn't have a nip. Then he'd be of no use to these people.

The liquor congenially burned down his throat. Poe took another two gulps, and feeling much better, replaced the bottle in his pack and began his hike to that house.

HOUSE OF SEVEN GABLES PRESS

The allusion on the rough wood sign was not beyond him. It made him wonder if his contemporary Nathaniel Hawthorne was behind this venture. He wasn't sure if this would be a beneficial eventuality. Even so, he was sure that a man who had felt his critical barbs upon Earth would be willing to forgive and forget in this new life. Still, Poe wondered, should I come walking up to this place with a scarlet letter "C" for "critic" pinned to my cloak, hoping that amusement will soothe all wounds?

Then again, he could hardly see a man like Nathaniel Hawthorne being party to this tripe, this terrible tawdriness . . . this "Tarzan" . . .

The house was a large one, albeit makeshift. It had a gothic feel to it certainly, what with chimney pots and gables, for God's sake. It stood separate from any other signs of civilization, and in truth, looked rather ridiculous in its juxtaposition with the regularities of the plain and the low forest. Nonetheless, it made Poe's heart ache. On Earth he had lived in cities all his life, and oh! how he missed the clatter of horse-drawn carts on cobblestones! The monoliths of brick and mortar with their cozy fires in soft bowels, filled with civilized bakery smells and the tastes of rich brew.

Off to the right was a small copse of trees and he heard the sounds of wood cutting. A heavyset, powerful-looking fellow with a square face and short hair worked hard at a stack of kindling. He was singing some song in a low voice that would alarmingly bellow out for a verse, then die down to a whisper. Some ditty about a "Yellow Rose of Texas." Sweat flew from his brow with each "chunk" of ax to log. At one point, as Poe stood observing this odd performance the man simply dropped the ax and began to shadowbox some surprise assailant. Then he again picked the ax up and proceeded with his task at hand.

"Pardon me," said Poe, making sure some yards were between him and this unusual individual.

The man swept around, ax cocked for battle, head sunk down in his shoulders like a turtle preparing to defend itself. He grunted something like "Crom."

Poe quickly held up hands empty of weapons. "Sorry to startle you. I'm merely a harmless visitor."

The man relaxed slightly, but his eyes stayed on guard. "Tarnation, mister," he said in a decided southwestern drawl. "You got to be watchin' whose back you sneak up on!"

" 'Sneaking' was hardly my intention," said Poe. "I assume that I am at the House of Seven Gables Publishing!"

The man put down the ax. "You bet! You here to buy a book maybe?"

"I am here for several reasons . . . alas, the purchase of a book is not one of them, though I am familiar with your product. Allow me to introduce myself. My name is Edgar Allan Poe, and I am seeking employment, amongst other things."

The man's face changed completely. "Holy pancakes!" Surprise and joy replaced suspicion. "Well, hot damn, put some long hair and a mustache on that head and you'd look just like that picture." The man slapped his hand against his thigh.

" 'To the tintinnabulation that so musically swells/From the bells, bells, bells, bells,/ Bells, bells, bells—' "

" 'From the jingling and the tinkling of the bells!' " Poe finished the stanza for him. It was always a thrill to find someone familiar with his work. Too rare an occurrence, but always appreciated. He smiled and nodded, basking in that big southern smile.

Before he knew it, he was pumping a big southern hand. "Mightily pleased to meet you, sir. Mah name's Howard. Robert Ervin Howard. You wouldn't have heard of me, not yet anyway. I'm from the twentieth century. And I write poems too!"

"Well, it would appear that I've found the right place."

"You have indeed. . . . Come on in and have yourself a drink. I just can't get over it! Poe! H.P. is gonna just shit himself!"

Poe allowed himself to be ushered into the house by the bear of a man. The southern accent made the hospitality all the more welcome—and the prospect of a drink put an additional roseate glow to the whole business. The man called Howard guided him around to the back of the large house—and Poe could see that there was another, single-level building beyond. "The latrine, I presume?"

Howard gave a hearty laugh and slapped his sudden bosom companion on the back. "Lordy no, Eddy! That's the Press. I'll show you later. Right now, we should get our stomachs around some booze."

Poe allowed himself to be led into a high, well-lit room with a long plank table, a sink, a stove, and a chimney place with a hanging pot that clearly served for whatever cooking or boiling that was necessary. Howard went to a cupboard and pulled out a jug and two tumblers. "Hope you don't mind ale—all of us have been getting gallons of it on our grails and we've been saving it up for something special. I reckon the visit of a literary giant can be termed real special."

"Yes. Ale would be fine."

With his thirst, just about anything would do, but Poe made no mention of that. He accepted the tumbler, allowed the brawny man to clink a toast, and then drank. It was dark and rich and yeasty, and he drank most of it in a few gulps—and his life of despair was momentarily forgotten.

Howard smacked his lips and belched. "We're all writers here . . . and let me tell you, you're gonna be appreciated. . . . All writers, except for Johann and his workers, of course."

"Johann?"

"Johann Gutenberg! That's how we got Gables Publishing going! Here you go, Eddy, how about some more brew?"

Poe gladly allowed his tumbler to be refilled. He drank deeply. "Fiction. You publish fiction. A most curious luxury in this world."

Howard's eyes burned. "It's the most important contribution we can make to mankind! How can a great man of letters like yourself even question that?"

Poe shrugged. "I suppose I have been concerned with other matters over the years."

Howard softened. "You just ain't never met up with other people to pool together and work, that's all!"

Emboldened by the drink, Poe said, "Doubtless, of course, you will want to publish my latest stories and poems!"

Howard deflated a little. "Well, Mister Poe, it just ain't all that simple. I guess we'd jump at the chance, if we had ourselves a regular magazine or something. You're gonna have to talk to Burroughs about all this. He's kind of in charge, since he's got a mind for business. . . . But for right now we just can't produce all that many books, and the ones we do produce we gotta be able to use for bartering so we can get the supplies we need. So that's why we got to produce books that are popular . . . that people like a lot, you know."

"Hence *Tarzan Resurrected*?"

"Yep. Folks are eatin' it up. Burroughs was right. The Ape Man is bringin' in most of what we need right now."

"I see. Well, perhaps some editing work, then . . ."

"Shit. Don't you worry none, hear? Edgar Allan Poe! I think we're gonna be able to find some work for you, if you want it." Howard suddenly lit up, and Poe was amazed at the valleys and heights between the man's dark moods and his congeniality.

The dialogue was suddenly interrupted when a tall, gaunt-faced man with a lantern jaw entered, holding a bowl and eating what appeared to be cornflakes and milk.

Howard leaped up. "H.P.! Lookie who we got here, just walked in off the River. Edgar Allan Poe! Eddy, this is Howard Phillips Lovecraft, but just call him H. P. for short!"

The gaunt man put the bowl aside and folded his arms, a chill suspicion in his eyes. "Edgar Allan Poe. It is a shame indeed," he said in an arch New England accent. "That we were not deposited upon this peculiar plane clutching Resurrection Certificates for identity purposes. So far I personally have encountered five Napoleon Bonapartes and no fewer than twenty-two Jesus Christs."

"Don't let old H.P. bother you . . . he's from the North." Howard stood and gestured animatedly at their guest. "C'mon, Lovecraft! This is Him. I ain't never wrong! He can recite his poetry!"

"Bob, Edgar Allan Poe's work was studied by scholars and aficionados for years. Simply because a man can recite verse, knows the details of a handful of stories and perhaps some biographical details, does not mean that he's the genuine article." Lovecraft sat down at the table. Despite his lecture, though, Poe could not help notice a quavering in the man's voice. He sensed that this man really would very much like to believe that he was Edgar Allan Poe . . . but why?

Poe shrugged and drank some more. "The proof is in the pudding, surely. My work will prove my identity, and it won't hurt to give me a try."

Lovecraft sniffed, leaned forward, inspecting the guest more closely. "You do have rather the aspect of the man, don't you? If you are indeed Edgar Allan Poe—then my honest and total apologies. You have to understand that I consider myself not merely a scholar of the writer . . . but my own meager work was influenced by that great and brilliant body of work he committed to print."

"I thank you!" said Poe. Such adulation! He felt very much in the company of, if not peers, then good companions. Nor was it simply the influence of the drink, either. "Could you tell me something more of your operation here . . . ? And perhaps we can devise a way that I can prove to you my worth."

"Just one second. I'll go and get the others. Reckon it's about coffee time anyway." Howard shook his head. "Edgar Allan Poe. Don't that just beat all." The man left, humming "Yellow Rose of Texas," pausing at the doorjamb a brief moment for a shadowbox, and then hunking on out toward the outbuilding to gather in the rest of the writers.

Poe suggested that Lovecraft join him in a drink, but Lovecraft demurred, citing the time of day. Poe asked the man about this influence he'd felt and how it was expressed in his own work, and Lovecraft smiled thinly, then detailed a body of short stories of darkness and mood, featuring lurking Dark Gods at the verge of human dimensions, hungry to return and devour.

Poe's large eyes grew larger in the telling. "I confess your words bring on a shiver or two." It was then that Howard stumped back in, triumphantly introducing Edgar Allan Poe to the other writers who'd been out helping Gutenberg. "This here's Frederick Faust, Mister Poe," said Howard, indicating the taller, larger of the two, a chiseled, good-looking fellow. "Or as he was known back on Earth to many readers . . . Max Brand. Thirty million published words. He's a writein' machine and a top-quality one!"

"Edgar Allan Poe," said Faust, congenially shaking Poe's hand. "I can't tell you what a pleasure . . . All I wrote is not worth one of your stories, one of your poems. I should far rather have been a great poet than a churner of slim adventure and doctor novels. . . . Perhaps you might look at some of my current efforts and give me some criticism."

"Ah, beware there," said Lovecraft. "Poe was known as a very harsh critic."

"Can't be any harsher on me than I am on myself," said Faust. "Wrote a lot of westerns, Mister Poe. Cowboys and Indians, ya know? Damn, but I yearn to turn out something great."

"I believe that my yearning was to keep body and soul together through my literary work," said Poe, "something in which I failed miserably."

"Can't get ahold of Burroughs. He's down the River a bit, building himself a ranch where he's going to live," said Howard. "Made himself a healthy amount of bartered goods already with the Tarzan book. This here, though, is Lester Dent. A.k.a. Kenneth Robeson. He's next up in line on releases with his character. What the title of your epic gonna be, Les?''

The man—another very healthy specimen of muscular manhood, Poe noted—took hold of the smaller Poe's hand and gave a firm handshake. *"Doc Savage on the Riverworld,* actually. Welcome, Mister Poe. Far as I'm concerned, the more the merrier.''

"Doctor Savage?'' said Poe, bemused.

"Doc Savage. It's the guy's name,'' said Dent, accepting a cup of ale from Howard. He shrugged. "Action character of popular magazines in the 1930s. Nothing to base an English lit course on—but an interesting guy. I don't know if Bob's filled you in on what we're doing here. Basically we're just trying to get people reading again. What we're writing isn't for just a pack of snobs in hallowed halls.''

With that Dent laughed, a full laugh that seemed to fill the room. "Actually there just aren't any more of those hallowed halls to fill. And I can't say that I miss them, to be right honest. What we are doing is looking for the average Joe with an extra stick of dreamgum or a bottle of whiskey to trade for a ripping good time that may educate them in the bargain.''

"You seem to be aiming only for English readers though—''

"Look, you have to start somewhere,'' said Faust, pouring himself a drink as well.

Poe cocked his head, considering. "Yes, indeed, you do, and far from being one of those snobs I have always advanced the cause of a good, well-told adventure yarn. May I cite *Ms. Found in a Bottle* or 'Descent to the Maelstrom' or 'The Gold Bug.' ''

"Shee—it,'' said Howard. "Mister Poe practically started detective and mystery and horror stories. I don't know if you realize it, sir. But a lot of those English professors say that you helped start up most of the magazines that gave us our livings on Earth.''

"Indeed,'' said Poe. "Well, it would seem that I've earned myself another drink, then, eh?''

Dent laughed, and Faust joined in as well. "Damn right.

Maybe we should roust old Burroughs to meet this fellow. Edgar Allan Poe! Bob, you know, there's a whole cask of this ale in the storage area, and we've got some sandwich stuff and some bread. I think we can put off work on the press today and get to know one another, eh?''

Poe lifted his cup, pleased. "Oh—and would any of you estimable scribes have a spare square of dreamgum?''

3

It was many and many a year ago,
In a kingdom by the sea,
That a maiden there lived whom you may know
By the name of Annabel Lee;
And this maiden she lived with no other thought
Than to love and be loved by me.

"Annabel Lee"
Edgar Allan Poe

As Poe thought, it did not take long for him to convince these writers of his depth of literary and editorial abilities by the sheer impact of his beautifully pronounced and managed words. He had always been adept at charming prospective employers with compliments and coos, and now, with a few good cups of drink in him, he waxed enthusiastic over this most marvelous project and how much he hoped he would be able to contribute to the enduring tales of Tarzan and Doc Savage, and perhaps this Conan fellow that Howard started to babble about after his third drink.

After a lunch of the promised sandwiches and yet more brew from the tapped cask, Poe was led on a tour of the facilities. He was first shown the modest rooms which the writers used both for living quarters and dens. "Pleasant, sunny—quiet," Poe observed. "What more could a writer want?" A ranch house for starters, like this acquisitive Burroughs, Poe thought. But he kept that thought to himself. First things, after all, first.

The writers then brought him out to the printing building that held the press. A bunch of German lads were busy working in one room, making paper, while in another more Germans yet were busy binding a new edition of *Tarzan Resurrected*.

Poe was guided to the center room, where he was introduced to Johan Gutenberg himself. Gutenberg, who seemed to have learned to use English well enough, albeit heavily accented, greeted Poe brusquely. "*Ja, ja, gut*. Another writer. You write the books, I print them. Good deal, *ja*." And then bustled back to work.

Poe, acknowledging that he knew very little about the ink-stained metal and wood that surrounded him, mentioned that it still looked quite a bit more advanced than the process he had read about that had produced the famous Gutenberg Bibles. Faust and Dent allowed that they'd introduced some concepts to the Germans, who had leaped on them eagerly and in fact had made improvements.

"Not exactly Franklin Mint," said Lovecraft, who had been persuaded to take a drop of sherry with his lunch. "But good enough for this place."

"You know, with all your writers," said Poe, "could you not introduce cheaper paper with thicker binding and develop a periodical . . . and thus decide from this the most popular tales and serials to print as books?"

"The man wants to reinvent pulp magazines," said Faust, grinning. "And frankly, so do we. . . . We're working on it, Mister Poe. Believe me . . . we're working on it. Why do you think we need more writers and editors?"

That pleased Poe immensely. Upon returning, he insisted that a toast be raised to the new project, *Gables* Magazine, and that for certain he would be happy to include a cryptogram department to surprise and delight the readers. By now the after-lunch dreamgum had set to work and Poe was feeling absolutely euphorious. After all these fruitless years of wandering this lonely world looking for friends and his dear Virginia, finally he had at least found the friends. And his resurrected wife, reunion with whom was his goal in this After-Earth? Well, the pain still gnawed, but was lessened again by faithful alcohol.

With the cask still half full, the writers settled down to drink and exchange experiences: It was Lester Dent who was called upon to explain how House of Seven Gables Press had come into being, and the man, who only took small sips of his foamy beer, told the story in a staccato yet compelling manner.

"I guess it helped that we were all along the same stretch of the River. What I wanted, first thing, was to find other writers. Hell, I don't know why. What good was it? Back when I was alive I did most of my writing in quick bursts, spending more time off exploring and seeing new parts of the world." He smiled. "Actually, back then writing was mostly just how I made my money. But after I looked around here for a year or so it became clear that writing was much more important to me than I had imagined."

He shrugged. "New York was worlds and a death away. I dunno. I suppose writing's not just in the blood, it's in the soul— Well, to make a long story short, I advertised. What I did was to write up signs and post them near grails for a few five-mile stretches along the river. What it said was: WRITERS' MEETING. Took a few of those up and down the river in the twentieth-century America area and I started to attract some writers that I figured were legitimate. They came out of curiosity, I guess, but most of them didn't seem to give much a damn about what I had in mind.

"Hemingway, he was too busy sporting and chasing women and exploring. Faulkner, he was busy drinking and dream-gumming. Steinbeck was busy trying to find out why he was here and bitterly complaining all the while. Likewise of most the other writers. I can't say, maybe they're writing again now, though most didn't seem particularly interested in it.

"What happened, though, was that H.P. and Robert had already talked about somehow devising a publishing scheme, and when I started detailing my ideas at the meeting, they were excited from the start. They came along and helped me with the meetings, and that's how we found Fred. Edgar kind of took it over, though, and that was fine by me since he seemed to have a better business head.

"'Look,' Edgar said to me one afternoon, 'what we're talking about here is probably already being devised some-where else. Rather than try to make something here, let's go down the river a bit and see if somebody isn't working on a printing press or something.' ''

Dent shrugged. "Well, all this had taken a while, and so did the searching. But a few years ago, damn if we didn't happen across this area and not too far down from English-speaking and-reading areas, which made it just prime real estate. Who should be here but Joe Gutenberg. He was just doing more or less what he did back home, so we printed some stuff with that, but then we started innovations. These guys found some ore around here, and it didn't take too much to come up with a press. Well, with what we knew, combined with Joe's ability, it wasn't long before we were cooking.

"Now, all along Burroughs had kept writing. . . . We all had, I guess. But we read his book, and since Tarzan was the most popular character we figured it was a natural for the first book. The rest is history. So what you see here, Mister Poe, is the beginnings of a writer's colony . . . and hopefully a publishing empire.

"Words, Mister Poe. Adventures and ideas—to keep alive the minds of billions. We've got plans . . . great plans. . . . And I guess we're real happy to have you with us."

All of which sounded just fine to Poe, and cause enough for another tapping of the cask and further toasts.

"So tell us, Eddie—what's your time on this world been like? What have you been doing?" asked Howard, his accent somehow thicker with drink.

"If you'll pardon me," said Dent, before Poe could answer. "I have to go down to the village. I will be back for dinner, and perhaps I'll bring back some dessert, eh? Welcome aboard, Mister Poe. Expect to start work tomorrow—when and if you feel well enough."

Poe toasted a farewell to one of his new benefactors and then thumped back down onto the bench. His mind seemed to be swimming with the remarkable combination of dreamgum and bear. Such volume of both . . . it had been a long time since he'd been able to indulge himself so completely. The rich colors of the room throbbed and hummed. The friendly, interested writer's faces hung like benign moons in a gentle sky. . . .

And oh! the stars were dripping in that sky like tears of fire. . . .

In words that rang with the diction of a poetry-reading triumph, that clanged with alliteration and sung with assonance and clustered with onomatopoeia, Edgar Allan Poe told his story. He told of his resurrection upon the banks of the River, and how he had believed himself mad for weeks, drifting away from the area in a kind of waking delirium. "It is my belief that I died from a brain lesion, not drink. I cannot deny that alcohol inflamed the wound in my sick brain—but had not that hole been there, I would not have died. I thought, you see, that I had been consigned to some bizarre hell and my weakened mind could not take the agony and therefore removed itself from my person. I wandered many, many days before I was at all myself again.

"By that time, alas, I was quite far from my time and my people, for how would I know that the resurrections would happen in batches according to race and lifetime and often even country! For when my senses returned and something of a realization occurred, my first thought was for my dear wife. I had a chance to be reunited again with her.

"Dear Virginia! Darling Sissy! I raced back in the direction I felt I had come, away from the tenth-century Chinese whose ministrations had brought me back to sanity. However, when I finally found dwellers of nineteenth-century America once more, for the life of me, Virginia Eliza Clemm Poe was just as lost to me as she had been when she expired that awful winter night of January 30, 1847.

"Since then," he said, after a long sepulchral silence that the writers observed as well, "I have searched for my dear one. This has been my quest on this world. To reunite our bodies and souls, for neither in this wretched shell have been complete since she passed away."

After further fortification with ale, he briefly outlined his wanderings which, while colorful, were touched by the melancholy of his spirit, in search for the dear cousin he had married when she was thirteen and whose life had inspired his greatest art.

When the last of his sibilant words lapsed to silence, the quietness was again observed by the moved writers.

Bob Howard's belch broke the mood. "That's so sad, Mister Poe! And I know just what you mean," the big man said, tears on his cheeks. "First thing I did was look for Maw. Found her too, but took a while. She's got herself a home now and I know just where to go to visit her. . . . But you know, Mister Poe, now that I got my buddies here and this publishing house . . . well, I don't think about Maw so much any more."

"That, Bob, and the fact that we get you laid regularly!" snorted Faust.

The big man blushed. "Hell! I even got myself a couple of regular girlfriends! You know, all in all, this place is a damned sight better than Texas ever was!"

Poe sighed. "I long only for my wife. My soul, my wife. I shall work here for a while, yes, and I do appreciate the asylum. However, you all must know that my destiny is not here . . . but in the arms of my darling."

Faust seemed to think this most amusing, and started telling about all the people he had met who were just as happy to be rid of their spouses from Earth. However, as though finishing the story had signaled to Poe that the tether to consciousness could be released further, Poe found his soggy brain drift away like a balloon—and then, *pop!*, it was gone.

He dreamed fantastic dreams.

He dreamed of mighty palaces on fantastic planets, of swordsmen and four-armed warriors and carriages that flew in the air. He dreamed of garish colors and exotic words and dashing handsome heroes and sweet, half-clad maidens. He dreamed in colors of fantasy and escape and excitement and he marveled, for somehow he knew he was the grandfather of these worlds. . . .

"Mister Poe!"

He was aware of someone shaking him.

"Mister Poe! You'd better wake up and get some water and some food inside you, then we'll put you to bed!"

Poe looked up blearily.

Bob Howard was hovering over him like some anxious ursine. "Out of my dreams, you wretched imitator!" growled Poe. His eyes groggily moved toward the man called Lovecraft, and his bile rose again. "Go back to your bad poetry and leave me in peace. Oh, Death, Death, Death—can there yet be no peace in Death?"

He reared up. "Gentlemen, listen! For I proclaim." Poe drunkenly shouted at the top of his lungs. "Death is a lie. A most foul and damnable lie!"

There was activity in the corner, and suddenly the man called Dent, the man with the savage doctor, walked up. "Hmmm. I was afraid of this. You two know this guy's history. . . . Why did you give him all the drink and the gum?"

"Because I am the great and magisterial Edgar Allan Poe!" said Poe. "Add a 'T' to 'Poe' and you define my true heart and soul."

Lovecraft shrugged. "One drunken day will surely not harm us. . . ."

Howard shook his head, clearly not in the best of shape himself. "Poor bastard seemed to need it bad."

"Ginny? You want to bring on some of that food and coffee. Maybe we can sober the great man up before we put him to bed. He'll thank us in the morning."

Poe stood and waved his hands wildly. "Villain! I detect sarcasm. . . . How dare you question the pain that has transfused my life from time immemorial. How dare—"

Poe was brought up short. For out of the alcoholic mists of vision, there moved an image that surely must be a ghost—and yet seemed as solid as these common and quite coarse writers that surrounded him.

She was small and she had brown hair and the most lovely of violet eyes. And yet, she was not so pale as she had been before. . . . She seemed radiantly healthy, and glowing with vitality.

"Hello, Eddy," said Virginia Clemm Poe, hands on her hips. "I see you haven't changed much."

4

While, like a ghostly rapid river,
Through the pale door
A hideous throng rushed out forever
And laugh—but smile no more.

"The Haunted Palace"
Edgar Allan Poe

The sight of her was like a slap of cold water. Poe emerged from his waking dream, sober and stunned. His eyes could not be mistaken, and the woman before him was absolutely no phantasm.

"Sissy! My darling wife?" he gasped. "Can it possibly be you . . . ? Can my search be over?"

"Maybe you'd better drink something that hasn't got alcohol in it, Eddy. And then we'll talk. Okay?"

"Darling. Let me take you in my arms. Oh, you don't know how my soul has longed for you. . . ." He staggered toward her.

She stepped back. "Eddy, you needn't be so melodramatic. We need to have an adult conversation, but only when you sleep this drunk off."

Stepped back, into the sheltering and protective arms of Lester Dent.

Disbelieving, Poe watched, shocked beyond words. The way this hulking barbarian held Sissy. The way this swine looked at her. Their relationship was all too clear. Poe sputtered for a moment and coughed, and only after a Herculean effort did coherent speech emerge. "This is truly Hades, and you are the Demon who torments me!" Fury washed over him, and before he knew what he was doing he flung himself at the writer.

Dent dodged, pushed Virginia safely out of the way, and then came back with a solid roundhouse that caught Poe squarely on the cheek.

Poe was slammed back over the table, and he hit the floor in a splatter and splash of ale.

The pain only woke him further. A soggy mess, he staggered up. He could not look at this terrible sight, though, and he spied a large container full of ale. He brought it to his lips and drank, and drank some more. No one stopped him. He drank to dull the heartache and the pain and would have drunk till the ale was all gone, had not a hand tugged at his shirt. "Edgar. . . Edgar please don't do this to yourself."

Hazily, he looked down and there was Sissy, looking imploringly at him. He grabbed for her and she stepped back, dodging him easily. Dent took her back again and stood between them protectively.

"I kinda wondered about this, but it seemed like too much of a coincidence," said Dent. "Then again, on a world where the kinds of things have happened that I've seen, I guess this is all pretty minor. Look, Poe. Ginny and I are happy. You can't hang on to what happened who knows how many years ago."

"But I have searched. . . lo! these long years . . . always for you, Sissy. . . . Always!"

"I'm sorry, Eddy, but he's right." She looked at him sorrowfully, but without regret.

"But, Sissy. . . our celestial love . . . our devotion . . . How can you forget . . ."

"You know, Poe," Dent said, "Ginny never told me the whole story, and you know I guess I'm one ignorant son of a bitch for not figuring out it was you she was talking about. Maybe it was because I never read much of your sick garbage. But I gotta tell you, you stinking drunk—you were one twisted asshole. And now I can see you're a pompous twisted asshole."

Poe stepped forward to attack him again, but Howard stepped in and grabbed his arm. "Mister Poe, some of us don't want you to get yourself killed here."

"You have poisoned my dear wife's mind! I can see it! I can see it all now!" Poe shouted.

"No, Eddy. I've gotten better."

Dent stepped forward. "Man! Mister expert in psychology! You marry your first cousin at the age of thirteen. Back where I come from we'd call you an incestuous pedophile! And then you subject the poor girl to years of drunken and drugged and morbid carryings-on. . . . And support? You little weasel, you should have worked harder. . . . No wonder the poor girl got tuberculosis and died."

Poe ignored him. He turned to Virginia again, his eyes imploring. "Come back to me, Sissy. My heart cries out for you."

"No, Eddy."

"But . . . this man is . . . is . . . nothing. My literary stature far surpasses his. . . . How can you possibly choose him?"

"I never told you, Eddy, but I never much liked what you wrote. I thought your poems and stories were much too cold." She looked up with admiring eyes at Dent. "Les, though . . . Now, Les can tell a story. . . ." She stroked his chest. "And he knows how to make a lady happy in other ways, too!"

It emerged like some terrible beast, spewed up from his throat: a howl. Edgar Allan Poe howled and wailed and screamed and tore at his hair. Worms seemed to be drilling through the chambers of his brain. The walls of this house seemed to be closing in on him like the sides of a casket buried deep in foul earth.

"Come on, Mister Poe," said Howard. "Take it easy. You're not the only one who's had a hard time. You shoulda heard what Maw told me when I found her!"

Insane with grief, unable to look again upon this foul excrescence of reality, Poe fled.

He rushed through the door into the dusk, his brain on fire.

"No," he wailed. "No!"

He staggered, and the pain seemed to rage through his head on fiery wings. It was just like the damp Baltimore night, rolling through the bars of Fells Point. Could this brain disease have returned, ignited again by this horrid revelation? Could it possibly snuff out his life again—this time for good? Here, though, he knew for certain what he had only suspected subconsciously through his art: that the soul could be not be submerged again in death, that it would return again and again and again, rotting and festering though it may be.

The River was in his nostrils, and he ran for it.

The water! The cool, cool water . . . To quench himself, to ease the agony, if only momentarily. . . .

He scuttled for the River and was almost there, when he was tackled from behind.

He fell down hard and was hammered onto the edge of

consciousness. With a sigh, he let go and drifted down into the dreamless dark.

5

*Is all that we see or seem
But a dream within a dream?*

*"A Dream Within a Dream"
Edgar Allan Poe*

"Doc! Hurry!"

The scream of the man called Monk reverberated through the drug sodden consciousness of the man called Savage. He bent his thews yet again, to the boulder, whilst all around him the other heroes lay in Lethe's grasp, the gases from Below filling their lungs. They were not dead, thanks be to God. However that doom would all append their fate soon, should this aperture to the Dark Lands not be closed.

From the gaseous ink of the well, a tentacle of the creature whose appellation was Cthulu rose up from the mists, questing.

Doc Savage pushed with all the might at his command.

Edgar Allan Poe scribbled madly.

With the primitive implements, writing was difficult but not impossible. He alone among the colony of writers was used to writing in longhand anyway, so in a sense the flow of his quill was an advantage.

He took a break, coming up for air, as it were, from the adventure. Taking the glass of ale nearby, he drank, though not deeply. Then he popped another stick of dreamgum in his mouth and chewed it thoughtfully. The writing of this epic seemed to have been aided by ale and dreamgum, curiously enough. . . . Though desperation and resolve kept his pen going.

It was Howard who had run after him that dreadful night, knocking him out. The next day it had been Lovecraft with the help of Howard, who had attended to him, weaning him off steady drink with food and tea and promises of dreamgum.

When his brain fever had finally broken, it had been Howard who had given him hope.

"What am I to do now?" he said. "The purpose of my life on this world is gone! And I cannot die!"

"Hey, friend. I can sympathize," the big man had said. "Tell you what. You do what us writers do. You write. You write it out. . . . We got paper and pens and food and we got ourselves a genius with some pain. And we got a printing press. Sounds like a good combination to me."

And thus Poe had realized that there might yet be hope, and vent himself in the process. If he could write a tale in the vein of the stories these men produced . . . and show his darling Virginia that he could produce a far superior story to the ones that this hopeless hack Lester Dent produced, then perhaps he might win her back. . . .

Yes! Again the words of E. A. Poe would ring out upon the consciousness of mankind! Only, their reverberations would not be so morbid, even though they had every bit of the literary merit!

Scribble, scribble, scribble!

The words poured forth as they never had before with this story. Howard had given him some of their writing and his Cimmerian hero Conan. Lovecraft provided truly splendid villains and was helpful in explaining the things in the universes of Doc Savage and Tarzan that he did not comprehend.

But Poe had supplied the genius, and he could feel it blistering through the drink and the dreamgum to take solid inky form! And a splendid tale it was! A tale of the attempt of the Dark Gods to take over this Riverworld, foiled only with great sacrifice by a new teaming of fictitious heroes made to breathe with the author's poetry made prose.

Poe took a deep breath and set back to work.

In an hour it was done, and he stacked the pages of the last chapter together, and clumped down the stairs to the common's hall. He did not often come down here, nor other places where he was likely to run into Virginia and Dent. Mostly, he took his meals in his room, or took long walks. However, his purpose allowed him to view the sight of the two together just enough so that it was not unbearable. And when she read this work of Art, she would see the error of her ways.

He found Howard and Lovecraft warming themselves by the fire and solemnly gave them the final chapter. They read the script quickly, and when they were finished, Howard spoke first. "Well, you know, like I said before, this ain't exactly the way I see Conan of Cimeria . . . but what the hell. It's good."

Lovecraft shook his head. "No, Bob. It's brilliant."

Poe smiled wanly. "Thank you."

"Now all we have to do is to get Burroughs to okay it," said Howard. "And we'll put it into production, right after *Doc Savage Meets Goliath*."

Poe wearily but happily followed the two out to the press. Burroughs was not there, but the second-in-command, Dent, was. Howard happily presented the man with the news and then the last chapter of *The Moans of the Heroes*, along with his opinion.

Dent shrugged. "I'll read it, I guess, but you know, can't say I cared much for the rest of it. Too wordy by half for me. Action, I say. You gotta keep that story moving. . . . And damn if I like the idea of Doc Savage writing verse!"

"But they're some of my best poems . . . ever!" said Poe.

"Could be, but you're taking vast liberties with *my* character," said Dent. "Yeah, I'll read it, but I'll warn you . . . Doesn't look like this is going to see print for a while."

"What?" said Poe.

"Nope. Showed the first half to Burroughs. He didn't like the bit about Tarzan getting buried alive and then resurrected in the land of ancient Greeks who try to bugger him."

"But it was so splendidly symbolic!" protested Lovecraft.

"Could be."

Poe was fuming. "Greatness will out. Give that back to me . . . I mean to show it to Virginia."

"She's already read it, chum. I showed it to her just like you asked me too. Fair's fair, and I'm sorry about the problems between us. I guess you were in the English books and I wasn't, but that doesn't make me resent you. Ginny read it, though, and she told me to tell you that 'The poor soul's morbidity cannot be shaken, it seems.' I don't believe she cares to read any more, Mister Poe. Now, you're doin' real good work editing for us, and I guess we'll publish stories and poems by you when we get the magazine rolling. . . . But you just don't have what it takes to write a good Doc Savage book, in my humble opinion. Nor in the opinion of the Boss.''

"Manure!" said Robert E. Howard.

"Utter nonsense!" said H. P. Lovecraft.

Quietly, Edgar Allan Poe twirled around and headed back to his room to pack.

Oddly enough, he felt nothing.

Absolutely nothing.

6

> *Quaff, oh quaff this kind nepenthe and*
> *forget this lost Lenore!''*
> *Quoth the Raven, "Nevermore."*
>
> *"The Raven"*
> *Edgar Allan Poe*

He was empty for a long time.

A numbness lay heavy in his soul. When he left that day, he had meant to travel far, far from that press and that colony of writers. However, sudden indifference took him only a few dozen miles down the River, where he found a group of Australian aborigines who suffered his presence without complaint. However, so diffident was Poe that he did not even share their Dream Time.

So it was that months passed, and when word came down the River in the form of a fearful American traveler that bad luck had fallen up the House of Seven Gables Press, Poe was not so far from the place in reality as he was in spirit.

"Nazis," said the man.

Poe was not familiar with the word.

"Let's put it this way. I was in the Second World War and I fought in France against 'em. National Socialist Party. Took over Germany in the 1940s. Now, it seems they've taken over the press. Damn shame, too. I was enjoying those books. Now look at the crap they're bringing out!''

The man fished inside a pack and brought out a book that Poe immediately noted was much neater in cutting, binding, and other elements of printing. He read the title out loud.

'' *'Tarzan Uber Alles'*?''

"Yes. Goddamn Nazi propaganda. They're turning the Gables into some sort of political machine.''

Poe studied the book for a moment, then returned it, thanking the man. He returned to the small tent he was using for his home, and meant to pop his full supply of dreamgum and drink his full allotment of alcohol provided by his grail today.

However, even as he lay down and reached for the stuff, something stayed his hand.

He remembered Lovecraft talking about racial purity, and how he'd admired fascism in his day. Poe was a bit adrift in political theories that occurred after his time—but the sound of this Nazi business rather chilled his blood. He'd never much liked black people, and he wasn't any kind of abolitionist, but he didn't particularly care for the kind of wholesale hatred and genocide he'd heard had been perpetrated by these Nazis.

Instead of chewing and drinking that night, he'd stayed awake most of the night, thinking. Thinking for the first time in a while on this world with a clear mind.

When the dawn broke, he started his journey back up the River.

7

Is there—is there balm in Gilead? tell me, tell me I Implore?''
Quoth the Raven "Nevermore."

"The Raven"
Edgar Allan Poe

He found Howard Phillips Lovecraft in a town three miles short of Seven Gables Publishing.

Poe had stopped to see if the people there—more fourteenth-century Germans—knew any more information about what had occurred at the writers' colony. They had taken him to a small house where a man swathed in bandages lay, and it was Lovecraft. Barely conscious.

"Poe! Poe! Gods, you've come back! Awful! Just awful!"

"Virginia . . . the others . . . are they all right?" Poe had demanded.

Lovecraft shook his head. "Burroughs is dead. The others—they have capitulated, although I don't know how long they'll be able to deal with churning out garbage for these villains before they try to kill themselves just to escape. Oh, I was wrong . . . wrong, Poe!"

Lovecraft told the story.

A group of forty men showed up one day about a month after Poe had left. In accented English they asked questions about the press and were given a tour after promising to trade supplies for a few books. Instead, upon completion of the tour, they took out weapons and took over the press. Burroughs was down to supervise that day. All of them fought. Burroughs was clubbed to death as an example.

"The two leaders say that they are Adolf Hitler and Joseph Goebbels, but Faust is sure they are imposters who were able to rally some old Nazis together. But their plan is sound. They mean to use our books and our characters to influence the readers of this world . . . and pave the way for domination of their philosophy."

Lovecraft told of his escape, after a severe beating when he refused to put pen to paper one day. "I was lucky and found a raft beached on the river. I just got on it and drifted. These poor people took me in, but I fear I cannot last much longer. Nonetheless, when I am resurrected, I will find my friends again. I spent too long in my Earthly life a recluse, and now have tasted of real friendship."

He took a deep, shuddering breath and continued. "And I know well now the full value of what I . . . of what we as writers do. . . ." The man sighed, and Poe gave him some water. "Our efforts, no matter how trifling, are a moral force, Poe."

Poe nodded. "My written words, I think, were my own salvation . . . surely the only good I ever did during my wretched years."

"And Virginia?"

"Virginia has renounced us and become the mistress of the man who claims to be Hitler."

"I see."

"I am sorry."

"So, I would think, is Mister Dent."

"Yes. I do believe he would like to speak to you . . . though I don't know what can be done. They are forty strong! Already they are seeking out writers of prose to do their work. Soon I suspect they will be able to kill Howard and Faust and Dent— and have their characters do their bidding. What can we do?"

"First, my friend, you must hang on. You must not die and be whisked a hundred thousand miles away. Second, you must wait . . . I shall endeavor to return."

Lovecraft promised to do his best.

Poe went to the leader of the German band and gave him all of his liquor and all of his dreamgum in return for the best care possible for his wounded friend.

He slept a short while and then traveled the rest of the way back to the House of the Seven Gables Publishing.

8

The sickness—the nausea—
The pitiless pain—
Have ceased, with the fever
That maddened my brain—
With the fever called 'Living'
That burned in my brain

"For Annie"
Edgar Allan Poe

Poe loathed the men on sight. They were officious, obnoxious martinets, particularly the two called Hitler and Goebbels.

Did it really matter that they were imposters? Surely the true individuals could not have owned more atrocious souls.

"Poe? Edgar Allan Poe?" said Goebbels. "I believe I have read some of your tales."

"Yes, I am a writer and editor of some note. And I seek employment." Poe had always had a talent for obsequiousness and praise, and he poured it on in full now, telling the Nazis how efficient everything looked now.

"Why do you want to work for us?"

"I will work for anyone who can pay my price in drink and dreamgum," Poe responded. "And besides . . . I worked here before and was rejected. It gives me great pleasure to thus thumb my nose at my previous employers, whom I understand are presently being held in captivity."

The man called Hitler smiled at that one. "Yes . . . yes . . . Joseph, he has a good cause to work here, and I do believe that I have heard of this man. He's known especially for his stories. . . . A man who writes well and works voluntarily is a great boon."

"Yes . . . yes . . . I agree. . . . But we must educate him in our cause first," said Goebbels.

"I confess that what I have heard of your philosophies only intrigues me. There must be some sort of order put on this anarchistic world. . . . And why not have the powerful, pure-bred races rule? I am such stock myself, and I can clearly see our superiority," said Poe.

Goebbels was not totally satisfied. He had some of his men drag Lester Dent up. Dent's eyes grew wide when he saw Poe. When he realized what Poe was doing here, they grew inflamed with rage.

"You bastard!"

"Perhaps, Dent," said Poe, "Gables Press will print what I write now."

"Traitor!"

"Enough. Put him back," said Hitler. "An extra chapter of *Herr Doktor Savage's Blitz* today, Herr Dent, or you shall be flayed mercilessly!"

Poe was shown to a comfortable room and provided with pen and paper. At dinnertime, he conversed comfortably with his new employers, and he saw his Earthly wife Virginia again, sitting beside Hitler. She had the grace to turn her eyes to the floor in shame, and whatever hatred for her Poe reserved fled in that moment. When he had the opportunity, he drew her aside.

"Virginia. We all must survive, yes?"

"Eddy... why have you come back?"

"To work." He looked at her with his piercing eyes and knew in a moment why she had done what she had done. "You do love him, don't you, this Dent fellow?"

"Yes."

He felt the familiar jealousy rage. How it easy it had been to let his violent emotions go unchecked—and yet, now, without the gum and the drink, he still felt the pain, but his intellect seemed more in control.

"That's why you went with this Hitler... to be near Dent, to help him as best you could."

"Yes. Eddy, I'm sorry. I was so young... and so sick all the time... I never grew up. I've grown up here. I've changed."

Poe nodded. "Now is the time that you can help Dent and the others. That's what I'm here for, Sissy. I didn't come here to work for these tyrants."

"Oh, Eddy..." Those bright eyes seemed suddenly so full of love again. He felt life again in his soul. "That's wonderful... I mean... What can I do?"

"How are these miscreants armed?"

"Swords. Bows and arrows. And clubs, of course. They speak wistfully of the wonderful guns and they used to own in their previous lives."

"Good. We have a chance, then. Sissy, we cannot beat them, but we can destroy what they would use—and in the confusion, escape with the others."

He told her his plan, and she breathlessly agreed.

Virginia, as it turned out, had full run of both the house and the press, and knew all the guards. Poe had been granted full privileges of the house. Together they stole down to the cellar where stores were kept, including several casks of the distilled lichen alcohol that Burroughs had insisted be kept "for possible medicinal purposes." Poe had requested access to them more than once, but had been denied, limited merely to ale. Now he was glad that had been the case. The stores were not under guard, and so it was easy enough to take the two small casks out.

"Bring the cask over to the Press, Ginny. Empty it on the dry pulp there. Then just as soon as you can, take a torch and set fire to it. Then I want you to immediately run to the trees and hide before the Nazis have any idea what you've done."

"What about you? What about Les, and the others?"

Poe grinned. "We'll meet you there."

She hugged him and kissed him on the cheek and then took the cask. He gave her a few minutes' head start and then took his own cask up to the main room.

Fortunately, it was empty of people. In one corner was a large pile of recently complete copies of *Tarzan Uber Alles*. He doused the pile with half of the cask of liquor and splashed the rest about the wooden room.

Then he went back to his own room.

His window had a perfect view of the Press. It was still dark inside. . . . No! A light! A wavering light. He heard the distant pad of footsteps as Virginia raced away into the night.

It was just a matter of time before the flames licked out of the windows, and the guards knew what was happening.

He went down to the common room, where he had glimpsed a pile of swords. The alarm was just a minute in coming.

"Fire!" cried a voice. "Fire in the press!"

Excited jabbers and shouted orders sounded in the night. He watched five men rush downstairs, keeping to the shadows himself.

Then he took four swords and a club and climbed back up to the second floor where he knew the writers were kept.

They had been thrown into the largest of the rooms for easy watching. Now, as he peered round the side of the hall, Poe could see that only one of the guards remained posted. . . . And the man seemed more interested in what was happening in the other building than in keeping alert to the events here.

Leaving the swords behind, Poe crept up behind him and brought the club down on the back of his head. The man fell with a satisfyingly final thud.

Poe quickly went to the door and took down the heavy latch that imprisoned the writers.

"Mister Poe!" cried Robert Howard.

"You!" said Dent. "What's going on!"

"I am effecting your escape. The House of Gables Press, I fear, must move on to safer harbor. Virginia has ignited the outbuilding and the Nazis are no doubt now attempting to put out the blaze. I, on the other hand, am about to ignite this structure, which should leave them with their hands full while we depart. Here, gentlemen, are swords. I suggest you take them up and pray to God that you do not have to use them."

Poe grabbed his own after Faust and Howard and Dent took theirs. He led them down to the main room. "Quickly, Bob . . . a lit log from the hearth fire."

Bob Howard wasted no time.

"But Virginia . . . how can you trust her," said Dent. "And why are you doing this, Poe?"

"First, my friend, Virginia did what she did to help you . . . which she is doing now. Faithfulness, it would seem, has different dimensions upon this world. And as for myself— perhaps I feel a responsibility for my literary bastards. . . ."

Faust chuckled. "Well, whatever. . . . Thanks."

Howard returned with the fiery brand.

"That pile of filth, if you please, Bob," said Poe, pointing to the stacks of *Tarzan Uber Alles*.

Howard grinned. "Sure thing."

The paper went up quickly, but they were unable to watch the full destruction. "Out the back and up the hill toward the trees," ordered Poe. "That is where we are to meet Virginia . . . and then hide."

"But Gutenberg . . . we'll need Gutenberg to start up again," said Faust.

"I know enough about presses now to start up again anywhere," said Dent. "Poe's right. We'll burn and run."

They raced out into the night, and up the hill. Poe could see the Press building burning like a gigantic match head, while the Nazis vainly attempted to toss water on it. Ah, but pulp could burn bright!

And not just in the hearts and minds of its readers.

"Gott in Himmel!" The cry broke out just seconds after a fist of flame rammed through the window of the gabled house itself.

Other voices started braying. Fingers were pointed.

"They've seen us! Hurry!" said Poe.

He raced, face flushed, toward the trees. It would not be long before they were pursued. . . .

The low trees were only a few yards away. As they hurried toward them, a swishing swished past Poe's ears.

"Arrows" cried Dent. "Damn, let's get the lead out!"

Just at the edge of the forest, Poe felt a blow on his back and knew he had been hit. He staggered but kept himself up and running. He followed the others, puffing and groaning. At first the piercing did not hurt and he thought it was minor, but by the time they were into the forest, and he realized that he was in shock . . . The pain was there, like a promise of a terrible storm.

"Les! Bob!" cried a voice.

"Ginny," said Lester Dent. "Come on! Hurry. You must run."

A figure separated from the shadows and joined them. "I've walked up these woods to the hills before. I know a cave where we can hide."

"Lead on, then!" said Dent.

Poe kept his pain to himself, managed to keep up, if lagging to the rear. Somehow, it seemed as though in this context his life of pain helped. He had weathered the stuff in his soul and his head; surely he could weather it now in his back.

The snarling voices of the Nazis dimmed behind them, and even as a fever of blood was taking over Poe's senses, Virginia led them into the cave.

"There's an exit on the other side if they find it. . . . But I suggest we stay here for a while," she said.

"They'll probably go back and fight the fire, for now," said Faust. "I could use a rest anyway."

"An excellent idea," said Poe. "And then perhaps you might assist me in removing this arrow." He staggered, and fell to his knees.

"Eddy," said Virginia.

"Mister Poe!"

They had no light, but they did the best they could under the circumstances. Still, it was a long and painful night, and by the morning, Poe had lost much blood.

When dawn touched the mountains, Frederick Faust returned from a quick scouting.

"Both buildings burned to the ground," he said. "Damned fine job, Poe."

"You will not forget what I told you about Lovecraft's whereabouts? You just go and get him and start somewhere else," said Poe.

Lester Dent knelt by him. "Hang on, chum. We need you too."

Poe shook his head weakly. "No. Having died before I can feel the final slide. Go and start again . . . I will find you . . . Or perhaps I shall start my own house. . . . Yes . . . that would be a fine idea, I think."

He choked and found his mouth full of blood. He let it leak out of his mouth and took a painful gasp.

"Still, you no doubt will have another press sooner and your Doctor Savage shall again be saving the minds and hearts of readers."

"Eddy, Eddy . . ." said Virginia. "Thank you. I'm so sorry. Find us, if you can. Find us . . ."

"An excellent idea. I never was much of a publisher anyway."

Poe could feel the life draining from him quickly, and yet even though he knew it was not the end, that he would be resurrected on the banks of the great River miles and miles away, he felt oddly at peace.

"Mister Poe," said Howard. "I wished I'd known how much my stories meant to people. Maybe I would have had a longer life. I'm just hoping now that you won't doubt that what you write has meaning . . . in ways none of us will ever know."

A wry, weak smile touched the corner of Edgar Allan Poe's mouth. "Doubt?" He shook his head. "Nevermore."

His soul dipped its oars into another old and familiar river. This time without dread.

Old Soldiers

Lawrence Watt-Evans

General George S. Patton looked out over his troops and smiled; they might not all be Americans, but they were a pretty good bunch, all the same—even the crazy Romans and Syrians. He'd picked the right place to stop.

When he'd first woken up back there, a couple of hundred miles upstream, surrounded by all those damn Germans and those Asiatics, whatever they were, there were so many Nazis and ex-Nazis that he'd thought he was in Hell. He'd helped get everyone organized, but then he'd looked around at them, at all those people who'd died about the same time and place he did, in the ruins of Hitler's Reich, and he'd realized that any minute they might notice that General George S. Patton, Jr., commander of the U.S. Third Army and high muckety-muck in the Allied army of occupation, no longer had an army backing him up.

And while he might have been the meanest son of a bitch there—or he might not, despite his reputation—there was only one of him, and a few dozen of them. The Asiatics didn't count, since none of them spoke a word of English, German, Latin, or any other language either he or the Germans recognized; it was between him and the Krauts.

So he'd announced that he was going to do a little scouting, and he'd headed downstream, grail in hand, and kept on going, looking for a better place.

When he'd finally found a group that spoke English they were Americans, all right, but from the future, the early 1980s, and they'd looked like a bunch of pansies. They were being bossed around by first-century Syrians, and he'd wondered how Americans—*Americans*—could do that. He'd thought about starting a rebellion.

Then he'd found out who the Syrian leader was.

He'd still insisted on some changes, and the Americans had backed him up, and here he was. They'd looked like pansies—but now, as he considered the army he commanded, he was well pleased with them. They'd turned out okay.

They were looking up at him, waiting. He spoke.

"Some of you may see me standing up here like a big shot, and you'll be thinking, Why should I get myself killed for him, or for the Emperor?" He paused dramatically, then shouted, "Well, you *shouldn't*! The Emperor and I don't *want* you to get killed, for us or anyone else. Nobody ever won a war by dying. You win a war by making the sons of bitches on the *other* side die."

A few men smiled at that, but most were too tense; they still just stared at him.

"Some of you may be thinking, Hey, if I get killed, it's no big deal—I'll just wake up somewhere else," Patton continued. "And if you're thinking like that, then you *will* get killed, because you won't be out there fighting as hard as you can, and you won't see the spear or club coming until it's too late. So what, you ask."

He stepped forward, to the edge of the platform, and shouted at them, "*I'll* tell you so what! You've got it good here, boys! I've seen what's upstream from here. You take a ride on the Dead Man's Highway, and you could wind up fuckin' *anywhere* on this whole goddamned River! You could wind up a grail slave to some bunch even worse than the ones we're fighting; you could be a prisoner of cavemen who cut off your legs so you can't run, you could be skinned alive just for fun by some barbarian pervert . . . You've got it good, I tell you! Nova Roma may not be the best damned country on the whole goddamn River, but it's the best *I've* seen in the fifteen years since we all woke up here bareass naked—it'd *have* to be, or I wouldn't have signed up here, and I wouldn't be ready to lead a bunch of good American boys into a fight like this. It's good enough that those bastards on the other side of the wall want to take it away from us, and it's up to us to make damn sure they can't do it! So when you go out there tomorrow, you won't just be fighting for me, or for the Emperor, you'll be fighting for a good life for *yourselves*!''

That got a cheer.

"So all of you get out there and do your damnedest to *get* those bastards, and to *not* die for your country!''

The cheer was a bit bigger and better this time, and Patton waved to the crowd. Soldiers shouted, waving their spears; Patton stepped back, smiling and waving, and then climbed down from the platform.

A messenger was waiting, bearing the white baton that meant she was on official business.

"What is it?'' Patton demanded. He still spoke English, from long habit.

"The Emperor wishes to see you, General,'' the messenger said in the same language, saluting.

"What, *now*?''

"Yes, sir.''

"Why?''

"I don't know, sir; perhaps he wishes to review the battle plans.''

"Shit,'' Patton said. "We went over all that.''

"I've delivered my message, General; what reply should I take back to the Emperor?''

Patton considered that for about three seconds, then shrugged and said, "What the hell, I'll come with you.''

Twenty minutes later the messenger scratched at the door-flap of a dragonskin pavilion as the guards on either side saluted Patton; the Emperor's voice called, "Enter.''

The messenger slipped aside, and Patton stepped into the tent.

"*Ave, Caesar Imperator,*'' he said, making a gesture with one hand that was a peculiar compromise between the sort of salute he had used back on Earth, and the old Roman one that prevailed here. He didn't shout the greeting the way a proper Roman was supposed to, but he didn't give a shit about that; he wasn't a proper Roman, he was an American, and the number-two man here.

"Hello, George," Germanicus Caesar, Emperor of Nova Roma, said, in English, from behind his desk. "Your pronunciation is lousy."

"Yeah, well..." Patton wasn't in the mood to continue the old argument just now—not when he should be getting ready to lead his men into battle. For over a decade the Emperor had been complaining about his pronunciation whenever he said so much as a word in Latin; Patton retaliated by correcting Germanicus's grammar. Germanicus might have been the heir to the throne, but he still spoke like a soldier; Patton might have been a soldier, but he'd learned his Latin from schoolbooks that had taught the formal speech of Cicero, and his teachers had had no tolerance for popular usage.

The schoolbooks, unfortunately, were for a dead language, so Patton's accent was abominable; Germanicus said he made Latin sound like dogs barking.

And since more than half the local population was twentieth-century American, Patton didn't really give a damn if his Latin stank; everyone here spoke either English or that silly Esperanto stuff that had a grammar even more degenerate than the Emperor's soldier Latin.

Germanicus rather liked Esperanto; Patton hated it.

"What was it you wanted, Manny?" Patton asked, in English.

"Close the flap and sit down," Germanicus said, indicating a folding camp stool.

Patton obeyed.

"Have a drink."

Patton hesitated, then accepted a wooden mug of bourbon.

"We have an embassy from the Five Scholars," Germanicus told him. "They came up the River a few hours ago."

Patton snorted. "It's a little late for that, isn't it?"

"Maybe not," Germanicus answered. "They want to surrender."

"Oh, for God's sake..." For a moment, Patton was too angry and disgusted to speak. Germanicus sat and watched as his best general digested this unpleasant morsel, and then gulped bourbon.

"All right, Manny," Patton said at last, "I know we have to accept it, I suppose—but just for the sake of argument, tell me what would happen if we didn't, if we went ahead with the attack."

"Many good men would be killed, for one thing," Germanicus answered. "You might be one of them."

"And I'd wake up a million miles downstream as good as new," Patton said, holding out his mug for a refill. Germanicus obliged, and picked up a mug of his own.

"That might be your best choice if the men found out you'd refused a surrender," he said. "Soldiers don't like fighting for nothing. Especially your Americans."

"They aren't *my* Americans, they're . . ." He stopped. Forty years wasn't that big a difference. He changed the subject and asked, "Would the Scholars fight?"

Germanicus made the open-handed gesture that was the Roman equivalent of a shrug. "They say they wouldn't—that they'd take poison and blow up their capital rather than suffer the ignominy of utter defeat."

"You believe them?"

"Not necessarily. I don't know what they'd do."

"You think the surrender's genuine?"

Germanicus sighed. "I do," he said.

"So what are the terms?"

"About what you'd expect—we can annex the Lands of the Five Scholars, the slaves will be ours to free if we choose. . . ." He paused questioningly.

"We free them," Patton said. "You know how I feel about that, Manny."

Germanicus nodded and drank. "No reparations, no war-crimes trials, no torture; all the Scholars to have the option of exile. Nothing fancy; they know they're beaten and just want to save their skins."

"We wouldn't torture them anyway," Patton pointed out.

"They don't know that—and besides, their own people might, if we let them."

Patton drank, then asked, "What did you tell the ambassadors?"

"That I'd give them a decision by morning."

Patton sighed. "So I suppose I'm commanding a goddamn army of occupation." He sipped bourbon, then added, "Again."

"So it seems, George."

"Another goddamn tease." He tossed off the rest of the bourbon and held the mug out for a refill. Germanicus obliged.

For a moment, the two men sat in silent thought; then Patton asked, "Are you satisfied with this, Manny?"

"With what?" Germanicus asked. "The surrender, or life in general?"

"With everything."

Germanicus didn't have to think about that. "I'm not," he said.

"Me neither," Patton said.

After a few more seconds of silence, he added, "Seems like we *ought* to be, though. I mean, we've got everything we need." He waved at the Emperor's grail. "It's just given to us, three times a day."

"It's not what we *want*, though," Germanicus said.

"No, it's not," Patton agreed, slumping back against one of the poles supporting the pavilion. Then he looked up. "So what do you want that you ain't got, Manny?"

"Roma," Germanicus answered immediately. "The *real* Roma. The one my uncle and that son of a bitch Piso cheated me out of when they got my wife to poison me."

Patton nodded.

"At least you got to build an empire here, though," he said.

"If you can call a thousand stadia of riverbanks and grailstones and huts, where I have to answer to an elected senate, an empire," Germanicus replied. "What kind of empire is less than a hundred stadia wide?"

"Better than *I* ever got," Patton muttered.

"What about you?" Germanicus asked. "What do you want?"

"What *I* want," Patton said, "is a real goddamn war. One that accomplishes something."

"We're accomplishing something. We're expanding the empire."

"Oh, yeah, but that's not what I mean. Sure, we free people, help them live a pretty good life—though it's not as if

we have much to do with that, since the grails provide everything we really need. But we're never going to free everybody,
because this damn River's just too long, and there's no way to
run a really *big* empire here, and while it was a challenge at
first, now we're big enough that nobody will mess with us—we
show up on the doorstep, and anyone who's got a worse
government than ours just surrenders to avoid getting slaughtered."
He snorted. "Either that, or they get slaughtered. Not because
we're so goddamned brilliant, but just because we outnumber
them a dozen to one."

Germanicus considered that. "This is only a suggestion," he
said at last, "and one I hope you won't consider, but maybe
you should sail on downstream and start over somewhere, if
you want a war that's not a sure thing."

Patton growled. "It's not that the wars are all guaranteed
wins—I mean, not *just* that—it's that they're so limited. I want
one where I can do something *new*. One where the enemy puts
up a real fight, yeah, but also one where I'm not limited to a
goddamn ten-mile front with that fucking River in the middle."
He emptied his mug again. "There isn't anything you can *do*
with this terrain," he complained. "And the men . . . well, the
men are okay, but there's no armor, no artillery, no goddamn
horses for calvary, the best we can do is those stupid wagons
and the grenadiers, and everyone else is just out there with
spears and axes, we haven't got any goddamn metals—what
kind of war is that?"

"A simple one," Germanicus said. "At least you've got
grenades, though—I didn't have those when I went up against
Arminio."

"Arminius," Patton corrected him absently. "And you had
forests and plains, you could move around, you could outflank—
it's like fighting in a goddamn garden hose here."

"We called him Arminio," Germanicus insisted. "I wonder
where he wound up."

Patton shrugged. "He probably wouldn't put up any better a
fight than these damn Chinese, or any of the others we've
whipped."

"Oh, I don't know—he was a fighter, Arminio was, not just
a slave-driver. You're a bit like him."

Patton grunted. Both men were feeling their liquor, and in Patton's case that meant growing less articulate. "I wish he were running the next country upstream—maybe he'd give us a real fight."

"Well, at least he wouldn't surrender as soon as he hears your name, the way that bastard Waldheim did."

"It wasn't my goddamn *name*," Patton said. "It was realizing he was outnumbered and outgunned, and that we weren't going to just roll over and die. And that half his men would've deserted and come over to our side. We've made life too easy here, Manny."

"Whatever it was, I have to listen to him in the Senate now. I wish he'd fought so we could have killed him. Or that I was really an emperor and didn't have to pay any attention to the Senate."

Patton nodded. "So you're pissed off because you didn't get to be Emperor," he said.

"And that lunatic son of mine *did*," Germanicus reminded him. "Emperor Bootsie. I wish we'd never called him that. And I thought old Uncle Tiberius gave the family a bad name—my own son made him look like the perfect example of traditional virtue!"

"You weren't there to pound sense into him."

"I'd have made a better emperor, that's certain!"

"And I might've made a good president, if my damn jeep hadn't turned over."

"If you'd been elected. At least I didn't have to worry about that." Germanicus grimaced. "I do *now*, thanks to all your countrymen, but I didn't in Rome."

"Big deal," Patton said. "Nobody's had the nerve to run against you yet, not seriously."

"Not yet," Germanicus replied gloomily. "I think Waldheim's working up to it."

Patton smiled drunkenly. "Maybe *I* should run against you," he said.

"Oh, shit, George, that's all I need!" Germanicus said. "What a way to ruin a friendship. Besides, I thought you wanted a real *fight*, not a lot of oratory."

"Then maybe I should challenge you to a duel," Patton

suggested. "The two of us fight it out with spear and shield, winner gets the empire."

"It'd probably turn into a civil war," Germanicus answered.

"Well, hell, what if it did?" Patton roused himself further. "Maybe that's just what we need!"

Germanicus stirred, considered, then shook his head. "No, George. Most of the people of Nova Roma don't want any trouble; if we try to stage a war they'll just remove *us*. Maggie isn't Plancina, but she'd probably be just as willing to poison me if I did anything like that. And when we were gone they'd probably elect Waldheim."

"Yeah, you're right," Patton admitted, sinking back.

"I'm sorry for you, George—you're as much a fighter as Flamma was."

Patton blinked blearily. "Who?"

"Flamma," Germanicus replied. "He was a *gladiator*." He pronounced the word in Latin, rather than English. "He was offered his freedom and retirement from the arena four times, turned it down every time."

"Gladiator," Patton said thoughtfully, using the English pronunciation.

"*Gladiator*," Germanicus repeated in Latin. "You know the word, don't you?"

"Of *course* I know the goddamn word, Manny!" Patton sat up. "It's the same in English as in Latin. I was just *thinking* about it."

"What is there to think about?"

"Well, for one thing," Patton said, carefully putting his empty mug on the emperor's desk, "why don't we have any?"

Germanicus frowned at him. "Because we don't have any slaves, George—you and all your fellow Americans saw to that."

"But, Manny," Patton said, "we don't *need* slaves, not here! Leaving out the crazies like Flamma, free men didn't want to be gladiators because they'd get killed. But this is the Riverworld—you die here, you pop back up somewhere else. Getting killed isn't a problem. Hell, this place could be fuckin' Valhalla—fight all day, and if you get killed, so what, you're back the next morning!"

"Somewhere else."

"So, the losers lose something."

"If we use volunteers, we'll use them all up pretty quickly."

"We'll put word out, all up and down the River. Anyone who wants a fight, here's the place to come."

Germanicus considered.

Finally, he said, "I have to settle the surrender terms, and you have an occupation to oversee; this can wait. But I *do* miss the Games. It wouldn't be Roma, but maybe . . ."

Building the arena went much faster than Germanicus had expected; apparently a good many of the citizens of Nova Roma were just as bored as Patton and himself. The inaugural games—which opened with a football match—took place a mere five months after the Lands of the Five Scholars surrendered and added several thousand people, mostly Ming Dynasty Chinese, to the empire.

After the football game (Red beat Green, 28–7) came the gladiatorial bouts, and Germanicus almost wept at the familiar spectacle. The weapons were stone and wood, rather than iron, but everything else was just as he remembered it.

Well—almost everything else; thanks to the Americans, the Nova Romans had the signals wrong, and insisted on using their silly thumbs-up, thumbs-down signs.

But it was close enough.

And there was George Patton, his stone-edged sword in his hand, facing off against a huge African with braided-grass net and bamboo trident; typical, that Patton had taken the role of secutor, the so-called "pursuer," when it was the retiarius, the net-man, who had the advantage.

Germanicus watched with interest—and then with dismay.

Patton had overestimated himself.

The African had him down in a matter of minutes, and should have looked to the imperial box for the signal—but he was new at this, they all were, and he was excited; he put the trident through Patton's throat.

Then he remembered to look, rather sheepishly, at the emperor.

*   *   *

Patton blinked, and sat up.

His grail was beside him, along with a stack of cloths, and the morning sun was spilling over the mountaintops.

He had died, obviously—but still, it had been . . . He groped for the right word.

"Good morning," someone said, in Esperanto.

Patton looked up, and found a welcoming committee of three men and a woman, one man Nordic, the others Asian in appearance. "You are in a land we call Shamballo," the Nordic said. "You need have no fear; we are peaceful here, and keep no slaves."

That was fortunate. "I'm glad to hear it," Patton said. He got to his feet and looked around, at the trees, the damnably familiar River, the grailstones.

Fun, that was the word—even though he'd gotten himself killed, it had been fun.

He hadn't had much fun since the Nazis surrendered.

He remembered how he'd always been taught that the noble Romans were partly beasts, that the arena games demonstrated as much. Maybe they were. Maybe *he* was a beast, fighting like that—but it had been fun, and it hadn't done any real harm. He'd lost Nova Roma, but still, here he was, alive and well.

This *was* Valhalla. He'd fought and died, just for fun, and been raised anew.

And he wanted to do it again.

"So," he said, getting to his feet, "what do you folks do for fun around here?"

Legends

Esther M. Friesner

The Lady of Colchis strode the length of the eastern battlement
and back, her gray eyes taking in every detail of the troops
massed on the riparian plain below. She folded her arms
beneath the weight of a cloak and stroked the copper serpent
bracelets entwining just above her elbows. The touch of their
gemmed eyes to her fingertips was strangely soothing. Each
facet, each tie taken from the stone, added to the sparkle of the
garnet, but did not—could not—truly diminish it.

I am the stone and the serpent, she thought. *I am the River
and the unseen sea.*

"Lady?" A deep voice, familiar, long held in secret contempt, woke her from her dabblings in philosophy. She whirled
around to face the towering warrior. The cloak, his gift,
impeded the smooth grace of her movements. It dragged at her,
held her back, like tiny hands clinging to the folds of a skirt
before—

"They have sent an envoy, Lady," the warrior said. He was
all deference. The armed men at his back who called him *sidi*,
Cid, lord, would never be able to say truthfully that Rodrigo
Diaz de Vivar was ever anything less than completely respect-
ful to the Lady of Colchis.

Knowing the hidden face of the truth, she wanted to laugh.
The truth was far from funny, yet in her breast was the hot,
swelling feeling that if she did not laugh, she would burst into
tears of fire.

"An envoy," she repeated. "They trust me that much?" Her

lip curled. "Aren't they afraid I'll serve their man as I served them, or the Theban bitch, or my brother?"

Rodrigo was a waste of irony. Plain-spoken, that was what he prided himself on bring: straightforward, honest, above the glib weaselings of courtiers who never held a sword's hilt or shed good hot blood. yet for the Lady to tell him the truth—that he was the worst sort of snob when most he scorned others for their snobbery—was to court a plain, straightforward, honest beating.

Now he simply shrugged and said, "This envoy is a woman."

The Lady of Colchis could not keep the look of surprise from flooding her face. Her slanting eyes flew wide open, her carefully plucked and penciled brows took wing.

"They send me one of their whores? I'll send her back in pieces!"

Rodrigo shook his heavy head. He brought to mind her father's boar hounds: thick-barreled, shaggy, murderous. "I doubt this is any sample of their camp whores. See for yourself. I have instructed her to wait for you in the great hall."

The Lady of Colchis inclined her head, acknowledging his words. Grape-black curls brushed her cheeks, set her flesh atingle. How long since she had known the last caress of such delicacy? Rodrigo's hands were blunt and hard as his manner. Rodrigo's time on the field of battle, in the service of his latest cause, was too valuable to waste on the nicer preliminaries of lovemaking. As she turned from him to seek out this strange ambassador she thought she heard the wild wind roar past her ears bearing his words: *I am a knight of Castilla. My life I live to serve.*

As the bull serves the cow, she thought. *Brisk, all business, sated, done.*

And she dreamed of other hands, hands that played a trill of golden notes from the taut strings of her body, hands that lingered, hands that led lips on to sweeter ventures lips that would not cease their tender explorations until she heard her own voice crying out to let her die, die now so drenched in pleasure that she was no longer Colchis' Lady but the slave of lips and hands and—

Treacherous hands. Betraying lips. Her own body turning traitor in service to those lips, those hands of his. Her body in turn betraying her mind, her heart, her very soul, until he had remade her in the image of his own unending treacheries.

Jason, my Judas.

The Lady smiled at her Castillian knight Rodrigo, guarding her thoughts. If he could read them, he would beat her again. Another time, not so long past, she had been fool enough to speak her mind straight out to the blunt-faced, blunt-mannered Castillian. Her words carried a hint of ironic humor touching on the virgin goddess he adored. She saw no harm in it. Mortals could not touch the gods in glory, so what harm lay in a jest at their expense? He disagreed. Since then she had become extremely careful to learn the names of all the gods Rodrigo worshiped, so that she would never misspeak herself again.

Not for the time being, in any case.

"Will you accompany me to the hall, *mio Cid*?" she asked, giving him her most dazzling glance, dark and liquid as the midnight sea. Using his old title was one of her lesser bits of calculated flattery.

"Our fighters are all within the castle precincts for the night. Now I must see to the sentries." He turned without further ceremony, leaving her to breathe cleaner air.

The way to the great hall from the battlements was long and winding, down twisting stairwells of stone streaked black and greasy with the smoke of torches. Here and there the way widened, giving on a niche where a weary archer crouched, eye to the slit in the stone, awaiting orders or any movement from the army on the plain. If she paused and placed her palms to the rockface, she could feel the castle hum beneath her hands like a hive of bees.

In the great hall, the hearth was laid with a blaze that drove the lingering chill from the high vaulted room. Still, the Lady of Colchis shrugged her cloak a little closer around her shoulders. Tapestries of her own weaving competed with those that were the work of grail slaves to banish the frosts that only she seemed to feel. None sufficed. If she ever died, she would die cold.

In a black oak chair with expertly caved lions holding up the arms, a woman sat and stared into the fire: the envoy. Sent for whatever unknown purpose by the besieging army outside, she carried a strange aura of tranquility along with her still-unknown message. At a time when the tension of battles past and battles sure to come infected everyone, from lowest grail slave to the most high within the castle walls, this newcomer seemed to have been born nerveless. She did not even know when another person had come into the room, though the Lady's booted footsteps on the flat stone floor echoed to the rafters.

The Lady of Colchis took the other woman's measure as she sat there, unaware she was no longer alone. Well, Rodrigo still had not lied. This was no camp whore. This creature hardly looked possessed of brains enough to spread her legs, if any man might want what lay between them.

She looks into the fire, but not as I do, the Lady thought. *Not many have the power to read the message of the flames, but nearly all possess the desire. She lacks even that. She seeks nothing in the dancing sparks—no hint of the future, no fantasy of the present. Those flat blue eyes of hers are almost as pale as a mirror of ice. All she sees is burning wood.*

Aloud, the Lady said, "Be welcome."

The envoy jerked her head up, startled. She stood, hands busy strangling each other in a nervous gesture, then spread the skirts of her ugly brown dress and sank into a clumsy curtsy. "Your Majesty," she said, bowing a head topped with a wispy knot of faded auburn hair.

The Lady laughed, meaning to set this poor awkward thing at ease. It was simply courtesy to a guest—for she saw at once that she had nothing to fear from the creature, and so might pass the bread and salt without a qualm.

"You are mistaken," she said, "I am no queen. I am called the Lady of Colchis."

"Medea." The name snapped out of the other woman's mouth like a lizard's tongue darting to snare a fat fly. Not bothering to rise from her obeisance, she added, "You cut up your brother to help Jason steal the fleece. You chopped him into little pieces and dropped them over the stern of the *Argo* so your father would have to stop to gather them up for burial, and you and Jason could get away.''

The Lady gasped as if her caller had reached up out of that preposterous curtsy and slapped her hard across the face. And yet there was no more meaning of malice or accusation in what the woman said than there was purpose to her fire-gazing. The Lady's soul trembled: she had never met a person who was all surface.

''So you know the legend,'' was all the Lady replied.

''Legend?'' For an instant the pale eyes flickered with interest. For an instant only.

''I doubt you'd have heard the truth of my doings, given where you come from.'' The Lady tried to sound jovial, as if humor might draw a measure of warmth from dead coals. ''You know as well as I that if I were merely a creature of legend, I would not be here now, speaking with you. Legends sleep on forever in books; only the once-living are . . . privileged to taste breath again in this world.''

''Oh.'' Nothing, not even a smile. ''I suppose.''

''Please rise,'' she said, forcing her voice to remain deep and level. The other woman obeyed. ''You have a message for me, I think?''

''Yes. From your sons. They say—''

''Wait.'' She did not want to hear a message from her sons. Not ever. Certainly not yet. ''First let me welcome you properly. I am no queen, but I am a king's daughter. I will have something brought to refresh you.''

Medea motioned to her guest to resume her seat in the lion chair. For herself she took a bench beside the fire. Slaves came when she clapped her hands. They did not come too quickly, but since the siege she had grown used to having to make do with fewer attendants. It was hardly worth the effort of beating the lazy ones anymore. Something seemed to have put her off beatings.

''Bring us the welcome offering,'' she directed the two thin, ivory-faced girls who answered her summons.

''Tea?'' the envoy asked. ''Do you have tea? I don't drink wine. I don't like any of the wine I've had here.''

''Tea.'' The Lady nodded, approving her guest's demand

with a nod to the slaves. They scurried away in a rustle of skirts. Silence rushed in like the tide to fill the hall when they were gone.

The Lady felt the silence like a still-heavier cloak across her back. Her guest sat prim and stiff, those soft, white hands now folded in the lap of her high-necked gown. Her bright-eyed, shallow glance held the chill of meltwater from the mountains in spring. If either was to break the silence, it would not be that scarecrow of ice.

"So . . ." Medea felt her gracious smile grow achy from using it so much, with so little true cause. "You had no trouble passing our ranks to reach me?"

"No." Nothing more was offered. Were those the eyes of a hermit crab deep in the darkness of that shell, or of a snake?

"I am surprised," the Lady pursued. "You don't look much like a messenger."

"I was always taught that if you can do a thing, you do it." The woman's voice rose to the edge of shrillness. "I can carry messages. Why would I have to look any different than I do?"

Ah! Was that a glimmer of wounded pride the Lady glimpsed behind the glassy eyes? Perhaps this thing was human after all.

"Forgive me." Medea's slanting glance offered apology and mockery at once. "When and where I was raised, the messengers who passed through battle lines were always men, sometimes the enemy's official heralds, always armored. Even if the fighters who serve me here and now come from other times and places, they still share this much: they expect an envoy to look the part."

"I carried a letter," the woman replied simply. She shifted a little and dug into one pocket of the ugly brown dress to tug out a much-folded piece of paper.

The Lady took it from her hand reluctantly. It was written by the hand of her elder son, Aeson, named for his paternal grandfather. It instructed the reader to abide by the honor of war to let this woman, his respected nurse, the Lady Issa, pass.

"Lady Issa," Medea repeated aloud. For a miracle, the other woman giggled, a stilted, brittle sound.

"That's what they called me. Not the 'Lady' part, at first, of course. When I found them, they were too young to be able to pronounce my name any better than that, and what do names matter here? They were children, just hungry children. I took care of them, and they grew. That's all."

"That . . . and this war." She handed back the letter. "So you were their nurse. How did that come to be?"

The woman shrugged her plump, slightly rounded shoulders. "I found them, they found me."

"You're fond of children."

Another shrug. "I don't dislike them. I don't think much about them one way or another, to tell you the truth."

"Did you ever have any of your own?"

"I never married."

"Yes, but—" The Lady of Colchis stopped herself. Here was territory where she must tread gently. In the honorable Rodrigo's keep she had met too many souls who shared their master's peculiar chimera of morality. For having given him her body and not her pledge she was somehow lessened before such men; and women. Not that Rodrigo had ever asked for any word of marriage. On the contrary, he gave her to know that if ever he had the luck to find his true wife Ximena again, things would change. Oh, Medea might still occupy his bed at his pleasure, but she must come and go from such service privily, keeping it secret even from the grail slaves. His chamber pot could be emptied with more fanfare.

It would be Thebes all over again, she thought bitterly. Only there no one had looked down upon her for having bedded Jason and borne his children with no wedding ceremony. When her lover leaped at the chance to marry the princess-bitch, Creusa, Medea would have lost no rank, no honor. Indeed, the three of them might have lived on amicably together, if not for the bitch's father.

That old fool Kreon! He feared my sons might usurp the fortunes of his daughter's whelps yet unborn. That was why he came at me with threats of exile. Well, I gave his fears a rest, didn't I? I did leave, as he demanded. More, before I left I made sure that no threat from my babies would ever touch his grandchildren. Her smile never reached her eyes. *If grandchildren could ever be born from a dead daughter's womb.*

Medea turned that false smile full upon her guest. Let mask

meet mask, she thought. "Well, Lady Issa, I should thank you for having brought them up so well. They have become leaders of men, I see, and able warriors."

"You are—glad of that?" The slightest degree of uncertainty made her words falter.

"I'm not glad of the war they've mounted against us—against me—if that's what you want to know. I'm not mad." Medea had studied her own image in the glass often enough to knew how her teeth dazzled, how her practiced airs had the power to charm and disarm. *What petty witchcrafts! And yet they are all I truly master. I could almost weep.* "The important thing is that they have grown up to be fighters. We always valued such at Colchis."

"This isn't Colchis," the woman replied in a voice too expressionless to register a care if this were hell. "It's all changed."

"Perhaps. But we shall manage to cling to what we hope will never change."

"Oh, everything changes here." The Lady Issa lacked all trace of a real philosopher's fire. No matter how her hostess might taken her remarks, it was fairly plain that she was only making idle chat.

"If you will." It was Medea's turn to shrug. "At least that thought gives me some hope."

"Hope?" It was a polite remark, no more than that.

Is there nothing on this world or beyond it, alive or dead, that can strike some spark of caring, of passion from this creature? Medea wondered. She recalled her king-father's champion—the one whom Jason had fought and vanquished in single combat, the one who later grew in legend into the unnumbered bronze-armored ranks of warriors sown from dragon's teeth. That man's whole life had been given over to serving her father until all trace of human feeling save battle-love was erased from his soul, his heart, his eyes.

I think I have finally found you your proper bride, Hydra, Medea thought.

"Yes," she said, still smiling. "Hope for change. This message you bring me from my sons—"

"You hope they've forgiven you." The woman's dead eyes turned again toward the fire.

"That would be a . . . comfort."

"You mean a relief." The words were tossed in among the flames. "It would be the end of this siege, the end of all the killing, all the blood—"

"*Is* that it?" Medea demanded, leaning forward suddenly in her chair, a raptor tensed to leap and grasp its prey. "Is that their message to me? That the siege is to end? That it's all over?"

The woman called Issa only said, "I suppose that will be for you to decide."

The Lady of Colchis sat back as if shoved by a giant hand. Bewildered, she asked, "What do you mean?"

"I am just their chore girl, these days." She said it without rancor, without any inflection of feeling at all. "I can't pretend to understand what they mean by their message. I told them when they charged me with delivering it to you, 'What sense can she possibly make of this?' They waved me away, saying, 'Oh, she'll know.' Now can I give you their words? The boys wouldn't write them down, and I'm afraid that if I go much longer without telling you, I might forget. I've memorized them, but they don't make sense to me, either. I thought they would at least do me the courtesy of explaining, but . . ."

"Tell me." Medea's fingers dug into the polished wood of the bench.

"They said, 'Tell Mother that if she ever could weave fire into wool, come now.' "

"Fire . . . into wool." The Lady of Colchis felt her lips go dry and crisp as paper, or as flesh burned off the bone. The other woman did not offer to repeat the message, nor was she asked.

The slaves returned with tea and cakes. The Lady of Colchis served her guest with her own hands, although her mind was far and far away. She noted with a slight shudder of distaste how Issa's bland expression finally kindled into lust at the sight of food. The red-haired woman crammed her mouth with sweet things as if she had no hope of eating ever again.

For herself, Medea took only a sparing portion. Pale-eyed

Issa's message had left her with no appetite. Besides, if she did not eat now, no matter; she would have ample opportunity later. There was no need to fret over foodstuffs so long as Rodrigo warded the castle's pooled grails. In this as in all matters touching war, he was an able administrator.

The Lady of Colchis' thoughts were not on food; not exactly. *Why do my sons besiege us, knowing as they must that we'll never lack for food so long as we have the grails? Oh yes, they can kill our men in open battle—and they have—but we can wait as long as they can otherwise. Why have they chosen this means of attack, turning aside from all others? There are some beings on this world whose knowledge of war goes so far beyond* . . .

She sighed, then shuddered. Who could say why they acted as they did? They were her children, born of her body, blessed or cursed with her subtle blood. For nine months she had been their world, for years after they had been hers. Even Jason had come a poor second to the love she felt for them. In the hour of the knife, it was that same all-devouring love that had wrapped her in its wings of madness and fire, driving her on to make the needed sacrifice. She would have been willing to swear before all gods that when the knife fell across their throats, her sons had silently offered her forgiveness, understanding. Why couldn't she understand them now?

Issa gobbled loudly, but she sipped her tea with inordinate delicacy. It was amusing even to the Lady, who had had so precious little to amuse her of late. She recalled a puppy she had once known back in Colchis, a whelp sired by her father's favorite boar hound: a cuckoo. The pudgy little thing grew up seemingly ignorant or indifferent to its purpose in life—to hunt, to rend, to die impaled on the boar's bloodied tusks. It preferred to shamble about through the women's quarters, earnestly imploring the attentions and caresses of the light-witted girls. It lived to make them laugh, and through laughter to find a few moments' forgetfulness.

Can you make me forget, Issa? Medea thought, watching the woman swill and sip, sip and swill. *Can your unconscious buffooneries make me forget how powerless I truly am? I, the black Colchian witch, powerless! Oh, there's a joke I've made myself. Why can't it let me laugh?*

The misfit boarhound was dead. One day he'd lingered too long with one of the king's favorite slave girls. The girl was kneeling on the floor, petting the beast, when Aeetes appeared, commanding her to rise and follow him to his bed. The dog uttered one of his halfhearted growls—he didn't want that delicious scratching behind his ears to stop—and took a few shambling steps after the king. Medea's father stepped forward to meet him, bronze-bladed dagger drawn. He clamped one hand around the dog's muzzle, jerked the beast's head up and cut his throat with one stroke. The dog turned piteous eyes up to his master and died with his own blood matting down the brindled fur of his breast and sides. When the slave girl gave a little cry of horror and compassion, Aeetes slapped her.

"Never worth much in the chase; small loss," he said, and yanked the girl's hair to reclaim her attention.

Medea watched it all. A child, she sat at a child's loom in the women's quarters and learned more than just the workings of wool. Her nurse, her teacher, was a Scythian. Some said the Scythian women were witches, every one.

But if she were any sort of witch, would she have been our slave?

And then: *They call me witch, too.*

There was the joke, a black joke that demanded blacker laughter. If Issa's message did truly mean what Medea imagined, soon she would have little time for any laughter at all.

The tea was gone, the cakes were demolished. The Lady of Colchis observed her guest lapping up the last crumbs from around her lips, then dabbing them primly with a cloth napkin. "I am glad to see you enjoyed our humble refreshments so much, Lady Issa," Medea said.

"I've always had a sweet tooth," she admitted. "But please, I already told you, my name isn't Lady Issa."

"It is to my sons." She rose from her chair. "And if I am going to see them again after all this time, I think I'd do well to adapt myself to their customs."

"You're . . . coming back with me?" Issa blinked.

"That was the purpose of their message: a lure." She wanted

to add *Isn't it?* but knew she had no hope of getting a straight answer from this creature.

The other woman looked put out, the first time Medea had seen anything like temper touch those doughy features. "If that was all they wanted, they might have said so. It would have been an easier message to remember, for one thing. And there I was, so worried I'd forget a word, or say a word wrong when for all I knew every syllable of their message was in some sort of—Oh, I don't know!—some silly secret code they still remembered from when they were little and you—" She paused, realizing perhaps that she had now said a word too many rather than too few.

"When I killed them?" the Lady provided.

Issa remained silent.

"What are you afraid of?" the Lady pressed. "It's the truth. Didn't they tell you the whole story?"

"Not at first." Issa gave up the words grudgingly, like one who dislikes divulging secrets; even secrets already known.

"Well, at last, then. But they must have told you sometime. Or if not, you couldn't help but know. I've learned, since my awakening, that the whole ugly story has passed into legend." Her laughter was more hollow than its own echo. "When I first accepted this . . . *blessing* of new life, I had the foolishness to imagine it was to be a second chance in all respects. What an infant I was! As soon as I knew myself—realized this was truly *me* again—she thumped her fists hard against her bosom "—*me*, in the flesh, and not some wandering ghost—I tried to gather all the promises a gift like this must fulfill."

"Promises—" The other woman repeated the word as if she'd never heard it used except coupled with *broken*.

Medea's ears pricked, catching this most fleeting of clues. Her slanting eyes sparkled. "So the same happened to you . . . whoever you were."

"Are. I told you: nothing changes here."

"So I learned. Perhaps it would have been better if we'd been reborn without knowing anything, not even our own names. But it seems as if the gods of all worlds are cruel. When I met others, freshly awakened like myself, and told them who I was, they refused to believe me. *Medea is as legendary as the unicorn!* they cried. So next I bent all my powers of persuasion to making them see that even legends must have some hook sunk in reality." Her mouth twisted in a wry expression. "I can be very persuasive."

"You wanted them to know who you really were?" Issa's cold eyes remained empty. "You must have known how they would react if you did convince them."

"Horror," Medea agreed. "Revulsion. Disgust. You might have heard the tales the Argives told of their sky-gods. It's only a father's privilege to destroy his children on a whim. My act was no whim, but try telling that to them!"

"But if you knew how they'd treat you if they believed, why did you persist?"

The Lady of Colchis could not help but let some measure of pity into the look she gave this plain, dull creature. "Because the legend I've become has more substance than the woman I was. It is the way of nature to let only the strongest live."

Issa's pudgy hands began to work themselves violently around a lump of invisible soap. "A legend . . ." Her smooth white brow furrowed as if with pain.

"Are you well?" Medea inquired. "Perhaps the food didn't agree with you. I have some herbal remedies—"

"No, no."

"Ah. I see." *So you've heard all the legend: How I used a false promise of rejuvenation to trick the daughters of Pelias into slaughtering their father; how I almost succeeded in poisoning Theseus, Aegeus' son. And if I had so many of the dark arts at my fingertips, did you never think to ask why Jason never found his fate at the bottom of a wine cup? Why it was my babies who had to pay the price for his whoremaster's eyes?*

Issa stood up. "Really, no thank you, I'm better now. I can take you to them, if you like."

Medea made a little bow that was half mockery. "By all means."

The slaves brought the woman's cloak. It was not so thick and heavy as Medea's, but it served its purpose. A guard conducted the two women to the great castle gate.

Rodrigo was waiting.

As I expected. The Lady of Colchis had to smile. *Predictable; supremely, stupidly predictable. I don't need to read the future in his entrails—much as I'd enjoy it!—not when he offers it to me with his every act.*

Of course Rodrigo was there to intercept them; he had his spies everywhere. Her father had been much the same. Knowing that she lived with a man tensely vigilant to root out secrets, she saw to it that she kept none. There was no greater pleasure she could deprive him of than denying him the chance to catch her in treachery. To deprive him of any pleasure had become for her the greatest pleasure of all.

"Where do you think you are going, Lady?" he demanded.

"This is the Lady Issa, the nurse who raised my sons," she replied. "They sent her to us with a message." Of course, he knew all that already, and so she was punctilious about repeating it letter prefect now.

"What is this prattle of fire and wool?" he demanded when she had done.

Medea shrugged. "No prattle, but a taunt in my face. You know the story, my lord: Fire woven into wool was how I killed her once. I made a bride gift for her with my own hands, a glorious robe shot through with golden thread spun from the Fleece itself. But when she put it on, the gold became threads of undying fire. She died in agony, burned to the bone alive."

The Lady of Colchis' lips curved up on one side. "Now my sons tell me she is back: Creusa."

"And what is that to you?" he asked. "You murdered her once. Do you think she will give you a second chance?"

"This world is built on second chances." The upturned corner of Medea's mouth twitched with dry mirth. "Perhaps it is past time to give her a chance to murder me."

His hand fell on her forearm like a judgment. "I hold this castle secure in your name, Lady. I serve only you by refusing to surrender. Your sons have no quarrel with me. I could have thrown you on their mercy long ago and saved the lives of many good soldiers. Will you now walk into their camp so easily, like a strayed sheep?" His grip tightened until she gritted her teeth together, refusing to let him see her pain. "I forbid it."

"No quarrel . . ." She turned her pain into laughter like the sound of shattering glass.

No quarrel! As Jason and his band of pirates had had no quarrel with her father, King Aeetes. The legend told of how it was a quest that brought the Argive ruffians to the Colchian lands—heroes all, kindred of the sky-gods every one. They sought the Golden Fleece, a talisman guarded by an unsleeping dragon. So the legend said.

Truth was often the greatest jest, bar none. The Fleece was in reality the sheepskin bags of gold dust sifted from Colchian streams, plundered by Jason and his horde from Aeetes' own palace. They had intended merely to scout the territory, to return with more ships, more swords if the land looked ripe enough.

Then she had seen him. The legend that it was Aphrodite's will, Eros' charmed arrow piercing her breast that made Medea fall so suddenly in love with the Thessalian freebooter. Well, let the legend call it by whatever name, the damage done was the same. Shameless as a bitch in heat, she sought him out, the golden-haired youth from the southern lands. Like him, she thought she would only scout the territory, creeping into the hall where he and his men slept. But as she stood over him, breathing the moonlight from his face, he woke and reached out his hand, and where he touched her left a spark of fire.

Creusa, forgive me; I learned the magic of undying flame from him.

She led him from the hall to her chamber. She led him from her bed to her father's treasury. Hydra stood watch, the king's champion. He heard the noise of their footfalls and couched his spear, ready. When she stepped out of the shadows and called his name softly, he relaxed. She engaged him in conversation, stealing the edge from his attentiveness just enough to cover the rumor of Jason's rapid step and spring. The Thessalian's bronze blade slashed clumsily across the champion's throat, but death gave no points for style. If one were as similarly blind to the niceties as was death, you could call that butchery a heroic, hand-to-hand single combat.

All that mattered to her was that Jason won. She looked down at Hydra as he lay in his own pooled blood, while her lover dragged the small, precious sacks of gold from the unwarded room. He had known her from a child, given her rides on his shoulders. (There was no love in his attentions to her—she had never entertained that illusion, even as a girl. He honored her father's blood in her, no more and no less.) She supposed that she ought to have felt something more than relief that he'd had the good grace to die quietly.

She had no quarrel with Hydra, just as Jason and his brigands had no quarrel with Aeetes. And had that prevented her from compacting in the champion's honorless death, in the sweet-tongued golden Thessalian's outright robbery of her father's hoard?

She often wondered if she would ever meet Hydra again, here, on this world of nightmares and miracles. *And if I do, whatever will I find to say to him?*

Her laughter filled the castle courtyard. Rodrigo's frosty eyes narrowed under beetling brows, weighing her sanity. "Our predicament amuses you?" His grip shifted to her wrist, his knuckles standing out white as she felt him grind the fragile bones together under his massive paw. Her laughter left her in a gasp. "Maybe I ought to let them have you. Maybe that is what I ought to have done from the first."

"Why didn't you?" It was a whisper forced out over the pain. His grip relented and she was free to chafe some feeling back into her flesh.

"I gave you my word as a knight and a man of honor." He spoke as if he believed all that, and she was hard-pressed to keep from laughing out loud again.

The Lady of Colchis gave her lord her most enthralling look. "My sons are also men of honor," she said. "In all the days of this siege, have they ever attempted to bring in the war machines that could level this castle around us?"

Grudgingly Rodrigo admitted she was right. "Still, what guarantee do you have they won't make you their hostage once they've got their hands on you?"

"A hostage? For what purpose? To take the castle?" She took care that her expression show only fondness for her lord, that there be no hint of condescension. "They only want the castle because it shelters me. If they do take me prisoner, their end's accomplished."

"And you will be dead."

Does he really care? she thought. *Or is this another show put on for the benefit of these soldiers, his witnesses? Or—*and she knew this to be the truth—*or does he only fear my death because he knows he cannot hold the castle without me?*

She remembered a time when the castle was hers alone; hers, held by right of wardship. Its true owner, its master builder, was long gone. Even his name was less than a whisper in her memory. She refused to think of it. She was happier so. Ever since Jason, she had never been capable of graciously accepting the fact that all her lovers, each and every one, always left her for a rival. Whether it was Jason's bitch-princess or Aegeus' bastard Theseus come home, Medea knew she invariably reacted . . . poorly.

This time her rival had been fairer than any woman, stronger than any son. This time her lover's new love could not be wrapped in burning wool or offered a poisoned cup. *How can you poison the River?* The River had claimed him—not with the final claim of death, perhaps, but with the more insidious siren song of exploration, adventure's promise, mystery's lure. *Water always sings to wanderers.* But before he departed, he left her the castle in trust and gave her the knowledge to keep it against a thousand Rodrigos.

And when Rodrigo came to our gates, with his army of ragged free-lances and hangers-on, I gave the castle to him—all except the knowledge of how to hold it without me. If they call me the Colchian witch, I might as well cling to this small measure of sorcery, eh? Oh, Medea, still with your taste for taking pirates to your bed! What was I thinking of? What is Rodrigo to me, truly; what have I made of him? A way to punish my wandering lover for having left me behind? A second Jason? A second chance?

A second chance.

"My lord," she said, putting on a face that gave away nothing. "Suppose I die. I might have died many times, before this. My sons' troops have weapons that don't discriminate one target from another. Arrows don't ask names. Do you think I never anticipated such an eventuality? I have provided for it, I assure you. To do otherwise—''

''—would violate the trust the castle's master placed in you. I know.'' Rodrigo made an automatic movement to stroke a beard no longer there. Medea idly asked herself whether that vanished crop of facial hair had improved his looks any, in the days when he'd had it.

So much I don't know about him, she thought. *So much I don't care to know. And yet we two are so much alike, in some ways. We are both chained to our legends.*

''Yes,'' she said smoothly. ''The master of this castle often told me how many stratagems he had to employ, how many sources of building materials he had to exhaust, how much plain hard labor he had to amass to erect such a structure.'' She glanced at the closed castle gate. The song of the River could still be heard even through the irontree wood. ''It would be wicked of me to throw all his labor away on a whim.''

''Then you see why I forbid you to go.'' He was rooted to his decision more stubbornly than Rivervalley grass. ''Even though you are the master of this stronghold, sometimes a good servant's duty is to compel his master to see his errors.''

She placed her hand in Rodrigo's, feeling the rough skin and dreaming, despite herself, that Jason's salt- and sun-toughened hands had never rasped her flesh so harshly. Still, she forced her lips into a tender smile.

''Once, Rodrigo—how long ago can't matter to us any more—once you served a better master than I. You served him faithfully, even when your enemies made him turn from you and banish you. I have heard from your men how your love for your master remained steadfast through all the years of your unjust exile.''

''The men who follow me here know too much of the legend and too little of me,'' Rodrigo said. ''I served my king Alfonso like any good knight. I took an oath to serve him. My first loyalty was to his brother Sancho, king of Castilla before him, dead by an assassin's hand.'' He gave her a look that left her uneasy. ''I knew that Alfonso was never entirely guiltless of his brother's blood, but there was no proof, and the realm needed a king. So I took my oath of loyalty to my new lord with all the rest of Castilla's knights. I kept my word. There was no love about it.''

No love. . . .

She felt her smile growing as stiff as dried honey. ''So we agree, you and I, that faith kept is better than love. I, too, gave my word. I promised to keep this castle secure, and so I shall.'' She stepped away from the gate, motioning for him to follow her.

Later, when the great gate of the castle had closed behind her, the Lady of Colchis settled Issa's light cloak around her shoulders and savored the breath of freedom. Ahead of her in the dusk lay the plain, and beyond that the tents of the enemy encampment where her sons awaited her.

Her sons . . . and one other.

Medea touched her bosom, where the dagger lay. It would be found, of course, and taken from her even before she set foot within her sons' tent. They would suspect something if she did not come bearing death.

Let them suspect, so long as they never know.

The dagger in her bosom was really a gift to her sons—such a fine steel blade, so rare! *After all, they've made me a gift of* her *blood for the second time,* she thought. *It's the least I can do by way of thanks.* The true death she carried lay elsewhere, in the slender wands holding up her hair. They were not sharp, no—such would surely be seen as weapons and taken from her—but the round, innocent-looking ornaments decorating the ends of the wands were in reality stoppers, and in the hollow heart of the wands . . .

Poison. How amazed she had been, a creature accused in legend of being mistress of a thousand venoms, to find herself on a world where none existed.

(Even the robe of wool and fire she had sent to Creusa was hardly that, when the legend was peeled away. She had gone to the bitch with her children's blood still on her hands, a madwoman to the eye of every sentry who feared the gods. Therefore she was holy. She spoke prophecy—or what she could make sound like lunatic visions—and they brought her to the princess because she made her rambling words just accessi-

ble enough for even the dullest guard to hear that she uttered
matters touching the future joy of their royal lady. And then,
while Creusa sat there with her cow's eyes fixed on the
northern madwoman, how simple to turn a trance-summoned
dance of insanity into the means of death!)

*All that I wove were patterns back and forth across the
bitch's chamber floor. All I did was dance, muttering things too
outlandish to be understood, but with the names of Creusa and
Jason spoken often enough so that the milk-fed fool didn't dare
order her guards to stop or silence me. The blood on my hands
was a good touch, too. I wonder if I thought of doing it or if
the faces of my slain babies really did whip my soul into the
night? So hard to know, looking back, where the legends end
and the world's notion of reality begins. And then, whose
reality?*

*So I danced, and used my madness—feigned or real—as a
blind through which I might peer around the room and find the
means to bring her to her death. If worse came to worst, I
promised myself I would grab one of the guards' own blades,
though I paid for it on the spot with my life. In the end, it was
simple. She liked her chamber well-lighted, the princess. Bowls
of burning oil stood on tall bronze stems, like flowers of fire, all
around the room. I saw my moment, seized two, and toppled
them at her. And while the oil soaked her wool bridal robe and
the flames joyfully lapped it up, I ran. The guards were too
stunned by their lady's plight—warm, fatty wool takes fire
well—to give me chase. They were all swept up into a madness
of their own—a madness to preserve their heads secure on their
necks when word of their fault in this murder reached the king.*

"*O Majesty, we were not to blame! A parcel arrived, the gift
of a glorious bridal robe for your regal daughter. She put it on
at once, delighted, and at once was devoured by the fiery
venoms of witchery woven into the wool by the black sorceress
of Colchis!*"

Medea chuckled to herself and patted the wands of her hair
like faithful hunting hounds. Soon they would be set on the
track of their prey. It had cost her days and weeks of solitary
madness, flirting with true insanity, but she had done it: she had
taken the daily ration of dreamgum from her own grail, chewed

it, swallowing as little of her own saliva as possible, spitting it into a holding vessel. When she had enough put by, she cooked it carefully over a flame, reducing it to a concentrate of demons.

There was a grail slave in the castle, a kitten-faced young girl, who one day ran shrieking and raging through the castle like a rabid lion. Rodrigo disapproved of dreamgum, saw to it that his most trustworthy lieutenants policed all grails, confiscating the noxious stuff (but the Lady's grail, oh no! Who would be so bold?). And a grail slave only got what was doled out by the master's hand. Therefore, this girl must be veritably mad. Why else would she find a knife and dash herself against Rodrigo himself? That was what Rodrigo said as he wiped the girl's blood from his sword. That was when the Lady of Colchis knew that her dreamgum-distilled potion worked.

As it will work on you, Creusa.

She crossed the plain without incident. As she expected, she was stopped by the outermost of her sons' pickets. "I am Medea," was all she needed to say. She was conveyed immediately into their presence, after only the shortest of delays. Her dagger, she was assured would be returned to her on her departure.

If they mean to let me depart, she thought as a guard held up the tent flap for her. *Only let me see the bitch's face again, give me a second chance to slay her, and I will die well pleased.*

The tent was huge and brightly painted, ringed with well-dressed, well-armed troops. She felt a curious swell of pride to see her sons made such masterful men. They sat in chairs of oak carved in the style they best recalled, their necks and arms bright with silver. Despite herself, she felt the tears rising to her eyes. *So this is what it means to face the might-have-been!*

The elder rose to greet her. Aeson's expression was unreadable. *He has no taint of Jason!* she thought, studying the dark hair, the level storm-gray eyes. And she marveled when she glanced at the younger, Iolaus, his father's cursed image, and felt all her heart go yearning out to him.

"Welcome, Mother," Aeson said without the smallest tint of irony in his voice. "Will you be seated?" He motioned toward the chair he had vacated. There were no others.

"I would rather stand," she said.

"Yes, standing is how I best remember you." Aeson turned from her and reclaimed his place. There was a small table between him and his brother where wine cups waited. He took one up and added, "With a knife in your hands. Do you remember? Iolaus?"

The golden head jerked away. She saw the broad shoulders of her younger boy tremble. Did he weep? She took a step toward him, but ghostly children tugged at her gown and held her back from the living child.

The hoarseness of her own voice startled he as she said, "You should know that I'm here on sufferance. I am expected back at the castle before the grails open to break tonight's fast. If I am not, my lord will conclude that you've killed me and resume the war."

"War?" How curiously familiar Aeson's voice! "This is no war."

Tell that to the dead, she thought. Aloud she said, "Then what is it? So much effort, why? Just to see me?"

"Why not?" Her own mannerism, that slight lift of the brow. "After Iolaus and I were grown, we came to wonder whether you or Father were among the resurrected souls. Our search began longer ago than I like to think, and it's only half succeeded. Unless...*you* might know where we can find him?"

"No." The word was dust. "If I did, I wouldn't save you the pleasure of killing him."

"Is that what you think we want? Iolaus, pay me! I wagered you she'd weigh us in her own balance." Aeson set down his cup, reached across the table, and gave his brother a companionable punch in the arm. The other stayed as he was, body averted, gaze fixed on the back of the tent. The elder looked at her again and said, "The Kindly Ones are less than kindly to kinslayers, Mother." He measured her with his eyes. "Or so the legends go. We merely wished to talk with you, if only to learn how you evaded the snake-whips they are supposed to reserve for those who shed blood of their own begetting."

"You will excuse me if I do not believe you," she said.

"But know that you may believe me with all certainty when I tell you that if you take my life, Rodrigo will take hers."

"Hers?" A moment's confusion stirred the cold sea of Aeson's eyes, then realization flashed. "Ah! Our nurse, you mean? Left behind as a hostage, no doubt. Was it your idea?"

The Lady of Colchis nodded. "He would not give me leave to go otherwise. And after your message, I had to come."

Aeson's mouth twisted, though it would take some stretch of the word to call that look a smile. He addressed his brother. "Iolaus, forget what you owe me; we're even. I thought she'd never take the bait." To her, he said, "My memory's not all I'd hoped. I recalled you as subtler, Mother. Although I see you still blame the whims of your own will on others. *He* would not give you leave? As if you were ever born to do other than take!"

She opened her mouth to shout *What can you know of how it is for me?* Across more than two thousand years the words were too familiar. *I do not do this to you, my babes, because I want to, but because your father's forced me to it. What can you know of exile? By ending your lives, I spare you. The fault is none of mine.*

Medea pressed her lips together, regained control. The twin wands in his hair were the promise that sustained her. "So it was all a lie, a trap. Creusa is not here. Now you will kill me, I suppose, and Rodrigo will do the same to the Lady Issa. It will mean nothing to you. You've wagered and you've won."

"We've wagered," Aeson agreed, "but we've won nothing except your loss." He poured more wine and slumped back in his seat. "You tell her, Iolaus. The nightmares still haunt you. You owe her more."

The golden head did not move, but Medea heard her younger son speak. His voice was soft and gentle, fragile as a breath of cloud. "We never lied. We never said we had Creusa. You simply assumed. We are not to blame for what you made of our message."

"What?" The fury rose in her breast. *Cheated! Cheated! I'll have blood for it!* "Then you lie now, saying you never lied. What else was I to think when your words were so clear—fire into wool?"

"What you did think: a rival. One who threatens to take away the man you hold so"—his voice broke on a sob— "precious. More precious than any other thing."

"You speak nonsense," Medea fumed, pacing the tent. "Riddles. If you mean your father, he's gone. I've neither seen nor heard of him anywhere on this world. If you mean the castle's true master, he's gone as well, and my rival for him flows not five spear-casts from this tent!"

"And you'd set the River herself aflame to sear away the wound she dealt your pride, wouldn't you, Mother?" Aeson's taunting words bit deep. "We mean neither of those men."

"Which leaves Rodrigo." The fierceness left her all at once. She felt drained. "Then you're mistaken, to call him precious in my sight; I never loved him."

"What has love to do with how dearly you prize things—this above that, what you love, what you truly value?" Iolaus' voice now seemed to come from a long way off. "You said you loved us often enough."

"Aeetes." Aeson ticked off names on his fingers. "Jason, Aegeus, all lovers who came after him until the day you died, all lovers who followed after Resurrection Day, the castle's master, Rodrigo—how many of the men you named yours did you love? Really love? Or were they just the solid bodies you needed to lend shape to the all-devouring cloak of flame that is Medea?"

"You're mad." She said it as simple fact, not accusation. "Both of you, mad."

Aeson shook his head. "We know madness—we've met with it many times since that first red hour with you. Children are quick studies. We learned to recognize it after that. Children are also practical beasts. We learned that madness is a more faithful weapon than the keenest blade."

"What do you—?"

"Oh, you know it's true, Mother. Wasn't it your own madness that brought you here to seek your rival?" He laughed at her. *"Here!"*

"Go back to your castle now." Iolaus turned to face her, and the force of cold hate in his eyes was a hammer to her heart. "She will be there, waiting. Do what you like with her—what you *can*. But if you had to beg him for permission to leave your own stronghold, do you think he will ever give you leave to harm his wedded wife?''

Her lips moved, yet she could not force the words to fill them. Both her sons were watching her now, avid and austere as the hawk about to stoop to its prey. She knew that her pain did not touch them; all that mattered was that they see her feel the pain. With a strength she'd never used before, she finally managed to pronounce, ''Ximena—?''

''You know how names can change here,'' Aeson said.

And she knew. ''Issa...'' A hiss, the sound of the Earth-snake's scales scraping over stone before it trickled back into its hole.

''The hostage you left behind so willingly, so eagerly.'' Aeson smiled. ''The price of your journey here, and this wonderful family reunion.''

''The rival you must dread so much. She has been alone with him for as long and longer than you have been here with us.'' Iolaus' hands were shaking like an old man's. They closed around his own wine cup and he drank until they were steady again. Fingers longer and finer than Jason's brushed away one carmine drop from beside his lips. ''How does it feel to set the knife to your own throat...Mother?''

She could not tell how she left the tent, how she found her way back across the plain. All she knew was that someone must have given her her dagger again, because it was a weight against her side. The stars made her path bright, but she ran in darkness. There were no tears to fog her sight, yet still the landscape fled to either side of her pounding feet in a blur. Even the grass seemed to send up mocking whispers in her wake, even the River's mighty voice turned snide and malicious in her ears. In her flight, the wands tore loose from her hair. One fell and was lost, but she clutched the other, pressed it to her bosom like some sacred thing, hiding it beneath her heart.

''Open!'' she shouted, pounding on the ironwood gate. ''Open now!''

One of her own men answered, drew the bar, let her in. The small portion of her brain not burning on the pyre wondered

idly how she must look to his eyes, to call up that much white
terror in his expression. She clenched her fists and demanded
that the hostage be brought before her.

Other soldiers came near to hear her wild orders. In all their
time of service to her and the Cid they had never seen her so. It
was the circle of their silent, stricken eyes that at last brought
her to her senses. She let her voice drop and passed a hand
through her hair.

"You will forgive me," she said, calmer, yet losing none of
her command. "Where I've come from—how they dealt with
me—" She knew these men would champion a helpless woman
sooner than one possessed, and trimmed her expression accord-
ingly. "I have learned things touching on the hostage that our
enemies so conveniently placed in our hands; treachery. My
lord Rodrigo must be told at once, from my lips only. But first
I must see her."

"Lady, as your desire, it shall be done," one of her own
men replied. "But treachery—? The hostage has made no
move against this stronghold or its garrison since your
departure—"

"Pure luck. If an adder glides past your naked foot, you
don't assume that all future serpents will be as courteous. She
did not lay to my return so soon. She thought her scheme had
time."

He showed his teeth in a soldier's smile. "She will learn she
has none." His hand closed on the hilt of his shortsword. "I
will fetch my lord Rodrigo. He is in the armory, taking stock of
our weapons. He will want for himself the honor of executing
this serpent among us."

"No." She was emphatic. "Not a word to him before I have
seen her. My interview with our enemies taught me more than
they bargained for. They weave their schemes tight, lies on
lies, with sometimes the glint of truth spied through the web. It
would be sin to execute the hostage if what they told me of her
proves to be only another lie, for whatever purpose." Her
stormy eyes held him as she added, "For all your faithful and
obedient service, I would spare you the shedding of innocent
blood."

They know my legend better than they know me, she thought, watching that circle of strong men shrink away from her words. *I used to think that was no good thing; now I know better. When I speak of the horrors attendant on shedding innocent blood, they tremble solely because the words come from my mouth. That's power, and power buys obedience. Innocent blood . . . seeing them, my sons, and the slip-tongued creatures they've become, who could ever think of them as innocent anymore?*

She made it clear to the men that Rodrigo must not learn of her return just yet. Until the grails opened in the morning, let him believe she was still in the tents of their enemies. The guards who had already seen her swore an oath of honor to keep the secret. (Rodrigo had turned honor into coin of the realm within the castle walls. Silently she thanked him for this useful tidbit of foolishness.) Only one man led her to the room where the hostage stayed.

She was not there. The man's face turned a telltale scarlet when Medea demanded where the bitch might be. He didn't even need to say another word.

Rodrigo's bedchamber was the master's room. He was not there, but she was. She gasped and pulled the bedclothes up to her small, plump chin when Medea entered.

The Lady of Colchis swept the room with her eyes. A decanter of wine was on the sideboard, beneath a display of Rodrigo's favorite edged weapons, but she recalled the bitch's distaste for wine. She turned to her man. "Bring tea." He was gone in a thought, asking no questions, closing the door behind him.

For a time the two women did nothing more than hold each other in the pale cups of their eyes. Then Medea said, "Does he know yet who you truly are?"

Issa shook her head. Her auburn hair, loosed from its bun, lay thin and dull to below her shoulders. "I never meant to— He was so— I couldn't protect— I never before—"

"Stop your chatter. I don't care if you fucked half the garrison." She relished the tiny tremor of shock that ran through Issa's body. "Ah, but what a surprise for him when he does learn with whom he's lain this night!"

"You . . . know?" Medea nodded. "And you don't care?"

"Oh, I *care*, Lady! I care very much. But not as you'd imagine. We made no promises of love, he and I, so I'd call him free. It's the promise that's most potent, hmm?''

"Oh, yes!'' Issa relaxed and even smiled. "The promise is everything,'' she said just as the door opened softly and Medea's man entered with the tea.

To administer the dose was not difficult. The lady Issa was occupied with putting her clothes back on, doing up her scraggly hair. Medea snapped the end from the hollow wand concealed in her bosom and deftly tilted the contents into the other woman's cup just before she poured the tea. She glanced at the wall where Rodrigo's display of armaments hung, and her eyes sparkled. Her own dagger was a comforting presence. *I hope her demons drive her there*, she thought. *It would be perfection. In everything he ever told me of his wife, Rodrigo never mentioned her having any knowledge of weapons. I, on the other hand— Yes, let her seize a sword! Then who's to call me liar when I collapse into a small, tear-damp ball of womanly fear; gasping that I only acted in self-defense?*

There was one chair in the room. Medea took it, leaving her rival to perch on the edge of the bed. They sipped their tea and spoke of Rodrigo, how masterful he was, how he never knew *no* for a woman's word. Before long, the Lady of Colchis noted with pleasure how a thin scud of cloud settled over the shallow blue eyes. *Soon . . . It only wants the pinprick to drive her demons out into the sun.*

"I don't begrudge him you,'' Medea said. "In fact, I give him as a gift.''

"A . . . gift?'' The woman blinked. "Like a piece of land . . . property. We were promised it, but he—'' The rest fell into inaudible mutterings.

"Of course, a gift. This is my castle, you know—not his—and even I hold it in trust for another. Someday, whoever commands this stronghold will command the River channel below.''

"He said—he said it would be ours.'' Issa's eyes darted from side to side. "He *promised*. Only then—''

Better and better. The Lady of Colchis forced herself to hold back a cry of victory. *Promised her the castle, did he? How*

*like him, giving what he hasn't got. Perhaps a broken promise
has an edge sharp enough to prod her where I want her to go.*

To her planned victim she said, "I need Rodrigo's arm to
help me hold it, but the rest of him—all yours. In exchange, all
I ask is that you use whatever influence you might have to
ensure that he continues to be a tractable vassal. I don't mind
losing him to you," she lied, "but I will not lose this castle to
him."

"Hot . . . so hot . . ." Issa began to sway, dabbing imaginary
sweat from her brow with flabby white hands. "Where is he?
This must be all a rumor. It's *ours*, he said it was *ours!*" Her
random gaze sharpened, homed on Medea. The watery blue
eyes sparked, flared, burned with penetrating cold. She sprang
from the bed. "And now is *she* going to have it?"

"Yes, *she* is," Medea returned, leaning forward in her chair.
She observed with glee the demons dancing in the other
woman's eyes. *Oh, feel the killing rise within you, Ximena!
Believe in your mouse-heart you are a match for me! Don't you
see the swords on the wall? Don't you hear the cold metal
singing your name? Dream how sweet it will be to sink one in
my blood. Try to move against me, bitch. Only try.* "*She* will
never let it go. I will not. It isn't yours anymore—never was,
no matter what he promised—but mine. Do you understand?
Mine."

The creature's moan rose to a bitter climactic wail. "Oh,
Mother!" she cried out, fast in the grip of the drug. "Mother,
how can you permit this?" She flung herself at the wall of
weaponry, tore loose a shortsword, and whirled upon a no
longer gloating Lady.

Medea threw herself from her chair just as the blade chopped
down. *The strength!* she thought. *Even to wield a blade so
small, the power in her arms—! I thought she'd grab a sword
and fumble, then I—* A second chopping stroke fell too close,
slicing the kiltcloth of her gown. She scurried across the floor
like a rat, suddenly desperate to get out of reach.

"It's all your fault, Abby!" the other woman keened, raising
the sword high. "He never would have broken his promise to
me if not for you. Greedy pig!"

Medea rolled aside in time to evade the downstroke. Then

she felt a warm wetness spreading from her shoulder and
discovered she had not been quite fast enough. She drew her
dagger, willing at least to face down the demons she had
conjured.

The door of the room slammed open. "What is this?"
Rodrigo demanded. Medea was able to glimpse the dead body
of her faithful soldier slumped in the hall outside before the
red-haired Fury whirled to face the towering knight and shout,
"I loved you, and you broke your promise to me. You gave it
to *her*! Oh, I *loved* you!"

Rodrigo reached for his sword. Medea had no more than a
moment to savor the possibility of her plan coming to fruition,
Ximena dead on Rodrigo's blade. But the Castillian's heavy
steel never even cleared the scabbard before the shortsword
sliced into his neck, sending the blood gouting. He tumbled
and she was on him, hacking at his head even though it was
clear he was already dead. The Lady of Colchis felt her eyes
swell with drinking in the horror as she attempted to inch her
way toward the door.

A hand seized her skirt, jerked her savagely back. She was
gasping into blue eyes empty of everything but blood. "This is
all your fault too." The other woman growled and panted like a
beast. "I never would have killed them if you hadn't abandoned me."

Gods . . . what am I seeing? Her words— Medea could not
move, transfixed by the ghost of her own legend. She touched
her face lightly, in a trance, half expecting her fingers to
discover Jason's features there.

"I never— Who—who do you take me for?" she asked.

Now the tears were streaming from the other woman's eyes.
"It *is* your fault, it *is!* If you hadn't died, he never would have
married *her:* fat, plain Abby, our stepmother. Emma said we
didn't need any stepmother. The farm he promised to leave us,
he was going to leave *her* when he changed his will. As if she
didn't have enough already, the sow! Emma told me you always
taught her that a promise is a sacred thing, made before God.
He'd broken too many promises already. For his soul's sake, I
couldn't let him break another. I never would have done what I

did if I'd had a choice. I loved my father! Oh Mother, Mother, why did you leave us?"

Whatever this demon-ridden creature was, Medea had one awful suspicion what she was *not.* Still, she had to ask: "Xi-Ximena?"

A scowl. "What did you call me?"

Very well, then, another try. Sometimes hearing one's true name could break insanity's most powerful hold, shatter a drug-tranced spell. "Issa . . . ?"

A harsh laugh. "Is that the best you can pronounce *Lizbeth* at your age Mother? Why, you sound like a child! Anyway, *he* always called me Lizzie." A line showed between her brows, grew deep as a chasm into oblivion. Head lowered like a bull about to charge, she took a step closer to the Lady of Colchis, and another. "They tried to blame me for their deaths, in court, but that was a lie. That was why they never could convict me. God knows where the real blame lies." Another step, the blade rising like a note of music. "And so do you."

In her mind, Medea called for the black chariot drawn by dragons with which the legends all dowered her. In her eyes she saw only the sword. Iolaus' words echoed in her ears: *We never lied. We never said we had Creusa. You simply assumed.* She saw his infant face and Aeson's reflected in Rodrigo's blood along the edge of the blade.

Her bleeding shoulder was beginning to set up a protest of pain. She was weary of second chances. Her arms spread wide, she embraced all that she truly was, letting the legend fall away like a too-heavy cloak. "The blame for their deaths is mine," she said for the first time in any of her lives, and bowed her head to accept the stroke of the sword.

Stephen Comes Into Courage

Rick Wilber

FIRST INNING
When a Man Falls, A Crowd Gathers

Stephen Crane takes three hard steps to his left and dives, glove hand outstretched, for the hard ground ball up the middle.

He is a fraction of a second late reacting, was too relaxed thinking that the Babe, pitching for the first time in a week or more and looking fit, would strike Reddie Buller out rather easily. Buller, after all, is one of the Brits and a cricketer more used to dealing with balls that skip off a sticky wicket than with a left-hander's fastballs high and tight. He certainly shouldn't be ready to handle the Babe's high hard one.

But handle it Buller has, swinging away on the first pitch as if he played this way all the time. He is a bit clumsy ordinarily, and cautious, much more suited to his task of organizing the chautauqua's military defenses than playing baseball. But to every man his hour—Reddie's swing is up the middle past the Babe, who can only wave at it futilely as it skips by. Stephen, scrambling toward it and then diving, only hopes to knock the ball down and hold the fellow to a single.

But the gods of this hateful place have other designs, and the ball takes a strange hop left to smack neatly into the kilt webbing of Stephen's mitt. For a brief moment Stephen lies there and curses at the thing. Damnation! Can't he do anything wrong here, isn't he allowed!

But then he thinks of the game, and his teammates, and rises to his knees, yanks the ball from the dragonfish-skin glove, and throws

262

hard to Lou over at first. Buller is out by more than a step, and the game over: Stephen's Red Stockings 8, Joseph's Secret Agents 7.

The Stockings shout congratulations to each other and Stephen as they run over to him. They were behind most of the game and figured to lose this one until Stephen's ground single in the eighth scored the go-ahead run. Now he's capped that off with this sterling play to hold the lead and win the game.

Stephen rises from the dirt and accepts the happy handshakes of his teammates. Second-baseman Nellie, who just translated in the month before after an encounter up-River with a dragonfish, is the first to reach Stephen. He throws an arm around him and grins widely.

"Great glove, Stephen. Damn lucky hop. Man, you're really on a roll. Just ride this hot streak while you can, OK? We're all having a good time."

"Right, Nelson. Right," Stephen says, and nods. But he can't find the heart to match his teammate's smile. It was a lucky hop. Too lucky, just like the single he hit the inning before, which should have been a routine out, but seemed to have eyes of its own as it skipped into the outfield and scored Pie for the go-ahead run.

This has been going on for months now, ever since he whimsically began this charming little chautauqua down the great River. Stephen has been getting nothing but lucky breaks, the fly balls dropping in for him, the grounders coming up smoothly, the pitches all seeming fat and huge and down the middle.

It is all too damn unlikely, and Stephen has come to hate it. It all feels preordained here in this unhappy second life, all neatly tied and knotted, things going along the way they are obviously meant to, planned to.

He hates that, abhors it, fears it.

SECOND INNING
An Open Boat

The *Otago*, a huge if ramshackle river-raft, drifts downstream at a solemn, steady pace, so that the shoreline seems to be moving by it, moving upstream, to disappear into the distant horizon, as if over a precipice, today disappearing into yesterday.

Stephen leans against the portside rail, takes a welcome deep breath, and works on unraveling the baseball he holds in his hands. He has already peeled back the sewn leather cover and now slowly pulls away the inner threads, occasionally snapping them and dropping a handful into the River.

Twice a day a baseball appears in his grail. The balls are from another era, far into his future, labeled with the names of a league and its president who are unknown to him. But the players on his team, many of them from that future, are glad to have the balls, overjoyed to have them, and Stephen understands that joy. It is the presence of the balls that convinced him to start this strange journey. It is the baseballs that have given them all a purpose to this strange new life.

Stephen finds it hard to figure why the balls are given to him. As a prank, once, in his student days at Syracuse, he ate the greater portion of one, chewing the coarse woolen string and washing it down with whiskey. Perhaps, he has thought, that is why they came his way now.

Or, more likely, he thinks, it's just the whimsy of the local gods. They want him to play the game here, and so this is their way of insisting. Like going down-River, their current is hard to resist.

He thinks again of how it went in yesterday's game, of the game-winning play he made, of the hits and plays over the past few months. There doesn't seem to be much resistance he can offer there, either.

He knocks the last parts of the baseball against the rail a few times, reminding himself with the tangible feel of the act that somehow this is all real, this new life. It is not a fever dream, as he thought at first it must be. It is not an invention; it is all too real.

He started this voyage of discovery as a simple way to travel the River, tell some stories, meet the people along its shores, perhaps even find Cora, his love from that first life. From that first day when he found Joseph, naked and shaking, fresh from a translation that followed a vicious attack from a group of

Tartars, it all seemed to fall into place. They could float down the River, pull in when it seemed safe, tell their stories, meet people, find out about this new life.

It would be, they thought, a way to learn more, to find new things to write about, the two of them working together on that, old friends together again. The stories they could tell!

And baseball was the wonderful excuse. The sport is known in some of the villages they come to, and fun and innocent enough for others, a respite from the fear and worry of this new life, so the chautauqua has been welcomed in most of the places they've tied the raft up.

There have been some tricky moments, of course, but Buller, who's been along from the first, has been up to them. He's instructed the men in the chautauqua and a good dozen of the women in hand-to-hand combat as well as some basic tactics. The instruction has proven useful.

Fights have broken out in a few of the towns where they've played, and near-riots once or twice. But Buller and the chautauqua's baseball bats and spears have always quelled the trouble.

Two months back the locals were involved in a territorial dispute with the next village down. The villagers assumed that the chautauqua was a trick to get them away from their stockade, so they decided to out-trick Stephen and his team-mates instead. They had the women and a few men come out to watch the game, and then in the third inning the rest of the men came boiling out of the stockade like ants to the attack.

The ensuing fight gave Buller a chance to prove that the daily practice maneuvers were worth the effort. Everyone pulled together smartly into a defensive square and the whole group of fifty marched steadily the half-mile back to the raft.

There were no lives lost; Buller made a point of that once they were aboard. Death didn't have the same impact here that it held in the old life, but avoiding it meant staying with the team, with the chautauqua, so Buller's remarks brought a huzzah from the crowd on the raft.

The whole thing seemed to have an extraordinary impact on Buller, Stephen thinks. The man has been considerably more self-confident since that day. Perhaps Buller's hard-hit ball yesterday was some sort of reflection of that new assuredness. That's all to the good; Stephen is happy for Buller, happy that the man is finding what he needs from this second chance at life.

Stephen wishes he could say the same for himself. It is the writing, or lack of it, that worries him so. He tosses the hard core of the ball into the River, as disappointed in himself as he is happy for Buller. Life here has gone well, really, and he should not be complaining.

He has been born anew, healthy, and perhaps that alone is reason enough to set aside his foolish worries and allow himself to enjoy it here. He lives, he breathes, he tells his old stories and he plays the game of baseball, what more could a sane man ask for?

He takes a deep breath, and appreciates even that simple act. There is no consumption here eating away at his lungs. The pain of that is gone, the helpless gasping for breath, the deadly rattle of labored breath.

For freedom, he thinks. For that, to be free, to struggle against an uncaring nature, to win and to lose, both. To live and to die. Freedom.

Then, he thinks, he would be able to write again, to create drama from the conflicts of this place. As it is, though, there is nothing to tell.

Stephen is convinced that the gods of this place control everyone, everything. His strange success at baseball is proof of that.

Oh, he admits to himself, he could always play it well, and God knows he loved the game in that earlier life. He laughs to think of how baseball and whiskey cost him his education at Syracuse, where he was asked to leave or face expulsion. Ah, the errancy of youth. He always did place batting and throwing above the tedium of his studies.

But here, he knows, his successes are too many, his skills too enlarged. Someone, he thinks, wants him to succeed at this chautauqua, someone of real power has made sure that he will. That someone, he is convinced, must be the same one who has brought them all back to this place, who controls them. It is a frightening, horrible thought for Stephen that all that he does, all that they all do, is controlled, designed for some larger purpose.

To be used and manipulated like this, to be a tiny part of some greater machinations, angers Stephen, frustrates him. Despite all the good that seems to be happening all around him, he fears the future, hates it. He shakes his head. Maybe there is a story in that hate somewhere, but he has yet to find it; instead he tells the old tales and lives each day as they pass down the river.

There is a rustle from behind, the patient puffing of a newly lit cigar. "Something has you upset, young Stephen?"

It is Joseph Conrad, his friend and co-owner of the Great River Baseball and Literature Company, who has come up quietly from behind.

Stephen turns to face him, smiles. "I'm just puzzling through the perversities of this place, Joseph. There are times I hate it so."

"Ah." Joseph nods slightly. "Yesterday's good fortune bothers you, yes? The happy hop . . ."

"Lucky hop."

". . . lucky hop. The hits that all seem to be safe for you. The winning. These things trouble you?"

"They're not natural, that's for damn sure."

"This is not a natural place, Stephen. We both know that. It is different. We are different. The rules here have changed, and so we must change, too. That is what we said when we started this little adventure."

He holds up his cigar at arm's length. "This delightful cigar, for instance, is quite out of place here, don't you think? The whole world is quite out of place, really.

"As we've said before, Stephen, you and I, we simply have to do with it what we can. We could die tomorrow, you know, and never see one another again. Let's simply enjoy it. After all," he says, "what choice do we have?"

Stephen turns away to look toward the shore, says nothing for a moment, then sighs.

"I know you're right, old friend. There's nothing for it, really, except to go on, make our way down the River, tell a few stories here and there, try to entertain ourselves and a few others as best we can."

"And play some of this baseball that you love so dearly."

"And play baseball," Stephen agrees. "There is that, at least. There is the game."

And Stephen smiles at Joseph, his good friend who has suffered, died, and translated back already once on this vicious world, who now calmly puffs on his cigar. Joseph's acceptance of all this, Stephen thinks, should be teaching him a lesson. Joseph is even finding things to write about here, has started some new stories, talks about a novel.

"It could simply be that you have been lucky, you know," Joseph says. "Or, Stephen, it could even be skill," and he grins at that thought before blowing smoke toward the shore.

THIRD INNING
The Upturned Face

A few hours later the River has widened and slowed so that it seems nearly a lake. The big raft barely moves in the sluggish stream, and the day has warmed to match the current's torpor. Stephen finds himself standing again at the favorite rail waving now to the passersby who have come to River's edge to watch the chautauqua float by.

The raft must be nearing Courage. As always, word has spread that the baseball chautauqua is coming. There will be another big crowd.

From what the people in New Hannibal told him after the game there yesterday, the raft should reach Courage by midafternoon. Stephen, Joseph, and the rest of the players will have the rest of the day to set up the site, line out the basepaths, build the small stage, and send out the criers to make the announcements.

And then tomorrow the chautauqua. Baseball at noon, right after the grails fill. The Red Stockings against the Secret Agents, with whatever players Courage can pull together getting a chance to play for either team. There are always a few. There are even times when the local town has its own team ready to play, and the Stockings and the Agents combine for an All-Star team to play against the local nine.

Tomorrow will be the one hundredth game for the chautauqua, and so a special event. The Red Stockings have done well on their journey, eighty wins against twenty losses. The Secret Agents, composed of cricketers mainly, are eager to improve on the twenty wins, and, as always, look to recruit new players from the towns.

Early on in the chautauqua, during a stretch of early-twentieth-century towns, they seemed frequently to run into talented teams from the towns they visited. On two occasions no one in the town had really realized what baseball talent was there until the chautauqua arrived.

In New New, for instance, the town had been busy fighting with its neighbor, a town full of Irish, and no one had thought about something so innocuous as a baseball game. Then, when they agreed to play, the townspeople realized that in their midst were Billy Hamilton, Willy Keeler, Pie Traynor, Wally Pipp, and Lou Gehrig. Working together, shoulder to shoulder, on the thick stockade, they had hardly talked about the sport, so busy had they been struggling to secure their town against the incursions from the village of Irish Celts down-River.

Putting together an entire team, the players of New New named themselves the Iron Horses, and clobbered the Red Stockings All-Stars, twenty to five.

When the raft pulled out the next morning Gehrig, Pipp, and Keeler were on board. The next day, in Kilkenny, the chautauqua had played baseball with the belligerent Irish, dividing up the locals between the two teams, and had a fine old time. The dancing afterward had been marvelous. Baseball diplomacy, Joseph called it, and it seemed to work.

That is the way it has gone in a year of travels. Picking up players as they go, losing others to village life. Ken Boyer played for six months before meeting a woman in New Louis two months back. He'd stayed behind then to make a home of it with her. Joe Jackson had done the same a month or so later.

Stephen thinks of the finality of that. They are traveling down-River only; they have no plans to retrace their path upstream, and the good-byes would be forever were this world not so vicious and the translations into new bodies so capricious. The Babe left the first time after only a month of play, staying behind in a little village that crowned him king and seemed to promise dreamgum, whiskey, and women forever.

After a few months of excess he'd been deposed and executed, and translated back to a village just a few days down-River from the chautauqua. He'd happily rejoined the journey, and seemed now, as a result of all that, to have at least a little firmer grip on his behavior. Stephen wonders how long that will last.

Tomorrow, after the game, Stephen and Joseph will recite from their work and enjoy a grail social as they do in each town. This part of the River is populated by those from the turn of the century or the first decades after, so both writers' work is known and respected. They speak to large crowds, grateful crowds in most cases, people who miss what these writers once offered them.

It hasn't always been that way, of course. In most towns, actually, the names of Crane and Conrad have been unknown. But good storytelling has been interesting to almost everyone, whether the words have come in English, Polish, or Esperanto. Many's the time that the locals already have their own storyteller, as well, and Stephen and Joseph make a point of including that person on stage with them. It has been quite amazing whom they've met that way, from the ancients to last week's wonderful oratory from Robert Burns.

They tried to entice Burns along on the chautauqua, but he refused, was happy in Kilmarnock and planned to make a life of it there with Clarinda. He talked of writing new poems, in fact. So tomorrow, Stephen guesses, will be its usual success. The noon grails, then baseball, then the evening grails before the storytelling.

At each stop on the River Stephen seems to do a better job of recalling his work. The shorter pieces were easiest to recall. "The Open Boat," "The Upturned Face"—those came back easily enough. He could reconstruct them even in the first few months after resurrection, back when he was still trying to find a way to make paper and ink.

That was a year ago now. And in the last nine months, since he found Joseph naked and mewling a few hundred miles upstream, Stephen has remembered more and more of the old work; "The Red Badge," of course, and "Maggie," and "The Monster," and any number of the poems.

For Joseph it has been more difficult. So much of it has had to come to him first in Polish and then, with nothing to write it down on except some slate and chalky rock they've found, he translates it again as he did once. It was a terrible frustration at first.

Joseph has been happier lately, though, with his new work helping that mood. It's almost as if the new stories help his memory to improve as they travel along. He tells Stephen now that he is almost ready to tell a whole new tale. "The Raft's Descent," he calls it. He lacks only the ending.

Stephen smiles each time Joseph brings it up, is happy for Joseph that he can create something new. Stephen wishes he could do the same, but the old times, the old characters don't seem to fit here, and Stephen isn't ready to talk about the new ones, not yet.

Still, telling the old stories works well enough for Stephen, and if Joseph can do something new, all the better. It works well enough either way. So now, each for their own reason, they float downstream, always downstream, entertaining and telling stories and playing baseball.

FOURTH INNING
Of Courage

There is a shout from the shore up ahead. A crowd is gathered, hands waving, an excited buzz of conversation drifts across the River. It is Courage, waiting for Stephen. He stands tall, waves to them across the water, and the shouting grows. The chautauqua is here!

Stephen puts on a smile and walks forward to where Joseph stands. The two of them look at each, nod, clasp hands for a moment. It is these moments that make the journey worthwhile.

Stephen turns and shouts to the players, calls them all by

their nicknames: Double-X and the Iron Horse and Black Babe and Nellie and all the rest.

"Fellows! We've arrived. Remember who you are! The Red Stockings and the Secret Agents, the best damn bunch of baseball players this world has ever seen. Let's have some fun here, fellows, but don't get us into trouble. Babe," and he points his finger at the grinning Babe Ruth, "can tell us what happens when we get into trouble, right?"

There is general laughter.

This is a wonderful team, no question. Stephen loves them each. Such talent, such players! He had no idea that baseball would come to this back in the old life. It's a wonder what these players can do. Nelson, at second, is a magician with the glove and a wonderful clutch hitter. The new woman player, Babe Didrikson, is a better athlete than most of the men. Josh Gibson, the black man who stands so quietly there in the back of the group, is the smartest catcher that Stephen has ever seen or can imagine, blessed with speed, arm strength, and hitting ability to match his cunning.

"Fellows," Stephen goes on, holding up his hands to quiet them down. "This is the most unlikely team that could have come together anywhere. You all know that. From what we know there are millions of people revived along this River's shore. That lovers and players of this one game would be able to come together like this defies any odds.

"But here we are, together to play this game for these fine people. I can only ask that you play hard, play fair, and let the best team win."

"And that'll be the Red Stockings, Stephen. You can bet on it," roars out the Babe, a little drunk already from the whiskey he found in the noon grail when the raft pulled in to use a stone.

The players shout in response, and their joy is reflected by the crowd on the shore as the raft pulls in.

The chautauqua is here! Baseball is here! For a day or two the hard realities of this new life are put away. For a day or two it is time to play a game, to enjoy this small portion of the second life. The players tumble off the raft and into the crowd.

Courage, it turns out, is a mid-twentieth-century town, the

first they've come to from this era in more than two months. Half the townspeople are blacks from gritty Detroit, the others rural whites. Josh Gibson is a hero here, and the Babe and Lou and several of the others as well.

It will go well here, very well, indeed. Stephen, walking off last with Joseph, feels good despite himself.

"It is a good thing we do here, Joseph. A good thing," he says to his friend. "I know I have these terrible doubts, this awful depression at times. But I see this and know we are doing something worthwhile for these people, at least."

"We bring these people joy for a day or two, young Stephen. That in itself is a fine thing. That so many of us enjoy doing it is rather much of a moral bonus, I should think."

Stephen laughs at that, at the thought of a moral bonus for playing baseball. Then he claps his friend on the shoulder and the two of them, happy enough for the moment, walk down the narrow path toward the town.

FIFTH INNING
A Girl of the Streets

Later, it is the fifth inning and the local team put together by Courage is actually winning, twelve to three.

Stephen has been just awful. He's booted two easy chances for ground balls, dropped an easy toss from Nellie Fox that would have turned the corner on a much-needed double play, and struck out twice. He's as happy as he can be.

This is what he wants and needs out of life, some bad hops, some mistakes and poor play and the struggle to succeed. This is much more like it, he thinks. This is life.

There is a sharp, low line drive in the gap between third and short. Didrikson dives to her left but can't reach it. Stephen, off at the crack of the bat, has time for two strides, no more, and then launches his body out full length to try for the ball.

He gloves it, has it in the mitt for a second, but then lands hard on the dirt and the ball pops loose from the impact.

Didrikson, coming up to help, grabs the ball and tosses it to second, where Nellie waits. At least they hold the batter to a single.

"You all right, Stephen?" Didrikson asks as she reaches down to offer him a hand up.

"Fine," he says, taking her hand and rising to smile as he rubs the dirt from his face. Reality, at last, he thinks. The real game, the real thing. Wonderful.

And then, as he brushes the dirt off his kilt, he looks up to see Cora.

Cora, his love, is walking across the open grassy meadow that separates the playing field from the thatched huts of Courage. She is wearing a kilt, tied at the waist, and no more. Even from here, Stephen sees in her the beauty that called to him a lifetime ago, when she ran a whorehouse in Jacksonville and laughed at him just once, just that once, to take his heart. "Cora!" he yells, and runs from the field, leaving the game behind. "Cora! Cora!"

She laughs to see him, and waves. His Cora, dark hair falling to her shoulders and over the tops of her breasts, long legs wading through the tall grass. His Cora, his love.

They meet, embrace, fall into the grass laughing and babbling like children.

In that other world, the one where they first met, they would have laughed and mocked the cliché they become here. The last thing Stephen wanted back in that life was a romantic vision of true love found. And Cora, when he found her running the Hotel De Dream, was no innocent ingenue.

He loved her for that, for her experience, her strength. It denied the romantic idea of love that was repulsive in the world around him. Their love was no artificial contrivance handed down from medieval court poetry, no invention of a culture bent on the denial of life's hard realities and the celebration of a chivalric code that murdered peasants in the name of God. Theirs was an honest love, a physical attraction that bound them in the act itself, in mutual heat and passion as well as a friendship bound together in conversation and admiration and honesty.

But here, now, he falls with her into the grass like a child of sixteen flush with romantic infatuation. He seeks to melt into her, making the two of them a single thing, a blazing fire of greedy need.

And Cora? "Oh, Stephen, Stevie, Stevie," she says to him as they roll in an embrace. "I've found you, I've found you, I've found you. My Stevie, my Stevie, my Stevie." Her litany says all she can manage to voice just now.

The intensity of their embrace finally eases, though they don't let go.

"Cora. God, it's you, it's really you! I can't believe it. You! Here!" Stephen says as they finally begin to settle down. He is on top of her there in the grass, lifts up his head, stares for a moment at the sky, an egg-blue heaven above them, a canopy over them, and then looks back to his love.

"Cora. I thought I'd never see you again, love. Ever. This world is so huge, there are so many people. I never dared think of it. And now you're here."

"Stevie," she says again, simply, and smiles up at him. He bends down to kiss her, starts on the lips and then moves to kiss her eyes, her forehead, her cheeks, her neck, that perfect white neck that he first saw that lifetime ago.

And he sees the bruises there on the side and the back of that ivory neck. They are faded, but must once have been mean, indeed, that is obvious to him.

"What are these, love?"

"It hasn't been easy for me, Stephen. This world can be so vicious. The cruelty..." She lets the thought slide.

"What have they done to you, Cora?" He slides off her, sits next to her, asks again, "What have they done? Was it someone here?" He thinks he can pull the team together and find the villain, kill him, send him elsewhere on the River. Or perhaps a slow torture, deny him the easy route of death.

But Cora explains it is not so simple as that. She sits up next to him, says, "I've come to warn you of him, Stephen. A few days' journey down-River. He's preparing to fight you, enslave you like he's done to others. You mustn't go there. I escaped a week ago to reach you, warn you. You must listen to me."

"Of course, Cora. Of course," he says, and then rises,

brings her to her feet. What has happened to his Cora? What has someone done to her?

He looks back to the field and realizes the game has gone on without him. Nelson waves at him, friendly. They are such good fellows, with him all the way.

He sits back down, pulls Cora to him there on the ground. They cross their legs, sit across from each other in the tall grass. He holds Cora's hands. "Tell me," he says to her, "Tell me about this monster."

SIXTH INNING
The Monster

She begins crying at first as she tries to speak: "Oh, Stevie. Dearest Stephen. For the last year, the longest year..."

She takes a breath, calms. Starts again: "When I came alive here, dearest, dear Stephen, I was so terribly confused. I had no idea what could have happened to me. Was this Heaven? Hell? I didn't know. There was such chaos.

"And Louis—Louis Botha is his name—was there to ease the confusion. He is a strong man, so sure of himself, and gracious, even warm.

"That very first day he took me by the hand and walked me away from the grailstone, away from all the others who were stirring and wandering in confusion.

"In days, just a few days, really, Louis began to organize us, pull us together. He is a natural leader, Stephen, was one in his first life, and fell into it so easily in this one. And he'd lived in the wild, in Africa. He knew how to survive. It was so easy to follow him. We began constructing some shelters, using bamboo and trees and the grass.

"With Louis leading us, dozens, then hundreds of us, we learned what to expect from the grails. We realized we were all in this same horror or heaven, whatever it was, together. It became an exciting time. The first few months were wonderful, in their own way. It was life, at least, and health, and youth. Exciting.

"And Louis kept me by his side, all the time. It started as friendship, nothing more. I still thought then that I would find you sometime soon, my love," and she smiled up to him.

"And then as the weeks went by his horror became more clear, his leadership more vicious. People of all kinds trickled into our kraal and joined us behind Louis's leadership. They were from everywhere, every when, Stephen. More of the Boers like Louis, a group of Romans from the time of Christ, and then some African blacks.

"Kaffirs, he called them, and welcomed them at first, dozens of them. Like all the others, they followed his lead, until one of them killed one of the Boers one day.

"They were building a new stockade wall, and the African, tall, majestic, a proud one, a chief from his own first life, was helping to raise a log when it slipped as it was being raised and one of the Africans had a leg crushed.

"A Boer, one of those close to Louis, came over with a spear and killed the African.

"Just like that. Killed him, the spear through his chest, said it was quicker and easier that way then to wait for the leg to heal. It was all so offhanded, so easily done.

"The chief went crazy, came screaming up to the Boer, pushed him down, struggled, grabbed his spear, still bloody from the first impaling, and stuck the Boer through the chest in just the same manner.

"There was pandemonium then, chaos, a huge fight broke out between the Africans and most of the whites. When it was over the Africans were all either dead, captured, or had run away.

"That day Louis changed. He has gathered his friends around him, leads everyone else through fear and intimidation, and roams our part of the valley to find more 'kaffirs' to enslave. There are dozens of them now, all slaves.

"I knew then I had to leave, this was not something I could take part in, though Louis still thought of me as his friend and confidant.

"Oh, Stephen, I tried to leave. I was foolish, at fist, and told him of my plans. I wanted to travel down the River, look for you."

She shuddered. "He kept me from leaving. Gently, at first, and then more strongly as I continued to mention it. This went on for weeks, Stephen, then months while he was building his little empire, more and more Boers trekking in all the time, hundreds of them finally. I realized he would never let me leave, I would have to simply sneak away, and so I tried to do that.

"I began constructing a raft, hid it near the shoreline as I built it. I could trust no one, they were all so blindly loyal to him by then. It took me much longer to build than I had thought, it was so much more difficult. But with vines and wood and bamboo I finally had something ready, something that would float me down-River far enough to be out of his grasp. Then, I thought, I could start a new life, start looking for you, my love."

She shook her head.

"He knew of my plans the whole while, knew of the raft, and just waited for me to try, then he and four or five of the other Boers, his commando, he called them, caught me as I pushed it into the River."

She stared at Stephen. No smile, no glimmer of emotion. "It has been hell since then, for weeks on end. I was a traitor to him, he says. I tried to die, I begged him to let me die. But he would only shake his head and tell me sorrowfully that he couldn't let me go.

"Then we heard of your chautauqua, Stephen. Travelers coming down the River told of your great raft and the baseball—baseball! I knew it had to be you, dear Stephen—and the storytelling.

"And Louis began a grand plan, Stephen, when he heard of who you have on your trip. Buller, your military man Redver Buller. They were deep enemies in that previous life, Stephen, your Buller and Louis Botha. They threw armies of men against each other in the South African War. Thousands died because of the battles these two fought. And, in the end, Louis Botha was forced to submit to Buller's armies.

"Now he sees this as a chance for revenge. He is deeply religious, still, sees all this as part of God's plan for him. He is convinced that God offers him this opportunity to right the wrongs of that past life.

"He wants to kill or enslave you all, and keep Buller alive through torture, a revenge for the lives of those Boers who died defending their land from Buller and his Englishmen.

"Oh, Stephen, he's a monster. He can be so reasonable and charming when he chooses, and then so utterly vicious by turn. It is only reasonable to him that the kaffirs should be slaves, and work for the Boers who are building a new society. This is what he told me evening after evening, me in my hut and he sitting next to me, talking on into the night, trying to win me back to his side. He would cajole me, woo me, and then beat me by turn," and she touched the bruises on her neck.

" 'A new great civilization,' he said to me many a night, Stephen, 'a place where white men can be free, where all can prosper.'

"I knew I had to find a way to warn you, dearest, and a few days ago the time finally came. He was gone with his commando on a raiding trip, trying to find more Africans to replace the ones who escaped or died. There was a storm that blew in from the River, dark-green lines of cloud that I could see from my hut. A huge whirlwind spun down from that cloud edge, a tornado that came right at us. It tore the village apart, huts flying about everywhere. After all those weeks it was suddenly so simple for me to leave. I ran."

She smiled at him. "I have walked for three days, dear Stephen, with no grail and almost no food, and now I am here, dearest, to warn you that Louis is coming, he is coming to attack you, to take Buller, make him a slave, since he says death is too easy for him here."

She has nothing more to say, can only stare at her Stephen and hold his hands.

He embraces her. "Dear Cora, dearest Cora," he says, and begins to walk with her back toward the game, toward the Red

Stockings and the Secret Agents and the plans they all must make.

SEVENTH INNING
The Bride Comes to Courage

It is a very simple ceremony, torchlit: the bride is dressed in her kilt, the bridegroom the same. Joseph Conrad is best man. Redver Buller is an usher along with Josh Gibson and Satchel Paige. In the audience are Lou Gehrig and Nelson Fox and dozens more, smiling broadly, happy for the moment.

Preacher Roe performs the ceremony, brings the couples' hands together at the end, wishes them life and love and happiness. They embrace.

EIGHTH INNING
An Episode of War

After the wedding, after the reception where the food and drink is plentiful, scouts come trotting back from down-River. A force marches toward Courage, will be there by mid-morning tomorrow. Buller smiles as he gathers his top lieutenants to discuss strategy. This is his chance to change the past. No Skion Kop here, no Majuba. This time he will defeat Botha, his nemesis, or happily die trying.

As the night progresses, men and women come up to the chautauqua camp offering to help in the fight. Not so many of them, two dozen or so, all of them Africans who have escaped from Botha's kraal and heard of the battle to come. This is, one of them tells Buller in Esperanto, their fight as much as anyone's.

Stephen is excited, frightened, exhilarated, all of those. This will be the first time he has fought, despite the books and stories that seem to hint otherwise. For the first time he will see a battle up close. Very close.

And, he thinks, his cause is just. If the coming battle has been prearranged by the gods of this place, then so be it. To fight here is, he thinks, the right thing to do, and he'll be doing it with Cora at his side.

He sleeps poorly for a few hours, and then he and Joseph and Cora and a few dozen more head off toward the woods, where they will wait for the enemy's approach.

It begins midmorning of the next day, and lasts for an hour or so, no more.

Buller and his men have fortified the small hill that sits south of the town. Skion Kop, he calls it, in honor of a tragic defeat in the old life that here he plans to rewrite.

There are about forty on the hill, and the force marching toward them numbers three times that many. Buller can see the tall, lean figure in the lead—Louis Botha.

Buller hopes that Botha walks into the very kind of trap he might have set himself in that previous struggle. Buller has only his forty on the hill, but there is another fifty, led by Stephen and Joseph, hidden back in the woods a quarter-mile inland from the hill, ready to flank the attackers and come up from behind to cut off a retreat.

And there is Buller's secret weapon, a third force of yet another fifty, waiting behind the stockades of the town. Buller thinks Botha won't think of them, will march right by the Riverside town and attack the hill, anxious to get at Buller and the English.

If he does, the force in the town will cut off that escape, and combine with the inland force to squeeze the Boers in a deadly vice, caught between three armies.

Of course, it isn't so simple as that once the fighting starts. Botha is no fool, and wary of the town. He sends a small force to attack it and find out how strong its defenders might be.

They attack by throwing flaming spears against the stockade and over the top into the village.

The defenders return the favor, and in so doing reveal themselves as kaffirs. It is Josh Gibson leading most of the villagers and a dozen more escaped slaves from Botha's kraal. They villagers stay behind their stockade walls, and this confirms Botha's impressions of their general cowardice. He leaves a strong commando of twenty men to harass the stockade and keep it busy, and brings the rest of his force up to attack the hill.

Buller watches this from the hill, and smiles.

The attack begins in earnest just as the noon grails flash and boom. The Boers charge up the hill, spears thrown over the top by men behind them to land in the English trenches.

Buller's men dodge the spears and wait as the Boers approach. A few moments more, a few moments more.

And they throw their own, and then, in what seems an act of foolish courage, they attack, coming down the hill with spears and baseball bats and shouts of encouragement.

At the same time, from behind the Boers on the inland side, Stephen and Joseph lead their force into the attack as well, moving in from the woods with spears raised, shouting. Stephen, running into battle, finds it incomprehensible in its chaos at first. He swings widely, sees a face crushed by the baseball bat he carries, parries a spear thrust and bashes another head, is cracked a good one on the head himself, falls to his knees, and is rescued by Joseph on one side and Cora on the other, who pull him back from the fight for a few moments before they look at one another, smile and then yell, and return to the fray.

At the stockade, the gates open and out come the townspeople, the Detroiters, all black and white together, armed with clubs and spears and borrowed baseball bats, Josh Gibson at the lead.

The small force of Boers that stands outside is overwhelmed immediately, those who survive the first onslaught running for their lives. Most do not make it.

The Boers are crushed between the three attackers. The overall numbers are nearly equal, but the Boers find themselves confused, unsure which way to turn to face the enemy. They fight bravely for a time, and there are losses on both sides, but they are surrounded and know it, and inevitably they begin to surrender.

In an hour the great battle is over. Dozens killed, dozens more captured, a few escaped. Botha is bruised, but otherwise unharmed. Buller accepts his capitulation in a small ceremony at the top of Skion Kop. Botha winces to hear the name of this small hill.

There is more than a little celebrating. The scourge of this part of the River is captured, his army destroyed.

Stephen is at first elated, euphoric. Cora can hardly calm him down. It was all very heroic, wonderful, glorious, not at all as he thought war would be.

Then Cora takes him for a walk back to the battlefield. The dead and wounded are strewn about in painful repose. Stephen, walking through the field, finds Lou Gehrig's body, the head bashed in from a club, the broken half of a spear still in his side.

Nearby lies Sliding Billy Hamilton, pinned to the earth with a spear through his chest.

And there, at the foot of the hill, lies Joseph. There is no mark on him that Stephen can see at first. He thinks Joseph might be sleeping, or knocked unconscious. He touches him, and there is still warmth.

He kneels next to his friend, reaches down to touch his face. Joseph's eyes open. He smiles, speaks.

"Something for you to write about now, young Stephen, eh? The ending of my story. The start of yours?"

Joseph falls into a deep cough, blood spurting from his mouth. Stephen brings him to him, hugs him, and feels the hardened burnt end of a spear emerging from Joseph's chest. He was speared in the back, and then the point broken off.

In a few minutes, Joseph, saying no more, dies. Stephen cries. He knows Joseph is alive again elsewhere on the River, but, still, he cries. It is an ugly, vicious scene here. There is the smell of blood, the stink of loosed bowels, and the beginnings of decay in the heat.

Stephen moves away from his friend, staggers to his knees, then throws up. He calms, the heaving eases, and he staggers back to the campsite with Cora. "Never again," he says to her, "never again that, Cora. My God."

She says nothing to him, but strokes his hair as he lies on his back, his head on her lap.

"My God," he says again. "How can we do this to one another?"

She has no answer to that.

NINTH INNING
The Red Stockings of Courage

The chautauqua is leaving this morning. Reddie Buller is now the manager of the Secret Agents. Babe Ruth will manage the Red Stockings. No one is certain how well that will work out, but the Babe promises to keep everyone in line, including himself.

Several of the Boers, deadly enemies the week before, have now joined the chautauqua. They are having some trouble with the idea of the black players as equals, but several practice sessions over the past two days have had a sobering effect on their assessment of who can play this game and who cannot. They have learned to avoid certain words: "kaffir" is at the top of the list.

A few others of the Boers have asked to stay on in Courage, and have been accepted there. The past is past, the new mayor says, and we need them in any event.

Mayor Stephen Crane leads the townspeople to the River's edge, where there are huzzahs, waves, tears, and excitement at the chautauqua's departure. Then Stephen, his arm around his bride, leads them all back to town. They have a lot to do, starting with rebuilding the stockade and then organizing the town's baseball team.

Yesterday a traveler in a dugout canoe came by with a message from Hannibal, up-River a few miles. The people of Hannibal had heard of the battle, and sent their congratulations and thanks; they would have been next on Botha's list. Also, the messenger added, the Elephants of Hannibal have challenged Courage to a game in two weeks. Stephen accepted the challenge, and now he must organize the new Red Stockings of Courage and have them ready.

Cora, dear Cora, is experimenting, learning how to make paper from the River reeds. She also has overhead the messenger request that Stephen tell more stories.

Stephen thinks he'll be pleased to do that. Last night, talking with Cora, he began a little something new. He thinks it's going to be quite a story, and Hannibal will get to hear it first.

"A Tale of Courage," he plans to call it.

Riverworld Roulette

Robert Weinberg

1

It was the silence, Jim Bowie decided, that bothered him the most on Riverworld. It was unnatural, unnerving. All of his life he had been surrounded by sound. Now, there was nothing.

At night, the forests should have been filled with noise. Many times, he found himself listening in vain for the hooting of owls, the incessant chirping of crickets. Where was the snap of a branch as deer stepped cautiously to water, or the raucous scream of the hunting cat discovering its prey? Such sounds did not exist on Riverworld. Only the hollow chattering of men broke the solitude of the dark.

Sighing, Bowie turned to the huge bonfire blazing nearby on the beach. Nearly sixty men sat clustered in a semicircle around the fire talking softly among themselves. Each man was armed with a dragonleather shield and hornfish sword. Hardened, grim-faced warriors, they looked ready for battle. Greek soldiers, under the command of Lysander of Sparta, the men served as the crew of the good ship *Unfinished Business*. Jim Bowie—notorious duelist, land speculator, knife fighter, and hero of the Alamo—was their captain.

His vessel was beached less than a hundred feet away, barely visible in the glow of the fire. Guarding it was its builder, the Norseman Thorberg Scafhogg; a Roman centurion who now called himself Isaac the Seeker; and a small party of Spartan volunteers. While no one expected any trouble, Bowie believed in preparing for any eventuality. Anything could happen on Riverworld, and very often did.

"Too damned peaceful," declared Davy Crockett, appearing suddenly out of nowhere at Bowie's side. Instinctively, the Texan's hand dropped to the huge knife at his belt. With a curse, he turned to his friend.

"Damn it, Davy," he declared angrily, "stop doing that." Bowie drew in a deep breath. "Ain't natural for a man to move so quiet. One of these days you'll catch me daydreamin' about Injuns and I'll slice you to ribbons before I realize my mistake."

"Sorry, Jim," said Crockett, chuckling. He sounded anything but. "Didn't mean to scare you none. Kinda forget myself sometime. The show start yet?"

"You arrived in the nick of time," said Bowie, gesturing toward the bonfire. A short, stocky blond man had just entered the circle. With a dramatic gesture, he raised his hands over his head. Immediately, all conversation ceased.

"Gentlemen," said Bill Mason, twentieth-century historian and organizer of the event. "Tonight, we offer you another evening of elucidation and entertainment by some of the greatest names in history. Please treat them with the courtesy and respect they deserve."

Bowie grinned at Mason's admonition. Normally, the Spartans were as well behaved an audience as anyone could want. However, the Somber Greeks were a pretty pompous lot and did not take well to sarcasm—a fact that had not gone unnoticed by another member of their expedition, the Athenian philosopher and teacher Socrates.

Master of a sharp tongue and biting wit that had gotten him into trouble more than once, the sage delighted in baiting his fellow travelers. So far, Bowie had managed to keep the peace. But each show presented a new challenge.

The amateur hours, as Bill Mason named them, took place every time they found a safe harbor. Despite the many billions of people inhabiting Riverworld, there were a number of small valleys devoid of life. Narrow strips of beach and forest without grailstones, they provided a welcome break from the frantic clash of cultures that normally filled their days.

Living off their stored supplies, the adventurers relaxed, repaired their boat, and engaged in athletic contests. At night, the more demonstrative members of the crew, under Mason's supervision, entertained the rest. Tonight was the tenth such show since starting their voyage over two years ago, and the historian had promised some special surprise events in celebration. Bowie waited in dread anticipation.

"Instead of our usual program," said Mason, as if replying directly to Bowie's worries, "I thought we would try something different. *Totally different.* For example, there will be no lectures this evening on justice and morality."

The Spartans cheered wildly, as that was Socrates' specialty. Mason waved his arms about for silence. "No magic tricks either, or tales of Spartan heroism. Tonight, we will engage in what was known in my culture as a hootenanny. A singalong."

"Sounds safe enough," said Bowie, turning to Crockett. But the frontiersman was no longer there. He had disappeared as silently as he had first appeared. With a shrug, the big Texan focused his attention on Mason. Somehow, he suspected, Crockett would not be gone long.

"Each of our entertainers has spent many long hours memorizing and practicing his song. Except for certain key words that create a certain resonance, we've translated the songs into Esperanto so that you can all understand the meaning. Listen to the lyrics as our performers sing them. Certain phrases, especially at the end of each stanza, are repeated again and again. These are the chorus, an idea freely borrowed from your own Greek theater. Once you think you know them, please join in. At a hootenanny, everyone participates."

Mason paused, drawing in a deep breath. "So, let's give a big welcome to our first performer. Davy Crockett!"

Whooping with delight, the Spartans banged their swords against their shields, creating a tremendous racket. Crockett, with his easygoing attitude and utter fearlessness in the face of danger, was a favorite of the Greeks. Smiling broadly, he entered the circle.

The frontiersman's gaze swept the crowd. His eyes met Bowie's for an instant and he winked. Mentally, the big Texan groaned. He prayed that Crockett wasn't going to sing the theme song from his television show. There was only so much torture a man could stand.

That both he and Crockett had become legendary figures

tickled Bowie's fancy. But the fact that Crockett had become immortalized in song as "King of the Wild Frontier" gnawed at his insides. The Texan hated to admit it, but he was jealous of his friend's fame.

According to Bill Mason, there had been a Jim Bowie show on that mysterious magical medium called television. Unfortunately, the historian couldn't remember a thing about the program, much less its theme song. Mason had dubbed the show "a flop." Bowie wasn't exactly sure what the word meant, but it didn't sound good.

Standing tall, Crockett started to sing. "Just sweet sixteen, that fateful night . . ."

Bowie sighed with relief. Instead of the ballad dealing with Crockett's exploits, the song told the tragic story of a young girl who died for love. Though Crockett was barely able to carry a tune, the words of the song rang true and clear. Much of the meaning was lost on Bowie, but what he did understand brought tears to his eyes.

By the time the frontiersman reached the third chorus, everyone around the bonfire was singing. "Teen Angel," they wailed dutifully, "Teen Angel."

Grinning merrily, Crockett finished the song with a flourish. He sauntered over to Bowie while behind him the Spartans thumped their swords against their shields in approval.

"Caught you by surprise, huh?" asked the frontiersman, his eyes sparkling.

"Sure did," admitted Bowie. "Mason teach you that ditty?"

"You bet," said Crockett. "He's been coaching a bunch of us for weeks. He calls the stuff rock'n'roll or somethin' like that. Though can't figure for the life of me what it has to do with rocks."

"Shhh," cautioned Bowie. "LeBlanc's getting ready to start. And, unlike you, the Frenchie's got a good voice."

Maurice LeBlanc was an odd combination of soldier and scientist. A veteran of the French Foreign Legion, he enjoyed a good fight almost as much as Crockett. His volatile temper had gotten him killed a half-dozen times on the River. LeBlanc believed in living life to its fullest, even if that meant dying more often than most people preferred.

Despite the violence in his soul, the Frenchman was also a dedicated mathematician and scientist. He had joined their party in hopes of finding one of his countrymen, Pierre de Fermat, who had lived centuries before his birth. According to LeBlanc, Fermat was the only one who could answer a question that had troubled mathematicians for hundreds of years.

As best Bowie could understand, the solution to the problem had no relevance to life on the River. Nor to much else of importance. The Texan couldn't understand why LeBlanc cared one way or another about the question, but he knew better than to ask. All of the crew members on the *Unfinished Business* were seeking answers that had escaped them during their life on Earth. On this voyage, you never questioned a man's dream, no matter how alien it seemed.

"My song," said LeBlanc solemnly, "is titled 'Satisfaction.' Though the words make little sense to me, I find myself in general agreement with the emotions expressed by the author. I, too, can't get no satisfaction. At least, not until my goal is realized. And liberty, equality, and fraternity exist everywhere on this mighty River. If you are ready, I shall begin."

Song followed song, each one feeding on the good feeling generated by the one before. They sang "Proud Mary," "Surfing USA," "This Land Is Your Land," and a dozen others. Oftentimes, many of the words made little sense to those present, but no one seemed to care.

Lysander of Sparta contributed to the mood by passing out all the bottles of wine he had confiscated from the crew for minor infractions of ship's rules during the past few months. By midnight, while they were not exactly drunk, neither were they particularly sober.

Bowie marveled over Bill Mason's seemingly inexhaustible supply of lyrics. The historian had once admitted to being a "trivia addict," which as far as Bowie could assert meant that he cluttered his mind up with as much useless information as possible. Still, tonight's performance topped any of Mason's previous feats of memory.

Socrates had just begun a spirited rendition of "The Times They Are A-Changin'" when the unexpected occurred.

A man's voice called out from the darkness. "Ho, the fire. I'm a traveler in distress. May I come forward?"

Instantly sober, fifty Spartans were on their feet, swords and shields ready. As was the knife in Bowie's hand.

"Advance and be recognized," Bowie declared. "I'll deny no man help if he needs it."

A solitary figure staggered toward the fire. He was nearly naked, clothed only in a dragonfish loincloth, his grailstone dangling from the thick belt around his waste. A lean, dark-haired man, he was dripping wet. He looked exhausted.

"My name is Paul Boyton," the stranger said, shakily. He spoke Esperanto with a heavy Irish accent. "I could use a bite to eat. And a drink of whisky if you can spare a nip."

Bowie waved the man over to a spot by the fire. Others brought him food and drink. The stranger attacked the supplies with a voracious appetite.

"I'm Jim Bowie. My tall friend here is Davy Crockett. The short, ugly fella is Socrates, the world's greatest philosopher. And so on."

"I heard your singing from the River," said Boyton, devouring a second sandwich. "While the words made little sense to me, they convinced me you weren't in league with *them*. So I decided to take my chances and swam ashore."

Boyton reached for a third sandwich. "I've been in the water for nearly two days without food or drink. Several times I almost gave up and let myself sink. But I refused to surrender. Those bastards most by stopped."

"Hey, Boyton," interrupted Crockett, "how's about you stop beating the bushes. Who are these friends you're talkin' about?"

"The Nazis," spat out the Irishman, as if pronouncing a curse. "and their thrice-damned leader, Adolf Eichmann."

2

In between sips of whiskey, Paul Boyton told his story.

"I was never one to sit around and do nothing with my

life," the Irishman began. Though I was born in Dublin, I was raised in the United States. At fifteen I ran away from home and joined the Union Navy. I never looked back.

"After the Civil War, I fought with the revolutionaries in Mexico and later in the Franco-Prussian War. Tiring of the military regimen, I then joined the famous Paris Commune, but that life wasn't exciting enough for me. So I worked for a time on a plot to free Cuba from the Spanish. When that fell through, I went to South Africa and mined diamonds."

Boyton took another swig of bourbon and reached for another sandwich. "Still in pursuit of my fortune, I captained the first lifesaving service in Atlantic City, New Jersey, and personally rescued seventy-one people. That record brought me to the attention of C. S. Merriman, a Pittsburgh manufacturer who had designed a special lifesaving suit for transatlantic steamship passengers. Merriman hired me to test his device, and I agreed.

"The watertight suit made survival possible in the harshest ocean conditions. In October 1874, I put the device to a stern test, swimming more than thirty miles from a boat at sea to Cork, Ireland. Six months later, I swam the English Channel, most of the way on my back, smoking a cigar.

"Don't seem proper," said Crockett, "a man spending so much time in the water."

Boyton nodded agreement. "Swimming was considered a foolish waste of time in my day as well, buy my exploits helped change that. I swam the Rhine, the Seine, the Tiber, the Missouri, and even the Mississippi rivers. Looking for excitement, I joined the Peruvian navy and blew up a Chilean ship by swimming out to it in the harbor and planting 125 pounds of dynamite to her side. Finally, I retired and set up a bar and grill in New York City. I died wealthy though somewhat bored in 1924."

"And woke up here on the Riverworld," said Bill Mason, smiling, "to face your greatest challenge."

"Correct," said Boyton. "Think of it, gentlemen. A river millions of miles long! What greater challenge for a man of my talents. It's my goal to swim its entire length."

"You're crazy as a loon," declared Crockett, no friend of water or bathing. "Why bother?"

"On Riverworld, why not?" countered Boyton. "From what you've told me of your quest, mine makes as much sense."

"Maybe more," said Bowie, grinning. "But tell us about these Nazi fellows in the next valley."

The smile vanished off the Irishman's face. "They're devils, pure and simple. I've encountered some pretty strange cultures swimming up the River. But none of them match those Germans for sheer ruthlessness."

"It doesn't make sense," said Bill Mason, frowning. "The Nazis come from my time, the 1920s through the 1940s, to be exact. According to all reports, the River's laid out in roughly chronological historic order. We're still floating through ancient times. LeBlanc did some calculations while you were drying off. He places the fascists ten million miles or more downstream."

"Moreover," interrupted the Frenchman, "in all of my reincarnations, I never encountered more than a dozen men or women from the twentieth century in one enclave. I suspect the gods of Riverworld planned this for a reason."

"Meaning what?" asked Bowie.

"Who am I to fathom the minds of gods?" asked LeBlanc, making it perfectly clear from his tone of voice that he felt perfectly qualified. "But, from what I have seen and our friend Mason has demonstrated many times, our modern friends are very comfortable with science and technology. They are not as overwhelmed by the marvels of our new home. I believe the gods fear what might happen if too many of them came together in one place. Perhaps they worry what they might discover."

"Well," said Boyton. "If those damned Nazis are any example, I don't blame the gods one bit."

"Why don't you continue with your story," suggested Bowie patiently. His companions were bright and inquisitive, but sometimes they talked too much.

"I've been swimming upstream for nearly two years now," said Boyton. "I could've gone with the current, but that seemed like cheating. I've always enjoyed a challenge. Usually, I swim from one valley to the next, spending a night in each new location. By and large, the reception I've encountered has been pretty friendly. Most people are fascinated by my attempt and have treated me well. With the spread of Esperanto, communication has rarely been a problem. It's been a good life.''

"The Nazis?" prompted Bowie.

"I'm coming to them," said Boyton. "Four days ago, I came ashore at the valley beyond this one. My reception was anything but friendly. As I made my way onto the beach, I was surrounded by a dozen men, armed with spears and swords. They demanded to know who I was and why I had come there. Their leader was a huge brute, eight feet tall and well over five hundred pounds. He carried a monstrous ax capable of smashing a man's head to a pulp with one blow. Several of the others called him Goliath, and I had no doubts that he was the legendary giant of *The Bible*.

"The titan was all for killing me on the spot, but several of the others persuaded him that their lord and master might want to question me. Thus I was brought before Adolf Eichmann."

Boyton paused, his gaze dramatically swinging around to take in the entire group. Master swimmer, he was also a master storyteller. "Goliath's size made him frightening. Eichmann's intellect served the same purpose. Of the two, I found the German the more horrifying. The giant was a creature of passion. Eichmann kept his desires under strict control. Instead, he never let his emotions interfere with his schemes. He was a cold, callous maniac. He was a true monster."

The Irishman downed his whiskey in a gulp. He should have been drunk, but his tale kept him cold sober. "A small, rat-faced man, Eichmann questioned me for hours. He expressed a great deal of interest in the civilizations down-river from his settlement. Feeling I revealed nothing he could not learn himself easily, I spoke freely and honestly.

"Evidently, what I described pleased the German immensely. Within a short time he was bragging of his plans to subjugate the 'mongrel races' surrounding his enclave. Eichmann planned to establish a Nazi empire, a "New Reich" he called it, ruled by his disciples. The monstrous truth behind that scheme I did not learn until the next morning."

"Just who are these Nazi fellas anyways?" asked Crockett.

Bill Mason grimaced. "The shame of the twentieth century."

Softly, dispassionately, the historian described the rise and fall of the Third Reich. By the time he finished speaking, a deathly silence had fallen over his companions.

Lysander of Sparta finally broke the spell. "The guard on the riverbank must be strengthened. We dare not let these monsters catch us by surprise." His features white, he rose to his feet. "I will return shortly."

"Thirteen million innocents killed," whispered Socrates. "The crimes of these Nazis stagger the imagination. And I thought someday to know the meaning of justice. Can such a concept exist in a species that permits such insanity?"

"Worst part is," said Boyton, "that now they're reborn on Riverworld, they plan to do it all over again."

"What do you mean?" asked Bowie. He could feel a cold, hard knot of rage forming within himself. The killing rage, as his brother named it. "What do you mean by that?"

"Eichmann questioned me until it grew dark. Finally, he wearied of the conversation. Hungry and tired, I was dragged off by his followers to a bamboo stockade inhabited by several hundred naked women. These poor unfortunates, I soon learned, were kept alive purely for the sexual pleasures of the Nazis. There was not one man in the entire prison. It was then that I started suspecting the worst. But the women, terrified by their captors, refused to speak with me. Not until daylight did I finally learn the full truth about the new Reich."

"Surely, suicide . . ." began Bill Mason.

"It takes courage to kill yourself," said Boyton. "More courage than these women possessed. Eichmann selected only those slaves who were terrified of dying. Anyone with real spirit never made it to the stockade."

"I don't like what you're saying," declared Davy Crockett, his eyes narrowing. "Tell me what I'm thinkin' about these Nazis ain't true."

Boyton sucked in a deep breath. "All too true, I'm afraid. I witnessed the slaughter the next morning. Dear God," and his voice cracked with emotion, "if I could only wipe the sight of it out of my mind."

"The valley was not a large one. It contained three grailstones. Or so I surmised from what happened at daybreak. The Nazis assembled shortly after sunrise and split into three groups. Watching them, it was obvious they had done this many times before. Two of the units marched off, presumably to other grailstones, while the third remained at the village.

"How many men in each group?" asked Bowie.

"Fifty or sixty," answered Boyton. "All of them big, powerful fellows, armed with swords and knives."

"They outnumber us three to one," said Bowie. "That's more than our crew could handle. Even with the element of surprise."

"Surprising them would be difficult," said Boyton. "The main compound is surrounded by a huge wall, with only one gate. They leave it open during the day, but it's closed at sunset. And guarded by Goliath."

"Bigger they are, the harder they fall," said Crockett.

"Under the watchful eyes of the Nazis, the women of the stockade were allowed to place their grails in the grailstone. As was I. Once we were herded back into our prison, our captors did the same."

"Going by your figures," said Bowie, frowning, "that left close to five hundred spaces in the grailstone free. Which meant there would be that many new people translated to the valley that morning."

Boyton nodded, his features white. "Make that nearly two thousand newcomers if you take into account the other two grailstones." His voice sank to a whisper. "Two thousand people every day."

Eyes filled with horrors only he could see, the Irishman continued. "At the usual time, energy flared and the five hundred new arrivals materialized into existence around the grailstone. A random sample of those who had died the previous day somewhere else on the River, now returned to life at a new location. But, for most, only for an instant."

"Madness," said Socrates. "Sheer madness."

"Not according to Eichmann," said Boyton. "His men worked swiftly and efficiently. They were expert slaughterers, having gone through the ritual so many times. Passing among the reborn, they slit the throats of all people of color. Red, black, and yellow, they died instantly. Not one was spared.

"Women they killed too, except for a few deemed most attractive. These joined the others in the stockade. In this Nazi hell, females provided sexual gratification and nothing more. Those who failed to satisfy were executed."

"What happened to the rest, the men they didn't kill immediately?" asked Bowie.

"They were herded together and placed in another compound not far from the grailstone. Still groggy from translation, most did what they were told without protest. After eating breakfast, Eichmann and several deputies cross-examined the captives. A few, likely recruits or resurrected Nazis, they allowed to live. All the others were dispatched.

"Later, the women of the stockade were allowed to retrieve their grails and devour the contents." Again, Boyton's voice grew shaky. "It was a vision of Hell. We ate surrounded by the newly slaughtered, their bodies still warm. Blood was everywhere.

"Afterward, the slaves split up into small groups, gathered together the corpses, and threw them into the river. Realizing this would be my only chance to escape, I broke away from my party and dove into the water. I struck out for the middle of the River, swimming underwater most of the time. A few guards tried to follow, but none of them came close. They soon gave up. Obviously, they felt I wasn't worth the effort."

"Why did you swim upstream?" asked Bowie.

"I came from downstream," said Boyton. "The two settlements beyond the Nazis are populated by members of the Church of the Second Chance. Nice people, but pacifists. They won't fight for any reason. My only hope of finding help to exterminate those vermin was upriver."

"Killin' thousands of people very day," said Crockett, shaking his head. "It don't make no sense. Why are they doin' it?"

"That's not hard to answer," said Bill Mason. "Eichmann has perverted the basic laws of the Riverworld to his own twisted aims. He's creating the so-called Nazi Master Race, not through breeding, but by selective extermination. It's ruthless and inhuman, but he's slowly achieving the results he wants, without anyone able to stop him.

"Each time a person dies on the River, they are translated

the next day to another location. As far as we can tell, these
rebirths follow no pattern. Anyone from any time period can
end up anywhere else. Eichmann is trying to assemble an army
of Nazis. So, every day he and his henchmen slaughter all of
the unwanted members of his colony. That ensures that there
will be a huge influx of newcomers the next morning. Since
millions of people die each day on the River, the supply of
fresh victims is never-ending. The laws of chance almost
guarantee that a few of the arrivals will qualify for membership
in Eichmann's empire.

"It's like sifting dirt on the River bottom hunting for gold.
You go through a lot of soil to find a few nuggets. Eichmann's
sorting through people, not rocks, but the principle is otherwise
the same. He's gambling against incredible odds but with an
unlimited bankroll. Call it a sort of Riverworld roulette."

"Still don't understand how he managed to get things started,"
said Crockett. "I can see how it works with all those people
bein' translated and still unconscious. But no way he and his
buddies could murder the original population of the valley so
easy."

"That's a question we'll probably never be able to answer,"
said Bowie. "Nor does it really matter. The real dilemma we
face is what are we going to do about it?"

No one said anything for a moment. Then, Socrates, the
conscience of their group, said what had to be said. "We set
out on this voyage to complete tasks not finished on Earth. Is
there any doubt among us that this colony of barbarians, these
Nazi madmen, must be destroyed? That they are part of
humanity's unfinished business?"

3

There was little debate over their course of action. Bowie
and Crockett were veterans of Indian wars and the Alamo.
Lysander was one of Sparta's greatest generals. Socrates had
participated in numerous battles both on Earth and Riverworld,
as had Isaac the Seeker and Maurice LeBlanc. They all agreed

there was only one way to defeat the Nazis. Unfortunately, there was no consensus on who should handle the most dangerous part of the mission.

Their plan consisted of two parts. First, they had to neutralize the numerical advantage of the Nazis. That could be done only by turning their boat up-River and recruiting warriors from the civilizations they had already visited. None of them worried about that.

Most of the inhabitants of this section of Riverworld originally came from the black kingdoms of Kush. Arrogant, proud warriors who had once conquered Egypt, they would be eager recruits in the upcoming battle.

The trip upstream would take several days, and it would require the entire crew of the *Unfinished Business* to battle the River's current. In the meantime, a small party of men had to infiltrate the Nazi camp. Boyton's description of the enclave made it quite clear that they needed a fifth column inside the fortress. Someone had to open the gate for the invaders. Otherwise, the battle would be a long and bloody one, without any guarantee of success. The problem was that everyone on the *Unfinished Business* wanted to go. And they all felt best qualified for the mission.

As captain of the expedition, Bowie made the final decision. As he expected, no one was pleased with his choice. Especially since he was one of the two men selected. The other was Lysander of Sparta.

"It don't make no sense," argued Davy Crockett. "You and Lysander are the only voices of reason on the whole damned expedition. Sending the both of you on a suicide mission is nuts."

Bowie shrugged. "You're just annoyed because I picked Lysander to accompany me instead of you. Can't say I don't understand your feelings. But Lysander ain't the talker you are. If those Kushites need some convincing, you and Socrates are the ones to do it. Bill Mason's got the smarts, but he ain't a fightin' man. Those black men respect you."

Crockett nodded. "I can't argue much with what you're sayin'. Me and the Kushite king hit it off pretty well. Got drunk and all that one night. And he did want me to stick around and marry his sister."

"Like I said," continued Bowie. "Lysander doesn't have a way with words. He's quiet. Too damned thoughtful to convince the Kushites to help. But he's tough as nails and a deadly fighter to boot. Other than you, he's the best choice to guard my back."

"I'm convinced," said Crockett, "but can't say I'm happy about it. Not a bit."

Bill Mason had other worries. He raised them with Bowie shortly before the *Unfinished Business* set off up-River.

"Lysander's a Spartan," he declared, sounding worried.

"No denying it," answered the Texan. "Something wrong with that, Bill?"

"I hope not," said Mason. "For your sake as well as ours. Don't get me wrong. I like Lysander a great deal. He's always stood beside us in all our adventures. But he was raised in Sparta, one of the most militaristic societies ever to exist. The Spartans truly believed that their citizens were more gifted than other people—that they were, in fact, a master race destined to rule. It's a view awfully close to Eichmann's."

Bowie frowned. "You think Lysander might agree with the Nazi program?"

The historian shook his head. "I don't know, Jim. I hope not. But anything's possible."

"Well," said Bowie, "I trust Lysander. He's never struck me as the type to betray his friends, no matter what the reason. In my gut, I know he's the right one to accompany me on this trip. Still, I appreciate the warning. I'll keep my eyes open."

"Eichmann's a devil," warned Mason. "Of all the Nazi leaders, he was the most ruthless. And the most cunning. He's a dangerous man."

Bowie smiled, thin lipped and without humor. "So am I, Bill. So am I."

4

Bowie and Lysander waited two days after their friends left before they set out on their own journey. Appearing too soon after Boyton's escape might seem suspicious. And Bowie was determined to spend as little time in the Nazi stronghold as possible.

They paddled smoothly, in rhythm, propelling the bamboo canoe swiftly through the water. It was hard, demanding work, with no time for talk. Which suited Jim Bowie just fine. A cold, white flame of anger burned deep within him. With all of his heart, he believed there could be no compromise with evil. The Nazis and their mad schemes had to be stopped.

His eyes narrowed as a wave of frustration swept through him. The Germans could and would be defeated. By his efforts or someone else. But it hardly mattered. Because on Riverworld, nothing really ended. Evil, like good, endured.

The simplest way to end the Nazi threat was to kill all those involved. Unfortunately, the next day all of the guilty parties would be reborn somewhere else on the River, free to start scheming again. Nor would anyone be aware of their true identities or their earlier crimes. To Bowie, it seemed quite unfair. Unlike the Second Chancers, he could not forgive and forget.

According to the Church of the Second Chance, mankind had been reborn on the River for a specific purpose. Members of the religion taught that the purpose of existence was to achieve oneness with God. Every individual was capable of reaching this personal salvation through love and total nonviolence. Life on Riverworld offered humanity a second chance at this goal. Freed from the burdens of finding food, raising children, and worrying about death, people could now concentrate fully on achieving immortality of the spirit.

Bowie had little patience with the Second Chancers. A man of action, he considered their philosophy of patience and harmony incredibly naive. Being a pacifist on the River seemed a sure guarantee of numerous resurrections. Humanity, on the whole, was not ready to forsake ten thousand years of violence no matter what miracles the gods of Riverworld produced.

Socrates had put it best: "If the gods preferred us to be sheep, they would have resurrected us with the minds of sheep. As we were returned as men, we must act like men."

Bowie's reverie was shattered by a nudge from Lysander's paddle. "I see the shallow inlet that Boyton described. And a party of well-wishers wait for us on the beach."

Six powerful men watched as the canoe headed for shore. One figure towered head and shoulders over the others. A giant with pitch-black hair and tiny piglike eyes that stared at the approaching craft with undisguised hostility. Cradled in his arms was the biggest club Bowie had ever seen. For their plan to succeed, this man had to die.

"Killing that monster might be a challenge," muttered Bowie as he and Lysander leapt into the water to steady the canoe as they brought it to land.

"Don't let his looks frighten you," whispered back Lysander. By now they were less than a dozen yards from the beach. "A man his size is slow and clumsy. Carrying that much weight, he will tire easy. His legs are his weak point."

"Sure the hell look like trees to me," said Bowie. Then there was no time for chatter.

As soon as they stepped out of the water, they were surrounded by the welcoming party. Each man was armed with both a sword and knife, and several of them carried spears as well. None of them appeared friendly.

"Who are you and what do you want?" asked a muscular blonde, an arrogant sneer on his face. "We do not allow strangers on our land."

"Then you boys should've posted a sign in the middle of the River," replied Bowie, in a slow, relaxed drawl. The possibility of sudden death always calmed his nerves. Especially since he knew that dying was no longer permanent. "Since there wasn't one, we decided to stop and look around."

"That answer is . . ." began the blonde, but stopped suddenly as Bowie pulled out his huge steel knife and began picking at his nails.

"I'm Jim Bowie," said the Texan, his tone pleasant. "My friend's Lysander of Sparta. Besides being one of the greatest generals in history, he handles a sword real well. Not a man I'd want for my enemy."

Lysander had used the momentary distraction caused by the appearance of Bowie's knife to draw his own weapon. He held his sword with the steady assurance of a man confident of his own skill.

Bowie chuckled and flashed his knife in the sunshine. "Those hornfish swords ain't bad weapons. But they don't compare to a real steel blade. In the hands of an expert, a knife like this can gut a man in a second. Spill his insides out all over the sand before he can blink an eye." Bowie grinned. "And I'm the best, boys. The very best."

"You are James Bowie?" asked another member of the shore patrol, sounding awed. "Inventor of the legendary Bowie knife? Who died with Davy Crockett at the Alamo?"

Mentally, Bowie grimaced. Escaping Crockett's legend was impossible. "One and the same," he answered. "My brother, Rezin, invented the knife. But I'm the one who killed six men in duels using it."

"Too much talking," interrupted the black-haired giant. He raised the huge club he carried onto one shoulder. "We gonna kill them or not?"

"Definitely not, Goliath," said the man who had recognized Bowie's name. Somewhat shorter than his companions, with dark-brown hair and eyes, he nodded his head in a polite half-bow. "I am Fritz Mueller. As a child, I read of your incredible exploits. I am honored to meet you."

Then, as if in answer to the mutterings among his fellows, Mueller continued, "Our leader, Herr Eichmann, was also a tremendous admirer of the American pioneers. I am sure he will be delighted to learn of your presence."

"Be glad to say hello," said Bowie, sheathing his knife though resting a hand on its hilt. "I've always enjoyed socializing."

As they marched up the beach, Bowie carefully studied Goliath. Up close, the giant was even more imposing than from a distance. His hands were immense, with fingers like sausages. His chest was twice the size of a normal man's and was creased with muscle.

Recalling Lysander's advice, Bowie paid close attention to how Goliath moved. His friend's assessment had been remarkably accurate. The titan moved slowly and without grace. He grunted in pain with each step, careful to avoid twisting his

ankles or knees. The Texan Bowie felt a little more confident.
He dared not underestimate the giant's incredible strength. But
he was by no means invulnerable. If David could kill Goliath,
so could Jim Bowie.

5

The Nazi compound was exactly as described by Paul Boyton.
It reminded Bowie of the forts of his time, and he wondered
idly if perhaps one of his contemporaries had helped construct
it.

A sturdy earthen wall fifteen feet high and five feet thick
surrounded the entire complex. There was a wood guardpost
every fifty feet, connected by ladder to the inside of the fort. A
massive ironwood gate provided the only entrance to the
compound. Boyton was right. Unless that gate was opened
from the inside, the Germans were safe from any outside
attack.

The settlement was approximately five hundred feet wide. In
its center was the ever-important grailstone, which provided
both food and drink for the inhabitants. On Riverworld long
sieges were impossible, as the defenders never ran out of
supplies. But the attackers, separated from their own grailstones,
did.

To the left of the grailstone was the stockade mentioned by
the Irishman. Bowie's gaze swept over it for an instant and then
moved on. The only way he could help the women imprisoned
there was by ignoring them. Still, he could feel their eyes on
his back as he walked silently past.

Directly across from the stockade was a number of small
cabins that Bowie surmised were the living quarters of the
Nazis. To the rear of the fort was a second large stockade,
empty of life. From Boyton's story, he recognized it as the
holding pen for potential members of the colony.

Eichmann's quarters, not particularly surprising to the Texan,
was the most lavish building within the compound. Etched on

one wall of the dwelling was a large twisted cross Bowie knew had to be a swastika.

He and Lysander were escorted to a small antechamber. There they remained, under the watchful eyes of a half-dozen armed guards, while Fritz Mueller went to report their presence to his leader. The German returned within minutes, his face glowing with excitement.

"Herr General Eichmann will see you gentlemen immediately," he proclaimed proudly. "He is honored to entertain such famous guests. Please, follow me."

For all of Mueller's courtesies, Bowie noticed that he didn't dismiss the guards following them.

Eichmann, short and slender when compared to his followers, had the warmth and personality of a snake. He reminded Bowie of numerous politicians he had known back on Earth. The only person who mattered to Adolf Eichmann was Adolf Eichmann.

After a glass of excellent brandy and a few pleasantries, the German came right to the point. "I'm told you carry a wonderful knife, Herr Bowie. Do you mind if I examine it?"

"Not at all," said Bowie. He pulled out the blade and handed it, hilt first, to Eichmann.

"You are quite trusting," said the Nazi, turning the steel weapon over in his hands.

"You've got the guards," said Bowie.

"That I do," said Eichmann. Still holding the knife, he smiled at the Texan. "And what would you think, Herr Bowie, now that I have your invaluable steel knife in my possession, if I commanded my men to execute the two of you on the spot?"

Laughing, Bowie shook his head. "I would think you were making an awfully terrible mistake, Mr. Eichmann. And, I don't think you're the type of fellow who makes mistakes."

"I'm not sure I follow your logic," said Eichmann, sounding puzzled.

"Sure, you have my steel knife. *One knife*. Ain't much good you can do with a single weapon. On the other hand, the *knowledge* of how that weapon was made . . ."

Eichmann inhaled sharply. "There is no iron ore on Riverworld."

"The blade you're holding says otherwise," said Bowie.

"And you made it?" asked the German.

"The secret of steel," said Bowie, calmly. "I know it. Kill me and you lose it. Forever." The Texan paused, letting his words sink in. "Mind handing me back my knife, now, Mr. Eichmann? I feel kinda naked without it."

"My pleasure," said the German, handing over the weapon. "My question was, of course, purely theoretical."

"Of course," echoed Bowie dryly.

Eichmann shook his head as if remembering something important. "In my haste to meet such a famous historical figure, I have ignored my obligations as a host. I am sure you and Herr Lysander would like the opportunity to relax after your journey. Herr Mueller will escort you to an empty cabin. We can speak again at dinner."

"Sounds right fine to me," answered Bowie.

They were safely inside the enemy camp. Now all that remained was opening the gate at the proper moment. Which, Bowie concluded, glancing at Goliath one last time, might be more of a challenge than he had anticipated.

6

Eichmann wasted little time after dinner making his proposal. "You possess a powerful secret, Herr Bowie," said the German. I possess the army to use it. Together, we could make our mark felt on the River."

"I've got the knife," said Bowie, leaning back in his chair. "I don't see no army, though. Fact is, this place seems a mite underpopulated."

Six of them sat in a huge chamber at the center of Eichmann's mansion. The Nazi chief, three of his top aides, Bowie, and Lysander. There was only one guard, Goliath, standing patiently by the door, huge club balanced on one shoulder. His gaze bore like a drill in the Texan's back, waiting for him to make the slightest mistake.

"It takes time to assemble a master race," said Eichmann. "Time and determination. Each day we come a little closer to realizing our dream of a new Reich, a new empire untainted by the blood of the mongrel races."

"You talk a lot," said Bowie. "But don't make much sense. You care to explain what you're gabbin' about?"

Eichmann rose from his chair and crossed his arms across his chest. "Mankind can be divided into two groups, Herr Bowie. The sheep and the wolves. The rulers and the slaves. You and I are wolves. As are all those here with us. We ruled back on Earth. We are destined to rule on Riverworld as well.

"Ever since my rebirth on this strange new world, I have been working toward this goal. Sheer providence brought me to this colony, where I was reunited with several officers from my Earthly existence. Together, we came up with a plan to re-create the Reich through a process of selective elimination. Slowly but surely we are assembling the core members of our new empire."

"Selective elimination?" said Bowie.

"The original inhabitants of this enclave were ancient Egyptians. Members of a civilization focused on death and the afterlife, they dwelt here in a state of shock and bewilderment. By all their beliefs, they belonged in the Underworld, living much in the same manner as they had on Earth. The fools could not cope with their existence on the River. It was not difficult to persuade them that somehow they had been detoured from their final rest by a malevolent god or sorcerer. And that only through a simultaneous mass suicide could they set the cosmic balance in order."

"Leaving you and your comrades the only ones left alive in the whole village," said Bowie, trying to keep his voice steady.

"Correct. And ever since then, we have maintained that status, adding to our population only those who share our beliefs, our goals, and our Aryan heritage. Plus a few other exceptional individuals, such as my friend Goliath. We kill all the rest."

"Pretty drastic way of buildin' an army, ain't it?" asked Bowie, his temper threatening to explode.

"Not really," said the German. "I know what you are thinking, but I am not an inhuman monster. *Killing means nothing on Riverworld, nothing at all.* It is, at best, a temporary inconvenience. Most of the ones we slaughter probably never even realize they died another time. We merely speed them on their next journey a little faster."

"What about the women?" asked Lysander, speaking for the first time.

Eichmann shrugged. "Sexual playthings, nothing more. Unable to breed, they are useless for anything else. Again, if they prefer, death brings them instant release."

The German sat back down. "After all, did not you Americans slaughter by the thousands the Red Indians in your move west? And was it not in Sparta that babies were left out on mountaintops to test their mettle? Do not preach morality to me, gentlemen. There is blood on all of our hands."

Bowie slowly rose to his feet, as did Lysander. "I'll need some time to think over what you said. Tomorrow morning I'll tell you my decision."

"That will be acceptable," said Eichmann. He paused for an instant as Bowie and Lysander headed for the door. "Remember, Herr Bowie. I can rule with your help. Or I can rule without it. In either case, I will still rule."

Back at their cabin, Bowie turned to his companion.

"Well, Lysander, what did you think of Mr. Eichmann's little speech. You havin' any second thoughts? Tempted a bit by his offer?"

The Greek general spat on the floor. "In Sparta, we valued strength and courage highly. But they meant nothing without honor. These men prey on the weak and the helpless. They are without honor. It will be a pleasure to bring them down."

"My thoughts exactly," said Bowie. "Better keep your fingers crossed that Crockett and our friends arrive here tonight. 'Cause otherwise, our meeting tomorrow with Mr. Eichmann ain't gonna be pleasant."

7

The whistling of a horned owl woke Bowie up from a dreamless sleep. Breathlessly, he waited for the sound to repeat. Less than a minute later, it echoed again through the darkness. Crockett's signal.

Sliding over to Lysander, Bowie was not surprised to find the Greek awake, his eyes glowing with excitement. "It woke me as well," the general whispered. "Dare we respond?"

"Better if we don't," said Bowie. "No reason for us to spell out our intentions. You wanna silence the guard at the door?"

"With pleasure," said Lysander, softly sliding his hornfish knife into one hand. Silently, he merged into the blackness at the front of their hut.

"Done," he declared a few seconds later, dragging a limp body into the room. "No one seems about. Perhaps this will be easier than we thought."

"I doubt it," said Bowie, pulling his knife free of its scabbard. "It's never easy."

As usual, he was correct. Goliath, Eichmann, and a dozen Nazis awaited them at the gate to the compound.

"Herr Bowie," said the Nazi leader, "I am very disappointed in you. Planning to leave without saying good-bye. Though, I must admit, I expected nothing less. You Americans were always a bothersome nuisance."

"That's us, all right," said Bowie, coolly. Eichmann evidently knew nothing of the raiders outside the walls. All of the guards from the gatehouses had joined him. The rest of the camp slept unawares. Which meant anything could happen. "Nuisances."

He waved the hand not holding the Bowie knife at Goliath. "Come on, big man," he beckoned. "Let's see how tough you really are."

"Kill the fool," barked Eichmann angrily. "And his friend as well."

With a roar of anticipation, the giant lumbered forward. His huge club whistled through the air, aimed directly at Bowie's head. But the Texan was no longer there. Moving with astonishing speed, he ducked underneath Goliath's reach and slashed the big man across one thigh.

Shrieking in surprise and pain, the titan lashed out wildly. This time, Bowie leapt up and over the blow. A streak of red appeared as if by magic on Goliath's chest.

"Get him, you idiots!" screamed Eichmann at his men, hypnotized by the fight.

"For Sparta!" shouted Lysander, and attacked. The Greek general, veteran of a hundred battles, used both a sword and knife with deadly results. Unlike his opponents, he was an expert at close-in fighting. In seconds, Nazi blood stained the ground.

Huffing and puffing, Goliath stood staring at Jim Bowie. Animal-like, the giant growled deep in his throat. Reaching down, he touched the wound on his chest. Bringing his fingers to his mouth, he licked the blood with his tongue.

Sweat trickled down Bowie's back. All he had done so far was make the giant mad. It would take a hundred wounds like the ones he had inflicted to stop the monster. And he had neither the time nor strength to inflict such punishment.

"Come get him!" screamed Adolf Eichmann, grabbing Bowie from behind. The German's arms snapped around Bowie's neck, jerking his head back in a death grip. Circling outside the Texan's field of vision, the Nazi had caught him completely unawares.

Desperately, Bowie slammed an elbow into Eichmann's gut. The German grunted in pain but refused to let go. Out of the corner of an eye, Bowie glimpsed Goliath stomping closer, massive club raised for a killing blow. If he couldn't pull free, Bowie was a dead man.

There was no time for finesse. Drawing back the hand holding the knife, Bowie plunged the blade deep into Eichmann's side. With a violent wrench, he ripped the weapon as far as he could across the Nazi's stomach. Blood and guts exploded against Bowie's back. With a hideous gurgling sound, the German collapsed to the ground, dead.

The pressure on his neck gone, Bowie rolled to the side just as Goliath's club came crashing down. The Texan bellowed in agony as the massive piece of wood glanced off his left shoulder. Fighting back tears of pain, he scrambled to his feet.

Goliath stood motionless, staring at the lifeless body of Adolf Eichmann. Slowly, the giant raised his gaze and looked around for Bowie. Madness glistened in his eyes.

"You killed the Master," declared the big man. Breathing deeply, he raised his massive hands to his face, letting his club fall forgotten to the ground. "He was the Master—the Master! I'll rip you apart for doing that."

Cursing, Bowie backed away from the giant. His shoulder hurt like hell. The club had probably broken several bones. His neck didn't feel that great either. And now, Goliath was mad, really mad. It was time for desperate measures.

Scrambling back, Bowie prayed that Goliath would remain motionless for a few seconds more. Thorberg Scafhogg had designed his knife to exacting specifications. Bowie only hoped this blade possessed the same traits as its Earthly model. His life depended on it.

Five yards away from the giant, he stopped. Drawing on hidden reserves of strength, Bowie straightened. "Here I am, big man. I'm through running. Time to finish this little duel of ours. Right now."

Goliath's eyes widened in berserk rage. Spittle dripping from his mouth, he took one step forward. Then another. Which was right were Bowie wanted him.

The Texan whipped back his arm and with all of his strength flung the Bowie knife at the approaching giant. Thorberg had crafted the blade to perfection. It turned one complete revolution in fourteen feet. And embedded itself up to the hilt in the giant's chest directly above his heart.

Goliath, his eyes glazed with sudden shock, stumbled two more steps forward before collapsing. He was dead before he hit the ground.

"Was startin' to wonder how you planned finishing the son of a bitch off," drawled Davy Crockett. "Glad I saw it with my own eyes. Wouldn't have believed it otherwise."

Wearily, Bowie turned to the frontiersman. "When did you arrive?"

"We were waiting outside for you boys to open the gates,"

said Crockett. "When I heard the ruckus, got a mite impatient. So, men and a few of the Kush warriors scurried over the wall. Provided Lysander some assistance, then opened the gate so the rest of our boys could join in."

Crockett waved a hand in the general direction of the Nazi cabins. "From the sounds of things, appears they've got the situation well in hand. Those boys from Kush are pretty mean fighters when riled. Don't think those Nazis stand much of a chance."

"Good," said Bowie, feeling dizzy, "since I'm gonna collapse."

8

By the time Bowie was feeling back to normal, events in the onetime Nazi colony had stabilized. The warriors from Kush had been unmerciful in their treatment of Eichmann's thugs. Except for the women in the stockade, none of the other colonists survived the night.

The next morning saw the beginning of a new era, as close to two thousand people materialized in the valley. Men and women from all sections of the Riverworld, they were perhaps the most varied mix ever to settle in one location. Red, black, yellow, and white, they came from a hundred different eras and places of origin. Oddly enough, they cooperated better than most. They all shared one experience in common—death—and seemed tempered by it. Within a week, they had the makings of a government in place and were dealing with the day-to-day problems of life on the River.

"About time for us to move on," Bill Mason informed Bowie one sunny afternoon. The Texan, the broken bones in his shoulder mending, sat playing solitaire on the poop deck of the *Unfinished Business*. Except for a small guard detail, the rest of the crew was in town enjoying an extended leave.

"No argument from me," said Bowie. "Death scattered the Nazis all over the River. I doubt if Eichmann will ever get another chance to put his master plan into action. And, if he does, somebody will swat him down again. At least, I hope so. In any case, no reason for us to stick around any longer.

"There is one last thing," said Mason, grinning. He waved a hand and Davy Crockett, Socrates, and Thorberg Scafhogg scrambled onto the deck. Along with them was an attractive young woman Bowie didn't recognize.

"Joan Vance, meet Jim Bowie," said Mason, performing the introduction. "Joan was one of the newcomers translated here. Like me, she's from the twentieth century. And like me, she's a real trivia buff."

Mason nodded to the others. "Gentlemen, are you ready?"

They formed the strangest quartet on Riverworld. Frontier hero, Greek philosopher, Viking shipbuilder, and twentieth-century historian. But it was the thought that counted. And the words.

"Jim Bowie, Jim Bowie, he was a bold, adventurous man. Jim Bowie, Jim Bowie . . ."

Bowie sighed with satisfaction, letting the song sweep over him. Let the others search for whatever they wanted on the River. He was content. No more unfinished business for him. At long last, he had this theme song.

Coda

Philip José Farmer

First I found Rabi'a. Then I found the artifact, which I think of as The Artifact. Which is more precious, Rabi'a or The Artifact? Rabi'a says that I do not have to choose between The Way or The Artifact. There is no choice in this matter between The Way and a machine.

I am not so sure.

My mind, the only truly time-traveling machine, goes back. And then back. And then it goes ahead of this very moment.

Here I sit on the rock that rims the top of the monolith. The sun burns the right side of my head and body. My mind burns too, but all over, burns to its center.

I am on the top of a two-thousand-foot-high granite monolith. It rises from the plain not more than a hundred feet from the Riverbank. The last hundred feet of the monolith flares out like a glans with the end cut off. That the monolith is phallus-shaped is, I think, accidental. But I am not sure that anything about this world is accidental. Even the contours of the mountains, which form the Rivervalley, and the course of the River may have both practical and symbolic meaning.

I wish that I could discern the meaning. There are times when I almost have grasped it. But that is as elusive as the water that forms the River.

The top of the monolith, my living space, my physical world, flares out to make a rough circle six hundred feet in diameter. Not much. But it is enough.

You cannot see it from the ground, but that circle is a cup. Within it is deep and fertile soil, fast-growing bamboo, bushes, and earthworms that eat rotting vegetable matter and human excrement.

In the center of this cup grows a giant oak. At the foot of the tree is a spring, the water brought up through the monolith from the ground-level source by whatever devices the makers of this world concealed in the stone. The water flows northward from the spring in a shallow creek. This broadens out into a lakelet and then cataracts through a narrow gap in the stone of the cup. Rainbow-colored fish live in the creek and the lake. They are about eight inches long and are delicious when fried or baked.

Not far from the tree is a grailstone.

I never needed much on Earth. Here I need even less, though, in a spiritual sense, I require more.

I am like the Dark Age Christian hermits who sat alone on high pillars for years in the African desert. They meditated most of the time, or so they claimed. They seldom moved from their sitting position. If so, they must have had running sores on their asses. I often get up and walk and sometimes run along the very limited circumference of my world. Other times, I climb this three-hundred-feet-high tree, leap from branch to branch, and run back and forth on the largest branches.

Mankind, it is claimed, is descended from the apes. If so, I have, in a sense, regressed to the apes. What of it? There is deep joy in playing on a tree. And it seems fitting to complete the circle from ape to man to ape. It also symbolically matches the circling of the River from North Pole to South Pole and back to the North Pole. What comes out must go back in. In a different form, perhaps. But its essence is matter. Spirit forms from matter. Without matter, spirit has no vessel. Of course, I do not mean The Spirit. Then the time comes when matter dies. Does the spirit also die? No more than a butterfly dies when it changes from pupa to imago. The spirit must go to a place where, unlike this universe but like The Spirit, matter is not necessary.

Or is this kind of thinking born of hope fathered by fear of death? Therefore, without validity.

Ten wishes do not make one piece of pie.

It seems, now and then, strange to utter "I," the first person singular. For so many years on this world, I called myself Doctor Faustroll, and everybody I met thought that was my true name. Many times, I truly forgot that my natal name was Alfred Jarry. The literary character I had created on Earth became me. And I had no individuality. Faustroll was just a piece of the all-embracing "we." But here, at this place on the River, somewhere in the north temperate zone of this planet, "we," which had been "I" in the beginning and then became "we," metamorphosed back into "I." It's as if the butterfly had regressed into the pupa, then again became the butterfly.

Is the second "I" superior to the first one?

I don't know.

Is any one place along the River better than any other place?

I don't know.

But I do know that we, my companions and I, traveled and fought for many years along many millions of miles of the River, going ever upstream, though often that way was from north to south or east or west as the River wandered and wound and writhed. But always, we went against the current.

Then we stopped to rest for a while, just as we had done throughout the journey when we were weary of the fighting and of sailing and of each other's company. Here, I met Rabi'a. Here, I stayed.

Ivar the Boneless, our leader, the huge bronze-haired Viking, did not seem surprised when I told him that I would not sail out with him in the morning.

"Lately, you seem to be thinking much more than is good for a man," he said. "You were always strange, one seemingly touched by the gods, a man with his brain askew."

He cocked an eyebrow at me, grinned, and said, "Have you become fainthearted because of the allure of this hawk-nosed, doe-eyed, dark-skinned woman you met here? Has she fired up your passion for woman? Which, I have observed, has never been fierce. Is that it? You would abandon our quest for a pair of splendid breasts and hot hips?"

"The physical has nothing to do with it," I said. "In fact, Rabi'a was a celibate all her life on Earth, a virgin, a saint.

Resurrection here did not change her mind about that. No, it is definitely not passion for her body that keeps me here. It is passion for her mind. No, not really that. It is passion for God!''

"Ah!" the Viking said, and he spoke no more of the matter. He wished me good luck, and he walked away.

I watched his broad back, and I felt some regret and some sense of loss. But it seemed to me that his loss was far greater than mine. Many years ago, he had experienced what I can only call a mystic moment. Out of the dark sky, while we were fleeing on a boat from enemies bent on killing us, something bright had seized him. That was evident though he would never talk about it. But, from that moment on, he lost his desire to conquer a piece of the Riverworld, rule it, and expand his holdings as far as his wits and his weapons would allow him. Nor did he ever attack a man or an entire state again. He fought only in self-defense, though there was much aggression in that.

His soul and body drove him always up the River. Someday, so he boasted, he would get to the sea at the North Pole and would storm the great tower that many said was there. And he would squeeze the throats of the tower dwellers until they told him who they were, why they had made this planet and its River, and how they had resurrected all of Earth's dead and brought them here and why they had done it.

His vow to do this made him sound simpleminded. In many ways, he was. But he was not just a cruel, bloodthirsty, and loot-hungry savage. He was very shrewd, very curious, and very observant, especially about those who professed to believe in the gods. Having been a priest and a sorceror of the Norse religion, he was skeptical of all faiths. Near the end of his life, while he was the king of Dublin, he had converted to Christianity. He was playing it safe just in case that religion might be the true one. It would not cost him anything.

He died in A.D. 873. After his resurrection in his youthful body on the Riverbank, he abandoned the Cross and became an agnostic, though he kept calling on Odin and Thor when he was in a tight spot. Lifelong habits die hard. Sometimes you have to die more than once before the habits die. That might be one of the messages of the Riverworld.

Ivar's character had changed somewhat. Now, instead of physical and temporal power, he wanted the power of knowledge of the truth. A step forward, yes. But not far enough. How was he going to use his knowledge? I suspected that he would be mightily tempted to wield the knowledge torn from the masters of this world—if he ever got it—for his benefit only. He wanted the truth, not The Truth.

Then there was Andrew Davis, the American physician, osteopath, and neuropath. He had died in A.D. 1919. But awakening on the River, though it had confused him, had not made him abandon his fundamentalist Church of Christ religion. Like so many believers, he had rationalized that the Riverworld was a testing ground that God had provided for those who professed to be Christians. That it was not mentioned in the Bible was only another proof of God's mysterious ways.

When he heard rumors that a woman had conceived and borne a male child, he became convinced that God's son was born again. And he had set out up-River to find the woman and the child. A few years ago, he had met a man who had known Jesus on Earth. This man told Davis that he had encountered Jesus again on the Riverbank. And he had witnessed the execution of Jesus by fanatical Christians.

Did Davis then admit that Jesus was just another madman who had believed that he was the Messiah? No! Davis said that his informant had lied. He was a tool of the Devil.

I believe that it was possible that, somewhere on this world, a woman did have a false pregnancy. And that the story of this somehow became twisted during the many years and the many millions of miles it traveled. Result: the tale goes that a woman has given birth in a world where all men and women are sterile. And, of course, the child must be the Savior.

Thus, Davis went with Ivar on his boat, leaving me behind. Davis did not care much about getting to the supposed tower in the supposed North Polar Sea. He hoped—longed—to find the son of the virgin somewhere north of here and to cast himself in adoration at the feet of the son. Who by now should be approximately thirty years old—if he exists. And he does not, of course.

After Ivar and his crew sailed off, seven years passed.

During this time, I met many dozens of groups of men and women who were going up-River to storm the tower. They were questioners and seekers after the truth, for which I honor them. One of them was a man who claimed to be an Arab. But some of his followers talked, and I found out that he was really an Englishman who had lived in the nineteenth century. My contemporary, more or less. His name was Burton, well known in his time, a remarkable man, a writer of many books, a speaker of many tongues, a great swordsman, a fabled explorer of many lands in Africa and elsewhere. His followers said that he had accidentally awakened in a pre-resurrection chamber made by those mysterious people who had made this planet. They had put him back to sleep, but he had had encounters with these beings since then, and they were out to find him. For what purposes, I do not know. I suspect that this story is one of many tales of wonder floating through the Riverworld.

If any man could get to the tower through the many seemingly insurmountable obstacles and seize the owners of the tower by the throat, this man could. At least, that was the impression I got. But he went on up the River, and that was the last I heard of him. Other questers followed him.

All this time, I was the disciple of Rabi'a, the Arab woman who had lived A.D. 717 to 801. She was born in Basra, a city on the Shatt-al-Arab, a river born of the meeting of the Tigris and Euphrates rivers. This was in the area of ancient Mesopotamia where the Sumerian civilization came into being and was followed by the Akkadian, the Babylonian, the Assyrian, and many others that rose and fell and were covered with the dust. Rabi'a's native city, Basra, was not distant from Baghdad, which some people tell me was the capital of a Muslim nation called Iraq in the middle twentieth century.

Rabi'a was a Sufi and well-known throughout the Muslim world in her time and later. The Sufis were Muslim mystics whose unconventional approach to religion often brought about persecution from the orthodox. That did not surprise me. Everywhere on Earth, the orthodox have hated the unorthodox, and there has been no change here. The not-so-strange thing is that, after the Sufis' deaths, they often became saints to the orthodox. They were no longer a danger.

Rabi'a told me that, for a long time, there have been Jewish
and Christian Sufis, though not many, and these are accepted as
equals by the Muslim Sufis. Anyone who believes in God may
become a Sufi. Atheists need not apply. But there are other
qualifications for becoming a Sufi, and they are very hard.
Also, unlike the orthodox, the Muslim Sufis genuinely believe
in the equality of women with men, a belief unacceptable to the
orthodox.

My many friends in late-nineteenth-century, early-twentieth-
century Paris (Apollinaire, Rousseau, Satie, and many others,
they were legion and legend, great poets, writers, and painters,
leapers from the orthodox into the future, where are they now?)
would be nauseated or would laugh scornfully if they knew that
I aspire to be a Sufi. I sometimes laugh at myself. Who is
better qualified to do so?

Rabi'a says that she has traveled The Path upward until she
knows the utmost ecstasy, seeing the glory of God. I might be
able to do so. No guarantee. She is my teacher, but only I,
through my own efforts, can achieve what she has achieved.
Others have done it, though they are very few. And then she
adds that my strivings may be for nothing. God chooses those
who will know The Way, The Path, The Truth. If I have not
been chosen, *tant pis, je suis dans un de ces merdiers, quel
con, le bon Dieu!*   Why am I, Alfred Jarry, once calling
himself Doctor Faustroll, mocker and satirizer of the hypo-
crites, the Philistines, the orthodox and the self-blinded, the
exploiter and persecutor of others, the dead of soul, the
steadfast and stick-in-the-mud people of faith . . . why am I now
seeking God and willing to work as I have never worked
before, to become a slave of God, not to mention a slave of
Rabi'a? Why am I doing this?

There are many explanations, mostly psychological. But
psychology never explains anything satisfactorily.

I had heard about Rabi'a for some time, and so I went to
hear her directly. I was the student and portrayer of the absurd,
and I did not wish to miss out on the particular absurdity she
represented . . . I thought. I hung around the fringe of the crowd
of her disciples and the eager to learn and the idly curious.
What she said seemed no different from what others of many

different faiths had preached. Talk of The Way and The Path is cheap, and only the names of those who founded the sects and of their disciples differ.

But this woman seemed to radiate something I had never detected in the others. And her words seemed to make sense even if they were, according to logic, absurd. And then she gave me a sidelong glance. It was as if lightning fastened us, as if positive and negative ions had joined. I saw something undefinable but magnetic in those black deerlike eyes.

To shorten the tale, I listened, and then I talked to her, and then I became convinced that what she was talking about was the essence of absurdity. But I recalled that it was Tertuallian who had written about his Christian faith. "I believe because it is absurd." That saying doesn't stand up to logical analysis. But then, it wasn't meant to do so. It appeals to the spirit, not the mind. There's a layer of meaning to it that is as hard to grasp as wine fumes. The nose smells them; the hand cannot hold them.

There is also a method of discipline which the Sufi master requires his initiates to obey. This is designed to lead the initiates upward physically, mentally, and spiritually. Part of it is taking nothing for granted just because it is traditional and conventional. The Sufi never accepts "everybody knows," "They say that..." Neither had I done that, but the Sufi evaluation method was different from mine. Mine had been to expose to ridicule. Theirs was to instill in the initiate an automatic method of looking at all sides of anything and, also, to teach the non-Sufi if that were possible. I had never believed that my satiric poetry, novels, plays, and paintings would illuminate a single person among the Philistines. I appealed only to minds that already agreed with me.

Thus, my schooling progressed under Rabi'a, though not very swiftly. I was her physical servant, bound to fetch and carry for her, attentive to her every waking moment. Fortunately, she liked to fish, so we spent many hours at my beloved pastime. I was also her spiritual servant, listening to her lectures and observations, thinking on them, answering her many questions designed to test my comprehension of her teachings, to see if I was making any progress. I was in bondage until I quit or I, too, attained the highest mastership and burned ecstatically with the flame of The One.

On the other hand, what else important did I have to do?

When Rabi'a heard me make that remark, she reproached me. "Levity has its place, but it too often indicates a giddy mind and a lack of seriousness," she said. "That is, a serious lack in the character. Or fear of the thing laughed at. Meditate about that."

She paused, then said, "I think you believe that you can attain a glimpse of The One through my eyes. I am only our teacher. You alone can find The Way."

It was not long after that that she decided to climb to the top of the monolith. There, if the top was inhabitable, she would stay for a long time. She would take along three of her disciples if they wished to accompany her.

"And how long, vessel of the inner light, will we remain there?" I said.

"We will let our hair grow until it reaches our calves," she said. "Then we will cut it off next to the scalp. When, after many cuttings, we have saved enough hair with which to make a rope long enough to descend from the top to the ground level, then we will leave the monolith."

That seemed a long time, but four of her disciples said that they would follow her. I was one. Havornik, a sixteenth-century Bohemian, wavered. He admitted that, like those who refused to go with her, he was afraid of the climb. But he finally said that he would try to overcome his lack of courage. He regretted that decision on the way up because he could use only his fingers and toes to cling to juts or ledges or holes in the rock, and many of these were small. But he made it to the top. He lay on the ground, quivering for an hour before he got the strength to stand up.

Havornik was the only one who was afraid. But he conquered his fear. Thus, he was the bravest of us all.

I wish that he had been as brave in his climbing out of his Self as he had been in climbing the mountain.

Or do I? After all, he might have saved me from my Self.

Three days after we got to the top, I found The Artifact. I was on my way to the little lake to fish when I saw something sticking out of the dirt at the base of a large bush. I don't know why I discerned it, since it was smeared with mud and protruded slightly from the ground. But I was curious, and I went to it, Bending down close to it, I saw the top of something bulb-shaped. I touched it; it was hard as metal. After digging in the soft earth around it, I pulled out something man-made. Made by sentiments, anyway. It was a cylinder about a foot long and three inches in diameter. On each end was an onion-sized bulb.

Very excited, I cleaned it in the creek water. It was black metal and bare of pushbuttons, slides, rheostats, and any operational devices. I didn't, of course, have the slightest idea who had made it or what it did or why it had been left or lost on this near-inaccessible peak. That day, I forgot about the fishing.

After an hour of touching it all over and turning it over and over and squeezing it, hoping to find a way to activate it or to open a section that would reveal controls, I took it to Rabi'a and the others. She heard my story, then said, "It may have been left here by accident by the makers of this world. If so, the makers are not gods, as many suppose. They are human beings like us, though they may differ in bodily form. Or it may be that the device was left here for some purpose in their plan. It does not matter who made it or what its function is. It has nothing to do with me or you. It can only be a deterrent, an obstacle, a stumbling block in The Path."

I was flabbergasted at this appalling lack of scientific curiosity—or any other kind. But, on reflection, I admitted that, from her viewpoint, she was right. Unfortunately, I have always been very interested in mathematics, physics, and technology. Not to brag (though why not?), but I am well-versed in these branches of science. In fact, I once designed a time-traveling machine that almost convinced many people that it was workable. Almost, I say. No one, including myself, ever built one to test its validity. That was because time travel seemed impossible according to the science of my day. Sometimes, I wonder if I should have built the machine. Perhaps time travel is impossible most of the time. But there may be moments when it is highly possible. I am a pataphysician, and pataphysics is, among other things, the science of the exceptional.

Rabi'a did not order me to get rid of The Artifact and forget about it. As her disciple, I was bound to obey her no matter how reluctant I was to do so. But she knew me well enough to realize that I would have to experiment with it until I gave up the search to determine its function. And perhaps she hoped to teach me a valuable lesson because of my willingness to veer from The Path for a while.

The third day after I had found the mysterious device, I was sitting on a branch of the great oak and staring at the device. Then I heard a voice. It was a woman's speaking a language I didn't know and had never heard before. And it came from one of the globes at the end of the cylinder. It startled me so much that I froze for a few seconds. Then I held the end near to my ear. The gibberish stopped after thirty seconds. But a man spoke then from the bulb at the other end.

When he stopped, a green ray bright enough to be seen in the daylight shot out. But it faded after four feet from the source, the bulb. It gave birth at the termination to a picture. A moving picture in which three-dimensional actors moved and spoke audibly. There were three strikingly handsome people in it, a Mongolian man, a Caucasian woman, and a Negro woman, each in a flimsy ancient-Greece-like robe. They were seated at a table the legs of which were curved and beautifully carved into the semblance of animals unknown to Earthly zoology. They were talking animatedly to each other and, now and then, into devices exactly like the one I held in my hand.

Then the images faded into sunlight. I tried to bring them back by duplicating the series of finger pressures on the cylinder just before they had appeared. Nothing happened. Not until at night three days later was I able to activate the device. This time, the images were no brighter, the device apparently automatically adjusting itself to the exterior illumination. The scene projected was of some place along the River and seemed to be during the day. There were the usual men and women in their towels, fishing and talking. They spoke in Esperanto. Across the River were round bamboo huts with thatched roofs and many people. Nothing of any great interest. Except that one of the men nearby looked remarkedly like a man in the projection of the first scene, the meeting at the table.

From this I deduced that the makers of this world—I had no doubt that they were the makers—walked among the Riverdwellers disguised as such. Whatever machine was recording this scene must be set in a boulder or perhaps in one of the indestructible and unmeltable irontrees everywhere on this world.

At the moment the scene was projected, Rabi'a and Havornik were present. She was interested, but she said, "This has nothing to do with us." Havornik, the Bohemian, however, was excited, and he was greatly disappointed when the scene faded out. I let him try his hand at reactivating the device after I had failed to do so. He also failed.

"There's some way to operate this," I said. "I'll find out what it is if I have to wear it out pressing on it."

Rabi'a frowned, then she smiled and said, "As long as playing with it does not interfere with your walking on The Path. It does no harm to have fun if you remain basically serious."

"All fun is basically serious," I said.

She thought for a moment, then smiled again and nodded.

But I became obsessed with operating The Artifact. When my mind should have been on Rabi'a's words, I thought of the device. Whenever I could, I retreated to the great tree or sat on the rim of the peak. Here, I experienced moments when I seemed to be on the brink of what I had written on Earth about God. That was the formula I had arrived at. Zero equals infinity. That was the formula for God, and, sometimes, it seemed that my soul—if I had one—was bereft of flesh and bone. It was close to realizing directly the truth behind that equation. I almost ripped off the mask of Reality.

When I told Rabi'a that, she said, "God is a mathematical equation. But God is also everything else, though The Spirit is apart from Himself."

"I can't make any more sense out of what you say than what I said," I replied.

She only said, "You may be approaching The One. But it is not with the help of that machine. Do not confuse it with The Way."

That night, while my companions slept, I sat on the rim and watched the bonfires far below. They were sitting or dancing around the flames or falling drunkenly on the ground. And then I thought of my years on Earth and here, and I felt pity mingled with despair for them. For myself and for my Self, too.

I had written many plays, stories, and poems about the stupid, the hypocritical, the savage, the unfeeling, and the exploiters of the wretched and doomed masses. I had jeered at all of them, the masters and the masses, for their failings and their low intelligence. Yet was it their fault? Were they not born to be what they became? Was not each one acting in accordance with what he could not surmount? Or, if a few did have perception and insight and the courage to act on these, were these not born to do that?

So how could anyone justly be praised or condemned? Those who seemed to lift themselves by their bootstraps to a higher plane were only doing so because their natal characters created their destinies. They deserved neither blame nor praise.

It seemed to me that there was no such thing as genuine free will.

Thus, if I, too, attained the ecstasy and the bliss of Rabi'a, it was because I was set on my course by my fleshly inheritance. And because I had lived so long. Why should Rabi'a or I be rewarded because God, in a manner of speaking, had willed it?

Where was the fairness or justice in this?

Those boobs and yahoos cavorting down below could not help being such. Nor could I or Rabi'a claim a superior virtue.

Where was the fairness and justice?

Rabi'a would have told me that it was all God's will. Someday, if I reached a certain plane of spiritual development, I would understand His will. If I did not, I was elected to be one of those doomed wretches who had filled the Earth and now filled the Riverworld.

On the other hand, she would say, all of us are capable of attaining union with God. If He so wills it.

At that moment, my restless gropings along the device seemed to have activated it. A green ray sprang from both bulbs, curved—it could not be true light—and met twelve feet beyond me. At the junction appeared a man's face. It was huge and scowling, and his words seemed to be threatening. After several minutes, while I sat motionless as if hypnotized by Doctor Mesmer, a woman's voice interrupted the tirade. It was very pleasant and soothing, yet somehow forceful. After another few minutes, the wrathful face relaxed. Presently, it was smiling. And then the emanations ceased.

I sighed. I thought, What did that mean? Does it have any special meaning for me? How could it?

Rabi'a's voice startled me. I turned and rose to face her. Her face looked stern in the bright light of the stars. Havornik was behind her.

"I saw; I heard," she said. "I can see where this is taking you. You are considering following the mystery posed by this machine instead of The Mystery posed by God. That will not do. It is time for you to choose between the Artifact and The Artificer. Now!"

I hesitated for a long time while she stood unmoving in body or face. Then I held the device out to her. She took it and gave it to Havornik.

"Take this and bury it where he will not find it," she said. "It is of no value to us."

"I will do so at once, mistress," the Bohemian said.

He disappeared into the bushes. But that dawn, as I was walking along the rim, weary from sleeplessness and wondering if I had decidedly rightly, I saw Havornik. He was climbing down through the gap in the stone through which we had entered this little world above the world. His grail was strapped to his back. The Artifact dangled on his chest at the end of a hair rope hung around his neck.

"Havornik!" I cried. I ran to the edge of the rim and looked down. He was not very far from me. He looked upward, his eyes huge and wild, and he grinned.

"Come back up," I shouted, "or I'll drop a rock on you!"

"No, you won't!" he shouted. "You have chosen God! I have chosen this machine! It's real! It's hard and practical and is the means to getting answers to my questions, not the imaginary being Rabi'a convinced me for a while actually existed! It is of no value to you, no consequence! Or have you changed your mind?"

I hesitated. I could follow him down to the ground and wrest it from him there. I longed for it; I felt crushed with a sense of loss. I'd been too hasty, too awed by Rabi'a's presence, to think clearly.

I stood there, looking down on him and at The Artifact, for a long time. If I tried to take the machine from him, I might have to kill him. Then I would be among many who would desire the machine and would kill me to get it, if they could.

Several times, Rabi'a had said, "Killing for the sake of material things or for an idea is evil. It is not The Way."

I struggled with myself as Jacob struggled with the angel at the foot of the ladder. It was no fixed match; it was hard and desperate.

And then I shouted down at Havornik, "You will regret that choice. But I wish you good luck in finding the answers to your questions! They are not my questions!"

I turned, and I started. Rabi'a was ten feet behind me. She had not said a word because she did not want to influence me. I, I alone, must make the choice.

I had expected a compliment from her. But she said, "We have much work to do," and she turned and walked toward our camp.

I followed her.